MOLLY CLA

TOUCH NOT

MARY 'Molly' Clavering was born in Glasgow in 1900. Her father was a Glasgow businessman, and her mother's grandfather had been a doctor in Moffat, where the author would live for nearly 50 years after World War Two.

She had little interest in conventional schooling as a child, but enjoyed studying nature, and read and wrote compulsively, considering herself a 'poetess' by the age of seven.

She returned to Scotland after her school days, and published three novels in the late 1920s, as well as being active in her local girl guides and writing two scenarios for ambitious historical pageants.

In 1936, the first of four novels under the pseudonym 'B. Mollett' appeared. Molly Clavering's war service in the WRNS interrupted her writing career, and in 1947 she moved to Moffat, in the Scottish border country, where she lived alone, but was active in local community activities. She resumed writing fiction, producing seven post-war novels and numerous serialized novels and novellas in the *People's Friend* magazine.

Molly Clavering died in Moffat on February 12, 1995.

TITLES BY MOLLY CLAVERING

Fiction

Georgina and the Stairs (1927)
The Leech of Life (1928)
Wantonwalls (1929)
Susan Settles Down (1936, as 'B. Mollett')
Love Comes Home (1938, as 'B. Mollett')
Yoked with a Lamb (1938, as 'B. Mollett')
Touch Not the Nettle (1939, as 'B. Mollett')
Mrs. Lorimer's Quiet Summer (1953)
Because of Sam (1954)
Dear Hugo (1955)
Near Neighbours (1956)
Result of the Finals (1957)
Dr. Glasgow's Family (1960)
Spring Adventure (1962)

Non-Fiction

From the Border Hills (1953)

Between 1952 and 1976, Molly Clavering also serialized at least two dozen novels or novellas in the *People's Friend* under the names Marion Moffatt and Emma Munro. Some of these were reprinted as 'pocket novels' as late as 1994.

MOLLY CLAVERING

TOUCH NOT THE NETTLE

With an introduction by
Elizabeth Crawford

DEAN STREET PRESS

A Furrowed Middlebrow Book
FM68

Published by Dean Street Press 2021

Copyright © 1939 Molly Clavering

Introduction © 2021 Elizabeth Crawford

All Rights Reserved

First published in 1939 by Stanley Paul & Co

Cover by DSP

ISBN 978 1 914150 49 4

www.deanstreetpress.co.uk

Touch not the nettle lest haply it sting ye,
Waly sae green as the bracken grows,
Love not the love that never can win ye,
For the bands of love are ill to lose.

To

MY ONLY AUNT

In the hope that she will
find in this book some of the
sort of country we both enjoy.

INTRODUCTION

OF *TOUCH Not the Nettle* the reviewer in the *Aberdeen Press and Journal* (24 August 1939) wrote, 'This is a romance with its setting in romantic country, for its many characters play their parts somewhere in Tweeddale within sight of the Cheviots, and the scenes of Borderland in autumn and winter are sketched by a loving pen', while an English paper, the *Burton Advertiser* (12 October 1939), highlighted the novel's universal appeal, describing it as 'amusing, romantic, sensible and exciting'. In this, her seventh novel and the fourth published using the pseudonym 'B. Mollett', Molly Clavering returns to the area around the village of 'Muirsfoot' and to the characters she created in *Susan Settles Down* (1936). Now, three years after novelist Susan Parsons married farmer Jed Armstrong and her brother, Oliver, married Peggy Cunningham, the daughter of the Manse, their quiet way of life is interrupted by the arrival of Amanda Cochrane, awaiting news of her husband, missing on a solo flight over the Amazon. The twist at the heart of the novel is the fact that, for good reason, she did not welcome the thought of his return. As with all Molly Clavering's novels, *Touch Not the Nettle* reflects the society of the day, its characters drawn from all strata, with a plot fuelled by sherry parties and gossip, the latter rendered on occasion very effectively in demotic Scots. Published at the outbreak of the Second World War, the novel was selected by a book club run by a Perth bookseller as offering pleasant reading during the long Black-Out nights.

Born in Glasgow on 23 October 1900, Molly Clavering was the eldest child of John Mollett Clavering (1858-1936) and his wife, Esther (1874-1943). Named 'Mary' for her paternal grandmother, she was always known by the diminutive, 'Molly'. Her brother, Alan, was born in 1903 and her sister, Esther, in 1907. Although John Clavering, as his father before him, worked in central Glasgow, brokering both iron and grain, by 1911 the family had moved eleven miles north of the city, to Alreoch House outside the village of Blanefield. In an autobiographical article Molly Clavering later commented, 'I was brought up in the country, and until I went to school ran wild more or less'. She was taught by her father to be a close observer of nature and 'to know the birds and flowers, the weather and the hills round our house'. From this knowledge, learned so early, were to spring the descriptions of the countryside that give readers of her novels such pleasure.

By the age of seven Molly was sufficiently confident in her literary attainment to consider herself a 'poetess', a view with which her father enthusiastically concurred. In these early years she was probably educated at home, remembering that she read 'everything I could lay hands on (we were never restricted in our reading)' and having little 'time for orthodox lessons, though I liked history and Latin'. She was later sent away to boarding school, to Mortimer House in Clifton, Bristol, the choice perhaps dictated by the reputation of its founder and principal, Mrs Meyrick Heath, whom Molly later described as 'a woman of wide culture and great character [who] influenced all the girls who went there'. However, despite a congenial environment, life at Mortimer House was so different from the freedom she enjoyed at home that Molly 'found the society of girls and the regular hours very difficult at first'. Although she later admitted that she preferred devoting time and effort to her own writing rather than school-work, she did sufficiently well academically to be offered a place at Oxford. Her parents, however, ruled against this, perhaps for reasons of finance. It is noticeable that in her novels Molly makes little mention of the education of her heroines, although they do demonstrate a close and loving knowledge of Shakespeare, Dickens, Thackeray, and Trollope.

After leaving school Molly returned home to Arleoch House and, with no need to take paid employment, was able to concentrate on her writing, publishing her first novel in 1927, the year following the tragically early death of her sister, Esther. Always sociable, Molly took a lively interest in local activities, particularly in the Girl Guides for whom she was able to put her literary talents to fund-raising effect by writing scenarios for two ambitious Scottish history pageants. The first, in which she took the pivotal part of 'Fate', was staged in 1929 in Stirlingshire, with a cast of 500. However, for the second, in 1930, she moved south and in aid of the Roxburgh Girl Guides wrote the 'Border Historical Pageant'.

Performed in the presence of royalty at Minto House, Roxburgh-shire, this pageant featured a large choir and a cast of 700, with Molly in the leading part as 'The Spirit of Borderland Legend'. For Molly was already devoted to the Border country, often visiting the area to stay with relations and, on occasion, attending a hunt ball.

Touch Not the Nettle, the title taken from an old Scottish ballad, was the last of the novels Molly published in the 1930s as 'B. Mollett'. Soon after its publication she joined the Women's Royal Naval Service and during the Second World War was based at Greenock, then an important and frenetic naval station. Serving in the Signals Cypher Branch, she eventually achieved the rank of second officer. Although there was no obvious family connection to the Navy, it is noticeable that even in her pre-war novels many of Molly's most attractive male characters are associated with the Senior Service.

After she was demobbed Molly moved to the Borders, to Moffat, the Dumfriesshire town where her great-grandfather had been a doctor. She had dedicated *Touch Not the Nettle* to 'My Only Aunt - in the hope she will find in this book some of the sort of country we both enjoy'. It was during visits to the doctor and his wife, her grandparents, that this aunt, Anne, sister to Molly's mother, had learned to love the Borders. Living in Moffat for the rest of her life, Molly shared 'Clover Cottage' with a series of black standard poodles, one of them a present from D.E. Stevenson, another of the town's novelists, whom she had known since the 1930s. The latter's granddaughter, Penny Kent, remembers how 'Molly used to breeze and bluster into North Park (my Grandmother's house) a rush of fresh air, gaberdine flapping, grey hair flying with her large, bouncy black poodles, Ham and Pam (and later Bramble), shaking, dripping and muddy from some wild walk through Tank Wood or over Gallow Hill'. Molly's love of the area was made evident in her only non-fiction book, *From the Border Hills* (1953).

During these post-war years Molly Clavering continued her work with the Girl Guides, serving for nine years as County Commissioner, and was active in the Women's Rural Institute. She was a member of Moffat town council, 1951-60, and for three years from 1957 was the town's first and only woman magistrate. Although president of the local Scottish Country Dance Association, her love of that activity did not blind her to its comic possibilities, realised in *Touch Not the Nettle* when Muirfoot's 'terrible spinsters', the Pringles, hold a class to initiate the locals into its mysteries. She continued writing, publishing seven further novels, as well as a steady stream of the stories that she referred to as her 'bread and butter', issued, under a variety of pseudonyms, by that very popular women's magazine, the *People's Friend*.

When Molly Clavering's long and fruitful life finally ended on 12 February 1995 her obituary was written by Wendy Simpson, another of D.E. Stevenson's granddaughters. Citing exactly the attributes that characterise Molly Clavering's novels, she remembered her as 'A convivial and warm human being who enjoyed the company of friends, especially young people, with her entertaining wit and a sense of fun allied to a robustness to stand up for what she believed in.'.

Elizabeth Crawford

CHAPTER ONE

I

"OLD age really must be creeping upon me at last," said Susan Armstrong. "I find more and more that what I most enjoy is a quiet evening at home by the fire, with a book—not necessarily of verse—and thou. Don't you, Jed?"

Her husband's only reply was the characteristic amiable grunt which had to do duty for all unimportant remarks, but Susan was not in the least disturbed by this seeming lack of enthusiasm. Practice enabled her to interpret the inarticulate sound as one of appreciation and agreement.

Though a book lay open on her knee, she had not been reading for several minutes while her wandering glance roved about the room, taking in every dear, familiar detail. It was only mid-September, but a dancing fire, all the more pleasant because it was not absolutely necessary, mellowed the cream-coloured walls to tea-rose pink, caught the great copper bowl of tawny dahlias, flickered across the rows of solid old calf-bound books in their low book-cases, and glimmered on the rounded surface of a lustre mug above them. Outside, the splendour of sunset had faded, leaving quiet skies of chill green darkening to deepest blue, and the light of a softly shaded standard lamp was reflected in the window-panes, mocking the colder brilliance of a rising harvest moon. Finally, with a feeling of deep content, Susan's eyes rested on the grey head and ruddy, weather-tanned face of her husband, where he lounged in a huge chair, knitting his brows over the *Scotsman* crossword puzzle. She had experienced three years of marriage, and in her opinion there was only one flaw in an otherwise admirable institution—it did not give her enough time to enjoy it to the full. This was probably, she had in fairness to acknowledge, less the fault of marriage itself than of her neighbours, who, in their hospitable desire to show approval of the match, invited Susan and her silent Jed to a continual round of dinner-parties with bridge to follow, dinner-parties without bridge, or bridge without dinner, never to mention luncheon, tea and sherry—all of which had to be returned in kind. An evening alone with Jed had now come to be a treasure all the more prized for its rarity, and she determined to savour each moment of this, the first in a fortnight of sociability, to the uttermost.

"Hmph," said Jed, and she realized that she must have announced her intention aloud.

"What did you say, Jed?"

"I only said 'hmph'," he repeated.

"Yes, darling, I know. I heard you. But I wanted you to translate it," said Susan.

"Well," he said, laying the *Scotsman* carefully on his knee, "I meant that if you talk such a lot about your quiet evening it's not likely to be very quiet after all."

"How rude of you. I'm sure I haven't been breaking the peace to that extent!"

"No, no. I like to hear your voice, it's kind of soothing," he assured her. "But you know how it is. You settle down—well, to a quiet evening by the fire, let's say—and ten to one something happens to interrupt it."

"Nothing," said Susan very firmly indeed, "is going to interrupt this. I won't allow it. It's far too good. I will not be disturbed."

Her husband grunted again, this time sceptically, and resumed his search for a word in seven letters which might mean a match.

Susan, knowing that her help would soon be needed, replaced her book with a piece of *petit-point* destined in course of time, if it ever reached completion, to cover the seat of an old pear-wood chair. She considered this work, which she had never dreamt of attempting in her single days, the hall-mark of a respectable married woman, as being decorative, restful and easily laid down at a moment's notice. She had just supplied Jed with 'lucifer' to fill the gap, when the door was gently opened.

"If ye please, sirr," said a very modest voice, "the steward's in the hall. Would ye speak to him a minute?"

Jed said nothing, but he permitted himself a teasing glance at his wife as he heaved his mighty frame from his chair and left the room.

"That doesn't count!" Susan called after him defiantly, and he came back to say:

"Not to you, maybe, but it's disturbed me."

"The steward comes down almost every evening," she said, as soon as the rumble of deep voices in the hall had ceased, and he was back in his chair again. "So it doesn't count."

"No?" he murmured annoyingly. "I'll bet you a fiver it's just the first interruption, and there'll be plenty more before you go to bed."

"A fiver's such a lot . . ." Susan was beginning, when the door was flung open, this time far from quietly, and the discreet voice which had announced the steward's presence cried, all discretion forgotten in excitement:

"If ye please, mem!"

"Yes, Robinia, what is it?" asked Susan, laying her work aside sadly. All too well she knew this tone of the very young housemaid who, the cook and parlourmaid having been given special leave of absence to attend a rally of the Women's Rural Institute in Abbey-shiels, was alone this evening in the kitchen and finding it dull. Robinia was a willing if unmethodical worker; she was as fresh as a daisy, with the same pink-and-white, newly washed appearance; but Susan feared that she would never learn the reticence proper to a well-trained maid. 'My own fault,' thought her mistress guilt-ily. 'I find her confidences so amusing that I haven't the heart to snub her. The Miss Pringles would be sorrier than ever for Jed if they knew how hopelessly I fail to keep Robinia in what they would call her Place!'

Thought of this criticism spurred her to add repressively, "You must not come and disturb the master like this, Robinia. If you really have anything important to say to me, I'll come to the kitchen for a moment."

"Ay, that'll dae fine. Come on," said Robinia, throwing in a perfunctory 'mem' as a sop to the proprieties. "Come till ye see the awfu' queer big beast I've found in the kitchen."

She rushed noisily away, and Susan, stopping as she passed Jed's chair to drop a kiss on his head and say gratefully, "Thank you for not even *looking* 'I-told-you-so', darling!" followed more slowly, hoping that Robinia's beast might not prove too alarming as to size or anything else. Vague, disquieting visions of some animal having escaped from the 'Grand Menagerie and Circus' which had pitched its tents for a week in a green meadow beside the river just outside their market- town of Abbeyshiels, floated through her mind; but when she reached the kitchen she saw nothing more disturbing than Robinia herself, searching frenziedly about the floor near the range, a lighted taper in her hand, the electric light not switched on.

"Eh," she lamented, "I'll be that vexed if it's a lossie. It's an *awfu'* queer great beast wi' a big face an' rollin' black een!"

This graphic description left Susan as puzzled as ever, and she was beginning to suspect that Robinia, bored with her own society, had invented the creature as an excuse to lure her into the kitchen, when a piercing scream made her jump wildly.

"Fegs," said Robinia, chuckling, and omitting the 'mem' altogether this time, "yon was a graun' loup ye gied! I thocht ye'd bash yer heid on the ceilin'!"

"Robinia," said Susan, with justifiable irritation, "you are not to scream like that and frighten me half out of my wits."

"Eh, but I've found the beastie," Robinia answered triumphantly, as if this were amply sufficient explanation, "Look, mem, an' ye'll can see it creepin' aboot." She flourished the taper, and Susan, stooping, saw by its wavering flame a very large insect running uncertainly about the whitened stone floor inside the fender, evidently far from satisfied with its surroundings.

"It seems to be some sort of beetle, but a very large one, certainly," said Susan, as comment appeared to be expected. But it did not meet with her housemaid's approval, for Robinia was tasting the sweets of discovery and looked for appropriate excitement in her audience.

"Beetle!" she cried, in high disdain. "Och, never heed for beetles. Look at its black een, ye can seen them rollin' roon' an' roon'! An' eh"—in an ecstasy of delighted mirth, "see till it noo, wavin' twa o'ts legs aboot!"

"Very interesting," said Susan tepidly. For her part, she felt that the entertainment was hardly worthy of these raptures.

It certainly did not compensate her for breaking into the evening which was to have been so peaceful. "But you'd better put the poor thing out of the window, it will only die in here."

"Is it touch yon? No' me!" said Robinia in horror. "Mebbe it'll bite me!"

"Nonsense," Susan's patience was exhausted. "Give me a towel and I'll do it for you."

And when the beetle had been set free, to fly off rather drunkenly into the night air, she said firmly: "You had better find a book and read it until bedtime, Robinia, and don't disturb us again, please."

"Ou ay. I'll hae a read of the *Friend*. Cook left it for me. There's an awfu' nice story o' Annie S. Swan's in it," said Robinia agreeably.

Susan, feeling curiously shattered, and robbed of all sense of peace, returned to the sitting-room.

"You've been a long time, surely? I was wondering if the beast had eaten you," said Jed, with a grin.

"It was a beetle." Susan picked up her piece of canvas and put in two stitches, but not in the tranquil, leisurely manner which she always thought *petit-point* deserved.

"A beetle! Good lord, I thought it must have been a gorilla at least," said her husband disgustedly. "A beetle!"

"Darling," said Susan, "if you value our love at all, you won't mention that insect by name again for a long time."

"All right, then, I won't. But all that fuss about a b—"

At this point the telephone's imperious trill cut short his remark with an appositeness not usually shown by that instrument—which is notorious, rather, for ringing at the wrong moment.

"Hell!" exclaimed Jed, simply and without rancour, proceeding very slowly towards the small table where it stood quivering with the fury of the strangled roar optimistically described in the telephone directory as a 'low-pitched burr-burr'. After a brisk passage with Exchange and Trunks, both of whom he regarded as deadly foes, he said suddenly, "Hullo, it's you, is it, Nora?"

The most unsuspicious wife in the world pricks her ears involuntarily when she hears her husband addressing a woman unknown to her by her Christian name in familiar tones. Susan could not help hearing the high-pitched, feminine voice, could not help wondering who its owner was and what she looked like, since Jed, always cautious of Christian names, appeared to know her well. That was the thing—advantage or disadvantage, she had never been able to make up her mind—about marrying one of those taciturn men—

they told you nothing, and expected you to know all they had left untold by instinct.

Instinct did not help her at all on this occasion, nor did Jed's growling 'Yeses' and 'Noes' enlighten her. His final and longest remark: "I expect it'll be all right, but I'll ask my wife and ring you up again, Nora," left her still in the dark.

"That was Nora Carmichael, " he said, coming back to the fire and kicking a log expertly into a blaze of blue and green and rose flames.

"Yes, I heard her name," Susan said with restraint. It was obvious that he had something to tell her, and she wondered whether it would hasten the process if she were to spring up, rush at him, and shake it out of him.

"My cousin Wat's widow," he added, before she could come to a decision. "You know."

"I *don't* know," cried Susan, in exasperation. "I never knew you had a cousin Wat, or that he was dead, or that he had a widow called Nora! How could I? You never told me."

"Didn't I?" He sounded mildly surprised at the omission. "Oh, well, I never could stand the woman, hardly saw Wat after he married her. She's got a voice like a saw and one of those long necks," he said simply, and he so evidently considered this a sufficient reason for never having mentioned her existence, that Susan only said:

"She sounds like a giraffe."

"A giraffe's a harmless sort of beast," he replied darkly.

"What did she ring you up for?"

"Well," he said, drawing a deep breath and pulling out his pipe and tobacco-pouch, "it's a longish story. She has a daughter, their only child—Amelia—Alicia—no, Amanda. That's it, Amanda—and she wants us to have this girl here at Reiverslaw for a bit. Not just a short visit, y'know. To stay a month or two."

To Susan the story seemed all too disagreeably short, but she gathered that there was more to come and held her peace, not without an effort.

"This girl Amanda Carmichael—she stayed here once before, just after she left school, rather a bonny girl," proceeded Jed, maddeningly deliberate. "Married one of those long-distance record-breaking flying fellows. Lloyd Cochrane his name is."

Susan knit her fine dark brows. "I'm sure I've heard that name recently," she murmured.

"Likely. He's gone missing, somewhere in the South Pacific or South America or somewhere," said Jed largely, "and Nora says the girl's fretting herself to a shadow—"

"No wonder, poor child!"

"No other wonder," he agreed, adding grimly, "She'll not have much of a chance to get over it—if he's really lost—as long as she has to stay with her mother."

Susan thought that she had never known Jed show such a strong dislike for anyone. His cousin's widow must be rather unusually tiresome and disagreeable in some way; and pity for the daughter, clinging desperately to an ever-fainter hope of her husband's safety, rose strong in her. It almost drowned her instinctive feeling that she did not want to have Amanda Cochrane here at Reiverslaw, a constant third to their serenely happy duet—almost, but not quite.

"Do you want to have her here, Jed?" she asked, trying to keep her voice non-committal.

"Want her? Good God, no, Susan! I don't want anyone else here," he said, with comforting vehemence. "It's only that I'm so damned sorry for her, poor thing." He ended in a shamefaced manner, as if confessing something disgraceful, "I—I was always fond of Wat, you know."

"Then, of course, she must come," said Susan. "Hadn't you better just ring up Mrs. Carmichael now and make arrangements? Our peaceful evening has been ruined, anyhow."

He gave her a long, slow look as he went to the telephone obediently. "Clinch it before we've time to change our minds and think better of it?" he suggested.

Susan sighed. "Perhaps, Jed. There isn't a doubt that marriage has made me a very selfish woman. Ring up quickly, because I'm repenting already."

"Here goes, then," said Jed, and lifted the receiver.

II

Susan found the house almost unbearably silent on the following afternoon. Jed had come in hot and tired, with straws clinging to his puttees and tweed jacket, to snatch a hasty luncheon and return immediately to the harvest field. The faint hum of voices from the kitchen wing, where Robinia was probably re-telling the story of the awfu' queer beast to a bored audience of cook, Elspeth and the woman who did the washing, over the cups of powerful tea which finished their meal, seemed only to aggravate the silence of the sitting-room. After opening several books and laying them down again, ruffling the pages of the newspaper without noticing even the headlines, and fidgeting for a few moments with her chair-seat, Susan went in despair to the wireless cabinet and twiddled the knobs. But the burst of arch French song, exquisitely articulated, from Radio-Paris, which assailed her ears made her hurriedly turn it off, cutting short the soprano singer in the middle of a piercing high note.

'It's because this unfortunate girl is coming tomorrow that I'm being so stupid,' she thought, moving restlessly about the room. 'I must pull myself together and not be so childish; but it's going to be horribly difficult when she's here. I'll feel a monster every time I speak to Jed—callous, unimaginative. It's a blessing that we aren't a demonstrative pair. Oh, dear, I'll hardly ever have a minute alone with him . . .' And then, against her will, she began to smile, remembering how he had said, "Thank the Lord she can't be with us all night, anyway!"—and she felt better.

Elspeth entering the room on noiseless feet, discovered her still chuckling, and by merely not looking at her, made her feel a fool.

"If you please, madam," she said correctly, "the boy from Easter Hartrigg has brought a message from Mrs. Parsons, as their telephone has broken down." Her tone conveyed adequately what she thought of persons who sent verbal messages by their boot-and-garden boy instead of writing a note, but Susan did not mind. She knew her sister-in-law's dislike of putting pen to paper very well.

"What is the message, Elspeth?" she said.

"Mrs. Parsons will be pleased, madam, if you would walk down this afternoon and have tea with her," she said, "as it is such a fine day, madam."

"Very well, I shall be out for tea," said Susan, only waiting until Elspeth had made a dignified exit in perfect silence, to dash upstairs in a most unmatronly fashion, dab at her nose with a powder-puff, pull on a hat and run down again and out of the house.

The sun welcomed her with the pleasant warmth of September, a westerly breeze ruffled the little loch across the road and sang in the reeds which bordered it. Laden carts were coming creaking up the fields to the stackyard, the horses' heads nodding, the tassels on their gay red-and-white ear-caps swinging in time, the harness jingling, the great plumed hoofs thudding. Empty carts, their drivers sitting bumpily on the edges, went downhill on a louder rumbling note. Shading her eyes, Susan looked at the small figures working among the stooks, the women in immense sun-bonnets like pale flowers, or huge shady hats of black straw. Jed was there in his blue shirt-sleeves, yielding a fork, towering above the other men. . . .

Suddenly she knew that no matter what superficial differences the coming of Amanda Cochrane might make in her life, it could not alter the fundamental fact of her happiness with Jed, her deep delight in this well-loved land all about her. If the house became too narrow to hold all three of them in peace, she had always this refuge of wide views, Cheviot's mighty humped back rising against the southern sky, the Lammermuirs fainting into the northern horizon, and between them the rolling country with its long ridges, its sheltered hollows where burns chattered over stones, the dark woods, the coloured fields, the friendly rivers; and over all the tremendous wide arch of the sky. Surely this Amanda, no matter what she was like, would find a measure of comfort simply from being in such a place, even if, as Susan was afraid, her husband was never heard of again.

"Poor child!" said Susan aloud, opening a gate into a meadow which ran down to the march between Reiverslaw and Easter Hartrigg, her brother Oliver's farm. The house towards which she was walking stood on a ridge facing her, but lower than Reiverslaw, so that beyond the trees which half hid its square outlines, she could see miles of rising ground, sloping up in the far distance to the dim blue Lammermuirs, impalpable as smoke on this hazy sunny day.

Except on higher ground where it was slow to ripen, the corn was being carried, and field after field was gradually left bare, the stubble shining silver blonde in the strong light, darkening almost to purple in the shadow. Down in the hollow the high hawthorn hedges hung, spiked branches burdened with reddening haws, a barberry bush was a glory of orange-tawny waxen fruit, and as Susan crossed the burn by large flat stones, she saw that a bed of watercress was still starred with its tiny white flowers. Now she was on her brother's land, going up through a stubble field thick with blue speedwell, smelling of the wild mint crushed under her feet. A covey of partridges rose and whirred over the hedge, a brown hare sat up to look at her before loping away to the coarse grass of a neighbouring meadow where he could lie securely hidden. Now Susan could see a small fair-haired figure in brown, waving a trowel at her from the rock-garden which was being reclaimed from wilderness alongside the house. It was her young sister-in-law, Peggy Parsons, married to her brother Oliver just a month before Susan herself had married Jed Armstrong, and already the proud and doting mother of a year-old son.

'Dear Peggy,' thought Susan, congratulating herself for the hundredth time on having a sister-in-law whom she had always liked, and for whom she had not had to whip a dutiful tardy fondness. It was an awkward relationship, and perhaps in their case things had been made easier by her own marriage. Still, it might have been difficult enough even so, with the house which Susan and her brother had struggled to make habitable, and in which they had spent a happy year together, only a few fields away, had Peggy been other than she was. 'But no one could possibly resent Peggy. She's like the Egyptian princess whose epitaph said that "she was sweet of heart".'

Peggy was coming to meet her, running down the field, the sun glinting on her bare head, the trowel still in one earthy hand. "*What* a long time you've been!" she called, as soon as she was within earshot. "I sent James with the message as soon as he'd finished his dinner, and he had it at twelve!"

"James must be an incredibly slow mover, then, Pegs, because I left the house immediately Elspeth gave me your message," said Susan, "and she's much too perfect to have delayed it. Curse her, she gives me an inferiority complex. I wish I could find an excuse for getting rid of her."

"Isn't she walking out with one of those horrible oily haired young men from the Abbeyshiels Co-op?" asked Peggy interestedly. "Perhaps she'll be getting married to him soon."

"I doubt it," said Susan. "The young man from the Co-op. isn't such a fool!"

"Well, never mind her, Susan dear. There's no need to worry about superior parlourmaids *here*," said Peggy. "I've got a new house-tablemaid, like a young cart-horse, and about as destructive. She only came five days ago, and she's broken something every day. And yesterday I told her she was to wait at lunch, and what do you think she did? Shut the dining room door, pulled out a chair, and sat down on it—to wait! Of course, Oliver began to laugh, and I had to tell her just to go away. She has done one good thing, though, and that was to smash the awful vase that the Miss Pringles gave Oliver and me for a wedding present. She managed that the day before yesterday."

"Never!" exclaimed Susan. "Not that funerary urn painted with mud-coloured roses and magenta leaves?"

Peggy nodded solemnly, her blue eyes dancing. "It was in about seven pieces, so Oliver took them out to the tool-shed and pounded them to dust with a hammer."

"I wish," said Susan bitterly, "that Elspeth had ever done anything half so useful! I can't lose or destroy the tablecloth the Miss Pringles gave us. I've spilt coffee on it, and tea on it, and I've encouraged Jed to drop burning ash from his pipe on it, and still it comes up smiling. Elspeth gets the stains out and mends the holes. It's my belief that she really admires the horrible thing, from the appalling regularity with which it appears on the tea-table. I've given up the struggle now. That tablecloth is indestructible."

"It was very unlucky for both of us that the Miss Pringles took to handicrafts and art combined just in time to give us specimens as wedding presents," said Peggy. "And you know, Susan, I feel as guilty as if I'd broken that vase myself on purpose. I suppose it's because I was so glad, and couldn't even sound grieved when Janet came weeping to me with the bits in her hand. I can't help feeling a little relieved that they don't owe me a visit."

They had reached the gate in the wall which led to the house, passing the rock-garden by a narrow winding path.

"How do you think it's getting on, Susan?" asked Peggy a little anxiously.

Susan looked at the masses of stone sticking grey heads from a sea of tangled weeds and alpine plants all run riot together. "You've cleared a lot," she said. "But what a business it's going to be! Does Oliver help at all?"

"Well, he's pretty busy at Wanside just now. Old Mr. Elliot leaves everything to him, you see," said the loyal Peggy hastily; "so I'm just grubbing by myself. But Father is coming up tomorrow from Muirfoot to do a bit. You know how he loves a garden, and this really will give him more scope than the Manse now."

"Scope? I should think so! This would give a gang of navvies scope, as you call it."

"It's fun. I like it," Peggy answered contentedly.

"You find everything fun, don't you, Peggy?"

"Yes, of course. But so do you, Susan! It was you who made me see that things are fun. Ever since I first knew you—can you believe that it's four and a half years now since you and Oliver came to Easter Hartrigg?—you've always thought so. Don't you still?"

"Well," Susan said slowly, "something has happened that I don't think is going to be fun at all. Never mind, though. Tell me how my nephew is? You haven't given me a chance to ask about young Oliver yet. Unnatural mother."

"Young Oliver is absolutely splendid, and he's got another tooth almost through, and no trouble at all; and he can very nearly walk. But we'll see him soon. He's out for a walk with Janet the cart-horse just now. I want to talk about you," said Peggy, seizing her sister-in-law by the arm and leading her to a teak seat cunningly placed where it was out of the wind but in the sun. "What *is* all this about you having some girl to stay at Reiverslaw?" And before Susan could answer she went on earnestly, "It's terribly, terribly good of you, Susan, but—a girl you don't know at all! Won't you hate it?"

"How did you hear about it so soon?" asked Susan, slightly dazed.

"Oh, Oliver told me when he came in for lunch. He'd met Jed this morning," Peggy explained.

"I see. What chatterboxes men are."

"Susan! You don't mind my knowing?"

"Of course not. I was going to tell you myself. It's rather a relief to find that you know. Did Oliver tell you all about her, poor thing?"

Peggy nodded. "I'm very sorry for her," she said soberly. "But it's you I'm thinking of. Won't you mind having her? I'm afraid I should."

"I expect we shall all three loathe it," Susan said more cheerfully than she felt. "Amanda Cochrane because she's been bundled off by her mother to a nice quiet place where she'll have plenty of time to brood—though I hope it won't take her that way; Jed because it makes him miserable to see anyone suffering and not be able to help them; and I because I'm a selfish woman who wants her husband's company all to herself even after three years of it."

"What nonsense! If you were selfish you'd have refused to have her at Reiverslaw at all."

"Oh, but I'm doing it with such a bad grace, Pegs! I hope no one else will realize that except you and me, but we know it. It's only to salve my conscience, because if I'd said no it would haunt me. Dear me, how I hate duty! 'Stern daughter of the voice of God'," said Susan, with a wry smile.

"The trouble is that if she—Mrs. Cochrane, I mean—guesses that it's the stern daughter who has made you do it, it will be so much worse for her," said Peggy, with one of the endearing flashes of shrewd kindness which she only showed to her intimates.

"Oh, I know. And by the time she arrives I hope I shall be in a better frame of mind. We may like each other tremendously, " said Susan. "And in any case, we can't help being sorry for her—I dare say that won't appeal to her, though. Probably a perfectly calm matter-of-fact attitude will be the best for all of us."

"You realize, don't you, that everyone will know who she is?" asked Peggy. "Lloyd Cochrane is an uncommon name; and his last flight was broadcast, and the news of his being missing."

"I never thought of that! Of course," said Susan thoughtfully, "it may be a good thing. At least, it will keep our more inquisitive neighbours from putting her through an examination about her husband."

"I hope it will stop the Miss Pringles," said Peggy, far from hopefully. "Oh!" in a different tone—"Susan! Here comes Noll!"

She sprang up and raced across the grass towards the gravel sweep in front of the house, where a perambulator, pushed by a sturdy young woman with deplorably untidy hair escaping from under a straw hat, had come to a standstill. Susan, following, saw the small alert face of the baby, who sat bolt upright in this equipage, break into a delicious, toothless smile as he caught sight of his mother; and she wondered with a pang whether she and Jed would ever have a son to stretch out his arms and leap like a trout at sight of her.

Young Oliver was a curious and not unattractive mixture of both his parents. His mother's blue eyes twinkled below downy dark brows and hair as black as Oliver's had been before it began to turn grey, and the funny, crooked smile was Oliver's. . . .

"Isn't he a fine big fellow?" said Peggy proudly. "And he does so want to walk and push his pram. And don't you think he's ridiculously like his daddy, Susan?"

"Ag-ag!" shouted young Oliver, bouncing up and down.

"Clever boy! That means 'Dad-dad'," Peggy explained. "Look, Susan, he's got Oliver's nose too, and that's such a comfort to me. It would be awful for a boy to have a turned-up thing like mine."

Susan gazed obediently but doubtfully at the minute button set in the middle of her nephew's chubby brown face, and tried in vain to see some resemblance to Oliver's beaky nose. "I'm sorry, Peggy," she was beginning, when Peggy gave a horrified gasp.

"Susan! The Miss Pringles!" she hissed, snatching the baby from his perambulator and flying with him into the house as if bloodhounds were at her heels.

The passionate desire for escape at any cost to which Peggy had so spontaneously yielded was a sensation all too frequently felt by acquaintances of the three Miss Pringles on seeing those notable women bearing down upon them. The Miss Pringles never merely arrived or came—their action was that of a small fleet of pirate vessels swooping on some rich prize and cutting it out from its attendant convoy. Susan, realizing that to run after her sister-in-law was merely to postpone the moment of meeting, since she was in full view of anyone approaching the house, resigned herself to immediate capture with a set smile determinedly fixed on her face.

The Miss Pringles, wheeling bicycles and attired in suits of very bright heather-mixture tweed, long and wide as to skirt, heavily belted and pocketed of coat, were drawing near in their usual formation—Miss Bell Pringle, the eldest of the redoubtable trio in the van, her sisters Jelly and Cissy side by side behind her.

"Ah, Mrs. Armstrong!" called Miss Pringle. "Your tablemaid told us we should find you here, so we just cycled over from Reiverslaw in order not to miss you!"

('One more mark to the score against Elspeth') thought Susan, as she murmured aloud that she was sorry they should have found her not at home.

"No matter," said Miss Pringle graciously, waving a hand in a yellow string glove which clashed violently both with her tweeds and her glowing complexion. "It is a glorious afternoon for a ride, and I said to the girls, 'Let us kill two birds with one stone, and see dear little Peggy as well as Mrs. Armstrong. 'So *here* we are—'

"Yes, *here* we are!" echoed Miss Cissy, the youngest, with a dreadful assumption of girlish roguery. "Like three bad pennies, hee-hee!"

Miss Jelly, who always went straight to the point, broke in: "And where *is* Peggy? I thought I saw her with you a moment ago?" her foghorn tones crashing through the light laughter of her younger sister.

"Oh, she—she had to take the baby in," said Susan, improvising rapidly. "It—she thought it was too hot for him in the—the sun, you know."

"Too *hot*? The sun?" cried all three Miss Pringles. "I thought he spent the whole *day* in the open air," added the eldest in disbelieving tones.

"Well, won't you come in?" said Susan, finding as usual that her tactics had failed. They almost always did where the Miss Pringles were concerned. Another burst of laughter from Miss Cissy greeted her remark, and Susan could only stare at her blankly until enlightened as to its cause.

"Dear me, it sounds so funny to hear you inviting us into Peggy's house as if it were still *yours!*" she cried gaily. "I hope Peggy doesn't mind!"

'Just the sort of thing calculated to engender a lively dislike between sisters-in-law,' thought Susan; but she answered with the gravity which she had found the only means of discomfiting Miss Cissy. "Oh, I don't think she will. I am sure she'd rather I asked you in than left you all standing about on the doorstep while I went in myself. Or would you rather be really formal and ring the bell?"

They stared at her so uncertainly that she felt a momentary compunction, which disappeared like mist in the sun when Miss Pringle said, before they had even seated themselves in the shabby, airy drawing-room, "I hear you are having the famous Cochrane's poor young widow to stay at Reiverslaw, Mrs. Armstrong?"

"How quickly news travels here," said Susan, much more mildly than she felt. "But surely it is a little premature to speak of her as a widow, Miss Pringle? Her husband may have come down safely, you know, somewhere about the upper regions of the Amazon, where it would be difficult to get news of him for a bit."

"But I understood that his aeroplane was lost over the sea," said Miss Pringle, slightly dashed.

"So it was thought at first, but there has been later news of his having been sighted," said Susan, realizing that she might as well tell them what she knew, as they were bound to find it out. "Apparently his 'plane was seen by a ship not far from the northern coast of Brazil, and they seemed to think that he had quite a good chance of reaching land safely, as he was flying strongly."

Human nature being what it is, the faces of the three sisters, far from showing pleasure, lengthened with disappointment at being deprived of this really choice titbit of harrowing news, which they could not now retail with an air of authority. They were good women according to their own ideas, their morals as rigidly upright as their long stiff spines; they were even kind at times; but in the passionate quest for news, their greatest interest, kindness was apt to go to the wall. So, although they wished Amanda Cochrane, whom they had never seen, no ill, they were disappointed to learn that she was not definitely the pathetic young widow of a hero. Susan, guessing all this, was conscious of satisfaction. It was always a triumph to get the better of the Miss Pringles, and she was quite unregenerate enough to enjoy it heartily.

When Peggy, in the flutter of nervous apology which she had felt from childhood in the presence of these terrible spinsters, hurried into the room, she found the uninvited guests seated bolt upright, glumly silent, while her sister-in-law chattered gaily about the splendour of the dahlias this season, the miserable weather they had had for harvest until the last week, and the thoroughly depressing state of foreign affairs.

"I'm so sorry, but I had to take Oliver upstairs," Peggy explained breathlessly, shaking hands all round. "How do you do?"

"Had to take Oliver upstairs?" cried Miss Cissy, girlishly puzzled. "Oh, you mean the *baby*! How silly of me!"

No one contradicted this last statement, and after a short but uncomfortable pause, Peggy, acutely aware that the eyes of all three Miss Pringles were darting about the room in fruitless search for their hand-painted vase, said, "I hope you won't mind, but Susan and I are going to have tea in the nursery today, with Oliver—young Oliver, I mean," she added hastily, to forestall a fresh outburst of girlishness from the youngest Miss Pringle.

"I assure you, my dear Peggy, that we have no wish to intrude," said Miss Pringle, with truly awful dignity, rising as she spoke. "Come, girls. We must go home."

"Oh, but please . . ." cried the unfortunate young hostess, scarlet with confusion. "Of course I meant you to stay, if you don't mind having nursery tea with us!"

"No, thank you, Peggy. Another time, perhaps, when you and Mrs. Armstrong have not quite so much to discuss," said Miss Pringle, incredulity and offence rampant in every angular line of her person. "*Good* afternoon."

She swept out, her sisters following in her wake, and all three managing to give the impression of shaking dust from off their shoes. Peggy, too horror-stricken to go and see them off, stood rooted to the middle of the drawing-room floor, watching them mount their bicycles and wobble haughtily away, while Susan gave a strangled cry and buried her face in a cushion.

"It's all very well for you," observed Peggy at last, when the final glimpse of heather-mixture tweed had disappeared round the bend of the drive. "*You* haven't broken their wedding-present or sent them away from your house without any tea!"

Muffled laughter was the only reply, and she began to laugh herself, but ruefully. "She'll tell Mother, and it will worry her so," she said.

Susan stopped laughing long enough to say consolingly, "Nonsense, Peggy. Mrs. Cunningham hasn't been a minister's wife all these years for nothing. Besides, she knows the Pringles only too well." Then she gave an involuntary chuckle. "Peggy! Their *faces*, when you said it!" she wailed.

The door was opened suddenly and Oliver Parsons, limping a little, came into the room. "I say," he said, "which of us has insulted the Jelly-bags? They whirled past me just now like a gaggle of geese, with their necks stretched out over the handlebars, and old Belly gave me a look that nearly shrivelled me."

"Oh, Oliver!" His wife rushed at him and flung her arms round his neck in a strangling hug. "It was *me*! And I didn't mean it!" Incoherently she poured out the story.

"Well, that's a pity anyhow," he said, patting her on the back. "You might as well have done it on purpose and got some satisfaction out of it."

"It's all very fine to be fu-funny about it," said Peggy, stammering in her agitation, "b-but I've always thought that Miss Pringle was a *witch*! And I don't mind b-betting that she'll pay us out for this—all of us!"

"Good heavens," said Susan indignantly. "*I* didn't do anything."

"You laughed, and I think she saw you," Peggy said with gloomy satisfaction. "Besides, she's always hated you because you wouldn't let her run you when you came here."

"But, Peggy darling," said Oliver, "this is just plain damn' silly, you know. Don't be a simpleton. What could old Belly or any of 'em do?"

"Wait and see," was Peggy's reply. "They'll get their own back. I know they will."

Nothing they could say would shake her from this belief, and when Susan left Easter Hartrigg to walk home she found herself, against all common sense, full of vague forebodings, with which in some strange way the coming of Amanda Cochrane seemed to be connected.

'Don't be an idiot,' she begged herself. 'You'll imagine you've got second-sight or something in a minute. What would Jed say? But I hope all the same that we won't regret having this girl at Reiverslaw.'

CHAPTER TWO

I

ON THIS same warm September afternoon the front at Southsea was black with holiday-makers, whose voices drowned all but the loudest efforts of the band playing in a kind of tin temple set among green lawns brilliant with flower-beds. The blue water, along the creaming fringes of which children ran shouting to their bathing elders, was fretted into a thousand points of dancing light by a soft breeze; the white wings of gulls flashed above white sails. Everyone, to the oldest who had to be wheeled across the Common in bathchairs, was out enjoying the fine day, it seemed; but to the really keen bridge-player weather is purely incidental, and the four ladies who sat round a table covered with a square of blue velvet, galon-trimmed, weighted at the corners by heavy gold, in Mrs. Carmichael's drawing-room, only noticed the sun when it was thoughtless enough to shine in their eyes.

"Poor child, in her present state of anxiety she did not feel equal to meeting even such old friends. No bid," said Mrs. Carmichael, after a swift glance at the cards held fanwise in one plump hand. She was a soft fluffy woman, irritatingly vague in manner, with soft grey hair, a small fretful mouth perpetually slightly open over protruding upper teeth, the rabbit mouth which by its misleading babyish softness of appearance so often beguiles a man into marrying its owner; a rosy, rather woolly complexion, and disconcertingly sharp blue eyes half-hidden by drooping lids.

Her guests, three hard-bitten bridge-playing women, looked as if they would have her totally at their mercy, and knew from bitter experience that it always turned out to be quite the other way about, at the card-table and elsewhere. A professed inability to remember what was trumps was one of the methods by which she baffled her opponents, and another weapon was her tendency to babble on irrelevant topics while bidding was in progress. Though they were sorry for poor Amanda whose husband was such a handsome young fellow, their chief feeling, as they heard her mother's plaintive words, was of helpless rage. She was their hostess, they could not in decency continue to bid without making sympathetic comment on the tragedy which lent Mrs. Carmichael a vicarious importance.

So Miss Hardcastle on her left, murmured, "I suppose you have had no further news?" when what she longed to say was a triumphant "Two hearts."

Mrs. Carmichael's sad shake of the head made it impossible to display anything so heartless, in another sense, as triumph, and Miss Hardcastle's bid was uttered in a depressed undertone.

"There is *still* hope, my dear Nora," said Mrs. Carmichael's partner bracingly, adding, "No bid."

"Very little, I am sadly afraid," sighed Mrs. Carmichael. "For my part I have *quite* given up hope of ever seeing the dear boy again in life. . . . What are trumps, partner? Did you say anything?"

"Nothing, and we have gone four hearts," replied Miss Hardcastle with commendable patience.

"*Four* hearts? Oh, I think I must double that," said the bereaved hostess brightly. "Now, who is dummy? Is it my lead?"

The game pursued its way to a not altogether unexpected conclusion with the declaring couple two down (doubled and vulnerable).

Mrs. Carmichael, preparing to pick up her next hand almost before it was dealt, said sorrowfully, "If only my poor child would share her grief with her mother, she would find it easier to bear. But then Amanda is so unlike me! I sometimes feel almost as if she were a *changeling*!"

Amanda, wandering reluctantly homewards through the narrow streets of old Portsmouth, was saying much the same thing to herself with rather dreary amusement. Nothing, it seemed, could make her feel in sympathy with her mother, and this awful uncertainty about Cocky had only driven them even farther apart.

'If only she wouldn't pretend so!" thought Amanda impatiently. 'But she's posed for so long that she has forgotten how to be natural with herself, far less with me. She knows how things were between Cocky and me before he left on this last flight, and still she persists in behaving as if I were broken-hearted. I'm not at all sure she isn't rather relieved that this has happened, it's so much the best way out from her point of view, and she doesn't know what I promised him when he went. . . . No scandal, Mother thinks; a decent display of grief, and the hero's young widow hiding her sorrow behind a mask of courage. Poor Mother! No wonder she has made up her mind that Cocky's dead. No wonder she gets so annoyed with me when I refuse to "give up hope", as I suppose she calls it to those awful bridge friends of hers. But how dare I believe that Cocky isn't alive still, when it's so impossible to imagine him dead? There's something ridiculous about the idea of Cocky being dead, though Mother seems to find it natural enough. Poor Mother! I can't really blame her for wanting to get me away to a safe distance where I won't be able to embarrass her. I wonder if I'll hate staying with Jed and his wife as much as I expect to? It can't possibly be worse than staying here in Southsea cooped up with Mother, and I don't mind very much where I am just now. Everything's horrible—haunted, unfriendly . . .'

Unbidden, there sprang to her mind, only dimly remembered, the picture of Reiverslaw and the country about it, the splendid sweep of the Cheviots, the spreading fields where slow teams ploughed long straight furrows, the lovely rivers, the dark woods clinging to hillsides. It was ten years since she had seen it, and so much had happened to her that she had never been conscious of wishing to see it again until now, when she was attacked by a longing so acute that she stopped short in the middle of the Common, deaf and blind to her surroundings. She did not hear the distant band or the shrill voices of the crowds on the front, she did not see the parched and trodden grass at her feet, or the far silken blue of the sea. She had suddenly remembered the particular place which she had loved at Reiverslaw, the narrow weed-grown church road which ran between high hedges down to the village of Muirkirk.

From the highest point of it the valley of Tweed lay in full view, misty with distance, blue with the smoke of Abbeyshiels, running away to the flat country about Berwick and the steely waters of a wilder sea. Amanda knew then that she wanted to go back there, to be free of streets and pavements and shop-windows, no matter how alluring, to hear only an occasional slow Border voice break upon the quiet of the countryside. If she could have gone to live alone in some small cottage, perhaps she could regain a measure of peace, she thought; she might be able then to rearrange her life, which for a long time had been muddled and stormy—swept about at Cocky's will; but there was an insuperable obstacle to that, if a sordid one: she could not afford it. Only by going to stay with her father's cousin Jed Armstrong, could she get away from her mother, and that was an immediate necessity.

She sighed and started to walk on slowly, thinking over what she had been told of Susan Armstrong. She had been taken to lunch on board a destroyer by David White, a friend of Cocky's, and one of her fellow-guests had been a very attractive Commander who, it appeared, was a great admirer of Jed's wife and a friend of her brother Oliver Parsons. From him Amanda had learned that Susan was in a class by herself, a nonesuch, a paragon . . . 'And that helps me *such* a lot!' was Amanda's ungrateful inward comment. 'I feel that I hate her without even having seen her! There's something so detestable about these perfect women. I suppose that man is or was in love with her, and expects everyone else to fall down and worship. . . . I hope that she won't be sorry for me; I've had enough of that from Mother's friends.'

In a gloomy mood she reached the flat which her mother called home, a top storey facing the front, and was not cheered by the tinkle of china and the hum of voices. The hum fell so abruptly away to an awkward silence as she entered the drawing-room that she had no difficulty in guessing that she herself had been the topic of conversation. Her loss was indeed a God-send to Mrs. Carmichael and her circle, but Amanda did not see it in that light. Irritated, she looked at the four elderly faces, unbecomingly flushed by much bridge and strong tea, and her greeting was of the coldest.

"Well, dear," said her mother in the tone of one addressing a fractious invalid, "have you been for a nice walk?"

"No," said Amanda with a gleam of wilful pleasure in the knowledge that she was about to shock them all. "I've been out to lunch with David White on board the Claymore. It was quite an amusing party."

There was another silence, this time of pure horror; Amanda wished that she could apply the time-honoured test of letting a pin drop, but she had neither pin nor time, for the three guests, in a pointed manner, as if to let her see that they, at least, knew what was becoming, rose, made their farewells and thanks and filed from the room.

Mrs. Carmichael, returning from speeding them on their long descent to the ground floor, lost no time in breaking into fluent reproaches.

"How could you do such a thing, Amanda?" she cried, her little mouth drooping at the corners. "Or if you had to, must you tell everyone about it?"

Amanda was lighting a cigarette. "Are you scolding me for going out to lunch, Mother?" she asked, "or for not telling lies about it?"

"It's no use being flippant, Amanda. In the circumstances you ought not to be going out at all."

"But what are the circumstances, Mother? I do wish you wouldn't persist in treating me like a widow before we know that I am."

"I don't know how you can talk in that heartless way, Amanda," said her mother, tears rising readily to her eyes, "With poor Lloyd gone—"

"Don't let us start on that, please," said Amanda quickly. "I refuse to believe that Cocky is dead, which I suppose is what you mean by 'gone'?"

('Oh dear, what a brute I'm being,' she thought miserably. 'Why must I always snap at her? Why can't I just keep quiet and let her go on?')

"My poor darling," Mrs. Carmichael was saying, richly sympathetic; "if you would only confide in your mother, your troubles would be halved at once! We must have *faith*, dear that whatever sorrow may come, it is from God and is for the best—"

"Mother!" cried Amanda passionately, revolted as she always was when her mother became sentimentally religious. All contrition for having been so sharp-tongued fled before this—to her—nauseating display of feeling which did not even ring true. "We won't drag God into this! Whatever has happened is my fault and Cocky's! It's too mean-spirited to turn round and blame God for it!"

"Well!" said her mother in a shocked indrawn breath. *"Well,* Amanda! I see it is useless to try to make you see this as I, thank God, see it. I wash my hands of it; you must struggle on yourself. I shall pray for you," she added nobly, but in a voice which expressed doubt of the efficacy of prayer when applied to anyone so lost to proper feeling as her daughter. "I shall *pray* for you, Amanda, night and day, that you may be given faith. More than that I cannot do, though I have tried my utmost."

"Very well, Mother. That's settled," said Amanda with a calm which hid her shaking horror of this scene, and unpleasantly reminded by it of a Revivalist meeting. "I suppose you want me to be given faith enough to believe that Cocky's dead? I am going to pack now, and you can pray for me in peace."

She slipped out of the room, leaving Mrs. Carmichael with hands clasped in mute forgiveness over the bag containing her bridge winnings. In the corridor outside, narrow and dark, she leant against the wall, struggling with the deadly sickness which after that sort of discussion invariably overcame her.

'At least,' she thought, when at last she was in her own tiny room, the door locked and the window flung wide open, 'at least I hope to be spared all these prayers and reproaches at Reiverslaw.'

II

"Well, here you are!" was Jed's obvious greeting as Amanda's slim gloved fingers were swallowed in his enormous clasp, and she wondered how she could have been so foolish as to think she might not recognize him, even after ten years, for he towered above everyone else on the platform at Berwick-on-Tweed. "Where's your luggage?"

"In the van. Could you find a porter?"

"No use. They're all too damn' lazy here. I'll get it."

He dived into the van, porters and guard and postmen spraying out on either side of him, dislodged by his great shoulders, and seizing a suitcase, hurled it out on to the platform at her feet, where it burst open to reveal a scattered collection of male underwear, a pair of striking purple sock-suspenders prominent on top of the pile.

Amanda began to laugh, even as she stooped to thrust the tumbled heap back into the case. Raising a flushed face she called: "This isn't mine! Look for two dark-brown expanding suitcases and a hat-box, and do be more careful with them!"

There was a scuffle inside the van, then, clearing a way with the suitcases and hatbox, which he brandished in either hand, Jed emerged triumphant.

"Got them!" he announced. "Come on, the car's outside." He swept Amanda, still laughing, before him, and it was only when he had thrown her luggage into the back of the car that she realized that she was still clutching a handful of gaudy pyjamas and the purple suspenders.

"Wait! Stop! Turn back!" she cried, as the car started with a roar and a violent jerk. "I've got some clothes here belonging to someone else!"

With another jerk the car stopped. "What's that?" he asked.

"Has anyone ever told you that you're an abominably bad driver?" said Amanda, accustomed to Cocky's smooth manipulation of gears and brake, and feeling as if her spine were sticking out through the crown of her hat.

"Bad driver? Me?" He stared at her innocently. "Was that what you stopped me for? To tell me? I've a good mind to make you walk."

"I wish I could." There was fervour in Amanda's voice. "But I didn't stop you to tell you what you can't help knowing. It's these— these clothes." She indicated the rainbow-coloured bundle on her knee. "Surely you didn't think they were mine?"

Jed glanced over his shoulder. "We needn't turn back, if that's all you're shouting about. Here's somebody coming to claim 'em!"

Amanda, twisting in her seat, also looked round to see a small man in a horrible bright blue overcoat and a green Homburg rushing towards them, gesticulating wildly.

"Oh!" she said in dismay. "*How* are we to explain? This is dreadful."

"I doubt it'll not be too easy," Jed answered; but he sounded as if he were more amused than worried.

As the figure drew near, he seized the things from Amanda's nerveless hold, rolled them up, and tossed them out of the window, to fall like a brilliant bouquet at their owner's regrettably green-suède-shod feet. "Here!" he bawled, before anything else could be said on either side. "You ought to take more care of your clothes. Might have had them stolen!" In the same instant the car jumped forward again with the clumsy bucking motion of a frisky bullock, and they shot off up the road, leaving Berwick, England, and the pyjamas' owner behind them. Amanda, for the second time in twenty minutes, laughed and continued to laugh as she had not for years; spontaneous laughter that brought tears to her eyes and threatened to degenerate into schoolgirl giggling.

Presently Jed's rumbling voice broke in on her mirth. "I got you out of that pretty neatly, didn't I?" he observed complacently.

Amanda's laughter was abruptly cut short by equally healthy righteous indignation. "You? But it was you who got me *into* it. It was all your fault," she cried. "*You* threw his suitcase at me. I only picked up the things."

"I'm sure I never told you to carry them off with you," he said severely. "We're not used to these goings-on here; you'll need to remember." Then he chuckled. "Lord, how angry Susan'll be when she hears!"

"Will she?" A note of apprehension sounded in Amanda's voice. "Does she—would she disapprove?"

"Disapprove? Susan? She'll be as cross as hell because she missed the fun," said Jed, chuckling again.

"Oh!" This shed quite a new light on the character of the unknown Susan, and as Jed seemed disinclined for further talk, Amanda was left to think it over in silence until the lovely peace of the evening stole on her senses, and she forgot to think at all.

The afterglow was fading from the sky, leaving it primrose and cold, unearthly green with wisps of almost transparent smoky grey cloud trailed across it. A tremendous full moon was sailing up above the eastern horizon in calm splendour, brightening almost with the passing moments; dark trees, separated from the road by wide stretches of grass, were motionless in the still air. There were beech hedges, trimmed to rounded elegance, on either side for miles at a time; the scent of stocks from red-roofed cottage gardens was blown in through the open windows of the car as they travelled. They crossed Till, running slow and sullen between cliffs crowned with woods, by a narrow high old bridge, and at last they were following the curves of kindlier Tweed, which swept in broad loops through the level water-meadows.

Jed had switched on his sidelights, though they were hardly necessary in this luminous northern twilight, and they picked out small objects, here a scudding rabbit's white bob-tail, there the savage green eyes of a marauding cat or a number of softer topaz twinkles that were the eyes of sheep staring over the hedge; the pale bark of an ash trunk, a cluster of vivid dahlias, robbed of all colour now that the sun was down, shaggy in front of a cottage. An owl flew over the car, stroking the air noiselessly with broad, blunt wings, on its way to hunt for mice in some near-by stackyard.

Now the fields lay open to right and left of the road, silvery and bare save where a few last stooks, not yet carried, cast long soft shadows thrown by the moon across the stubble. Stacks stood ghostly behind the hedges, palely gleaming, like tall, narrow, windowless houses. steep-roofed, thatched with straw, or round like solid towers. They turned into a narrower, rougher road, bordered with hawthorn and elder bowed down by heavy bunches of ripening purple berries. They were gradually climbing, and before them rose the ridge on which Reiverslaw stood, with the Cheviots, fold on fold, far and faint behind it.

"Nearly there," said Jed.

Amanda, calling herself all sorts of a fool for being so sensitive, sat forward, her hands tightly clasped, her heart beating fast and thick. In a very few minutes she must meet Jed's wife, and a great deal seemed to hang on their meeting. If she and Susan were antagonistic towards each other her stay at Reiverslaw would be wasted in petty irritation, and she might as well have remained with her mother. Not until now had she realized fully how much she was depending on these simpler, more sympathetic surroundings to possess again not only a degree of happiness, a little of the joyful serenity which she had never known properly except in fleeting moments, but her self-respect. Her mother had been right in saying that she needed faith, but it was faith in herself, in her ability to be master of her fate, which she lacked and must regain if life was ever to be worth living. She was so deadly weary of keeping up the defensive pose of hard, polished flippancy which she had adopted as a guard for her shrinking, hurt, inner self . . . She shook her head impatiently; by this time she ought to have learned not to hope for anything from others. Why should Susan Armstrong's like or dislike of her have any real influence on her? 'It's this place,' she thought. 'Making me soft and childish. I mustn't let it get hold of me like this, or I'll be worse off than ever.'

As they swung in between white-painted gates, Jed would have seen, had he looked at her, that her face had hardened to an expressionless calm; but he was intent on something else, peering before him into the half-dark of the tree-shadowed drive, which the moon was not high enough to light.

"What the devil?" he muttered, stopping the car in his usual abrupt fashion.

"Couldn't you *warn* me when you're going to . . ." began Amanda, only to break off as an extraordinary combination of sounds, which the car's engine had previously muffled, smote on her ears. Gruntings, squeaks, a dog's hysterical barking, wild female laughter and the crashing of heavy bodies through undergrowth made a background to a man's voice, hoarse with rage and mirth, roaring, "Head 'em off, can't you? Head the brutes off! Not *that* way! To the gate, for God's sake! Damn 'em for worse than Gadarene swine!"

"What . . ." began Amanda again. Beside her Jed's chuckle sounded. "Just watch," he advised. "You'll see some rare fun in a minute."

There rose a shriek: "I've lost my shoe!" answered by another of: "My *precious* roses! They're trampling all over them! Never mind your shoe!" And there burst simultaneously from the shelter of a small shrubbery an enormous elderly sow and numbers of small squealing piglets, two young women in evening dress with skirts hoisted to their knees and a man flourishing a rake. From the bushes still echoed a volley of well-chosen oaths uttered with speed and precision, and accompanied by a loud snapping of twigs and small branches.

"There you are," said Jed with simple pride, switching on the headlights to illuminate the scene more fully. "Pigsticking at your very door. How's that for sport?"

Amanda had no time to reply, even if she had not been dumb with amazement, for the taller young woman, clearing a flower-border in a flying leap, screamed, "Jed! If that's you, for heaven's sake get out and help us! Those vile pigs of yours have made the most appalling mess of the garden."

"Not I. Bad for them to be chased, and bad for me to run after them," said Jed unmoved.

"You brute!" This was evidently addressed to Jed, but as in the same moment she turned and dealt one small porker a resounding blow with the stick in her hand, there was reasonable ground for confusion.

"That's my wife," said Jed with pride.

"What?" cried Amanda, craning out of her side of the car. *"That?"*

He nodded, pulling a pipe from his pocket and proceeding to fill it, heedless of the exhortations to "Come and *help*!" which rent the air on all sides, for by this time two men in dinner jackets had also burst from the shrubbery.

"Eh, ma dallies!" suddenly bellowed the man with the rake, from his tone of personal bereavement the gardener dashing off into the distance once more.

"Hadn't you better help them?" suggested Amanda, only to wish that she had not, for without hesitation Jed let in the clutch and, furiously sounding his horn, drove full upon the assembled multitude of pigs and humans with instant and gratifying result. The pigs melted away into the darkness to an outburst of grunts and squeals, while their pursuers leapt wildly to safety.

Jed once more stopped the car, got out, and looked along the drive towards the gate. Amanda, following, was in time to see the drove sweep through the entrance, with a fleeting form, rake in hand, after them.

"That's done it," he said with satisfaction, and was instantly surrounded by four dishevelled and indignant persons demanding what he meant by it.

"Well, I've driven out your pigs for you. What more d'you want?" he asked. "You're a fine-looking lot. Tinkers in evening clothes."

He turned to the silent Amanda. "That ruffian with the limp's my brother-in-law, Oliver Parsons," he said, pointing at one of the dinner-jacketed figures, now brushing moss and dust from his trousers with passionate care. "And that's his wife Peggy with the yellow hair and one shoe off. And the next is Larry Heriot. I don't know what he's doing here, anyway. He ought to be too tired with looking after his harvest to be chasing pigs at this time of night; and you've seen my wife already. She looks about the worst of the bunch."

Amanda's eyes met the glance of the tall woman who was trying vainly, as she advanced, to tidy her hair and stop laughing.

"W-welcome to Reiverslaw," quavered Susan Armstrong, holding out a grubby hand.

III

'A nice hostess I must seem,' thought Susan, as her hand was shaken without much enthusiasm by her guest, 'but I'm *blowed* if I'm going to apologize for looking like this! After all, the pigs could hardly have been left romping about the garden.'

Aloud she said, restored to her own humorous gravity, "Shall we all go into the house? I think that drinks are indicated."

The suggestion was a popular one. They trooped in, but once inside there was a curious drifting away, accompanied by murmurs of "I could do with a wash", and "I *must* do something to my face . . ." which left guest and hostess facing each other in the sitting-room, rather at a loss for conversation now that they were so unexpectedly *tête-à-tête*.

"Have you had dinner?"

"Yes, thank you. I dined on the train."

"Then won't you have a drink? And do you smoke?"

"Please. I should like a whisky-and-soda. Very weak."

It was exactly like a page out of one of those horrid little books which contained useful questions and answers in a foreign language, thought Susan, pouring out whisky, adding soda, handing the filled glass and the cigarettes.

Amanda for her part was wondering with unreasonable disappointment just why she had expected so much of Susan. She was quite ordinary, though nice to look at in an uncommon way, so tall and dark, with the mouth curved for laughter and those serious eyes. There was nothing to dislike about her, but not a great deal to like, either.

Susan, striking a match and lighting their cigarettes, was seeing Amanda Cochrane fully in the bright room. Not very tall, but slender to thinness, which gave her an air of height, she had beautiful feet and ankles, was beautifully made altogether. Her hair, now that she had pulled off the brown felt hat which had partially covered it, shone pale as platinum above a small face, pale also, except for skilfully applied rouge. Her eyes, heavily shadowed by thick gold-tipped lashes, were unexpectedly brown. She looked pretty, smart and tired to death.

On impulse Susan said quickly, "I didn't mean to have all these people here on your very first evening. There's something so tiresome about coming from a journey and having to meet a whole collection of strangers. But my brother and sister-in-law found themselves dinnerless owing to the collapse of their kitchen range, and Larry Heriot just appeared."

"It doesn't matter a bit. I really thought you'd been very clever," said Amanda, "and asked them here to help to break the ice. I feel rather an incubus, you know."

"What nonsense! Jed is out all day, and you will be company for me, I hope."

Amanda looked at her straight in the eyes. "Did my mother write to you and tell you that I was a fragile creature, distraught and unbalanced, to be treated with tender care?" she asked suddenly.

"Yes. I'm afraid that she did, but don't let it worry you for a moment. I haven't the faintest intention of looking after you, and to avoid temptation I tore up her letter and burned it," said Susan. "Oh, here they are, all coming to drink like jungle beasts at a waterhole! Would you like to stay, or would you rather just vanish? I don't mean to ask these polite questions after tonight, so make the most of my politeness."

"Then I'd like to go to bed, please," Amanda said promptly.

"You shall. Come with me; I'll take you up by the back-stairs and we won't meet the crowd. Blessed back-stairs! What should we do without them in this trying life?"

Susan led her swiftly up, along a passage and into a cheerful room where a fire burned and green-and-white chintz showed off the polished surfaces of old mahogany.

"I gave you this room because it looks out to Cheviot. You can lie in bed and see it," she said, going to the window and pulling aside a curtain. Moonlight streamed coldly in, and outside it was so bright that trees showed their branches and leaves, flowers had not lost their shapes, and delicate black shadows lay sharply etched over lawn and drive. A cow lowed from one of the near fields, and an owl hooted loud and eerily in a tall elm beside the gate. Apart from that, there were no sounds but the innumerable small rustlings which never cease on the quietest night.

"Good night," said Susan. "I hope you will sleep well. Breakfast is round about nine."

"Good night." Amanda stood stiffly in the middle of the room watching until Susan had closed the door behind her, then she drew a deep breath and stretched her arms wide. It was lovely to think that no one would disturb her, that the room was hers alone. Even when she stayed in the Southsea flat she had often had to share her mother's room if Mrs. Carmichael happened to be feeling wealthy enough to pay a maid who slept in. Since Cocky had left on this last flight, she had asked Amanda every night if she would really rather sleep alone, and had been hurt when Amanda said yes, she would.

Every night Amanda had been acutely conscious of her mother's presence in the next room, divided from her by a thin inner wall, so different from the solidity of Reiverslaw. She *must* be lonely in the night, Mrs. Carmichael had insisted, without . . . after being accustomed to . . . delicately she would break off, her words trailing away into significant murmurs. Lonely! After seven years of marriage it seemed to Amanda an exquisite loneliness which she would never want to exchange for the society of anyone, mother or lover—or husband.

At last she relaxed, and turning to her suitcases, began quickly and neatly to empty them. Almost at the bottom of the second, her fingers encountered something hard laid in between the folds of a tweed skirt. Frowning a little in bewilderment, she drew out a square silver frame, and the frown changed to a deeper one of anger. It was just like her mother to steal in and hide Cocky's latest photograph among her clothes, where she would not find it until she came to unpack.

Amanda looked coldly at the handsome, reckless, self-confident and wilful face of the picture, and found herself unmoved. Perhaps, though, it was as well that her mother had chosen this photograph and not the old one, taken in the early days of their engagement. Cold and dead as her heart seemed, Amanda was glad not to have to look at that younger Cocky tonight. It was difficult to keep one's memory from harking back to forbidden things like those enchanted days before she had discovered how utterly unsuited they were. Cocky, and this was so typical of him, had never discovered it at all. It was strange, thought Amanda, standing with the silver frame cold to her hand, that instinct, which so often gave warning of danger, seemed to fail when passion, physical attraction, propinquity—call it anything but love!—hurried two careless young creatures into marriage. No inner voice counselled caution, and if older people said 'Wait', they might as well speak to the wind. Older people, however, had entirely approved when Amanda Carmichael and Lloyd Cochrane announced their intention of getting married. The church had given its beautifully worded blessing, and added warningly that whom God had joined together, man must not put asunder.

Amanda sighed, took the photograph from its frame, and slowly tore it across and across, dropping the pieces of stiff cardboard into a waste-paper-basket beside the writing-table. When her cases were empty she put the untenanted frame into one, and turned the key on it. Tomorrow her luggage would be taken away to a box-room, the basket would be emptied, and the fragments it contained burnt. She was not going to begin her stay at Reiverslaw with this reminder of her husband where she could see it, however shocked her mother might be. The dead—and she obviously considered Cocky dead—were sacred to Mrs. Carmichael, even their photographs holy, no matter how much she might have disliked them in life. Amanda smiled, remembering the hideous likeness of her mother's most-hated aunt, which, now that Aunt Ruthie could not any longer annoy her by calling her a hypocrite, occupied an honoured position on her chest of drawers. "Poor Mother!" she said aloud, with less irritation than usual. "I wonder how she ever came to have a daughter so unlike her? I hope she realizes how much fonder of each other we are when we're apart."

A fine new feeling of freedom possessed her as she undressed and bathed, nor had it left her when, wrapping the quilt from the bed round her, she switched off the lights, drew back the curtains, and sat down by the open window. For hours she sat there motionless, watching the stars wheel into place round the dark cup of the sky, vaguely comforted by their presence and the thought of her own insignificance. When she crept stiffly to bed, it was to fall immediately into a deep sleep untroubled by dreaming, from which she awoke unwillingly, roused by a heavy tattoo on her door.

CHAPTER THREE

I

IN ANSWER to her drowsy "Come in", the door began slowly to open, apparently through the agency of a laden tray which appeared, wobbling so that the china on it rattled, round the corner, and remained there alone in mid-air while Amanda rubbed her eyes, staring sleepily. After a pause, the tray began to move forward, followed, rather to Amanda's relief, by a very young housemaid, daisy-like in pink print, with a snowy apron and cap. She steered the tray safely to the bedside table, set it down a little too definitely, and announced cheerfully:

"Here yer tea . . . mem. An' the mistress says are ye wantin' yer breakfast in bed?"

Amanda sat up, shook back the heavy pale curls from her face and looked at the window, still uncurtained and open. It was a fine fresh morning, the sky a hazy, almost colourless blue, the Cheviots veiled in mist which half revealed their noble flanks. Carts were going past jingling and creaking to an undercurrent of men's voices talking slowly and companionably. The air carried a burden of country scents: late roses, wet grass, a hint of wood smoke, and earth just warmed by the sun.

"I wonder what they'd like me to do?" murmured Amanda half to herself, longing to be up and out, yet knowing that to many hostesses a guest who insists on appearing for breakfast is an unmitigated nuisance.

"Och, there's naebody lies in their bed at Reiverslaw without they're gey hard-up," said Robinia.

'Hard-up?' thought Amanda, puzzled. 'Why on earth should anyone stay in bed because they were hard-up, and why should the maid know they were anyhow?' But she gathered that to go downstairs for breakfast would be quite in order, and sprang from bed with an eagerness to face the day to which she had long been a stranger.

In the dining-room she found Jed and Susan already at table. There was a delicious smell of coffee from the machine over which Susan brooded like a hen with one chicken; there were brown eggs, a home-cured, home-grown ham, pink and white with a spicy brown crust, on a side table, a dish of grilled trout, caught, Susan announced, by Oliver yesterday afternoon, on a hot-plate. There was porridge made of coarse- ground meal milled at the Abbeyshiels mill from local oats, rich cream, primrose-coloured fresh butter, a brown loaf, scones, and honey in the comb.

"Heavens! What a feast," said Amanda, sitting down. "Yes, I'll have porridge, please. I feel greedy this morning."

"Grand!" said Jed, giving her a small bowl, pouring cream lavishly over its contents, heedless of her protests that she would become grossly fat. "You fat? You look like a needle!"

"Not very prettily put," murmured Susan, still engrossed with coffee-making. "*I* should have said a willow-wand, myself. And very nice it looks, too."

Jed grunted something which sounded like "Fancy work. Comes of writing novels," and Amanda heard him and paused with her spoon half-way to her mouth.

"*Do* you write novels?" she asked.

"I only wrote two, and they weren't at all successful," Susan said peacefully.

"Wait a minute! I've got it!" cried Amanda in great excitement. "You must be 'S. Parsons'. You wrote *Partners for the Lancers*!"

"Yes," admitted Susan. "I did."

"I loved that book," said Amanda, staring at her wide-eyed, as if she had not seen her before. "Really loved it, I mean. Read it and read it until it was almost in shreds. And you wrote it?"

"'And did you once see Shelley plain'?" said Susan, smiling. She waved a hand at her guest. "Behold my public, Jed!" And to Amanda: "Dear Public, how awfully gratifying it is to hear that you have read it, poor book! To judge by its sales, I should have thought that no one had ever heard of it. We'll talk about it later, Amanda. Don't spoil Jed's appetite. He's always terrified when my books are mentioned in case I should suddenly go mad and start on another."

"I don't know why you don't," said Amanda.

"I'm too busy living at first-hand just now. I was an onlooker when I wrote that book. Here's some coffee. I hope it's drinkable, but I am not at all clever with this infernal machine. My hand lacks cunning."

Amanda took the offered cup, and said, remembering something: "Why did the nice little maid who brought my tea tell me that no one stayed in bed for breakfast unless they were hard-up?"

"Ah!" said Susan. "So you've struck it already, have you? The language difficulty, I mean. It always used to worry me, too, the way the people here seemed to plume themselves on being 'hard-up' or 'shabby', speaking of it without a trace of decent reticence. Such a lack of proper pride, I thought, and so different from what one had been told of the Scots character."

"But what did she mean, then?"

"D'you mean to tell me you don't know that it means ill, sick?" Jed interrupted. "I'd have thought you'd have heard your father use the words. As for Susan, pay no attention to her blethering, she knows the language as well as I do myself by this time." He pushed back his chair and rose, looming enormous in the small room. "Well, do you two want to go to the show at Gledesmuir today?"

"Jed! Is it really Gledesmuir Show? Of course we want to go," said Susan. "Do you hate a picnic lunch?" she added hastily to Amanda. "I hope not, because the food provided at the Show is abominable, and the atmosphere in the marquee could be cut in slices with a knife."

"It's more than the meat could be, last year," said her husband with a grin. "And the butter had to be helped with a teaspoon. Better get them to pack some lunch, and don't forget the beer. I'm going up to see the steward. We'll start after the post's been." He tramped out.

Susan laughed. "Orders for the day," she said.

"You don't mind?" asked Amanda.

"Mind what? The orders? Oh dear me, no. Why should I?"

"Oh, I don't know." Amanda stirred restlessly in her chair. "I'm not good at having orders given to me, and somehow I should have thought you wouldn't be, either. I mean, you didn't marry young enough to take kindly to it, after being your own mistress for so long."

Passing over the fact that she had taken her brother's orders, often much more unreasonable and tiresome than a husband's, during most of her life, Susan said lightly,

"Probably I find the change restful, and it depends so much, don't you think, on who gives the orders? Jed's almost always coincide with my own wishes, so perhaps I am lucky, but I can't imagine him riding rough-shod over me even if they didn't. It isn't his nature, masterful man though he is."

She rose as she spoke, to put an end to the discussion, for it was plain to her that Amanda was on the verge of making one of those hasty confidences, usually regretted almost before uttered, which have the unfortunate effect of causing the too-impulsive utterer to look with loathing on her unwilling confidante ever after.

"I must go and see cook," she said, "and arrange about lunch, not forgetting the beer. Will you do whatever you like—write letters, or go into the garden, or anything, until the post comes? He is generally here by half past ten, so, giving Jed twenty minutes with his precious *Scotsman*, we'll start about eleven, I expect. Don't forget thick shoes and a coat, because Gledesmuir is right up among the hills, and it will be quite cool."

'Thank heaven I didn't say any more,' thought Amanda, blissfully unconscious that there had been any purpose in Susan's quiet departure to consult her cook. 'This place is having a most demoralizing effect on me, I want to babble everything I always have kept to myself; but she must be an understanding sort of person if she wrote *Partners for the Lancers*. I don't know how I was so silly last night as to think she was ordinary. . . . Oh, lord! I suppose I'd better go and write to Mother before I forget . . .'

The letter took so long that she had only finished it when Elspeth, rustling in starched print, bore the letters and papers into the sitting-room on a salver. Close at her heels came Jed, accompanied by a peculiarly woolly black dog of dubious ancestry, with a coat like a sheep-skin rug and brilliant eyes peering roguishly through a ragged forelock. He gambolled up to Amanda and made a playful snatch at her newly-written letter, which she saved by springing to her feet with a shriek.

"Down, Bawtie, down, sir!" Susan, who had also entered cried ineffectually.

"What an odd name—" began Amanda, and:

"Well, after all, he's a damned odd *dog*!" said Jed, ripping open the bundle of newspapers. "Did you ever see such a brute, Amanda? Have three shots at guessing what he is."

"He's a spoondle, or a refoundler, if you prefer it," said Susan, "and he was called Bawtie after a beautiful but wicked gentleman, the Sieur de la Beauté, who was Warden of the Marches for a bit, and was commonly known as Bonnie Bawtie. He's a very charming dog indeed—at least, he can be. There are times when I would willingly slay him with my own hand."

The spoondle—or refoundler—smirked at her after the manner of the dog who is not certain that a remark made by his humans is in good taste. Then, as she pulled one of his long ears, he gave a forgiving wag of the plumy tail, which swept a cigarette-box, an ash-tray and Jed's pipe from a small low table on to the floor.

"The wee man!" said Susan bitterly. She and Amanda bent to pick up the scattered cigarettes, and Bawtie, highly delighted, made a swoop at their defenceless faces, passing a long moist tongue over each like a sponge over a slate.

"Ouf!" cried Amanda, dropping the handful of cigarettes and hastily standing erect.

"Are you not a dog-lover, Mrs. Cochrane? I am so fond of our dumb friends," said Susan, pushing her dumb friend violently from her.

"I hope I love the meanest of God's creatures," said Amanda with equal gravity, "but your wee man has just removed all the powder from my nose. And do you think it can be good for him to eat cigarettes in bulk like that? What about nicotine poisoning?"

"Brute's got the digestion of an ostrich," growled Jed from behind pages of the *Scotsman*.

"It's a pity that Bawtie is so sophisticated. He loves the taste of powder, the more expensive the better," said Susan. "Catch him ever trying to lick Jed's face! I suppose we'd better go and repair damages."

They came downstairs again a few minutes later freshly made up for the outing, hastened by prolonged blasts from the car's horn, to find Jed sitting in the driving-seat alternately pushing Bawtie back from his knee to the seat beside him, and sounding a fanfare.

"Apparently we are meant to sit behind," murmured Susan, and got in after Amanda had negotiated a lordly basket, covered with a dinner-napkin of glossy whiteness, which occupied most of the available space. "Do you mind?"

"Not a bit," Amanda assured her. "Shall we nurse the basket, turn about?"

"We'll put it on the floor," said Susan, and promptly did so.

"Mind the beer," said her husband anxiously as he started the car, quite smoothly for once. "It's bad for it to be jolted."

"The beer. That's all he thinks of. We may suffer the most brutal discomfort as long as the precious beer is safe," said Susan, giving the basket a surreptitious but vindictive kick. "If you mention the beer again, Jed, I'll throw it out of the window, every single bottle."

II

Apart from a few impulsive curvets and caracoles executed by the car, which caused the picnic basket to bounce against their ankles, the occupants of the back seat endured very little discomfort as they were carried over winding roads towards the misty hills.

Though the woods still wore their sombre green of summer, with only an elm here and there turning clear pale yellow, or a horse-chestnut drooping golden-brown fans them as they passed, there was a feel of autumn in the air, a look of autumn in the hazy blue distances. The hedges were richly coloured, great bunches of crimson haws hung on the hawthorns, the long spiked branches of the barberry bush were weighted with waxen tassels, orange, vermilion, tawny; elders added a splash of shining black fruit, purple-bloomed. In bare fields where the stooks had been carried, the stubble shone. Where they passed a row of cottages in village or steading, the little trim gardens were brilliant with dahlias of all colours, looking almost too big for the tiny plots where they nodded their heavy heads, with the hot orange of marigolds with lavender and pink and blue-mauve Michaelmas daisies, with hollyhocks so tall that they reached almost to the roofs above, of mellow red pantiles or slates shining with a green and purple sheen in the sun. Then ran down into a broad valley where the links of a little river coiled between level green pastures. Beyond the low ground the hills rose again more steeply now, for these were the lower slopes of the Cheviots; and in a fold of the green hillside, backed by a cluster of trees, was a house and farm-steading, looking out across the river.

"What a lovely place to live!" exclaimed Amanda, enchanted by the sudden glimpse of the house and its surroundings, the bare hills at its back, the valley below.

"Yes. I sometimes wish that Gledewaterford were my house," said Susan, "until I see Reiverslaw again. Larry Heriot lives there."

"This is Glede Water," said Jed over his shoulder, as they crossed it by a narrow bridge of grey stone, humped steeply in the middle with embrasures in which foot-passengers must stand to let a vehicle pass; "and that'll be Larry, off to Gledesmuir for the show," he added, as a red car nosed its way between high stone gateposts below the house. and turned into the road a little way ahead of them.

"Lucky man," said Amanda, her eyes still fixed on his house, white walls shaded by a spreading lime tree, tall chimneys with a curl of blue smoke rising from one, vivid against the hillside behind it, and a corner of old-walled garden. "If I were a millionaire I'd buy it from him."

"No you wouldn't," broke in Jed, whose ears were evidently very sharp this morning, "because the Heriots have owned it and farmed it for hundreds of years. A Heriot went to Flodden from here, and they're as proud of it as Lucifer. Larry wouldn't sell it if he was starving."

"He'd be a fool if he did," said Amanda.

"It's a very lonely place in winter, especially for a woman. They've been snowed up at Gledewaterford for weeks on end," said Susan. "I don't imagine that Ruth Heriot cares for it much, and there isn't any doubt that she would be less queer if she lived nearer other people."

"Who is Ruth? Mr. Heriot's wife?"

"No, his sister. She keeps house for him, and breeds dogs in her spare time," Susan told her.

"Heavens! What an appalling hobby," murmured Amanda absent-mindedly, twisting her head as they swept past the gates to get a last view of the place. A huge old rowan stretched branches heavy with bright berries and leaves beginning to turn to the rusty reds and tarnished bronze tints which in a week or two would transform it to a tower of flame, over the crumbling wall by the gate-post; the dusky shapes clustered beside the garden were ancient yews. The car turned a corner, and she sank back with a sigh.

"We'll take you there some day," Jed promised. "Though they're not exactly keen on visitors. It's an interesting old house; used to be a rest-house for the monks of Abbeyshiels, or something."

Privately Amanda thought she would prefer Gledewaterford to remain a mystery, just sighted, never seen at close quarters; one of those castles perched on hills of glass beloved of fairy tales, unattainable, alluring. She wondered if the Prince who reached the castle after toiling up those smooth slopes was ever disappointed? But in a fairy-tale, of course, achievement always fulfilled expectations, which was the whole difference between those lands of enchantment bound in stiff red or green covers, and real life. "When I go there to tea or some dull festivity," she said to herself, "it will just turn out to be another rather lonely farm with an old house, not nearly so pleasant as Reiverslaw."

They were following Glede Water, the road turning and twisting just above its bank, and rising steadily with every mile. Now the nearer hills, which had closed them in, fell behind them, and they had a sight of higher crests, wave upon wave rolling away on either side to the far distance where they faded into the paler dimness of a faint blue sky. They crossed the water again by another hump-backed bridge, crept through a tiny village dignified by a church with a slender steeple which was Gledewaterhead, and took a road even narrower, unfenced, innocent of tarmacadam, guided by a rickety signpost, its one arm announcing in staggering, ill-painted characters, 'Gledesmuir', and underneath in smaller letters, as if of minor importance, 'Newcastle', which gave Amanda a shock of surprise, for it seemed impossible that a track so small and rough as almost to be part of the moors through which it wound, should ever bring a weary traveller to the noisy, dirty streets of Newcastle-on-Tyne.

Quite suddenly, when Glede Water beside them had dwindled away to no more than a burn seeping through moss and peat, running small and very clear, creeping round great boulders, they ran into a great shallow cup high among the hills which reared their splendid heads all round its circumference, a cup filled with pale golden light to the brim, so lovely, so remote, so alien to the modern world, where progress had come to mean mass-production and the race to arm, where science and art were turned to purely material advantages or to destruction; a lump rose in Amanda's throat as she gazed wordlessly at it For a long moment it seemed unearthly, an exquisite mirage, or a flashing glimpse of Tir-nan-Og, that land of heart's desire. . . . The moment passed, and she was able to see it as it was, a place of wild beauty, but no longer enchanted.

Dark purple-brown of fading heather, tawny bog and russet bracken broke up the great stretches of bent, that strange coarse grass, more grey than green, harshened and stiffened by the restless winds for ever singing through the wiry blades, the tips so white that in certain lights it looked like a fall of snow. Up here the tiny Glede was wider again, but very shallow. Other burns, fine as threads at a little distance, meandered to join it. Sandpipers perched on sun-warmed stones in the water, uttering their plaintive cries, and a pair of water-ousels, the white patches on their breasts conspicuous, flitted downstream. Through the car's open windows and roof came the clean damp scents of moor and bog, borne on a breeze that was sharper on this upland than in the fertile, arable country they had left behind them.

Amanda felt very grateful to Susan for not having spoken to spoil her perfect moment. It did not enter her mind that Susan, although she had often been there before, herself felt that at her first sight of Gledesmuir, every time she came so suddenly upon it, her eyes were rapt in the old fairy power of glamour. So she only turned her head at last, and blinking a little, as if dazzled, smiled at Amanda. Long afterwards they knew that from this moment began a friendship based on mutual understanding, born of that silent sympathy of emotion too instinctive for thought.

"Is—is this Gledesmuir?" asked Amanda.

"Yes. We go right across to the far side, where there's a tin hut. If you look you can just see the end of a dirty marquee appearing."

They were not the only people on the lonely road this morning. Every now and then Jed sounded the horn and slowed down to pass flushed and breathless cyclists bent over their handlebars, rosy girls in bright-coloured, badly made coats over cotton dresses, young men with serious red-brown faces, hot in their Sunday suits of black or navy blue, with their hair plastered down under tweed caps. Other men in similar costume could be seen making for the show-ground across country, walking with a long easy lope which looked deceptively slow, for these were mostly hill-shepherds, who could cover rough moorland all day at the same pace without a quickening of breath. There were cars, too, and even an occasional elderly pony-trap bearing a full complement of buxom women and old men, who seemed about to overflow the confines of their small vehicles, so closely were they packed.

"A good turn-out today," observed Jed, as they neared the tin hut perched on the southern rim of the moor, and saw the other cars standing in a row along the road. A crowd, composed mainly of solemn men with shepherds' crooks in horny hands, handsome black-and-white collies sidling at the heels of their masters' heavy hob-nailed boots, and ubiquitous small boys moved and stood and moved again with the purposeless air which an amiable crowd so often has, behind a dry-stone dyke running up over the moor from the road. The hut, huddled beside it, formed one side of the entrance to the show, while the other was composed of a stout, elderly person armed with a roll of tickets, from which he tore one and pressed it into the hand of each who entered, at the same time relieving them of a shilling per head.

"Tits, man!" he was roaring to a saturnine shepherd as the Reiverslaw party approached. "What's a bob tae you? Has yer wife no' got a bakin' o' girdle scones ben the hut that'll tak' firrst prize the day—forbye ye'll get eatin' them tae yer tea after! Come awa' noo, and let's see yer siller!"

"Is it me get eatin' them?" retorted the shepherd. "If the wife disna keep them in ablow a glass case for an exheebit, she'll be savin' them for the Weemen's Institute tae ta'te. Here's ma shullin'." He paid and passed in ahead of Susan and Amanda, who, leaving Jed to deal with the door-keeper and exchange loud pleasantries, joined the crowd on the short, sheep-bitten grass, sweet with wild thyme, round the door of the hut. There was a good deal of noise and laughter, but it lacked the stridency which makes townspeople's voices, raised in mirth or conversation, grate so unpleasantly on the sensitive ear. Up on Gledesmuir the broad soft accents seemed to melt into the air, and even the coquettish yells of young ladies exhorting their chosen swains to do their utmost in a foot-race died before the far-off hills could echo them.

"I shall have to go in and look at the scones and jelly and butter and knitting and things," said Susan, indicating the doorway of the hut, round which the feminine portion of the gathering swarmed like bees outside a hive. "Robinia's mother lives near here, and is certain to be showing *something*, and Robinia will want to know all about it when we get home this evening. But you don't need to, of course, unless you like."

"I *do* like. I haven't ever seen anything quite like this before," was Amanda's eager reply, and together they battled their way into the crowded place, with a mass of others, and a certain amount of good-natured jostling given and received in excellent part.

Long trestle-tables ran down the middle of the hut and round three sides, and these were covered with a bewildering variety of country produce and handcraft. From the passionate interest aroused by every item, it was plain that the entries were entirely local, and greater pride in their handiwork could not have been shown by the partial relatives of the exhibitors had the show been 'The Highland' itself.

'It's pathetic,' was Amanda's first thought as she watched an old woman, in a shapeless black hat dating from the last days of Victoria's reign, hovering over a dreadful tea-cloth embroidered in loud magenta and orange on a pink background of coarse linen, and beaming all across her lined face. "Ay, my granddochter, a' her ain work. She's an awfu' clever lassie," she said to a neighbour. Amanda changed her mind. 'It isn't pathetic at all. It's really rather wonderful, in these days when everything is centralized, and buns come machine-made out of a baker's shop, and hardly anyone knows what a churn is used for! I suppose, sooner or later, these little shows will die out, but I hope it won't be for a very long time. When they go, the last struggle of lonely country places to keep their individuality against the draw of the towns will be over.'

She said something of this to Susan, who nodded. "Yes. That's why I love to come to a show like Gledesmuir," she said. "I like the honest pride in their own work, and the knowledge that it is all done in remote shepherds' cottages and lonely hill-farms. They don't care a bit for outside opinion, so long as they know that their efforts are appreciated or envied by their neighbours. There's no exploiting, no playing to the gallery here, no real publicity. If you're fool enough not to like the show you can keep away, no one will miss you, because you're only an outsider and onlooker anyhow. Jed, of course, mourns that everything is altered the worse since he was a boy, that women no longer feed their children on porridge, or salt salmon to last them through the winter, and in a way he's right. The meal-ark, which used to be almost the whole store-cupboard, has fallen from its high estate and given way to 'baker's breid' from a cart! But as long as they still keep up this sort of thing the old spirit won't die out."

"It does seem a pity, though," murmured Amanda, "that they should put such really fine work into such ugly things doesn't it? Look at this blouse, for example." They gazed silently on the garment to which a first-prize ticket had been pinned. Of poor cheap material in a crude shade of blue, made without much regard for the existing fashion, it was exquisitely embroidered, tucked and gathered.

"Oh, well! The girl who made it will be the envy and admiration of all her friends, and when she puts it on to walk out with her 'lad' he'll think her beautiful and be as proud as a peacock," Susan consoled her. "Don't waste your pity on her, for she'll be quite happy, having nothing to compare it with but others of the same cut. Come and help me to look for Robinia's mother's socks and scones."

Obediently Amanda followed her, and they were bending over an array of socks, knitted in intricate patterns, each pair vieing with the next in colour and thickness, when a deep woman's voice said gruffly:

"So you *are* here. Larry said it was your car we saw just as we came out of our gate."

"Oh, Ruth!" Susan said, without, it seemed to Amanda, any very great pleasure. "How are you?"

"Much as usual, thanks. A bit sick of the frowst in here among these ghastly woollen goods," returned the tall woman whose thinness, allied to big bones, combined to give her a gaunt appearance; but her face had a kind of haggard good looks, marred by the discontented expression which had pulled down her mouth at the corners and drawn deep lines from nose to upper lip. She spoke without troubling to lower her loud gruff tones, and several far from friendly glances were darted at her when she continued: "Did you see ever a more loathsome collection of hand-made garments and tray-cloths? Must have been executed by colour-blind women, what?"

"The work is quite beautifully done," said Susan, rather coldly, and her voice, though low in pitch, was clear as single notes on a wood wind-instrument in contrast to the other's.

"You're not going to pretend you admire 'em, Susan? Tact can be carried a bit too far, you know. Come on, tell the truth and shame the devil."

"I *do* admire anything that shows such excellent workmanship," said Susan, and added, "My dear Ruth, if tact can be carried too far, so can your kind of truthfulness. Never speak the truth except when it's unpleasant, might be your motto. And now, don't let us bicker. Here is Amanda Cochrane, Mrs. Cochrane, the daughter of Jed's cousin Wat Carmichael, who has come to stay with us for as long as she can bear it. Amanda, this is Miss Heriot, she lives in the house which you thought so charming, you remember?"

Amanda, who had been listening with faint amusement to this passage of arms, tempered with respect for Susan's calm refusal to be browbeaten, bowed and smiled politely but without enthusiasm. Heaven alone knew what the awful woman might say next! Miss Heriot, however, gave her a glance which spoke quite plainly her contempt for anyone who was so obviously ornamental and nothing else, and nodded in an off-hand manner.

"You can have a damn' good time here if you hunt," she said carelessly, "But I don't suppose you do."

As this appeared to be a statement rather than a question, Amanda did not trouble to reply, and a rather awkward silence fell on all three, broken at last by Susan.

"Where's Larry?" she asked.

"Outside somewhere," said his sister indifferently. "If the bar's open in the luncheon-tent, that's where he'll be. He's never very far away from whisky."

'More unpleasant truths, I should think, judging by Susan's eye,' thought Amanda the onlooker. 'But what an awful thing to say! If his sister is always like this, I wouldn't blame "Larry" for spending his time in a bar—any bar!'

When they had succeeded in forcing their way past batches of scones, crusty loaves, neat glass jars filled with darkly glowing bramble jelly or the pale translucent pink of apple, past collections of vegetables scrubbed to unnatural cleanliness, past the small exhibits of the school children, and were again in the open, it seemed that Miss Heriot had not been correct as to her brother's whereabouts, although the luncheon-marquee was already doing a roaring trade in liquid refreshment, behind its curtain of grimy canvas. For Susan said with pleasure "Why, there he is, with Jed and Oliver!"

Amanda, looking in the same direction, saw a number of youths gathered about Jed, who was trying his skill at a peculiar form of quoits, consisting of throwing iron rings into a small hole in the ground. With him was a dark man limping slightly when he moved, whom she recognized as Oliver Parsons; and another, slighter but with well-built shoulders in an equally well-built but disgracefully shabby tweed jacket, who must be Larry Heriot. He glanced towards them as Susan spoke, and Amanda was conscious of a sudden sympathy with him, a sort of kinship, for in his jaded but reckless air she read her own outlook on life. Perhaps she did not carry the marks so clearly in her face, but they were there, scored deep on heart and mind. How could she fail to recognize another like herself?

"Larry!" called Susan, and he came up to them with a smile.

"So you've come out of that scrum alive? And not a hair disarranged. Wonderful creatures, women," he said, looking from her to Amanda.

"What on earth are you boys doing?" Susan asked indulgently. "I can't think why you allowed Jed to start that. He'll never be torn away from it now."

"Allow him? Oliver and I couldn't stop him. Can anyone stop Jed if he's set on doing something? As soon as he clapped eyes on it he had to try it, and now he's well in the running for the kitty. Best score of the day so far, and the runner-up any number of points behind," said Larry Heriot. Again he looked at Amanda. "Aren't you going to introduce me?"

"I thought you met last night. Amanda, this is Mr. Heriot—Mrs. Cochrane," said Susan. "And you *did* meet last night."

"An introduction thrown out in the middle of a pig-hunt doesn't count," he said. "Mrs. Cochrane never knew I was there last night. Did you?" Without giving Amanda time to answer, he went on to her, "I say, come and see the collies being judged for points, it's quite worth it. All their masters are as jealous as hell."

"Lunch in the car in half an hour!" Susan called after her, as Larry Heriot put a hand under her elbow and whisked her away.

CHAPTER FOUR

I

ONCE out of range of his sister's disapproving, smouldering eye, which Amanda could almost feel scorching her back, his pace slackened.

"I saw you all right last night, if you didn't see me," he said.

"Did you?" said Amanda, who knew this opening gambit by heart.

He was not in the least discouraged by her lack of interest. "I did. It was a grand sight—your face, I mean. You looked at us as if we all smelt like the old sow!"

"Dear me," murmured Amanda, who was not going to permit herself to be disconcerted, though a hint of natural colour, faint but becoming, added itself to her discreet touches of rouge. "I didn't realize that I showed my feelings as plainly as that. I'm so sorry."

"Don't apologize," he said airily. "You're looking the same again now."

"Then I'm afraid what you see must be just my normal slightly disagreeable expression," said Amanda coldly. "Shall we go and see the collies? Because if you don't mean to, I shall go back to my own party."

"It's all right. I'm not drunk," he assured her, seizing her arm, from which she had already shaken his hand several minutes earlier.

"I didn't suppose you were," said Amanda, now thoroughly bewildered—he really was a very odd person—"but do you always find it necessary to tell people that you aren't?"

"Well, I very often am, you see," he answered, staring at her deflantly.

"Oh," said Amanda blankly, for this was quite beyond any of her former experiences. Men, she had found, were much more liable to deny it flatly, even when their condition was obvious to the most unsuspicious.

"Want to run back to Susan—and Ruth?" he asked.

Amanda looked at him, saw the unhappiness that lurked behind contempt and defiance, and was again made aware of his strange likeness to her. Just so had she often felt, though, because she was a woman, she succeeded in masking it more cleverly. "No, I don't. But I don't want to stand here missing all the fun of the show just to hear you making an ass of yourself," she said.

At that he put his dark head back and laughed without bitterness. "You're all right," he said, in a relieved tone. "Come on and we'll look at the 'collie-dugs'."

More than the collies were on show when they reached the length of wall which served as props for the judges and onlookers, in front of which a number of stout stakes had been driven into the ground, each with a demure, glossy, black-and-white sheepdog, groomed as never in its hard-working life before, tethered to it. For parading up and down under the eyes of the sorely puzzled judges, and causing hysterical outbursts of jealous rage on the part of the younger and more emotional collies, was Oliver Parsons, leading Bawtie as if in a show-ring at Cruft's. Bawtie, a natural comedian, was enjoying the sensation he caused to the full, and quite saw the humour of the thing as he pranced along, waving his plumed tail and rolling his eyes.

"Good for Oliver!" exclaimed Larry Heriot. "He swore he'd do it, but I didn't think even he would have the nerve!"

There was sad confusion among the judges—sober, elderly shepherds with a deep sense of the importance of their exalted position. On their decision hung the opinion of the whole countryside as to the merits of the collies shown, and now they were confronted with this strange woollen animal, solemnly assured by Oliver that it was a pedigreed Bolivian sheep-dog, and expected to pass judgment upon it. Amanda, though rapidly becoming helpless with stifled laughter, could not help pitying them, for their furrowed brows and frequent anxious conclaves showed their perplexity. At last one, more frivolous or less gullible than his brethren, put forward the suggestion that "the wee black dug wad need tae be disqualified for his tail".

"What's wrong with his tail?" demanded Oliver indignantly, but the other judges had thankfully seized on the excuse, and gave as their undivided opinion, "He doesna juist carry it richt, d'ye see, sirr?"

"You fellows don't know a decent dog when you see one," said Oliver, in tones of disgust. "They all carry their tails like this in

Bolivia. Come on, Bawtie, my man, this is no place for us. We're not appreciated."

A voice from the ranks of the deeply interested spectators called after him as he turned haughtily away: "Ye'd best tak' him hame tae Bolivvy an' show him there!"

"Well, that makes a quid Jed owes me," said Oliver, chuckling to Larry and Amanda. "How are you this morning Amanda? As only brother of your cousin-in-law, I propose to call you Amanda. All right?"

"Yes, of course. Why not?" Amanda found his easy friendliness very engaging. "Does your sister know that you've been making a fool of her dog?"

"As a matter of fact, she doesn't—or didn't. Here she comes now, though, and I should say by the look of her that Jed must have given the show away," said Oliver rather guiltily. "Well, they say the best defence is attack, so I'll try to prove it. Hullo, Soosan loove! Do you know they haven't had the sense to give your Bonnie Bawtie a prize?"

"What have you been doing with my dog?" cried Susan, and Bawtie rose on his hind legs and leant against her with an imbecile expression of bliss. "The *poor* wee man, then!"

"Poor wee man! Why, hang it," protested her brother, "he enjoyed the fun better than anyone—a damn' sight better than the judges! He's a born clown. You might try him in a circus when farming gets so hopeless that even plutocrats like Jed have to give it up."

"Jed," said Susan severely, but with a twinkle in her eyes, as her husband silently drew a crumpled one-pound note from his trousers pocket and handed it to Oliver. "Jed, you won't be a plutocrat for much longer if you go on making these idiotic bets. Don't you know by this time that Oliver will do anything for money?"

"Thank you, dear sister. I suppose you imagine that because you're tainted with the love of filthy lucre and married Jed for his money, it runs in the family?" said Oliver. "I wish I had Peggy here to stand up for me."

"Why haven't you? Where is Peggy?"

"Her mother wanted her to go down to the Manse for the day and help entertain the Women's Guild, or some such body," Oliver explained. "That's the worst of marrying into the Church, you find

yourself involved in the most peculiar activities. Dash it all, I sometimes wonder if I'm not just an unpaid curate in plain clothes."

But such a burst of sceptical laughter greeted this last absurdity
that he shrugged his shoulders, murmured that the world knew little
of its greatest men, and announcing to Susan that he intended to
honour her by sharing her picnic lunch, wandered away towards
the car.

"I seemed to read 'beer' in his eye," said Susan, as they followed.
"You'd better not let him get too long a start, Jed. Oh—and, Larry,
Ruth told me to tell you that she's had to go home to feed her dogs,
so will you lunch with us too, and we can drop you at Gledewaterford on our way home when we leave?"

It was a little disconcerting, on reaching the car, to find it the
centre of interest of a small but excited crowd of boys with, on the
outskirts, one small girl weeping bitterly.

"Eh, the puir gentleman!" she sobbed.

Pushing the swarm aside, Jed advanced to the car and looked
in, followed rather anxiously by Susan. Oliver lay huddled in the
back seat with closed eyes, a bottle of beer foaming freely over him.

"What the devil—" began Jed.

"Eh, he's shot himsel'!" squeaked one small urchin. "We heard
the bang! It wis juist like the pictur's at Abbeyshiels!"

"Shot himself? Don't you believe it," said Jed. "Watch me." He
opened the door and made a grab at the beer bottle.

"No you don't!" shouted Oliver, sitting erect at once. "That's
mine!"

"He's no' deid! Ach, nae use waitin' here!" Amanda heard the
disappointed crowd mutter, and they melted away like snow in
summer.

"Would someone kindly explain what all this means?" asked
Susan. "Oliver, why is the car swimming in beer? The place smells
like a pot-house."

"Dear Susan, if I've told you once I've told you a hundred
times *not* to buy these rotten little bottles with corks," said Oliver.
"You ought to get screw-tops, and then perhaps your unfortunate
guests, exploring your luncheon-basket in search of sustenance,
won't suddenly find themselves shot by a cork which the heat of

the sun on the bottle has caused to fly out. Do I make myself quite clear? Screw-tops are the thing."

"It serves you right for being greedy," said Susan. "And you'll have to sit a long way off. I don't care to eat in an atmosphere so powerfully reminiscent of a brewery."

"Funny, isn't it," observed Oliver to Larry Heriot, as he removed himself with his bottle down-wind from his sister, "how women will spray themselves with scent, adding that alluring touch behind the ears which is guaranteed—see advertisements—to make men fall madly in love with them, and yet have the effrontery to pretend that their delicate nostrils can't stand the smell of good, honest beer?"

"Amanda, you'd better start to eat while he's still talking," said Susan, paying not the least attention to him, "for once he begins it's like a plague of locusts. Peggy doesn't starve him, either, though you mightn't think it. He's put on weight since he's married."

"That's just jealousy because you've got skinny," retorted Oliver, and then bit his lip. Amanda saw Susan shake her head at him, saw Jed's quick glance at his wife, and wondered what was the matter, and if she ought to introduce a fresh topic, since weights did not seem a very good choice for some reason.

The fresh topic was provided for her before there was any appreciable pause in the conversation, and she seized it all the more readily because her curiosity had been aroused.

"Look," she said, gesticulating with a ham sandwich. "Can those possibly be bookies setting up their things over by the refreshment-tent? What on earth are they doing here?"

"They'll be taking bets on the hound trail," said Larry Heriot, as if it were the most natural thing in the world to see five unmistakable bookmakers on Gledesmuir, planting placards proclaiming them to be 'The Old Firm', or 'The Man Who Never Lets You Down', and already beginning to bawl, "Two to one the field!" in tones of brass.

"Will someone please explain?" asked Amanda pathetically, looking at Jed for guidance. "All this is Greek to me. What is a hound trail, and why must it have bookies?"

"It's run on the same principle as a drag," said Jed. "They send a man with a bag out over the course, and hounds are loosed on the trail, and the rest's like any other race. The first home wins, and if there's a big entry the bookies pay place-money as well. There's a lot of betting done on it, I believe. The hound trail is a feature of Gledesmuir Show—it's a Westmoreland sport really, not done at all in this country, and that's why it is such a curiosity here."

"Oh! Can I back a horse—I mean a hound?"

"Back the whole pack if you like," he said generously. "One of them's bound to win."

Thus encouraged, Amanda was quite prepared to rush at once to the nearest bookie, who was intoning the odds against one Challenger, evidently the favourite; but, "Plenty of time yet", and "They won't start for *ages*", the others assured her, and she resigned herself to waiting. As ham sandwiches were succeeded by biscuits and cheese, and they in turn slowly disappeared to give place to dark damp slabs of gingerbread, rich with treacle, stuffed with almonds, and a huge thermos of coffee was unpacked from a basket which seemed bottomless, she grew more and more impatient. Suppose they missed the start? It was all very well for the others, who had seen the hound trail before, but this might be her only chance; and still they sat there callously munching, sipping coffee, lighting cigarettes with a maddening air of having all time at their disposal. She had not felt so youthfully angry and in a hurry since the days when she had fidgeted to leave the table and return to her toys in the nursery.

II

Larry Heriot, after watching her ill-concealed impatience with amusement for some moments, finally sprang to his feet. "Come on, Mrs. Cochrane. You've finished, and so have I," he said. "Let's go and see what the odds are now, and leave the greedy ones to tidy up."

"It was kind of you to take pity on my childish impatience," said Amanda, as they walked away.

"I was getting sick of listening to their gabble, anyway," he said ungraciously.

"But you'd have been better to go by yourself, in that case for I shall probably 'gabble', as you so prettily call it, and be an even greater infliction," she pointed out.

"It's not so bad when there's only one of you, and I can always tell you to shut up."

"Really, Mr. Heriot, you are a most astonishing person," said Amanda, laughing. "You don't bother to be polite for politeness' sake, do you?"

"Waste of time," he said.

"I suppose the habit of shouting the truth at each other runs in your family," she said thoughtfully. "Like being musical or mathematical. I seemed to see a—a trace of it in your sister."

"Oh, Ruth? She thinks I'm the most awful liar," he said, and Amanda's 'gabble' was quite successfully cut short by this remark, for which she was unable to find any suitable reply, though she thought that family life at Gledewaterford must be a little difficult, with both members so prone to outspokenness. And what did their unhappy visitors do? But of course Susan said they hardly saw anyone. . . .

"You think I'm not fit for decent society, don't you?" he asked suddenly.

"Does it matter to you what I think?"

"Not much."

"Then why did you ask me?" Amanda said angrily, and checked further argument with an effort. "I don't propose to take part in an exchange of vulgar abuse with you under the name of truth," she added loftily, after a simmering pause. "It is really too childish, and spoils the lovely afternoon."

"That's only because you know you're beaten," he told her, but she was not to be drawn.

"Quite possibly," she agreed. "You know there's a familiar ring about this pleasant little chat of ours. It smacks of Ethel M. Dell, don't you think?"

"There you go again, slippery as an eel, off on to something else as soon as you hear anything you don't like," he said sulkily. "You're all the same—smooth, and pleasant, keep off the grass, don't let us say it if it's disagreeable. Spare our feelings at all costs."

"Oh, don't be so ridiculously rugged!" cried Amanda. "All you need is a horsewhip to slap your boots with, and you'd be complete! It's one of the few advantages of civilized society that people take pains to be agreeable!" Then, with a change of tone: "Oh, there are the hounds. How lovely!"

On the edge of the open moor, the centre of an ever-growing crowd, were several taciturn men in riding-breeches, each holding one or two couple of fox-hounds, large, serious creatures with enormous feet, gently waving sterns, drooping tan ears, and melancholy faces. They looked, at first sight, too mild to chase even a mouse; but every now and then one would raise his jowl and utter a whimper, another would add a bell-like note of protest, and there followed a full-mouthed outcry for a second or two which belied their air of meekness. Their names ran through the crowd like wind through a field of barley: "That's Challenger there! Eh, he's a graun' big hound!" . . . "See to Warrior, then." . . . "Captain's a bonnie dog, is't no'?" . . . "Randall" . . . "Ranter" . . . "Mountain Mist's my choice" . . . "Fleetfoot'll win for sure."

"Well, what's your fancy?" asked Larry Heriot suddenly. Evidently he had decided to stop sulking, rather to Amanda's relief.

"I don't know," she said helplessly. "I wouldn't dare pick one myself, and they all look more or less alike to me."

"I'll give you a tip, then, if you'll take it. D'you see that wee quiet one standing with his head hanging? That's Enchanter, and he's not known here, so you should get five to one. Unless he falls over a cliff or gets drowned swimming Glede, he ought to win. Don't go making a noise about it now, or you'll shorten the odds, maybe. I'll take you to a bookie and you can put your money on quietly."

After the transaction with two bulbous-nosed gentlemen in bowler hats who called themselves Joe and Jack Parmiloe, The Boys You Can Trust, in the course of which Amanda handed them five shillings and received a dirty card in exchange, they walked back to hounds, now being gathered for the start. Susan, with Jed and her brother, were there now, and Oliver turned to ask Amanda, "What have you done about it?"

"Backed Enchanter," said she in a conspiratorial undertone and was astonished at their looks of dismay.

"Who put you on to him?" demanded Jed. "He's no use at all. Never followed this trail before, never won anywhere else."

"Larry, it was too bad of you," said Susan reproachfully "Surely *you* should have known better?"

It came to Amanda, swift as an unexpected blow, as she turned to see him smiling sardonically, quite unabashed, that he had known better, that he had wilfully misled her from some strange malicious impulse. 'Why?' was her first instinctive angry thought. 'What harm have I done him?' She shied away from this at once like a nervous horse. To start feeling hurt and angry with anyone was at once to render herself vulnerable, as she had been long ago; and she, of all people, ought to be able to understand the queer, warped pleasure which he would take in hurting. She had not been altogether guiltless of the same rather mean, small-spirited offence. 'But I wonder what has made *him* like that,' she thought, even while she was saying carelessly, "Oh, it will teach me not to throw my money away another time. I haven't a doubt that it will be very good for me to see poor Enchanter come limping in, the very last of the also-rans."

"It's a rotten trick," Oliver Parsons said angrily.

"Perhaps he'll win, Amanda, and then you'll have the laugh on everybody," consoled Susan.

They all ignored Larry, who had ostentatiously turned his back and was looking at the hounds, his shoulders hunched almost to his ears.

"Here comes the man with the bag," said Jed. "They'll be off any minute now."

Across the moor a man was coming towards them at a slow run, a sack jumping and jerking behind him on the rough ground like a live thing. He reached the outskirts of the crowd and dived among them, and in the same instant hounds were loosed. With a clamour like a peal of bells jangled madly, they were off, muzzles to the trail, sterns up, ears flopping, a medley of white and tan and black streaming away over heather and bent and rushy bog.

"Come on to the road, it's higher. We'll see them from there as soon as they've crossed the low ground," shouted Jed, leading a rush of eager spectators. Amanda, flying behind him, had time to see from the corner of her eye Larry Heriot marching into the dark interior of the refreshment-marquee, and she hoped that it was remorse that he was about to quench, but doubted it. Then all her thoughts turned to the excitement of the trail, and forgetting the surly, spiteful Larry, she caught up with Jed just as he reached the road.

"You'll need to watch for your Enchanter," he roared at her.

"I don't care a bit which one wins!" she screamed back at him. "It's quite thrilling enough just to see and hear them!"

"That's the spirit," he said approvingly, tugging at a pair of field-glasses which he had jammed into his pocket, and which were resisting his brute-strength attempts to drag them out.

"Oh, do be quick!" cried Amanda, dancing with impatience. "Here, let *me* try, you'll only tear your coat!"

Together they struggled with the refractory glasses, disentangling them triumphantly just as Susan and Oliver came to stand beside them.

"You don't need these things," said Oliver. "Unless you're blind. Can't you see them going along the hillside beyond the burn there?"

Amanda gazed at the green hill facing them, scarred still with the remains of a Roman road, while from behind her the bookies' brazen chanting rose high. "Challenger leads! Three to one the field! Three to one bar one!"

"Yon's no' Challenger, it's Mountain Mist," said a gruff voice, its eagle-eyed owner following some object as yet invisible to Amanda.

"Oh, why can't I see them?" she cried, and even as the words left her mouth she realized that the dim white shapes floating against the green so fast, so effortlessly, that she had supposed them to be seagulls, were the leading hounds. "I never imagined they could move so quickly," she murmured.

The crowd surged backwards and forwards from one point of vantage to another, and still hounds swam soundlessly over the distant moor, coming round in a half-circle to cross Glede Water and be lost to view again in the hollow.

"Back to the starting-point. They finish there!" said Oliver, and they joined the scramble past the hut again.

It seemed a long time after that a small boy shrieked on a piercing treble note, "Here's ane o' them noo, comin' doon the brae!"

A single hound, bedraggled and patched with mud, was coming steadily down the steep slope to the finish. Behind him, above a grey wall, appeared another and yet another, and after them the ruck, pouring and flowing over the high dyke like water. But the leader was too far in front to be caught, and now he was near enough for them to see the lolling tongue, and a roar went up to the skies.

"Enchanter has it! He has it! Enchanter wins!"

III

"I don't think you'd better wait for Larry," said Jed later with a jerk of his head at the marquee, now full to bursting. "Oliver'll give you two a lift back, and I'll get Larry out and see him home."

"Very well," said Susan, and she and Amanda got into Oliver's shabby little car.

"Did you enjoy it?" she asked, when they were bumping down the road, the sinking sun sending shafts of glory across the breadth of Gledesmuir. "You scored a triumph, winning on Enchanter like that. Aren't you pleased?"

"Yes, I am, rather," Amanda confessed. "And it has been a wonderful day, except that I found battling with Mr. Heriot a little tiring."

"Oh, poor Larry, you mustn't mind him. He has a grudge against the world and his fellow-men, which must be more tiresome for him than for us. We *can* get away from him, he can never get away from himself," Susan said equably, in her soft, grave voice. "There's some dark secret in his past, no one knows what, except that it has something to do with women—most dark secrets have, of course! Ruth Heriot is rather given to throwing out hints about it, and I dare say she doesn't let Larry forget."

"All the same, he played a dirty trick on Amanda," Oliver threw in. "It's no thanks to him that she won instead of losing."

"After all, he *did* give me the tip. But don't let's bother about him," begged Amanda. "The evening is so beautiful. . . ."

As they passed the gate to Gledewaterford, however, her thoughts returned to him for a moment, almost against her will, and she wondered if Jed would succeed in luring him from the 'whisky-tent'. They were never to know the means Jed did adopt, though Susan and Oliver guessed that they were probably a mixture of brute force and cajolery; but that he had safely delivered Larry to the tender mercies of his sister was obvious from the outburst of victorious electric horn to which he treated them as he rocketed past them like a driven cock-pheasant a mile or two from Reiverslaw.

"It's a damn' good thing," said Oliver grimly, emerging from the grassy edge on to which he had driven to give his brother-in-law passage, "that Jed drives mostly in his own county! Everyone knows him and gets out of his way—they're all so rotten at it themselves, anyhow, that they give each other a wide berth."

Jed, unrepentant, was waiting for them at the door when they arrived. "Come on, Amanda, you're for it," he said jovially, hauling her bodily out of the little car. "There's a policeman in the sitting-room waiting to see you."

"A policeman!" Amanda's hand went to her throat, blood left her cheeks, where the rouge stood out startling clear now, like twin flags of bright colour. "Is it—news do you think?"

News of Cocky, she meant; Cocky, to whom she had hardly given a thought for a whole day.

Susan, who had sprung out also and laid a hand on her arm looked at Jed with deep reproach, almost with anger. "Jed," she said, "that was not a good joke. You should really be more careful."

Jed's honest distress was pathetic. "I forgot," he mumbled. "Amanda, I'm sorry. I forgot."

"It's all right, Jed, really it is. Please don't look like that," said Amanda, who had steadied herself by this time. "Only—you see—I'm—expecting news."

"Of course, my dear. We know that," said Susan, her light touch conveying what no words could of sympathy and comfort. "But I don't think that a policeman is likely to bring it—if there *is* a police-man here?"

"There's a policeman all right, and he wants to see Amanda," answered Jed, with a rather shamefaced grin. "I thought it'd be a joke to give her a fright."

"Your sense of humour is a little crude, darling," said his wife. "Not unlike Larry Heriot's when he told Amanda to back Enchanter. She must be getting a pretty opinion of Border jokes—and manners."

"Oh, don't be severe," said Amanda. "And Jed's jokes aren't spiteful, I'm sure, as I fancy most of Larry Heriot's are."

"No, he isn't spiteful," admitted Susan. "He's just rather like Bawtie—a bit apt to do the wrong thing, but awfully well-meaning."

"Thank you," said Jed, whose meekness was already wearing off. "Come on, Amanda, and interview your policeman."

With Susan and Oliver close behind, he ushered Amanda into the sitting-room, where a young member of the County Constabulary stood turning his flat-topped hat round and round in large hands, stiff with embarrassment and importance.

"Here's your criminal," was Jed's happy introduction. Susan began to laugh; Amanda, still a little dazed by the shock she had had, looked bewildered; and perspiration broke out on the nervous policeman's ruddy brow. He mopped it, gazed earnestly into his hat, seemed to discover his official manner inside it, and drew a small note-book from a pocket of his tunic.

"The Berwick polis," he began huskily, and cleared his throat. "We was notified frae Berwick-on-Tweed," he started, more confidently, "that a young man wished tae lodge a complaint against a leddy wha was seen tae drive aw a' frae Berwick in a caur bearin' the number o' Maister Armstrang's o' Reiverslaw. Said young fally . . . man . . . accused the leddy o' stealin' his claes—or, I should say, o' purloinin' severial articles o' wearing ap-apparel."

"I say, what odd things you steal, Amanda," said Oliver, from the door where he had propped himself the better to enjoy the entertainment. "I shouldn't have thought you'd have stooped to anything below the family jools, the diamond tarara, or the ill-fated ruby from an Indian temple."

"I didn't have much choice, you see," Amanda explained. "A strange suitcase was flung at my head out of the guard's van by dear, kind Jed, who was collecting my luggage; and the wretched thing—it was made of cardboard or papier-mâché at best—burst open and strewed the—the wearing apparel on the platform. So I picked it up, officer," she went on, suddenly realizing that it might be more politic to address herself directly to the Law rather than Oliver, "and very kindly replaced the horrible gaudy things in the case. That is, I thought I'd put them all back; but Jed hustled me out to the car, and it was only after we'd started that I found I still had some of them, including the most staggering pair of sock suspenders. Then he ran after us shouting, and Jed stopped and threw his clothes out at him—"

"What on earth did Jed want to chuck his clothes at the fellow for?" Oliver wanted to know. "He seemed to be wearing all of them when he got here, anyhow."

The policeman, who had been writing copiously in his note-book, paused, read what he had just set down, and proceeded hurriedly to scratch it out.

"*Don't* make it any madder than it was, Noll!" begged Susan. "You've quite mixed Amanda up, and she was getting on famously."

"If she's innocent, interruptions shouldn't worry her," retorted Oliver. "But it strikes me that she's a bit too glib and circumstantial for innocence. What do you say, officer?"

The policeman ceased to scratch in his note-book and scratched his head instead. "It's kin' o' confusin', is it no'?" he said. "Mebbe if the leddy was tae feenish . . . ?"

"Nothing confusing about it," said Jed, who had kept silence until now. "You heard Mrs. Cochrane say that I gave him back his clothes—pyjamas and things they were that he should have been ashamed to own. What more does he want?"

"Seemin'ly he's o' the opeenion, sirr, that you an' the leddy wadna hae stoppit had he no' rin efter ye," suggested the policeman delicately. "Forbye he's sayin' ye assaultit him, flingin' the claes in his face, like, the way they blindit him, an' he fell doon in the road an' cut his troosers."

"Well, I don't wonder he was blinded by his pyjamas," Jed agreed. "I've never seen such colours before. But as for the rest of it, it's all damned nonsense, and you can tell the Berwick police to tell *him* that if he's looking for trouble he can come to Reiverslaw any time he likes and he'll find it here easily enough."

The policeman permitted himself a small, discreet smile. "I doot it'll no' get that length, sirr," he said indulgently. "It wad juist be a try-on for damages. I'll pit in a wee report that it was a' a mistake an' that'll be the last ye'll hear o't."

"Well, if it's all settled you'd better come and have something," said Jed, "after rushing up the brae at full speed to arrest us. Coming, Oliver?"

They left the room, and Susan said, laughing, to Amanda, "The old lawless spirit is still in Jed to such an extent that he's quite disappointed because there isn't going to be a row."

"You and Jed are awfully well suited to each other, aren't you?" Amanda said suddenly, as if she had been following her own train of thought.

"Yes, I suppose we are. I hadn't consciously thought of it before," said Susan, struck by the question, wondering where it was leading. "You see, I liked him so much always—at least, not quite at the beginning, because I'd never met anyone of his kind before—but always from the moment I began to understand him. And that must be half the battle, don't you think?"

"The whole—or practically the whole of it, I should say." Amanda's voice was hard. "If I were you, I'd start appreciating what being well suited to your husband means right away. It's rather uncommon."

Susan, about to protest, changed her mind. She had seen the shadows painted by fatigue and strain under the girl's eyes. Instead she said in a deliberately matter-of-fact manner, "I'll take your advice and start counting my blessings every day. And now, my dear, I don't want to fuss you or try to be motherly, but you look tired. I'm afraid Jed really did give you a fright just now, and you've been on the move all day. And do you realize that you only arrived last night? Wouldn't you like to go to bed, and I'll have dinner sent up to your room?"

Not once for years past had Amanda ever yielded to the admission that she was worn out, and since Cocky had left on his flight, she had resisted all her mother's nagging efforts to make her do so. Her nerves, taut as the string on a bow ready bent, would give way utterly if she once relaxed her vigilant watch for signs of breaking in herself. Now, suddenly, came the blessed knowledge that it would not matter if she did break down, for no one would intrude on her privacy, mental or physical. She could cry herself blind and say that she had a bad headache, without having to endure covert glances of meaning, gusty sighs of sentimental sympathy.

"Yes, please," she said, "I would."

Susan nodded. She had no intention of pressing her guest to rest, however great her need; but she was intensely relieved by

Amanda's decision. 'It will do her more good than anything else if she *does* cry when she gets to bed,' was her thought.

"I'm going to run you a boiling-hot bath and pour in gallons of eau-de-Cologne," she said cheerfully. "It's so extravagant to empty whole bottles into one bath that it makes you feel good at once."

Following her upstairs, as on the previous evening, but already without the sense that the tall, slender figure leading the way was a stranger, Amanda said, "But if it's *your* eau-de-Cologne and extravagance, and *my* bath, will it benefit me?"

"All the more, if you have any conscience at all. It ought to give you a delightful pang of guilt as you wallow," Susan assured her.

IV

Perhaps it was the fragrant bath, perhaps the strong hill air which she had breathed all day, but Amanda found herself too stupefied with sleep to think, or even to cry; and at nine o'clock Elspeth, carrying down her tray, reported that Mrs. Cochrane was sound asleep, with such pride that she herself might have been responsible for it.

"I'm glad to find that Elspeth is almost human, after all," murmured Susan, when the maid had left the sitting-room. "Even she isn't proof against the pathos of Amanda's position."

Jed moved uneasily in his chair, and burst out, "It was damned clumsy of me this afternoon, Susan. Don't know what made me forget that the poor girl must be always waiting to hear. But she's so hard about it that I suppose I just didn't remember."

"Hard? Yes, she does give one that impression," said Susan thoughtfully. "Certainly she's completely disillusioned. It's defensiveness, I'm pretty sure. She's living under the most frightful strain, and she's afraid of breaking down. There's misery at the back of it, too, and I'd like to know the cause."

"The cause?" Jed stared at her. "Why, isn't it cause enough that she doesn't know whether her husband's dead or alive? Except that by this time he's pretty certain to be dead," he added gloomily.

"Oh yes, there's plenty of cause," said Susan. "Only, I said there was misery. It's quite different from grief, you know."

He stirred again, upset by her sombre look. Susan was strange this evening, and he didn't like it. "Look here," he said, "if having her here is going to trouble you, she'll have to go. I'll not have *you* miserable."

"Darling, I'm not miserable—only sorry for Amanda. You don't want me to be unsympathetic, do you?"

"I don't want you to be miserable," he repeated doggedly. "And there's another thing. What did Oliver mean when he said you'd got thinner?" He glared at her, his eyes, hiding anxiety behind a fierceness which did not deceive her in the least, brilliantly blue.

"*What* a nice colour your eyes are," said his wife irrelevantly. "Oh? Don't you think I look nicer like this? I was much too fat before. And did you notice me misusing that ill-treated word 'nice'? Some-one must really invent another word instead of it, though how an adjective which means 'over-particular' or 'fastidious' or 'precise' ever came to be such a changeling, I can't—"

"It's no use trying to put me off with a lot of rubbish about words. Are you thinner than when we were married?"

"Well, yes, a little. Just a few pounds—nothing. It's really only Oliver's jealousy because he used to have the best figure, and he *has* got heavier, Jed, and I'm very glad. He was like a rake when I was looking after him," said Susan. She did not look at him, but continued her *petit-point*; and after a pause, with a discontented growl, Jed picked up a book. The slight tension had gone from the atmosphere, to Susan's relief.

Knowing his tenacity, she was not astonished, though much annoyed with Oliver, whose fault it was that the subject had ever cropped up, to have him hark back to it again, much later that night, when she was lying in bed, half-asleep, but aware in every nerve of his powerful arm holding her to him. "If you go on losing weight I'll ring up Dr. Jamieson and get him to come and vet you," he muttered into her ear.

"Oh, bother my wretched weight. I want to go to sleep, and I'm *so* comfortable!" moaned Susan.

"Will you swear you're all right?"

"Of course I'm all right, darling. How could I be anything else when I'm so gloriously happy?" she whispered.

His arm tightened round her. "Darling . . . Susan . . ."

"Oh, Jed, my love . . ."

Was it because she had lost this ecstasy when her husband left on his last flight that Amanda bore the look of haunted misery which Susan had seen in her eyes? No, never, never! She could never have known it. . . . Poor Amanda, thought Susan, well might she be miserable, if she had never walked those starry heights where passionate love and trust and perfect comradeship went hand in hand. What could her marriage have been?

CHAPTER FIVE

I

THE autumn days slid by and passed from September into October as quietly and easily as the burn by which Amanda was wandering slipped along beside the high hedges. Down here in the hollow, the boundary between Reiverslaw and Easter Hartrigg, there was no wind, and the soft mellow sunshine touched the coloured leaves, the rich clusters of haws and berries, to a brilliant passing glory. It was one of those still days promising rain, when the air was so crystal-clear that even human eyes seemed to have borrowed the keenness of an eagle's sight, seeing the tiniest distant detail of the varied landscape sparkling and unblurred.

The stubble was not golden any longer, but shone with a rosily silver sheen which melted to soft purples and grey-browns wherever a dip in the ground held shadows. A low grassy hill, rising from among russet woods some miles off, was suddenly brightly emerald green, a jewel set in tarnished copper. Stacks in a row on the ridge behind Easter Hartrigg caught the light on their rounded blonde sides, and flung blue shadows over the field in which they stood. The Lammermuirs faded into violet against an almost colourless sky, their wild hidden glens marked by stains of a deeper tint. The red roofs of cottages and barns, a wisp of blue smoke from a farmhouse chimney, a glimpse of white roughcast wall between the thinning leaves of a little wood—all added notes of sudden colour. And closer at hand, Amanda saw the green-leather jerkin worn by Susan, who was picking sprays of barberry destined to fill a huge copper urn in a dark corner of the hall. She fitted so well into the picture, as she tugged at the thorny branches drooping under their weight of painted waxen fruit which touched her bare dark head, that Amanda, much too lazy to help, watched her with artistic pleasure warmed by affection.

Now that she was beginning to know Jed's wife, she was slowly realizing why so many people loved her; but no one, she thought, with better reason than herself. The delicate detachment of Susan's manner did not come from a cold heart, but was the respect which she showed to other people's reserve, and which she expected of them in return. 'Dear acquaintance' must always describe her most admirably to all but those few, her inner circle, for whom she had let down the barriers of her reticence. Amanda knew that Susan liked her, she knew even better that Susan would never presume on that liking to ask a single question. And for that very reason Amanda would have told her everything, except that she felt it would trouble her too much, and so spoil the lovely peace of Reiverslaw.

She saw now, quite plainly, that Susan was the heart of the place; it was her personality that changed what might merely have been rural dullness to an exquisite serenity, she who had breathed fire into Jed Armstrong and given him a new fineness of perception, she whose mixture of gravity and gaiety made life under her roof run like an air for an old ballad; and if the heart were distressed, all the house would feel it and droop.

Amanda hoped that Susan did not think her ungrateful, secretive—which was undoubtedly what her mother felt; but remembering that it would be hard to find two women more different than Mrs. Carmichael and Susan, she was comforted. As the days drifted into weeks and no word was heard of Cocky, no trace found by which he could be supposed to be either alive or dead, Amanda knew a curious suspension of feeling—a breathing-space in which she lived only for the present, and hardly thought of the past or worried about the future. It was the peace of a backwater from which she might be washed into the stormy sea at any moment, but it was a respite to be deeply grateful for.

Only one thing really disturbed this peace, and it was that sordid, nagging, niggling shortage of money which often is harder to bear than sorrow or disaster. It was useless to apply to her mother, whose never-dying faith in those tempting circulars which urge the readers to take shares immediately in a new gold-mine of unparalleled wealth, or an oil-well richer in petroleum than any yet sunk, or a mushroom-farm acres in extent, had dissipated as much of her late husband's money as she could lay hands on. And Cocky, of course, had gone off blithely, leaving his wife penniless, but sure to be all right because she was in her mother's care. It was a little difficult to know what to do, for she could not linger indefinitely here, and whether Cocky ever came back or not, she would have to find some sort of job—and untrained women had very little chance in the competition to earn.

"I can type, of course," she said thoughtfully, and realized too late that she had spoken aloud, and that Susan, who had come nearer while she was thinking, was now looking at her quizzically.

"And I thought you were admiring the beauties of nature!" she said. "Have you suddenly been overtaken with a violent urge to type?"

"No," Amanda answered soberly. "Not exactly. But I shall have to do something about trying to make a little money. The drawback is that though I type quite well and quickly, I know absolutely nothing about shorthand. Those horrible little squiggles and squirls never made sense to me, but you can't get a secretarial job without them very well."

Susan did not answer at once, and Amanda had time to be afraid that she might be going to offer her money to stay at Reiverslaw as the companion of whom she was obviously in no need; but it was plain that she did not yet know Susan very well.

"No, it's awkward, isn't it, Amanda?" she said finally, frowning slightly as she sometimes did when perplexed. "Besides, you couldn't get a satisfactory job of that sort here, and you don't want to leave us yet, do you? Jed and I hoped that you would stay at least until you had some definite news."

"That is what I'd like to do," said Amanda. "Whatever I may have to hear would be so much more bearable if I were with you." It was the first time she had let Susan hear her gratitude in words. "But . . . I can't do anything without some money, even a little. I'm down to my last five pounds, and there's no more in the bank."

She made this statement as quietly and unemotionally as the remark which had shown Susan so plainly that she did not want to go. A more superficial listener might have thought that she did not care very much about either, but the woman who stood close by on the brink of the burn, looking at her over a great sheaf of burning barberries, understood all that was left unsaid, and liked her for not saying it.

"But surely—your father must have left you something?" she asked.

Amanda shook her head with a rueful smile. "Mother is life-rented in almost all of it, except what was left to her outright, and what I did have I—well, I was younger and very careless, I'm afraid."

"I see."

A silence fell, broken by Susan's clear voice speaking again. "I believe, you know, Amanda, that I may be able to do something," she said. "Your typing ought to be turned to good account, I feel sure." She paused, thinking, her eyes on the water running ceaselessly past. Suddenly: "I've got it! I knew there was something in the back of my mind!" she cried. "Jed was talking to me only the other day about an old racehorse owner and trainer who has written his memoirs and wants to publish them, but they'll have to be not only typed but pulled into shape a bit first, and probably expurgated, because he has no idea of style or form or spelling or anything; and he won't trust his precious papers to any professional typewriting agency because he's quite certain that they'll steal his best stories! Amanda, this is our chance! Would you do it?"

"Would I do it?" Amanda's eyes were shining. "Susan, I won't insult you by asking if you've made this up just to help me—"

"No, don't. I can hardly see myself, even in my most philanthropic mood, sitting down and inventing a whole volume of horsy reminiscences just for you to type them," said Susan. "Let's go straight home, and I'll get Jed to ring up this old Mr. Makepeace at once. I know he'll trust his book to someone recommended by Jed—and under his eye, too! We must hold out for at least two shillings a thousand words, Amanda. Actually I'm sure there will be no difficulty about the price, and you should get more for doing the necessary editing."

"Two shillings a thousand words!" Amanda echoed dreamily. "Why, that will be nearly ten pounds, unless it's a very short book."

"It will be *long*, and you'll earn every penny you get," Susan assured her, as they started towards Reiverslaw. "This won't be a charity job, let me tell you, unless on your part."

"I'm glad of that. I'd hate to think that I only got something to do because your friends were sorry for me." Then a thought struck her and she stopped walking with a cry of dismay. "Susan, I haven't got a typewriter any more. I—I sold mine."

It would have been more accurate to have said that Cocky had sold it when he was short of ready money, and had not thought it necessary to tell her until the transaction had been carried through and the money spent, but she did not. Where was the use? The important point was that she no longer owned a typewriter.

"Don't let that bother you. There's one in the house somewhere," said Susan easily. "It's old, and it isn't a portable—in fact, it looks like a small harmonium, but I use it occasionally, so I know it works all right."

"Oh, thank you . . ." began Amanda; but Susan was walking at a brisk pace and would not listen.

"Do hurry," she said. "I shan't know a moment's ease of mind until Jed has rung up Mr. Makepeace. I have terrible forebodings that he may be negotiating with a rival firm while we dally here!"

The sun was already dipping below the western horizon, leaving long level streamers of rose-red light lying over the higher ground, towards which sheep were moving steadily in long, orderly lines, following the instinct which always takes them uphill in the evening. Already the hollow where the burn ran was mysteriously grey, a goblet filling with shadow; the trunks and lower branches of trees were dark while the topmost leaves were banners of gold. High on the ridge stood Reiverslaw, house and steading and tiny church, floating in clear amber light. There was a sudden whistle of wings over head, and three mallard flew over, making for Reiverslaw loch, long necks outstretched like spearheads cleaving the air, the drake's gleaming with iridescent green and blue as the sun's last rays caught it.

"Lovely!" murmured Amanda, short of breath though she was, for Susan was going up the hill like a deerstalker. "What a place to go home to."

"I know. I feel like that every time I leave the house, even for a walk," said Susan, who did not appear to be suffering from breathlessness at all. They reached the top and gained the road, which formed the backbone of the ridge, through a white-painted hunting-gate. "Oh, *blow!*"

"I *am* blowing, curse you!" panted Amanda.

"I didn't mean that. I see someone coming this way, riding, that's all," said Susan, with a laugh and a groan. "And I *won't* be stopped. Oh, worse and worse, it's Ruth Heriot! Waylay her, Amanda, and bring her in to tea if you must. I'll sneak back into the field and get to the house that way, through the steading." She pushed the gate open again and slipped away behind the hedge, calling back to the bewildered Amanda, "Tell her I'm afraid Bawtie will try to bite her horse and get kicked!"

As Bawtie was not with them, but had chosen to accompany Jed on a much more interesting and odoriferous walk round fields on which manure was being spread, it seemed a very thin story; but Amanda was not required to tell it at all, for Ruth Heriot, enormously tall and thin on her tall horse, said at once, "I saw Susan escaping in a hurry, didn't I?"

"Yes, you did. She had to tell Jed to telephone to someone," said Amanda equally bluntly, for if Ruth Heriot liked the plain truth, she should have it.

Antagonism flashed between them, swift as summer lightning. The gaunt woman, a towering black silhouette against the homing sky, looked down contemptuously at the slight figure of Amanda, smart even after a cross-country scramble, with her primrose-fair head gleaming uncovered. Amanda stared blandly upwards, evidently feeling at no disadvantage.

"Frightened of Satan?" said Miss Heriot gruffly, touching the horse with her heel, on which he turned his head and snapped at her boot, yellow teeth bared, wild eyes rolling.

"Satan? No, I've never thought about him much—oh, you mean your horse," said Amanda, all innocence. "No, I'm not afraid of him, thank you."

"That's a good one! You thought I meant the devil, did you? Ha, ha!" The hoarse laughter rang loud through the still air, drowning the soft lap and hiss of water as it met the reeds round the little loch. "It's about as rich as you backing the worst hound of the lot up at Gledesmuir the other day! Everyone's laughin' about it. You must have felt a damned fool!"

"Not in the least, thank you," Amanda said sweetly. "You see, the hound won, and I made some money on him. Quite good odds."

"The devil you did. Beginner's luck, of course. You'd better be careful what you back at the races next week."

"If I go, I shall be very careful indeed," Amanda promised, still smiling. "And only take tips from Jed or Oliver, or someone who knows a little about it."

"That's a hit at my brother, I suppose?" Ruth Heriot's sallow face showed a red danger-signal in either cheek. "Well, I'll tell him. We'll both laugh like hell if you lose."

"I'm sure you will laugh like the proverbial sewer," Amanda agreed, knowing that she was more than this woman's match in sharpness of tongue, and careless of her enmity because it seemed so entirely without ground. "And by the way, Susan said I was to ask you to come in to tea."

"No. I've got to get back and feed my dogs. Tell Susan I'll look out for her at the races," said Ruth Heriot, and without a word of farewell rode on.

Amanda went slowly down the road to Reiverslaw, passing the cottages where children home from school played at the doors and men too old for work stood warming their stiff joints in the last of the sunshine now gilding the lichen-crusted roofs of the steading on her left. Cows were back to the byre; horses, their day's toil ended, were being led to the troughs to drink, dipping their broad velvety noses deep in cool, fresh water. A pail clattered, a collie yelped; from somewhere behind the solid stone-built barn came a clear, tuneful whistle. Everything was peaceful with the sense of fulfilment of an honestly spent day over; even the slight noises were homely and in harmony with the evening's mildness. To come back to a place like this and call it home, she thought, was what she would like better than anything in the world, for Amanda had made the discovery that she loved the land and all that went with it. However hard a farmer's lot might be in these days of foreign wheat, foreign eggs, and meat, milk-marketing boards and all the cumbrous machinery of governmental supervision, there was something real and vital in a life like this, something worth while.

"Where's Ruth? Wouldn't she come in?" asked Susan, when Amanda, after washing her hands and reducing her hair to its ordered curls, came into the warm sitting-room.

"She had to go home and feed her dogs," said Amanda, and, suddenly remembering something: "Jed, please, are we going to the races?"

"The races?" said he, as if he had never heard of the sport. "I thought you wanted to start in and type old Makepeace's book. You'll get plenty of racing in that."

"Oh!" Amanda remembered something more important than the wish to annoy Ruth Heriot by winning vast sums of money, and looked penitently at Susan. "What an ungrateful pig I am, Susan! And you rushed home to ask Jed to ask Mr. Makepeace to . . . is he going to let me?"

"I don't know what you're talking about," said Jed, digging in his pipe with a knife and the intent air of a terrier at a rabbit-burrow. "You speak so fast. Do you, Susan?"

Susan ignored him and spoke to Amanda. "Yes, it's all settled, and he's coming to luncheon tomorrow and bringing his sacred manuscript with him. Apparently he doesn't trust even the post-office to convey it safely. And, of course, we're going to the races. We always do. Pay no attention whatever to Jed."

"I wasn't," said Amanda, lost in a rosy vision of moneymaking by various means, backing outsiders among them.

"And I think you're both absolute darlings to bother. Thank you both."

"I'll tell Makepeace to take his book away with him again, mind, if you go betting all your money in advance on the tote," threatened Jed.

"Oh, but I won't. I'm going to be very, very careful," said Amanda. "I shall type Mr. Makepeace's book most exquisitely, and only back the horses you tell me to—unless I see one I like very much. And I mean to win a lot, and tell the Heriots," she ended. "And we'll see who will laugh *then*!"

"You women" muttered Jed disgustedly, but a smile broke over his face. "You'll not be taking any tips from Larry at the races, I suppose, Amanda?" he said innocently. "No? He's usually on to a good thing or two. Remember the money you made on the hound trail."

"That," said Amanda darkly, "is one of the things I am remembering. Most particularly."

II

Peggy was kneeling in the middle of the nursery floor, surrounded by small, fluffy woollen garments, and watched with intense interest by young Oliver from the combined chair and table which was his own piece of furniture, and which, being provided with wheels, could be moved about the room by an indulgent parent, or even, by convulsive efforts on his part, made to stir an inch or two.

"Really, Oliver," said his mother, pushing the golden hair from her eyes and looking at him severely, "you grow much too fast for any self-respecting baby. Look at these clothes, sir! There's hardly one of them big enough for you now, and if I don't start to knit at once for you, you'll have to become a nudist—and winter's coming on, my precious!"

"Ag-ag!" shouted young Oliver delightedly, hurling a woolly dog of dubious whiteness in her direction. "Boo-oof!" he added, charmed with his own cleverness. "Boo-*oof*!"

"Clever boy!" said Peggy, equally charmed, and giving him back his dog, which he instantly flung from him again. "No, don't throw it *any*more, darling. I'm busy."

'I ought not to say "don't" to him, of course. It's supposed to give him repressions or something,' she thought, as if repressions were an infectious ailment like chicken-pox. 'But he doesn't seem to have got them yet'—as the dog once more fell to the floor with a thump. 'This time I really will not pick it up, and if he yells, he must.'

Young Oliver, disarmingly, did not yell. He hung over the side of his low chair as far as the straps which confined him allowed, and chuckled joyously, trying to touch the floor with his finger-tips. "Boo-oof!" he said. "Ag-ag! Boo-oof!" And then, tentatively, mouthing a new sound to hear if it pleased him: "Mom-om. Mom-om!"

"Oh, you darling!" cried Peggy, scrambling up, running to him, and falling on her knees to hug him. "You darling! You said 'Mum-mum', didn't you, my beautiful clever one? Say it again, Oliver! 'Mum-mum!'"

But Oliver, wiser than the wise thrush, refused to spoil his triumph by singing the song twice over. The first fine careless rapture was good enough for him, and it had brought the chief person in his little world so close to him that he could seize her shining hair, always a desired treasure, in both fat paws.

"Oliver! You're hurting!" Peggy tried to disengage the clutching hands, but as she was intent on doing him no damage, and he did not care in the least what pain he caused her, it was an unequal struggle, only ended by the ringing of the front-door bell, which was a delightfully infrequent noise in a house where most people walked in without ceremony, and succeeded in distracting his attention for a moment. Peggy, smoothing the tangle to which her child had reduced her hair, listened also, with foreboding, to the crash and scream that followed the ring. Too evidently Janet, disturbed while washing up the breakfast dishes, had let several of them fall in her agitation at the prospect of answering the bell.

"Oh dear, I shall have to go myself!" murmured Peggy, absent-mindedly handing Oliver the woolly dog, and hearing it thrown down as she flew to the stairs. "I *hope* it isn't the coffee-pot again!"

Speeding down, she saw Janet crossing the hall from the pantry, several pieces of earthenware in one large red hand, while with the other she rubbed her eyes. The unmistakable sound of a loud sniff came to Peggy's ears, and she smiled ruefully. Janet still broke something almost every day, still wept at the unaccountable awkwardness of breakable articles which slipped from her clumsy hold to smash themselves on the floor. Now, hearing her young mistress's light, hurrying steps, she halted, looked up, and began to sob loudly.

"Eh, the coffee-pot's smashed itsel'!" she wailed. "An there's a leddy at the door!"

It was difficult to tell from her woeful tones which was the greater calamity. Peggy bit her lip and said, "Really, Janet, you mustn't be so dreadfully careless. Throw the bits away and I'll go to the door. And do try not to break anything more today."

To a renewed outburst of sobs from the retreating Janet Peggy opened the door and found Amanda standing there.

"Has something awful happened?" she asked at once. "I thought I heard someone crying. Not you, anyhow, Peggy, I'm glad to see, on this fine morning."

"It's only Janet. She's broken another coffee-pot," explained Peggy.

Amanda looked puzzled. "Surely—somehow I shouldn't have thought you were so severe as that," she said.

"Oh no. It's her tender heart. She always cries, poor Janet. Her days are spent in tears and breakages in rotation. But the coffee-pot is rather a special smash, being bigger than most things, and she has broken three already. And Oliver threatened to buy a tin one, which she feels would be so shameful that she will never hold up her head again. He calls her 'Jeanneton Casse-tout'—after the girl in *The Cloister and the Hearth*, you know."

"I don't know. I could never struggle through it" said Amanda. "But the name seems to suit her. Isn't she very expensive?"

Terribly," Peggy said with a groan. "But she's devoted to Oliver, and takes him out in his pram so proudly—I mean young Oliver, of course . . ." she broke off, as Amanda looked more puzzled than ever. "Though I'm sure she would wheel *both* of them without a murmur! She adores young Oliver, but her adoration of 'the Commander' is mixed with terror. . . . So I don't know how I could send her away."

"Don't. Buy her a tin coffee-pot and Woolworth china and keep her," was Amanda's advice. "But I came here to ask you something, not to give you advice which you probably don't want."

"Come up to the nursery and ask me there," said Peggy "I do love to be asked something, it makes me feel so important What is it?"

Amanda, sitting down in a chair close to young Oliver's handed him his dog and said, "I want to know what I should wear to the races tomorrow, Peggy. Or, rather, I've only got my black suit, so there's very little choice, but I want you to tell me if it will *do*. If it won't, I shall have to stay at home."

"Susan's far better about clothes than I am," began Peggy diffidently.

"'Yes, but, don't you see, it sounds so dreadfully like crying poverty when I ask Susan," said Amanda. "She knows I haven't any money, and I hate to be always drawing her attention to the difference between our means. Now, I don't feel the same about coming to you, because you aren't awfully well off yourself, and understand the trials of the poor."

Peggy nodded. "I know. I hardly ever talk about money to Susan either. I'd hate her to feel that she was luckier than I am. Not that she is," she ended stoutly. "Perhaps we're both too sensitive. Money isn't really so very important."

"It is when you haven't enough of it," said Amanda. "Ought I to go on picking up this toy for your child, Peggy? I'm sure it's bad for his character."

"Oh, it is. Terribly," said Peggy cheerfully. "Don't pick it up again."

"What if he roars?"

"Let him. But he won't, the lovely lamb. He hardly ever roars," said his proud parent. "Let's take him down and put him outside in his pram, and I'll tell Janet to bring us a cup of tea to the drawing-room, where we can watch him through the window."

"You haven't told me yet whether my black suit will be all right for tomorrow," said Amanda, when they were seated in the shabby, sunny drawing-room, and Janet had blundered in with a tea-tray and blundered out again, like a bumble-bee against a window-pane.

"Of course it will. It's beautifully cut and very plain and smart."

"What are you going to wear?" asked Amanda.

"Well, I was brought up on navy blue—so lady-like," Peggy explained. "Mother's very old-fashioned about clothes, and being a minister's wife, she has never had much scope. But tomorrow I'm wearing new tweeds; sort of turquoise blue, that Oliver gave me for my birthday. Only I'm not sure about my *hat*."

"What's it like?"

"Very bright green. Oliver says it won't do."

"Oliver is perfectly right. I've got an idea. Will you change hats, like people on a bank holiday? I'll give you a dark-brown one—very smart with your blue tweeds, and you'll give me the green one, to brighten up my black suit. I don't want to look as if I were in mourning," Amanda ended hardily, on a defiant note.

"Of course you don't," Peggy agreed, "and I'd love to exchange." She poured out second cups of tea, they talked for a little about nothing very pleasantly, and Amanda left to walk back to Reiverslaw, the question of clothes satisfactorily settled.

"I do like her, Oliver," said Peggy when her husband came limping in for luncheon. "I wish she could be happy—like us."

"But you don't really think it's possible, Peg, do you?"

"No," she admitted. "I don't believe that even Susan and Jed are as happy as we are. You see, we've got young Oliver."

"Did you give Amanda a glass of sherry?" was her husband's practical question as he lighted a cigarette.

"No. Tea," said Peggy guiltily. "I quite forgot about sherry."

"Oh, my sweet! You're still very much the minister's daughter, aren't you?" he said with a shout of laughter. "I believe you feel quite wicked about the races."

"Of course I don't. How absurd!" she said indignantly but she blushed as she said it, and, still laughing, he tucked her hand under his arm and led her into the dining-room.

Amanda, remembering that Susan had said she was going to see an old man in one of the cottages between Reiverslaw and Easter Hartrigg, decided to walk the longer way by the road on the chance of meeting her; and just as she reached the little school, where the children were playing or eating their midday 'pieces', she saw the tall elegant figure come out of a cottage near by. She waved and called "Susan!", but the shrill voices of the children as they moved slowly round in a circle singing drowned her cry. Susan had not seen her; she was standing watching the children's game. The words came clearly through the still air:

> "The farmer wants a wife,
> The farmer wants a wife,

Hi-o, my daddy-o,
The farmer wants a wife!

"The wife wants a child,
The wife wants a child,
Hi-o, my daddy-o,
The wife wants a child! . . ."

'Why,' thought Amanda in surprise and consternation, 'I believe that *is* what Susan wants! She looks so—so wistful—' And it seemed to her that she had no right to take Susan unawares with that look on her face. She retreated round a convenient corner until there was a lull in the monotonous shrill chanting, then came out and called again:

"Susan! What luck to catch you! I've just been to see Peggy!"

This time, to her relief, Susan was prepared to face anyone; was, indeed, talking to the school-mistress, who had come out of her neat little house and was leaning on the green gate, deep in conversation.

The magic word 'Hallowe'en' was in the air as Amanda joined them, and the children, their game forgotten, had crept closer and closer, all ears at the sound of it, which brought memories of ducking for rosy apples, plates of brown nuts, false faces, turnip lanterns grinning from dark corners.

"Of course I won't forget, Miss Simpson," Susan said finally. "You must come up to Reiverslaw and have tea with me a little nearer the time, and we can make all the arrangements then. Mrs. Parsons will want to help too." She nodded pleasantly and took her leave, the children scattering again for a last outburst of shouting before the afternoon's lessons, the school-mistress retiring gratified to her house. She was staunchly Labour in her political views, but always forgot to be aggressive when Toryism was represented by Susan Parsons, who never seemed to be on her dignity, but behaved so entirely naturally that she was conflictingly described as 'a real lady' and 'just as common as oursel's' by members of the opposing parties, to their mutual satisfaction.

"We must remember not to make any other date for Hallowe'en," she said, as she and Amanda went briskly towards Reiverslaw; "and Jed will have to go to the children's party in the school whether he wants to or not. Perhaps you would judge the fancy dresses, Amanda? It saves such a lot of heart-burning if we can get someone to do it who can't be accused of partiality." Her voice was calm and even, her expression gravely humorous as usual, and if Amanda had not seen her a few minutes earlier she would have laughed at the mere idea that Susan could have anything in life left to wish for.

III

"Kind of you to wear my colours—very encouraging," said a voice at Amanda's shoulder, and she glanced up from her race-card to see Larry Heriot, wearing an overcoat and riding-boots, smiling ironically at her.

"I'm sorry if I seem stupid, but I don't know what you mean," said Amanda. She spoke coldly, having neither forgotten nor forgiven him for the trick he had played her at Gledesmuir Show. All about them a well-dressed crowd shifted, broke into small friendly groups, gathered to watch horses being saddled, or eddied about the bookies and the more impersonal windows of the Tote. Underfoot the trodden grass was dry and firm, promising good going; overhead a wind sang above the race-course on Monkrig, marked by white fences sprinkled with hurdles and stout steeple-chase jumps. Though the sun shone, there was a nip in the air which made Amanda very glad that she had not been too proud to accept the loan of Susan's silver fox. The green hat, small and smart, was perched on her fair head, the black suit was so well-cut that only she knew that this was its fourth season of hard wear. In spite of the presence of Society, she felt that she did not look dowdy, and she had been well-disposed towards everyone until Larry Heriot spoke to her.

"Didn't you know I was riding this afternoon for old Makepeace?" he said. "His colours are black with an emerald green cap."

"Oh, I don't mind wearing Mr. Makepeace's colours in the least," said Amanda with a slight but noticeable emphasis on the name.

He laughed. "So you've still got a grudge against me for the hound-trail, have you? Trust a woman to keep it up. You won on Enchanter, after all, but I suppose if I gave you the winner for every race this afternoon you still wouldn't forgive me?"

"Thank you, I don't require any tips from you," said Amanda, "Jed is helping me, and I've picked out one or two for myself."

"Well, I dare say you could get your own back on me by telling me your own choice, if I was fool enough to risk my money on it," he said, "for I don't suppose you know much about a horse, do you?"

"Not a great deal. It has four legs, and a head in front, and people put their shirts on it, don't they?" asked Amanda, all dewy-eyed innocence.

"Look here," he said suddenly, "I *will* give you a tip, a real good one—"

"Please don't bother. I shouldn't back it."

"I say, you dislike me pretty thoroughly, don't you?"

"I don't really think about you at all," said Amanda untruthfully, "but of course your mean spitefulness has rather stuck in my memory, in the same way that a slug leaves a horrid slimy sticky trail over anything it touches. Oh, there's Susan looking for me. Good afternoon, Mr. Heriot. I do hope you won't fall off Mr. Makepeace's horse going over those nasty high jumps."

She walked away, thinking with immense satisfaction, 'Perhaps that will be a lesson to him!'—but before she had gone three yards her arm was seized, and he was there glowering at her with a dark face of fury.

"Can't you take a joke at all?" he said savagely, shaking her a little as he spoke.

"Is it your idea of a joke to make a scene in the paddock?" she asked. "It isn't mine."

He dropped her arm as if the touch of it stung him. "You—you put me in a rage," he said, so simply, as if that explained and excused him, that Amanda had to stare at him, completely taken aback.

"But you're like a naughty child in a tantrum," she exclaimed. "Surely you don't just give in to your temper like that? It's—it's hardly to be believed."

"I do, though," he said; "that's why it isn't safe to rouse me." He spoke with a sort of sullen complacency which made her long to box his ears. "It runs in the family."

"Amazing!" murmured Amanda. She had always supposed that Cocky had allowed his temper—or temperament, as his flatterers preferred to call it—more freedom from restraint than any other man; but his rages were never given rein when anyone whose opinion he valued was present, and they paled into mere childish outbursts in comparison with Larry Heriot's, which were obviously so pandered to that they took no heed of either time or place. Larry's would have been almost magnificent in their carelessness as to what his audience might think if it had not been that she suspected him of deliberately lashing himself into them, of playing to an awe-struck gallery of which she refused to make one. So she now added calmly, "I really do want to go and find Susan. We've got some bets to make on the Tote, so you'd much better go and find someone else to be angry with."

This time he let her go without argument, and she threaded her way towards Susan through the crowd, past the cluster of noisy bookies, past the ring where steeple-chasers were being led to and fro, their glossy coats half hidden by bright blankets, their lovely sure movements a poem of grace and strength, past the little knots of grave, even solemn, men, who stared vacantly at their cards and muttered almost inaudible words out of the corners of their mouths grudgingly, as if each were a pearl of great price and might be stolen. Susan was talking to three weirdly attired elderly women whom Amanda had no difficulty in recognizing, from graphic descriptions given her by Oliver and Peggy, as the Misses Pringle. Their three heads, on long scrawny necks, crowned by astonishing felt hats, nodded animatedly and in perfect accord, as if all pulled by one string; their voices came cutting through the confused hum of other speech with pea-hen stridency.

Introduced in Susan's quiet manner, Amanda was instantly aware of three pairs of needle-sharp eyes making a rapid survey of her appearance, approving the black suit, pausing in shocked surprise as they reached the gay green hat, before the eldest said in a dreadfully significant tone, "Ah yes! We have all heard of you, Mrs. Cochrane."

Not knowing the proper reply to this always rather embarrassing remark, Amanda smiled politely, and felt relieved when Miss Cissy, the youngest, cried eagerly, "Didn't we see you talking to Mr. Heriot just now?"

"Yes," said Amanda.

"I suppose he told you *all* the winners?" pursued Miss Cissy. "He knows *such* a lot about the gee-gees, the dear things!"

Uncertain as to whether the dear things alluded to were the horses or Larry Heriot, Amanda only said, "No. He didn't tell me anything, Miss Pringle; but why don't you go and ask him yourself?"

There was a great fluttering amongst the three sisters, Miss Cissy crying, "Oh, I *couldn't*!" in a tone which made Amanda wonder if she would not presently put her finger in her mouth, so childish was it; while Miss Pringle boomed loudly, "I *strongly* disapprove of young Heriot, and will not permit the girls to have any dealings with him!" And then Susan's clear voice saying: "We must go, Miss Pringle. I know Jed will be looking for us. Are you coming, Amanda?"

"Did you do it on purpose?" she added, as soon as they were out of hearing. "Larry Heriot's name is like a red rag to a bull where Miss Pringle is concerned, you know. She hasn't a good word to say for him."

"I didn't know," said Amanda. "It's the first thing in his favour that I've learnt about him."

Susan glanced at her quickly, but said nothing; and the next moment they were beside Jed, and it was time for the second race to start.

The afternoon passed pleasantly, and quite profitably for Amanda, who, by dint of what Oliver called 'shocking flukes', succeeded in backing two outsiders at long odds, both of which won. The first, she insisted, had a nice kind face; and the second, while being led round the ring, had twice stopped just in front of her, tossed his head, and pawed the ground, a plain invitation to back him. She enjoyed it all; the brilliant colours of the jockeys as the sun caught them sweeping round the far side of the course and glinted on their mounts, the splendid lift and spring when they came over the jumps, the maddening thud of flying hoofs, the heavy breathing from wide red nostrils, the smell of trodden turf and the sharp tang of sweat-darkened coats as they came in, all combined to sharpen her senses so that the freshening wind stung more keenly, the sky above shone more blue, the clouds flew across it faster even than the galloping horses, chasing their tremendous shadows over the wide green circle of the course.

"What's your outsider for the last race?" asked Jed, coming up to her in the members' enclosure with a wide smile. "Any more horses with kind faces? I wish you'd pick a kind one for *me*."

"There are two I like," said Amanda seriously. "I don't know whether they are outsiders yet or not. A nice grey horse like a rocking-horse and a big black one."

"Well," he said teasingly, "grey's fine and easy to follow all the way round. You'll be able to see exactly where your horse is lying."

"That's what I thought," said Amanda. "Then I'll back the grey. Let me see what his name is—"

"'Glenlogie'. I'm backing him myself," said Jed with suspicious obligingness. "I'll put your money on for you if you like," and he went off, leaving Amanda to follow, and to wonder why he had been so eager for her to follow her fancy in this race.

When she looked at her card, and then at the board where the starters and jockeys were posted, she knew, and was furious. For opposite Number 5—'Glenlogie's' number—appeared the name of Mr. L. Heriot.

'How funny he thinks he is!' she thought. 'And now I don't want my nice grey rocking-horse to win after all.'

Hurrying to the Tote, she put a great deal more than she could afford on her other horse, the black 'Fireater', and, feeling a little better, joined Jed and Susan, Oliver and Peggy, when they all met to have a hasty glass of sherry before the race. Even when Ruth Heriot said in her loud jeering voice, "Well, Mrs. Cochrane, I hear you're backing Larry to win, in spite of Gledesmuir!" she only smiled amiably.

Her placid reply, "Oh, Jed did that for me. I suppose he thinks he ought to support home talent. I've backed Fireater on my own," caused Oliver and Jed to exchange quick looks of amusement behind the women's backs, while Ruth Heriot's face showed the flush of ill-temper, and Susan began to talk to Peggy about something else.

This race really did mean more than the others, she realized, as she went down from the stand to get a place by the rails where she could see the finish at close quarters. If only another jockey had been riding Glenlogie, how gladly she would have backed him! Even now, something about the gallant grey, as Larry Heriot steadied him for a gallop to the start, caught at her throat. Amanda, knowing next to nothing about horses, had perceived something of Glenlogie's quality, his stout-heartedness, his will to win. On his back, spare and well-knit in black, the emerald cap the only flash of colour about him, crouched his jockey, as eager to win as he.

Fireater whirled unnoticed past Amanda, the rest followed; there was the usual pause while they were being placed at the start, on the far side of the course; then a bell rang, a flag ran up, there was a breathless shout, "They're off!" and the coloured jumble swept round by the white rails, resolving itself, as they came up the straight on the first lap, into separate horses ridden by distinguishable men. Grey and black and emerald stood out clearly among the others. Glenlogie, lying sixth, was going easily and jumping with lovely precision: Amanda forgot to look for Fireater's scarlet and white, forgot Larry Heriot, forgot everything but the little grey horse.

"Oh! I hope he wins!" she cried to Oliver, standing beside her with glasses to his eyes.

"He ought to, if you mean Glenlogie. Larry's riding him magnificently and he's jumping like clockwork," he said. Then, lowering the glasses to stare at her, "I thought you were backing Fireater?" he said.

"Well, I am. But I want the grey to win," Amanda answered defiantly. "It isn't his fault that the Heriot man's riding him!"

"Here they come again now. Only two more jumps, and—by Jove! Glenlogie's in front—"

A roar, increasing in volume with the thundering hoofs, began to go up: "Glenlogie! Glenlogie!"

The last jump now, with Glenlogie as fresh as paint, and Larry Heriot's whip-hand idle, while other jockeys were applying the necessary encouragement of heel and lash; then, rising to it, Glenlogie, soaring in mid-air like the flying horse of the Arabian Nights, was knocked into by the maddened chesnut whose rider had forced him to this final effort, and all in a second, with a horrible mingling of hoofs, a glimpse of frightened eyes and flying mane, the chesnut was down, and had brought Glenlogie with him. Fireater, clearing jump and fallen, raced on, with whip plying hard, to pass the post an easy first.

But Amanda never noticed him. While Jed and Oliver with faces grown grave, muttered, "Nasty fall," while Peggy clung to Susan in horror, and voices behind them said, "Are the jockeys damaged?" she was crying: "Oh, the horse! The poor horse! Is the horse hurt?"

Navy-blue-clad ambulance men, springing, it seemed, from nowhere, were running to the spot, a veterinary surgeon had also added himself to the hurrying figures on the course, when a sigh like a sudden breeze shivered over the crowd. Glenlogie, shaking his head, had got to his feet, and a capless jockey in mud-plastered black was sitting up on the grass waving the ambulance men away. The chestnut, limping, was led in, but his jockey lay still, and presently a stretcher was brought, and a slow procession began to make its way towards a waiting ambulance.

"I hope you're pleased with your win," said Ruth Heriot's harsh voice, vindictive as if Amanda had engineered the accident.

Amanda turned her back and said to Susan: "Can we find out if the jockey has been badly hurt? I—I don't believe I care much for racing after all."

Jed, who had moved away, was back with the comforting news that the chestnut's rider had broken a leg, but was otherwise all right. "And hadn't you better see how Larry is, Ruth?"

"Give me your ticket and I'll collect your winnings for you," said Oliver as Ruth Heriot went slowly off.

"I don't want them," said Amanda, shuddering.

"Don't be an ass. Fireater had nothing to do with the smash. He'd have been second, anyway," said Oliver, and his sound common sense restored Amanda's values and proportions. She meekly gave him the flimsy slip of paper, and went on with Susan and Peggy, hoping that she would not see Larry Heriot or his sister again.

Nor did she until she was standing beside the car, feeling quite secure, for among the hundreds of cars all ranged in long rows on the grass it seemed impossible that she should ever find anyone she knew; even Jed and Susan were still in the distance, hunting for their own, and had not seen her waving to attract their attention.

It was then that Larry Heriot spoke to her, and, turning, she realized that his red car was in the line behind Jed's, and quite close. 'It would be,' she thought, and said crossly, "I wish, if you must speak to me, Mr. Heriot, that you wouldn't always creep up behind me and give me a fright each time!"

"I was afraid that if you saw me coming you'd bolt," he said. "That's why I took you unawares."

"Why *should* I bolt?"

"Didn't you ill-wish Glenlogie and me in that last race? I felt sure you had. I had time to think about it as we came down together." His face was paler than usual, and wore a haggard look that made him quite uncomfortably like his sister, but he sounded only faintly, sardonically amused.

"No, I didn't," Amanda said gently. "I know Glenlogie should have won. I didn't want you to, before the race, but once you were off, and riding so well, and he's such a—noble horse—I couldn't help hoping he would win."

"In spite of his jockey?"

"Yes," said Amanda. "In spite of his jockey. It was very hard luck that you were bumped like that at the last fence. I was dreadfully afraid that Glenlogie was hurt."

"Not me? You didn't care about me?"

"Well, you didn't have to ride if you didn't want to, but Glenlogie hadn't any choice," explained Amanda.

"I see. That's one way of looking at it, certainly, and fair enough," he said. "I'm rather glad you didn't hope Glenlogie would come down. He's a grand horse, you know. Good-bye."

"Good-bye," said Amanda, and got into the car.

CHAPTER SIX

I

"IF THAT's a postcard from Miss Pringle on top of the pile, I don't want it," said Susan, as her husband picked up the letters.

"Right," he said amiably, tearing the postcard to small pieces and flinging them into the waste-paper-basket without hesitation. "No, nothing for you today, Amanda."

Susan left her seat at the writing-table to forage in the basket. "Really, Jed dear, there are times when I despair of you. Bawtie is hardly more destructive," she said, putting the bits together as best she could. "You *know* she'll only 'postcaird' me again if I don't read this one. I was speaking figuratively when I said I didn't want it. You mustn't be so literal. Amanda, you're doing nothing at the moment; come and tell me what this is about. After struggling with Mr. Makepeace's masterpiece—how odd that sounds!—you should be able to decipher anything. It *looks* like 'I have a pig to poke at you', but of course it can't be, even from Miss Pringle!"

"It's upside down," said Amanda, after a long look.

"No, really it isn't. That's what her writing always makes you think at first. I know I've got it right way up. *Jed* ought to be made to translate it," said Susan fiercely. "Great hulking brute, sitting there grinning!"

Amanda, who was studying the postcard intently, exclaimed, "It isn't a pig, Susan, it's a party. 'I am having a little party'"

"Oh, those little parties!" Susan groaned. "But go on, go on. Tell me the worst."

"I can't quite get the next bit," said Amanda, knitting her brows. "Oh yes, it's something about dancing. Would that be possible?"

"Anything," said Susan with conviction, "is possible where the Miss Pringles are concerned. I know now what it is. A country-dancing class. Would you like to go, Amanda? It will be quite dreadful, I know, without even setting foot in the room. But would you?"

"I'll try anything once," said Amanda, and added, laughing, "She's asked Jed too."

"I'm not going—I can't. I've got a sale on that day," he said at once.

"You don't know yet what day the party is."

"I've got a sale to go to on the same day as the party," he insisted, and nothing would shake him, not even Amanda's suggestion that it might be a Sunday.

"Do they really expect to get men to go to that sort of thing?" asked Amanda.

"I know one who'll go; you couldn't keep him away from it," said Jed with a wicked grin.

"Who is it?" Amanda was interested, but sceptical.

"Oliver. He's dead keen on everything they get up."

"Oliver? What nonsense! He doesn't mean it, does he, Susan? Oliver wouldn't—"

"Yes, I'm afraid Oliver would. You've no idea, no conception, what Oliver will do," said Susan gloomily. "He'll certainly go if Peggy can't stop him, and he'll behave abominably throughout. It gives me cold shivers down my back when I think of it."

"I've got to go down to Abbeyshiels." Jed rose and flung the mangled remains of what had been a neatly folded newspaper on the floor. "Do you two want to come?"

"I can't, Jed," said Susan. "I've got to go and see Peggy about the school-children's Hallowe'en party this morning, and the shepherd's daughter is ill. I promised to look in and see her too."

He nodded. "All right. What about you, then, Amanda?"

"I'd like to, unless Susan wants me for anything? No? And I'll walk part of the way back," said Amanda. "I need exercise badly. All the cream and things I eat here are making my skirts too small for my waist, and that must not be. Wait for me, Jed, won't you, until I get a coat?" She ran from the room.

Jed stood knocking out his pipe on the palm of his hand, a habit of which the Misses Pringle considered that a wife would have broken him long ago. "Amanda's looking a lot better," he observed at last. "She's been here three weeks now, isn't it?"

"More than four, and she seems to have settled down as if she liked it," Susan said, "which makes me think that she can't have enjoyed living with her mother."

"Nobody would. Has she ever mentioned her husband to you at all?"

Susan shook her head. "Not once, but I'm sure she must have given up all hope of ever hearing of him alive by now," she said. "It may even be a relief in a way. That kind of hoping against hope, if she *is* hoping, must be agonizing."

"Poor lass," said Jed. "Wouldn't she be better to talk about him a bit?"

"Perhaps, but I can't force her confidence, Jed dear. Don't you see, she's been suffering that from her mother? It's because we leave her alone that she's beginning to trust us."

"You're a clever one, aren't you?" he said, smiling at her. "I wish you were coming to Abbeyshiels. The front seat of the car's all wrong without you in it."

"What a pretty speech! Thank you, darling. I shall be thinking about it and preening myself all the time I ought to be concentrating on the party and Mrs. Hogg's 'hard-up' daughter," said Susan. "There's Amanda in the hall, waiting. Haste ye back, as they say."

They had gone half-way to Abbeyshiels when Amanda said suddenly, breaking a companionable silence, "I suppose I'll never hear anything about Cocky now."

Coming on top of his remark to Susan, this was startling, but Jed's habitual slowness to answer stood him in good stead. He had passed a row of cottages, swerving to avoid a dirty white hen which pecked about in the middle of the road, oblivious to traffic in its hunt for treasure, before he said, "I doubt there's no hope for him now, Amanda."

"You don't think there's still a chance that he may be somewhere up-country in the wilds?" she asked nervously. "One hears of such things happening, of people being hurt, and found by some remote tribe and not getting back to civilization for months. It's seven weeks since Cocky went."

"I should say the odds are about a million to one against," he said pitifully, but refusing to hold out false hopes. "You'd better put it out of your mind."

"If I could only know for certain!" she cried with impatient misery. "It's the not *knowing*!"

"Yes, I know. That's the hard bit. I suppose it's what you pay for marrying a man with a dangerous job like that. You'll just have to bear it!"

"If I *knew*!" she said again, but too low for him to hear. Then, resolutely turning her face to him, "I'm sorry to have inflicted my—my woes on you, Jed. It's a shame."

"I'm sorry I can't give you any comfort, Amanda," he said. "You're damned plucky about it."

"But you do comfort me—you and Susan," she said. "You'll never know what it has meant to me to be at Reiverslaw with you both all this ghastly time. I sometimes think you've saved me from going mad. . . . Now let's talk about something else. Shall I have time to do any shopping?'

"I've got to go to the mill; it'll take me a bit, I expect," he said, following her lead with relief, "but I wouldn't have thought that anyone used to London could do much shopping in Abbeyshiels."

"I like it," she said eagerly. "It's fun. All the shop-people know me already, and ask for you and Susan; and the butcher gives me racing tips—I've never dared to confess to him that I don't do anything about them—and the draper has a beautiful marmalade cat that sits among the knitting-wools, and no one minds. I don't believe I'll ever enjoy shopping so much anywhere else."

"Well, here we are, then," he said, stopping the car in the open space in front of the old Town Hall, "and as you're so keen on the shops here, you might go into that tobacconist's at the corner there and get my tobacco for me. You needn't pay for it if you just say who it's for."

A cool breeze from the west was blowing along the ridge on which Reiverslaw perched, but down in the valley, where the old town sprawled by the river bank, it was windless, air full of mellow warmth, and a faint blue haze, rising from garden bonfires, hung over the houses. The grey stones of the ruined abbey, broken arch, which even yet had a hint of matchless symmetry, empty, pointed windows, the crumbling remains of the stately tower, were gilded by the late-October sun. The pleasing melancholy of a fine autumn day seemed to have laid a hush on Abbeyshiels, broken only by the cooing of pigeons and the ceaseless voice of the smooth-flowing water near by, until a car, sounding its horn to warn the leisurely pedestrians of its approach, swung round a corner into the main street, and as if at a given signal the town awoke to the normal activities of a week-day morning.

Amanda wandered down to the waterside, where she stood for a moment to watch an angler casting from a boat in the reach above the bridge; the movement which swung the heavy rod and landed the fly just where he wanted it to fall as easy, as smooth as the water below it. There was a sudden flash of living silver as a salmon rose, a shower of sparkling drops, rainbow-hued, fell from the sleek, arched body, and it was gone again. The fisherman cast patiently over the spot where it had been, and presently Amanda turned back to the town.

II

With her few small purchases, including Jed's tobacco, dangling from one hand by strings, she decided to go into the 'Plough and Horses', where they made surprisingly good coffee. It had been a coaching inn in its early days, and could still boast the archway leading to a spacious stable-yard alongside the door. Amanda liked the hotel, and the lounge with its small-paned windows set deep into the wall above panelled window-seats overlooked the Town Hall and the Corn Exchange, where she could see Jed when he came back to meet her. At this time of the morning, except on market-days, she was almost certain of finding it empty, and it was with the faint unreasonable feeling of resentment which overcomes the mildest on these occasions that, pushing the door open, she saw a pair of legs in riding-breeches and muddy boots extended across the floor from a large chair which hid their owner.

"Bring me the same again, Archie, and look sharp. I've got to get back," said a voice from the chair, which Amanda recognized. She jumped at the sudden sound and pushed against a table, which squeaked protestingly as it moved.

"For God's sake don't make such a damnable noise!" said the voice irritably.

Amanda's colour rose, a dangerous sparkle appeared in her brown eyes. Deliberately she pushed the table a good deal harder, and this time produced a really satisfactory squeaking groan.

"What the hell—" said the voice, and as its owner got to his feet in anger Amanda marched forward and confronted him.

"Since when has the 'Plough and Horses' belonged to you, Mr. Heriot?" she asked with most misleading sweetness. "As you seem to be so entirely at home here, perhaps you will ring the bell for me?"

"It's you, is it?" Larry Heriot uttered a short laugh, but moved to the bell beside the fire and pressed it, keeping one finger on it while he nodded towards a chair. "Sit down, won't you?"

"So it *does* belong to you?" murmured Amanda, laying her parcels on a table and beginning slowly to pull off her gloves, but without a glance at the chair. "And by the way, I think I asked you to ring the bell, not to make a noise like a fire-alarm. I thought you were so sensitive to noise? You appeared to be, only a minute or two ago."

"We're being very witty this morning, aren't we?" he drawled, relinquishing his attack on the bell. "Well, if you're not going to have a chair, you'll excuse me if I sit down, won't you?" He sank into the depths of the chair—the only really comfortable one in the room, Amanda noticed—and stretched his legs out again.

She crossed to the window and stood there looking out at the sunny open space in front of the Town Hall, where all the streets in Abbeyshiels converged, and presently little astonished at the delay, "They are taking a very long time to answer the bell, aren't they? Or do they object to your method of ringing it?"

He did not answer her directly, but got up and, going to the inner door, flung it open and shouted violently: "Here, Archie, Kate, Watson! Where the devil have you all got to? There's a lady here waiting to be served! ... That ought to bring them," he added, turning, flushed with vocal effort, to look at Amanda, seeing her only as a small slight shape outlined darkly against the clear glass. "They should be shot for not attending to their business better than this." Evidently he was now trying to be conciliatory, though his manner was brusque, his dark face sullen.

She had no time to decide how to take this ungracious overture when a small pear-shaped man trotted into the lounge on short legs, a nervously ingratiating smile twitching his mouth.

"Now, Mr. Heriot," he began, washing his hands in the air before him. "Now, this'll never do, ye know. Never at all. Ye'd be best to just take the road an' away back to Gledewaterford, and not miss your dinner, eh?"

"Soft soap, Watson. You can save your breath," said Larry curtly, "and attend to this lady. You've kept her waiting long enough."

The landlord's face cleared as he caught sight of Amanda. "Dear me, miss—madam, I should say—I'm sure I'm verra sorry, extremely sorry. It'll be coffee ye're wanting?"

"Please. If it doesn't take too long. I don't want to keep Mr. Armstrong waiting," said Amanda.

"You're in luck, madam, for the pot's on the fire this minute to make it," cried Watson eagerly. "I'll take the order ben myself. Can ye stop five minutes?"

He turned, plainly eager to make his escape, but Larry's voice caught him just as he reached the door. "Bring me a double whisky-and-soda at the same time, Watson."

"Oh, now, now, Mr. Heriot!" said the landlord unhappily. "We'll not start to argy before the leddy, surely?"

"There's no question of arguing. I gave you an order."

"I'm sure Mr. Heriot doesn't want to keep you from ordering my coffee," Amanda broke in, out of pity for the little man, "and if you will bring enough for two, perhaps he will keep me company."

She nodded at the door as she spoke, and Watson thankfully slipped through a narrow crack with an eel-like agility which his build made ludicrous. The door closed very softly behind him, and an oppressive silence fell on the lounge lake a blight.

'Gentlemen of the Guard, fire first,' thought Amanda, wanting to giggle from pure nervousness. Not that she was in the least afraid of Larry Heriot or of any man. Rage, abuse, threats of violence, even tears, she could withstand any or all of them. Seven years of marriage with Cocky had taught her almost everything there was to know about the meaner side of masculine character; but this waiting for him to blow up was rather trying.

When he did speak it was in a voice disarmingly gentle.

He had, she realized suddenly, a peculiarly charming voice when he was not shouting. It was the first time she had considered that he owned any charm at all.

"I suppose I ought to be grateful to you for showing so much interest in me?" he said beguilingly, so that for an instant, off her guard, she was deceived, she had almost avowed it. Then she saw the glint in his eyes, and shrugged her shoulders very slightly.

"Interest—in you?" she said carelessly.

"Yes. Your reforming zeal wouldn't be being let loose on me—no woman's ever is on any man—unless you were interested. Or is 'intrigued' the word you'd use?"

"You have made a mistake," Amanda said coolly. "My interest, if any, is in Watson. I wanted to save him the distress which he felt, and you quite obviously didn't, at the thought of making a scene in my presence."

"I'm damned if you haven't got the most amazing nerve I've ever seen in anyone, man or woman!" he cried in frank astonishment that Amanda's severity had to be tempered a little with softening. "There you stand and tell me to my face that you interfered for *Watson's* sake!"

"Why not? Surely that didn't require so much courage as you seem to think?"

He hesitated a little, then said shamefacedly, "You're such a little creature, I could break you in half with my left hand, and I've got a murderous temper. It might frighten anyone."

"I know. You told me that before," said Amanda, "but murderous tempers are nothing to me. I know how to deal with them." She spoke lightly enough, but a sudden involuntary shiver shook her, and the colour left her cheeks. It dawned on him then that she must have suffered at someone's hands, that she was far from being the brittle Dresden china figure he had imagined. There was a tremendous will concealed in the slender frame. For the first time in years he was honestly ashamed, not of his temper, which he felt she would excuse, but of the capital he had made out of it, his deliberate working himself into a fury to cow more timid men.

"I beg your pardon," he said, and this time she knew he was sincere. "I won't do it again—not before you, anyway. It wouldn't be any good, now that you've seen through me."

Amanda smiled. "Here comes the coffee," she said, "so you can prove that you mean what you say by not bullying poor Watson, and sharing it with me."

"I will, if you'll let me pay for it."

She had not wanted this, for she did not feel that she would care to be in his debt even to this unimportant extent; but that was only ungenerous caution, fostered in her by her distrust of almost everyone she met. "Thank you," she said sedately. "It's very kind of you—and after I was so rude to you, too."

He waited until Watson had set the tray down beside her, and, taking up the money which Larry flung silently on the table, had sidled away again, before he said, "I was rude first, remember."

"Oh, I remember!" Amanda gave a sudden delicious gurgle of laughter. "I'm hardly likely to forget. Here's your coffee, and to sweeten it I'll confess that I seem to provoke evil tempers in people, so that it really was quite as much my fault as yours."

He did not contradict this, as most men would have, but sat stirring his coffee and staring thoughtfully at her out of eyes which, she noticed with a quite disproportionate interest—for what were his eyes to her—were darkly blue.

"Like the missel-thrush?" he said at last. "That's supposed to bring wild weather with it. You know it's called the storm-cock in some parts, don't you? I've always thought I was like that. Perhaps we're two of a kind?"

This, Amanda thought, was progressing much too rapidly, and in a direction which might very well lead to trouble. "Very possibly," she said briskly. "Storm-cocks are fairly common, human as well as missel-thrushes. I must fly, or Jed will lose patience altogether and go without me, and I'd hate to have to walk eight miles to Rieverslaw and arrive too late for lunch. Besides, haven't you got to go? Your sister will be—"

"Ruth? Oh, she's gone off in the car on a round of visits in England," he said absently. "It doesn't matter when I get back. I'll just jog quietly home and they'll give me something to eat when I get in."

"So you're all alone at Gledewaterford?"

He nodded. "I don't mind. You don't have to pity me," he said.

"Pity you? My dear man, I don't consider that you need any pity," said Amanda. "I was rather envying you, if you must know."

"Don't you like being with them at Reiverslaw, then?"

"Oh, but that's different. I love it, but it isn't anything more than a delightful interlude."

"If I ask Jed to bring you to Gledewaterford some day, will you come?"

"Of course. We'll all three come," Amanda promised. "I should like to see Gledewaterford again."

"What a nice chap Larry is when he's not in one of those black moods of his," said Jed when, after a short talk beside the car, they had started homewards, leaving him standing looking after them. "I always think he's better without Ruth. They must get on each other's nerves a bit."

"Jed, I wonder what *is* the matter with him? This grudge that he has against everyone and everything—what has caused it? Do you know?"

"No," he said, "I don't. There's always been gossip, of course—bound to be when a man is like Larry. I believe he had a love-affair that went wrong, or something. But I'll tell you who can supply you with all the information there is—and more. The Miss Pringles. Better ask *them*."

"You know perfectly well that I wouldn't do that," said Amanda indignantly. "I hate gossiping old women, and I certainly never pry into other people's secrets."

"No?" he said annoyingly. "You've been letting Susan put you against them. She can't stand 'em, you know. Never could. They're three very nice well-meaning women," he concluded virtuously, "and I don't know why so many people object to them. I'm sure I don't."

"All the same, I notice that you don't exactly jump at their invitations," said Amanda. "If you aren't very good, and if you don't take the dreadful, blind corner that we're coming to more carefully than usual, I shall tell Susan how much you like the Miss Pringles, and she'll make you come to their country-dancing class with us!"

III

"Step-together-step-hop! Step-together-step-hop! Now with the music! Thank you, Miss Hamilton."

A tripping measure, struck up by a tinny piano, and accompanied by strange uneven shuffling sounds, followed these words. Oliver, standing in the passage outside the back door of the Kaleford village hall, hired by the Misses Pringle for their dancing class, straightened his shoulders and glanced, self-consciously at the white tennis-shoes with which, by Miss Pringle's express demand, his feet were covered.

"Well, girls, are you ready?" he asked.

"Oliver," said his sister anxiously, "for the last time, I beg you not to behave badly."

Peggy began to giggle. Oliver sighed. "I came here to be taught how to dance by Miss Pringle," he said patiently. "Come on, let's join the merry dancers. My feet are itching."

Flinging open the door, he seized the astonished Amanda by the hand, and before she could resist had curvetted with her into the middle of the hall in a series of gazelle-like bounds, greatly to the inconvenience of several ladies of all ages, and one sad elderly man, who were proceeding round the floor to the strains of the piano, conscientiously muttering, "Step-together-step-hop."

"Oh, Commander Parsons! You *have* come, then, and brought your women-folk with you, too," said Miss Pringle, springing up to them flat-footed in a pair of the largest and dirtiest canvas shoes which Amanda had ever seen. "This is splendid! Such an addition to the class. Dear little Peggy, too! So glad to see you."

"Peggy is, legally, all the women-folk to whom I can lay claim, Miss Pringle," said Oliver, deadly serious. "This is Mrs. Cochrane, who is staying at Reiverslaw—"

"Ah yes; we have met. Dear, brave girl to come. Far better than hiding your grief at home," said Miss Pringle, as she squeezed Amanda's limp hand in her own damply sticky one. Amanda immediately felt that she hated her, and knew why Peggy always said that the Misses Pringle roused all her worst feelings.

"And the other," Oliver continued firmly, "is]ed's wife, and, properly speaking, her place is by her husband's side, not gadding here. However, she felt that she really could not *resist* your invitation"— this in such an appallingly life-like imitation of his hostess's own gushing manner that his three unfortunate companions trembled lest she should recognize the parody and take offence—"so here we are," he ended, "ready to dance till we drop. Are you conducting the class yourself, Miss Pringle? Surely an authority like you is not a mere *learner*?"

Miss Pringle, gratified, bridled. "I felt," she said confidentially, "that however competent I might be to take the class, Commander Parsons, it would be *wiser* to have an outsider. I'm *sure* you agree."

"Very prudent," said Oliver with a wink at Peggy, who promptly crept behind Susan in the hope that she might laugh unseen. "And what dances are we performing this afternoon?"

"At present we are concentrating on our steps, at my suggestion," said Miss Pringle, "as so many of the class do not appear to know them." Her vulture's eye lighted on several people in turn, each of whom shrunk guiltily and shuffled her feet. "Presently, when I think we have mastered them, perhaps Miss Fleming will let us go on to a dance; but she is very, very strict—aren't you, Miss Fleming?" This to a meek and unassuming little woman with mouse-coloured hair, who made deprecating noises and tried to look amused and fearless.

"Well, since we are all gathered now," said the mistress of ceremonies, "shall we go on with our lesson? A circle round the room, please, and the music ready. Step-together-step-hop, remember, everyone. Now, Miss Fleming!" She plattered to her place in the circle like a duck.

Susan whispered to Amanda as they dutifully fell into line, "You will note that the relegation of authority is *purely* nominal, my dear Mrs. Cochrane!"

"'Step-together-step-hop!'" was Amanda's reply.

Round and round they bumped, until, when Peggy was gasping that she was exhausted, and Miss Jelly Pringle resembled a wine-flavoured jelly, not only in name but in the hue and consistency of her quivering pendulous cheeks, Miss Fleming, with a terrified glance at the eldest of the sisters, ventured to call a halt. Before that lady could collect sufficient breath for speech she said hurriedly in a nervous squeak, "Very creditable indeed for the first lesson. I think we could quite well go on to a dance now."

"*Ex*-cellent!" panted Miss Pringle, joining her in the middle of the floor and darting highly critical glances at the remainder of the class. "Those—of you—who are not—yet—perfect in step-work—can-always-practise-at-home!" she finished with a triumphant rush, having by this time got her second wind. "And what dance is it to be, Miss Fleming? Now, I should like to suggest—"

"May we have *The Nut*, please, Miss Pringling?" called our Oliver boldly before she could suggest the dance which she and her sisters had been learning in private to confound the others. "I mean Miss Flemmle." In an undertone to Peggy he added, "See what comes of divided authority. I've got their names all wrong now!"

"*The Nut?* Well, yes, I suppose—" began Miss Pringle, so doubtfully that it was instantly and enjoyably plain to all that she did not know it.

"Or if you think that too old a favourite, how about one of the more advanced ones? *The Draggle-tailed Lassie*, or *Tak' the Road, my Gudeman's Comin'*, or *Swallow the Poker*?" suggested the graceless Oliver with enthusiasm. "*Swallow the Poker* is a grand dance, don't you think?"

"Peggy," muttered Susan, clutching her sister-in-law's arm with one hand and her own forehead with the other, "he's at it again. Where did he learn anything about these dances? Can they possibly be real?"

"Of course they're not real," said Peggy in a choking voice. "*The Nut* is, so I suppose he put it in to confuse them, but the rest are all his own. Oh, I should never, never have let him come!"

"I think he's perfectly marvellous," said Amanda dreamily. "I hope he gets them to do *Swallow the Poker*. Surely even Miss Pringle can't swallow *that* one?"

It soon became apparent that Miss Pringle, who had never succeeded in believing that that charming Commander Parsons, so much more pleasant than his sister, who had married little Peggy Cunningham from the Manse, not a match in any respect, could possibly be anything but what he seemed, delightfully enthusiastic about all her plans, was entirely deceived.

"Why, you *naughty* man!" she cried, shaking a bony playful finger at him. "You must be an *expert*! Too, too bad of you to come and make fun of our poor little beginners' class! *Can* we do one of the fascinating dances he has suggested, Miss Fleming?"

"Oh, do, *do* let us!" squealed Miss Cissy, running from her place with girlish excitement to stand, her hands clasped imploringly under her chin, in front of the bewildered Miss Fleming. "Just *one*?"

"I'm afraid," began that nervous instructress unhappily, "that I don't know any of the dances this gentleman has mentioned—at least, not by those names."

"Ah!" said Oliver. "I expect you call *Swallow the Poker* by its other name—*Fill 'Em Up With Toddy*? Of course, the names vary so much in different parts of the country. No? Well, probably the pianist may have heard of *Fill 'Em Up With Toddy*? Oh, surely?"

But the soured spinster at the piano, who between bursts of rapid playing sat chafing her fingers to make them supple, put an end to the ridiculous discussion by announcing acidly and genteelly that she hed no mewsick for any of these dences except *The Nut*.

"*The Nut* let it be! Miss Pringle, will you honour me by being my partner?" said Oliver, leading her to the top of the room. "We'll show 'em how it should be done, eh?"

Wild horses nor red-hot pincers could have torn from Miss Pringle the admission that she did not know it. With magnificent composure she took her place opposite her partner. "Miss Fleming said she, "perhaps for the sake of others who may not be quite, quite sure of the dance, you would just run through it for us very quickly? Just a *hint*, you know, to guide the rest of the set."

Oliver's grin said 'One up to old Belly' as he caught his wife's eye; but he did not mind. He expected, by the end of the dance, to have scored so heavily that Miss Pringle's slight temporary gain would count for nothing.

He was right. *The Nut*, danced to a light-hearted tune in jog-time, is a simple measure, but its performance requires that at one point two men and one woman balance in line, hand in hand, while the remaining woman dances in and out under their raised arms in a glorified and more complex version of that favourite game at children's parties, 'Oranges and Lemons'. Exccuted with skill and neatness, this evolution provides the main attraction of an otherwise commonplace dance; and Susan, who was naturally graceful and had attended various harvest-home gatherings, played her part adequately, while Peggy, light as a fairy, tripped daintily under the two arches of the living bridge with easy elegance. Even Amanda, handicapped by her total ignorance of the technique of Scottish country dancing, and gasping with suppressed laughter, made a fairly good showing for a beginner. But the spectacle of Miss Pringle, large-footed and clumsy, bouncing her relentless way through the dance, was a severe test of gravity and politeness. "Like a camel diving into a rabbit-hole," as Oliver described it when they were allowed a moment's rest, and he had sunk, mopping bis brow, on to a bench beside Amanda and his wife.

"Or an elephant at a bee-hive, trying to get in, and looking a little pained because the entrance wasn't bigger," was Amanda's more elaborate contribution.

"No, no, my child. That would be]elly. She's the elephant," Oliver reproved her. "And, like the elephant, she never forgets; long after everyone else has forgotten *Swallow the Poker* she'll dig it up and want to dance it. Just you wait. But old Belly is pure camel. What other creature has that long, intolerably superior face and that expression of finding its fellow-creatures too low for recognition? What—"

"Explaining the dance to our little visitor from the south, I see," said the voice of Miss Pringle herself, cutting short this peroration, and she sat down firmly on the last few inches of bench, regardless of their discomfort.

"No, I was talking about camels," said Oliver gently, while the girls sat in guilty silence, looking at their feet.

"*Camels?* Surely a very odd topic?"

"Oh, not really, you know. Interesting beasts, camels" said Oliver, still more gently. "Something awfully human about 'em. And then, here we are, skipping about two by two, like the animals going into the ark."

"Oh," said Miss Pringle rather stiffly. "I see. *How* amusing of you! But I do not care for camels, personally. There is something revolting in the idea of all those stomachs."

"Susan," said Peggy in a quavering voice, feeling Amanda shaking at her side, and anxious to divert attention from her—"Susan, are you going to the party that Larry Heriot's giving?"

Susan, who had just come up at that moment, having escaped with difficulty from Miss Jelly's searching questions on the origin of the dances so glibly rattled off by Oliver, nodded. "Oh, I think so," she said. "Aren't you?"

"Yes. Only—only, I can't help thinking it's rather funny of him to have it when Miss Heriot is away," said Peggy. "If you say it's all right, then it must be."

"Ruth doesn't give him much encouragement to have one, does she? You know she never asks anyone to the house, and if Larry does, or someone happens to be passing and goes in, they don't get a very warm welcome," said Susan. "I often think that it's that isolation that sends Larry into those queer moody tempers of his."

"Oh, my *dear* Mrs. Armstrong, if you are speaking of Larry Heriot, you must, you really *must*, allow me to contradict that!" Miss Pringle, whose long ears, in spite of Oliver's determined chat, had caught most of this, broke in, and proceeded to contradict without waiting for any permission, "His poor unfortunate sister doesn't ask people to Gledewaterford because she *dare* not, in case they should arrive and find him *completely* intoxicated. He has only himself to blame for his 'isolation', I think I heard you call it. If he is having a party in Ruth Heriot's absence, I shudder to contemplate what it will be like. Positively a *drunken orgy*! I certainly would not go, nor permit the girls to do so, and I very strongly advise you to stay away."

Upon the stricken silence which followed the clear soprano voice of Amanda was heard saying, not altogether innocently, "Oh, have you been invited too, Miss Pringle?"

If she hoped to embarrass that notable woman she was disappointed.

"I have *not*," replied Miss Pringle with more emphasis than ever. "That man knows better than to ask me to attend his carousals. I *have* been to Gledewaterford, when I knew he would not be there, to see his sister. I have nothing against *her*, poor woman. But he has never dared to come near *my* house. He knows that he would be *turned* from the door without *hesitation*."

No one attempted to argue the point with her, and, foiled in this, she left them, and flapped her way across to Miss Fleming, calling energetically, "Now, all you *lazy* people, what about another dance?"

"What I can't understand," Amanda murmured in astonished tones, "is why someone hasn't murdered her long ago."

"Ay'm afrayd, Mrs. Cochrane," said Oliver mincingly, "that our little circle does not altogether meet with your approval."

"I don't admire your girl-friend a bit, Oliver!"

"Admire her or not," said Susan, "we've got to go back to tea with them after this. I suppose we should be thankful that she doesn't consider us disreputable enough to be turned from her door."

"There is nothing I'd enjoy better," declared Amanda. "One of these days I shall try it, if I have to get Larry Heriot himself to escort me!"

"Oh, she'd hale you in and leave him gnashing his teeth on the doorstep just to make it a bit more pointed," said Oliver cheerfully. "You can't get even with Belly by those crude means. It needs something a lot more subtle."

At last the class was dismissed. "We meet again at the same hour next week," announced Miss Pringle, "and though Miss Fleming cannot spare us more than one afternoon in the week, *I* shall be only too pleased to hold a practice on *any*day."

Strangely enough, this handsome offer roused no eager acceptances. Murmurs of "So sorry, too busy, the Rural—the Women's Guild—my Guide company—my husband . . ." were heard on all sides, until even Miss Pringle had, regretfully, to give up the idea.

"*Such* lukewarmness, such *lack* of real interest!" she mourned, as, having marshalled those fortunate ones who were going to her house for tea out of the hall and down the road she led them in at the gate. "Now, if they were all like *you*, Commander Parsons, what a splendid class we should have!"

Oliver made suitable mumbling noises in response, but his wife and sister, walking close behind, thought he sounded unusually distrait, and he fell back almost immediately to join them.

"Look there!" he whispered, nodding towards the gaunt weather-beaten house which they were so unwillingly approaching. "That window, left of the front door. Do you see what I see?"

Obedient, but puzzled, the two stared hard at the window in question, then turned faces wild with surmise and expectation to him. For in full view, his profile clearly recognizable even to a short-sighted person at that close range, was the outcast Larry Heriot, not only firmly established within the Misses Pringle's sacred dwelling, but engrossed in talking to their parrot, and, if his expression were a true indication, teaching it bad language with a considerable degree of success.

"Oh! Oh!" Peggy's voice rose to an uncontrollable squeak which was literally nipped off by Susan, who hissed in her ear, "Don't spoil it. Where's Amanda? She *must* be shown at once!"

Amanda was bringing up the rear of the procession with Miss Fleming, the mouse-like instructress, but she wasted no time on ceremony as soon as she had caught sight of the tableau in the window, to which the others drew her attention by frantic nods and furtive pointings. Running like a hare, she drew abreast of them, gasped "Quick! We must have ringside seats for this!" and fled on to take her place beside Miss Pringle.

That lady, serenely unconscious of the violation of her home, was discoursing on country dancing to her remaining guests, the melancholy elderly man, who appeared to be deaf, and his wife, while Miss Jelly and Miss Cissy, on his other side, threw in remarks, downright or sprightly in accordance with their natures, whenever their elder sister gave them a chance, which was not often. On marched this vanguard, right to the door, and still Larry Heriot was unobserved by Miss Pringle, though at the last moment, as they were actually entering the house, Miss Cissy saw him and uttered a bleating cry of horror and outrage.

"Bell!" she gasped. *"Bell!"*

"A moment, Cissy, please, and kindly remember that I am not deaf," said Miss Pringle testily, and heedless of the warning, rushed on her doom. "I think, if we *all* left our dancing-shoes and coats in the little morning-room," she said, and flung open the door on her left, "they will be less in the—" Her voice died in her throat, and she remained standing in the doorway, speechless for once, her eyes starting from her head, as the audacious intruder came to meet her with outstretched hand.

"How d'you do, Miss Pringle? Forgive me for barging in like this, won't you?" he said cheerily. "I thought the dancing-class was here in the house, but your maid said I was too late, anyway, so I waited to see you. Thought of joining the class, you know—good exercise and all that. Shakes up the liver. By the way, that's a jolly bird you've got there. Knows a lot, doesn't he? What a flow of language he's got! Why, it'd make a bo'sun's mate pale to hear him. Did you teach him all he knows yourself?"

While her sisters waited, quivering with indignation, to hear her scorch the horrible man (who must have been drinking, of course, or he would never have dared to come) with a few well-chosen words; while her guests held their breaths in anticipation of the fire and brimstone about to rain on Larry Heriot's unrepentant head, there was a silence so profound that everyone jumped when a loud raucous voice from the parrot's cage exclaimed: "What about a nice cup of tea? Kiss-me-quick, dear! Eh, ye'll catch it!" Only the last sentence seemed suitable to the occasion, but Miss Pringle, to her sisters' horror and her guests' disappointment, seized on the first.

"You'll—you'll stay and drink a cup of tea, I hope?" she said feebly. As she explained afterwards, it was beneath her dignity to wrangle with the man when he had been admitted to the house in her absence through Martha's stupidity, who must certainly never let him in again. Besides, there were her guests to consider. She could not let them suffer the awkwardness of seeing him driven from the doors, when they all knew him; but, alas, the explanations fell very flat, and for once her younger sisters felt that, after all, Bell was really no better fitted to deal with a difficult situation than they. It was a long time before she regained her dominion over them, nor was it ever entirely unquestioned again, for the seeds of rebellion were sown that afternoon, and sprang up to bear the most astonishing fruit.

CHAPTER SEVEN

I

"I'm BEGINNING to think perhaps it is rather a pity that Larry has chosen to have a sherry party," said Susan, some days after the tame ending to Miss Pringle's sensational dancing-class.

"Oh, I don't know." Jed, as always, was very lenient. "You could hardly expect him to ask people to a tea-party, after all."

"No, I suppose not; but it seems to—well, to encourage him if we go, and he does drink more than he should, Jed."

"He's been better lately," Jed pointed out.

"That's because Ruth isn't at home. I sometimes think it would be better for both of them if they didn't live together."

"No doubt about it, it'd be better for Larry. I'd take to drink myself if I had to have that woman with me all the time," said Jed, this time so far from leniently that Amanda looked up from her book in surprise.

She was glad enough to have her thoughts diverted to the subject of Larry Heriot, for, though she pretended to be absorbed in the printed pages, her mind kept on returning to the letter which she had had from her mother only that morning.

You must really stop being so childish, and make up your mind that poor dear Lloyd is gone (her mother had written). Gone! If she meant 'dead', why couldn't she say so? *And buy yourself some black clothes* (using what for money?)—*which would be only decent. I can't understand you, Amanda; it seems strange that my daughter should be so insensitive. Surely you must realize that your position, as neither wife nor widow, is very ambiguous, and must give rise to all sorts of speculation even in the country and where people don't know you. Here I am constantly being questioned as to what you mean to do and there is no doubt in my mind that your proper place once you have stopped being so obstinate about Lloyd being alive, which is* quite *impossible after more than two months, is with your mother. Would you like me to come to Reiverslaw for a few days, though I can ill afford the journey, and we can talk it all over quietly?*

And so on for several pages. 'Heaven forbid that she should come here,' thought Amanda, looking round the pleasant, peaceful room, made doubly so by the wild wind which raged outside and drove frequent showers of rain to batter at the windows. Her mother's haste to assume Cocky dead seemed almost indecent. Legally, he was still alive, and would be for months to come; after which, if there was still no word of him, she supposed drearily that there would be small discreet notices in the daily papers to the effect that Lloyd Cochrane's widow prayed leave to—well, to consider herself a widow, in fact. But David White, his lifelong friend and faithful admirer, still undisillusioned after knowing him for so many years, thought he was alive; and she would never really believe Cocky dead unless or until some proof of it were discovered—wreckage of his 'plane, something tangible.

Round and round went her thoughts, doing their squirrel-in-a-cage performance. It was far better to try not to think of it at all, to keep her mind blank, or fill it with other things which had no personal concern for her, or at least did not touch her nearly. Such as Larry Heriot, for instance. . . . She had something to think about there, remembering a conversation which she had had with Watson, the landlord of the 'Plough and Horses', only the day before. Going in for her usual cup of coffee, to pass the time while Jed was about his affairs and Susan was being fitted for a coat and skirt, Watson had bustled to serve her himself. As it happened, she had not seen him since the morning when she had found Larry in the lounge, and he had spoken of it.

"I was *that* sorry it should've taken place with you there, miss—madam," he had burst out. "Only for you saving the situation, as you might say, we would have had words again. Poor Mr. Heriot, as fine a young gentleman as you could find in the country until he took to this drink. I knew his father well, and I wouldn't like it said that I'd encouraged the son to bad ways. That's why I'll not serve him with more than a couple of drinks in a morning, madam. I know he'd have to go a good way to get more, for he quarrelled with the 'Black Bull', and the 'Swan' won't have him in the place since he kicked up a row there one day when the Farmers' Union Commytee was meeting there. So you'll excuse me for mentioning it to you, madam, but I'm very grateful to you—and so should Mr. Heriot be if he stops to think for a minute where he's heading. I see all sorts here in the 'Plough and Horses', and I know when a man should drink and when he shouldn't. If Mr. Heriot went on a blind—excuse me, madam—like other gentlemen, now and then, there'd be little harm done; but this everlasting determined quiet nip-nipping'll be the ruin of him. D.T.'s is the least he can expect. *Good* morning, madam. Many thanks. . . ."

What was the cause of it? Apparently he had not inherited any alcoholic tendencies, nor had he always been as he now was. It seemed to have started so suddenly as to argue a definite cause; and then he was worse when his sister was at home. . . . "Oh, I give it up!" she said, unconscious that she had spoken aloud, until Susan said:

"Yes, I found it almost impossible to get through it, and I thought I could read anything."

"I wasn't speaking about the book," confessed Amanda. "I was thinking, not reading—though probably because you're right, and it is a dull novel. Such dreary people who never seem to come to life, so that rape and murder and suicide are quite unimportant because you really don't care what happens to them."

"Author's puppets, remember. They have to dance when he pulls the strings, and to his tune. But why did you say, 'I give it up'? You sounded so puzzled," said Susan. And, as Amanda hesitated, added hastily, "No, don't tell me if you would rather not! I didn't mean to pry"

Amanda laughed. "My dear Susan, I should think that you and Jed are the least prying people who walk the earth! I was wondering about Larry Heriot, and why he has 'taken to drink', as they say."

"No one knows," said Susan. "Though, of course, Miss Pringle and her dear sisters are bursting with theories about it. It's completely wrop in mystery. I begin to wonder if Larry knows himself, or if he hasn't just given way to a weakness that was always there, from sheer boredom."

"I don't think that can be right," Amanda answered slowly. "Really I don't. I think there was some reason for it, and that if it could be discovered and cleared up he'd stop again. It isn't as if he enjoyed it, you know, Susan. He has such a desperate look sometimes."

"Well, if you can discover it and reform Larry you'll be doing a service to the whole neighbourhood." This was Jed suddenly joining the discussion. "We're all getting about fed up with taking Larry home, dragging him out of pubs and pushing him in at his own door, and getting no thanks either from him or his sister."

"Reforming has gone out of fashion," said Amanda, struggling with a yawn. "It belonged to Victorian days, when women were all pure and good, and all men were alien creatures of a lower nature altogether. Now they know too much about each other for any woman to try to reform a man successfully."

"It is still attempted," murmured Susan, rather drily. "You have only to tell a girl that a man is a bit of a rake to see her eyes light with interest."

"Very young girls, though, Susan. They haven't recovered from all the romantic novels they devour, which show the heroine as the rake's guiding star and guardian angel," retorted Amanda. "We all go through that phase, but it doesn't last."

"What about you, though?" Jed objected. He had been following the argument carefully, and now pointed out the weak spot in it with glee. "What about yourself, Amanda? Look at the interest *you* take in Larry."

"Oh!" Amanda said airily. "That certainly isn't reforming zeal, Jed. It's fellow-feeling. Larry Heriot and I are two of a kind. He said so himself, and he ought to know."

And without giving him a chance to continue, she said good night to both, and slipped out of the room, with a last mocking smile and a blown kiss in Jed's direction.

II

"She talks a lot of rubbish, doesn't she?" he said at last. "Does it make any sense to you, Susan? For I'm damned if it does to me."

"She talks a good deal without telling you anything, but I don't think it's rubbish. There's a lot of rather bitter philosophy in what Amanda says, and it must come from what life has taught her—nothing very pleasant, I'm afraid, from the scraps she occasionally gives away in those cynical remarks. I hope she isn't too much interested in Larry, fellow-feeling or not. It's supposed to make one 'wondrous kind', isn't it?"

Jed moved uneasily, hunching his broad shoulders. "I don't care for all that sort of abstract talk," he growled. "Things have got twisted, somehow, since she came. They never were before."

"She told me that Larry had said she was like the storm-cock, bringing bad weather with her. More Larry," said Susan. "There's too much Larry. But you like Amanda, Jed. You know you do."

"Oh yes, I like her," he said grudgingly. "But I want things to be open and straightforward, without all these hidden meanings and hints. Nothing's the same, Susan. Even you and I have changed a bit."

"Perhaps we were too placid and contented, and she's roused us," said Susan. "We could learn a good deal from Amanda, I fancy."

He looked at her resentfully. "What could she teach you? You're a better woman than she is."

"If I am, it's only because I'm a happier woman," said his wife, and she looked at him very sweetly. "I'll tell you one thing that Amanda has taught me, Jed: that I am even luckier than I realize to be married to you."

She was sitting close to him on a low stool, and now, without speaking, he stretched out his hand and laid it, strong and comforting, over hers, clasped on her knee.

"We've never talked very much about these things," said Susan, looking down at the sinewy hand on her own. "There's never been any need. But I want you to know that you've never shocked or disgusted me, never made me feel cheap or ashamed—"

"For God's sake, Susan! Why should I do any of that? No decent man would!"

"Then what sort of a man is Lloyd Cochrane?"

He shook his head. "Don't know. Never saw him. All I know about him is what I've read in the papers. Fearless pilot and all the rest."

"He must be selfish and faithless and boasting and mean-spirited," said Susan.

"How d'you make that out? It's not canny—"

"Quite easily, Jed. Oh, can't you see?" she cried. "Because Amanda *has* been shocked and shamed and disgusted over and over again, until she is sick of everything. You can see it in her face, hear it in what she says. And I hope with all my heart," said Susan defiantly, "that he really *is* dead."

III

The November morning was not actually wet, though a thin mist trailed and swirled about the ridge, blotting out all view from the windows of Reiverslaw beyond the nearest fields; but hounds had met at the cross-roads not far from Easter Hartrigg, and Amanda was determined to go out and look for them.

It was a ghostly day, the red and brown and golden trees looming through the haze like fires through smoke. Walking in the middle of the narrow road, Amanda could barely see the hedges, from which all but the last few coloured leaves had fallen, though they were still gay with berries, and every twig was jewelled with drops of moisture. Even sound was muffled, until cattle lowing, the chirr-chirr of quarrelsome partridges in a stubble-field behind the hedge, a cock-pheasant's arrogant crowing, the high yapping bark of a collie and a man's voice calling him, all blended into the strange eerie silence. Suddenly a louder and more cheerful combination of noises broke on her thoughts—the ring of shod hoofs, the clink of bits and stirrups, and out of the mist appeared a hunter's face, long, gentle and surprised, with a flash of scarlet glimpsed above the twitching ears. Amanda, standing aside on the grass, realized that she had met the hunt, jogging somewhat disconsolately along the road. Behind the whip came hounds pattering sedately, passing in a blur of dirty white and tan and brown, and more pink coats heralded the huntsman and second whip, the Master, and a medley of followers—trim women with bowlers set on incredibly neat hair and exquisitely cut sober habits; an occasional girl riding astride; a crimson-faced small boy, capless, on a stout pony; lean, keen-eyed leather-faced men. None of them knew Amanda, though most gave her a glance—friendly, curious, or merely indifferent—as they passed. And it seemed that she knew not one among them, even by sight, when a dark face, with a bowler slanted over one eyebrow, smiled down at her from the heights, and she found herself smiling back at Larry Heriot.

"Hullo," he said, drawing in to the roadside close to her, while the tail of the hunt drifted by, to be lost immediately in the milky veil of the mist. "Did you come out to see us?"

"Yes," said Amanda. "Haven't you—haven't they"—her mind searched madly for the proper word, and pounced on it just in time—"haven't you found?"

"Devil a fox in the whole country for all we've seen this morning," he said. "Are you going anywhere special, or will you turn and walk a bit with me?"

"But you'll lose the hunt," said Amanda.

"I can easily catch them up again. They're going down to draw the Muirkirk covert," he said carelessly. "And I only meant to take half a day, anyway. I'll have to get back to Gledewaterford by lunch-time."

"It's a long time since I saw you to speak to, though we've passed each other on the road once or twice," he went on, when he had got off his horse and was walking beside her, with the faint sounds of the hunt dying in the distance ahead. "At Miss Pringle's tea-party, it was."

"Do you mean to go to that dancing-class?"

"Do you take me for a damn' fool? Of course I'm not going near it. It was just an excuse to see if she would really turn me out of the house when she found me there. Someone told me she'd threatened to; but it all fell very flat, I thought."

"Yes. I was disappointed," she said. "After all I had heard about Miss Pringle, I did expect her to show her mettle when she discovered an—an impudent interloper teasing her parrot."

"It just shows that you should never believe all you hear," he answered sententiously.

"I don't. But in this case I'd already had a taste of Miss Pringle's methods—very *fortiter in re*," she said. "And it seemed to me that they might be applied to you, for you really deserved to be sent away tealess at least, when you only went there out of spite."

"You're always so hard on me," he complained. "Were you like that to your husband? Because, if you were, no wonder he took to flying to get away from you."

Such delicate regard had been shown for her feelings since she came to Reiverslaw, that no reference to Cocky, hardly even to flying, had ever been made in her presence; and she had felt this unobtrusive care wrapping her round, protecting her from every possible source of grief or embarrassment Now it was torn from her so suddenly, by a hand so brutally heedless, that she shivered as if an icy wind had struck her. She was speechless under the assault of the callous words, and though her feet continued mechanically to carry her on along the narrow road, she did not see her surroundings. But her ears still rang with his last remark; she thought that she must hear it always, for at least part of its horror was that, if it were not entirely true, it still approached the truth nearly enough to hurt her sharply.

"Please . . ." she stammered at last, all her defences down for the moment. "Why must you? What have I done to you always to choose me to be spiteful to? Please—"

"For once," he said, taking her arm and leading her out of the way of a large puddle into which she was blindly stepping, "I am not being spiteful at all. Hard though you may find it to believe—in fact, I can't expect you to believe it—I said it for your own sake, not merely to gratify my unpleasant instincts."

Again she shivered, and he shook the arm which he still held. "Now listen to me, Amanda," he said, "and think me all the brutes you like. You've been kept in cotton-wool, no doubt with the best intentions, by Susan. I'm right, aren't I? No one has been allowed even to say the words 'your husband', far less to talk about him. And what good do you think that's going to do you?"

"It was to escape having to talk about him that I came here," she said. "My mother never stopped, and it was driving me mad."

"I remember meeting your mother once. I can guess how she talked about him—'poor, brave boy', what? And 'my poor little girl a hero's widow'? Well, you needn't be afraid I'll take that line with you."

Indeed, the thought of his doing so was so utterly ridiculous that Amanda gave a shaky laugh which was more than half a sob.

"But you're going to talk about him now, whether you like it or not," he went on relentlessly, his grip bruising her arm. "If you don't, I will. You've got a whole cats' home in the bag, all fighting like tigers, and you can let 'em loose on me. Why not? We're two of a kind, remember. You can say things to me that you could never had said to that husband of yours. To start with, what was wrong with him?"

IV

"Why should there have been anything wrong with him?" cried Amanda, making a last wild effort to maintain her silence. "After all, he is my husband, and he's missing. Isn't that enough to distress me and make me hate to—to have his name dragged into conversation by outsiders? I hardly know you. We've only met a few times."

"Very pretty. Quite a good performance, considering that you've had no chance to rehearse it," he said. "It's no use lying to me, though, and you know it. We aren't strangers, either, however few times we've met. I know you, and you know me. Stop pretending that you're hoping he'll come back, and tell the truth. You're dreading it, aren't you?"

"Yes," said Amanda, with a dry sob.

"You poor little wretch. And that's the worst of the tiger-cats safely out of the bag. He must have given you a hell of a time, one way or another. I know he must, so you may as well tell me about him."

"It doesn't seem fair. If he does come back, no one ought to know them. And if—if he's dead, why shouldn't the things that I've kept to myself for such a long time die with him?"

"Because if you bottle them up they won't die," he grimly. "As nobody knows better than I. If I didn't, do you suppose I'd have had the damnable impertinence to speak to you like this?"

"Yes, I do suppose it. I don't believe that the fear of being thought impertinent would stop you from saying anything outrageous," said Amanda. Her cheeks were wet, she imagined with the mist blowing coolly in their faces, until she suddenly realized that the drops trickling down to fall on her white waterproof were both hot and salt. 'I must be crying!' she thought, in dull amazement. 'This is the first time I've cried for years!'

"I dare say you're right. People are always kind enough to tell me that I'm not hampered by any scruples of decency or good breeding," he said. "But I'm a very safe person to tell secrets to, because even if I passed them on, I'm such a disreputable character that no one would ever believe 'em. Well, I won't bother you any more, if you'd really rather suffer the torments of the damned in silence. Let's talk about something else."

"It's too late now!" Amanda's voice rose almost to a wail, so that his horse, uneasy, pricked his ears and gently nosed at his master's sleeve. "Don't you see that I'll *have* to tell you now, whether I want to or not? I can't keep it to myself any longer!"

"I know, I know," he said, so soothingly that her tears ran faster than ever.

"You don't know! How could you? I've been married to Cocky for seven whole years! I was just twenty-one, and he was twenty-four—"

"Poor lass. Was it as bad as that?"

"Oh, Larry! Oh, Larry! It was awful. People talk, of things being hell, but this—and it was partly my fault. Perhaps if I'd been easier at first I might have made him better. I don't know. But it was such a shock—not so much that he was unfaithful, for women always ran after Cocky, he was so handsome and gay and amusing—not even that he used to boast about them to me, compare me with them . . ." She shuddered uncontrollably. "But he was—was shifty about other things. Money, and business deals—everything. He just hasn't got a conscience or a heart. I suppose it isn't his fault that he was born that way? And people loved him and were taken in by him. There was David White, who's never let anyone say a word against Cocky, and still thinks he's the finest thing ever made, and me the luckiest woman in the world to have married him! He even cheated David. The only thing he didn't cheat about was flying, and I thought that might save him, only he drank such a lot that they were beginning to say he wasn't safe in the air, even. This flight was a last attempt; if it were successful he was to get a good job—and, as it was, no one would put up enough money to finance it. David did what he could, and we had to take every penny we had between us. Cocky mortgaged his life insurance, it was all he had, because everything he made was spent at once; and I sold out what was left of the money my father left me. Before this flight was arranged I was going to divorce him, I'd gone to my lawyers about it and it was all settled. I couldn't stand it any longer. There was always plenty of evidence! I was living with my mother in Southsea, I'd left him finally and he knew it. Then one day he came to see me—Mother must have helped him, she was fond of him, anyone who played up to her could get her on their side—and she didn't want to be saddled with a daughter who'd been through the divorce court—"

"Hold on a minute, Amanda. *You* wouldn't have been through the divorce court. Don't be childish. You were the injured one."

"Oh, but Cocky wasn't going to let it go quietly undefended. He'd have brought a counter-charge, or whatever the horrid thing is called—"

"Were you ever unfaithful to him?"

"In thought, often. Often!" she said passionately. "Not in—in any other way. But I'd been careless. You know—or perhaps you don't, because you're a man—that a woman has to do something to salve her self-respect a little. Other men showed quite plainly that if Cocky didn't appreciate me, they did. And I fooled about with them enough to make it sound not too good if it came out in court. . . . Anyhow Cocky came to the Southsea flat, and Mother had seen to it that I was alone. He wanted me to take him back, give him a last chance—another last chance! In the end, because I knew that I was partly to blame, I promised that I would when this flight was over, and we settled all the money business—for the flight, I mean. He promised me—oh, all the usual things. No more women, no more drink, no more trickery. He went away, and I was—not happy, for I knew I didn't love him, but fairly peaceful in my mind. A sort of 'port after stormie seas' feeling. And then—oh, Larry! This is the most horrible bit of the whole sordid business! He went straight off to another woman, told her how neatly he'd managed to get round me, and how the money for the flight was safe. She told me after he'd gone. How they must have laughed at me for the fool I was, the two of them!"

Larry Heriot, looking at the wan face swollen with tears that she turned to him, seeing the bitter smile of self-mockery that twisted her mouth, swallowed some unprintable words. "Go on," he said hoarsely.

"There's really no more to tell. He's gone. Only—do you wonder now that I dread hearing he's alive? I promised to go back to him—"

"He's not alive," said Larry confidently. "Can't be after all this time. You can be sure of that."

"I can't be sure. That's what haunts me—that, and knowing how horrible it is to hope that he's dead. But Cocky isn't dead," said Amanda, with dreary certainty. "You don't know him, you can't understand, but he had far more hold on life than most people. He always said that he wouldn't die—"

"That's absurd, my dear," he said gently. "You've let him become an obsession. It's like a nightmare, and you've got to wake up out of it."

"This is the kind of nightmare one doesn't wake out of," said Amanda. "It's no good. I'm sure you mean to be kind, but unless I have some sort of proof, I won't be able to believe that Cocky's dead. Everything in my life is at a standstill until I know one way or the other."

She pulled off a glove and lightly touched her cheek. "I feel *raw* with crying, but it's done me good. It has been a relief to tell you. You knew it would be, and you were right. That's because as soon as I saw you, I knew that *your* cupboard had a skeleton in it too. Would you like to tell me about it? Let me see the bones? It might take my mind off my own ugly skeleton."

"The cats in my bag or the skeleton in my cupboard aren't fit for you to see," he told her, in a hard voice.

"Is that quite fair? After you've dragged out mine?"

"Fair or unfair, I'm keeping mine to myself. You've forgotten, haven't you, that I don't feel bound by such trifles as fairness? Besides, in your case you're not to blame. It's quite the reverse with me."

"I was partly to blame," she said, very low. "I know that I raged and nagged and pleaded, and probably drove him on, when if I'd been a little better at managing him, and hadn't thought so much about my own pride and self-respect, I might have saved him, poor Cocky."

"Well, I'm not going to tell you my secrets," he said. "If I'm ever driven so hard that I can't keep quiet any longer, it's to you I'll come. Once you've heard them, your opinion of me will have reached rock-bottom."

"Suppose I heard them from someone else?" she insinuated. "Wouldn't that be far worse?"

His face darkened, then he laughed. "No use, my dear. I'm proof against even your wiles. And I say, Amanda! What a sight you are!"

"Whose fault is that? But, Larry, I do feel as if part of the awful weight had been lifted," said Amanda. "And—oh, look! We've walked right out of the mist. The sun's shining down here."

Talking and walking slowly along, the horse's hoofs a peaceful accompaniment, they had come to lower ground, and all the wide country rolled away below them, only the hills remained shrouded impenetrably in cloud. A field near at hand was being ploughed, the long straight furrows shining silver in the pale sunlight that caught their ridges, the hollows deep purple. Amanda watched the slow pairs moving up and down, the horses' mighty rounded quarters straining with each lift of their plumy hoofs, the wise heads nodding. Above the field flew golden plover, filling the air for a moment with plaintive piping as they passed and vanished. The painted woods glowed in the light, their tarnished golds and russets deepened and enriched by recent rain; a field of turnips shone vividly green where everything else had taken on the more sober hues of early winter.

"You've come a long way from Reiverslaw," said Larry. "You ought to be getting back now."

His hand was still on her arm, reminding her that she had come farther this morning than any mere matter of miles. An exhausted peacefulness possessed her spirit, the quiet of the countryside fell on her heart like balm, and she owed it to him. Impulsively she turned and looked at his grave face.

"I can't begin to thank you," she said.

"Don't try, then," he said brusquely. "I knew I was the only one who could be any help just then, the only one brutal enough to force you to it. That's all. I don't flatter myself that you'll find any more use for me. I've done my bit. You'll have to help yourself now."

"You—you aren't very gracious," began Amanda. "Oh! Here comes a car, and you say I look so awful! I wish I could hide—"

"I wish you could, too," he replied grimly, as, a car full of women, curious faces and waving hands seen at the windows, flashed past and was gone. "That was the doctor's wife from Kaleford, taking the Miss Pringles for a drive. Now they *will* have something to talk about. Here we are, me holding your arm, you with the tears still on your face. It's a fair cop this time."

"I don't mind," said Amanda. "I didn't think that you would. It's none of their business."

"Everyone's business is theirs," he said. "It doesn't matter for me, but you won't find it so funny when those tongues begin to wag, and you're the subject. I'm going to send you back now. I'll see you at the sherry-party next week if not sooner."

He mounted and rode off, frowning. There was no reason whatever against his walking down a country road with Amanda Cochrane. The whole world might have known of it, for all he cared; but he would not have liked the world to see her tears, and of all persons in the world, the Misses Pringle least. They could make a story out of a turn of the head, and obvious traces of tears were rich material for them to handle. So he frowned, and growled below his breath names which would have caused those blameless but rather faded flowers of spinsterhood to shrivel away altogether if they had heard them.

CHAPTER EIGHT

I

AMANDA, sitting back in the shadowy corner of the sofa nearest the fire, watched Susan making tea. It was a pleasant, gracious sight of which she never tired. The lamps were switched but the curtains, not yet drawn, showed the gathering darkness, the sky lighted only by the evening star, behind Susan's dark head as she sat on the window-seat with the low table in front of her, ladling smoky-scented China tea from an old Sheffield-plate caddy into the earthenware tea-pot of darkest blue like the night sky itself.

"Hullo, Susan! Had to pawn the silver tea-pot already? I didn't know that times were as hard as all that," said Oliver from his deep chair in front of the blazing fire. Elspeth, setting a covered dish of hot scones on the table, curled her nose scornfully, and was plainly only restrained from sniffing audibly by her enormous sense of decorum.

"The Queen," said Susan, looking at her brother repressively, "favours an earthenware tea-pot, and what is good enough for Buckingham Palace will surely do for us at Reiverslaw." And when Elspeth, embodied disapproval, had tripped noiselessly out: "My dear Oliver! If you only knew what a fight I had with Elspeth over being allowed to make the tea myself, far less use this old china tea-pot, you'd have been tactful enough not to mention it! I was determined not to drink another cup of the dish-water she calls tea, and only yesterday Jed threw a whole cupful of the horrid brew into the fire and almost put it out, as Amanda can tell you. Hence this charming domestic scene."

"It's all vanity. You know you look nice sitting there playing with silver kettles and spirit-lamps, with your lily-white hands straying among the tea-leaves," retorted Oliver. "Where is Jed, anyhow?"

"Here he comes now," said Peggy, who was perched beside her sister-in-law, as Jed's tall figure tramped past the window.

In a minute he had come into the sitting-room, unconcernedly leaving a trail of mud across the carpet, and smiled silently but amiably as he took his place at the table, for he utterly refused to balance a cup on his knee.

"You'll have to change, Jed, remember," said Susan, pouring out tea into white cups on which green dragons sprawled.

"Change? What for?" he demanded indignantly.

"Larry's party. Have you forgotten it's this evening?" asked Peggy. "Look at Oliver in his church suit, and me in my new black dress!"

"Gosh! I'd forgotten all about it. I don't think I'll go. There's plenty of you without me," said Jed, getting to his feet to carry her cup over to Amanda, and to offer her scones.

"Now, Jed, it's no use beginning that," said Susan, unmoved. "Your navy-blue suit is laid out on your bed in the dressing-room, and as soon as you've finished tea you'd better go and put it on."

Jed nodded, and asked resignedly, "Will I have to shave?"

"Well, as I strongly suspect you of not having done so this morning, I'm afraid you will," said his wife. "It's your own fault."

"I had to see the shepherd this morning," he said, as if that explained it. "Is this party going to be a big crush? I'd have thought that old clothes and a bristly chin wouldn't be noticed at Glede-waterford."

"I should notice it," said Susan. "Peggy, have a scone, won't you?"

"Oh!" said Peggy suddenly. "I nearly forgot! I give you three guesses. Who do you think are going to the party? It's no use looking at Oliver, Jed. He doesn't know who I mean."

"Give it up. Tell us," said Oliver lazily, helping himself to a slab of home-made cherry cake.

"Miss Jelly and Miss Cissy!" cried Peggy, in her excitement at being the bearer of such astounding news dropping her half of the scone, which was immediately wolfed by the ever watchful Bawtie, crouched on the floor at her feet. "Yes, really!"—as the others looked disbelieving. "It's absolutely true, not a rumour. I met them bicycling on the road this morning when I was out with young Oliver in his pram, and they told me themselves. Miss Pringle has gone away for a week or more—'visiting friends in the south,' they said. She left the day before yesterday, and Miss Jelly said that as they had entertained Mr. Heriot to tea, she didn't see why they shouldn't accept his invitation in return. They were on their way to Abbeyshiels to buy frills and bits of ribbon and things to make themselves grand for the party. What do you think of *that*?"

"My hat!" said Oliver, drawing a deep breath. "Mutiny in the Jelly-bag camp! What on earth will happen to them when old Belly gets home and hears about it? Do you mean to tell me, Peggy, that you, the wife of my bosom, had this priceless bit of news up your sleeve and never let me in on it? I thought at luncheon that you were wearing a particularly irritating smirk, and now I know the reason."

"Pig," said Peggy. "I don't smirk. And it was worth saving up, to see all your faces just now."

"You know," Susan said uneasily, "I don't like the sound of this at all. If the party gets a bit riotous, think what a harvest of gossip they'll reap! No, I don't care for it. It has a bad smell to me. And where has Miss Pringle gone, Peggy, do you suppose? The only 'friends in the south' I have ever heard her mention are those doggy people near Carlisle whom Ruth Heriot knows. Just imagine if she has hurried off there to tell Ruth that her brother is having a party while she's away? There's trouble brewing in this for someone."

"Now, Susan, look here." This was Jed's placid rumbling voice, restoring common sense to the disturbed atmosphere. "That's all guess-work. You don't know where Miss Pringle's gone, and you don't know that Ruth's anywhere near Carlisle."

"It's a premonition. I feel like an oracle," said Susan dreamily, lifting the lid of the tea-pot and peering into the steamy depths in a witch-like manner.

"If an oracle ever had a face as shiny with steam as yours is, I don't believe anyone'd have paid attention to it," said Oliver, with brotherly brutality. "You girls had better go and bedizen yourselves while Jed and I smoke a pipe in peace."

"Jed will have to smoke while he changes," said Susan, rising as she spoke. "We're starting just before six."

"I don't start for anywhere until I've heard the first news," said Jed, with the firm flatness to which his wife always yielded gracefully when she heard it in his voice. "We'll leave as soon as the weather report is finished."

"That's more like an oracle," said Oliver approvingly. "What's more, it has every chance of coming true. I'm with you, Jed, every time."

The three women exchanged glances which spoke more eloquently than words their opinion of a sex which clung together so consistently, and drifted out of the room.

II

Amanda dressed with unusual care for Larry's party. Somehow it seemed an important enough occasion to require her smartest frock, her most careful make-up. Her toilet was not completed when she heard the cultured voice from Broadcasting House announcing below that before he read the weather forecast for tomorrow here was one S.O.S. Susan and Peggy had gone downstairs, the car had been brought to the door, and still she lingered dissatisfied, looking at her reflection in the long glass which showed her a figure fashionably slim in dark brown, a gleam of pale hair under a high-crowned hat swathed with green and blue, a pair of over-bright dark eyes.

Then the radio was switched off, footsteps sounded in the hall, and she picked up a pair of gloves and hurried down to take her place in Oliver's car, wedged in between him and Peggy for she had chosen quite firmly not to go with Jed and Susan, and Peggy had backed her up.

"Never mind if it is a bit of a squash," she had said. "We'll be all the warmer, and it's our turn to have a share of Amanda."

It was charmingly put, and Amanda appreciated the kindness of heart which had prompted the words. Peggy might quite easily have said the truth, bald, unvarnished: "Let Susan and Jed have a chance of being alone for once." But her version of the truth was always a pleasanter one than Ruth Heriot's. . . .

Packed in as they were, there was very little to be seen of the run to Gledewaterford, nor did the feeble glimmer shed by the lights of Oliver's wheezing elderly Morris do much more than make darkness visible. They shone, it seemed, where they pleased, the wavering beams now catching the top of a hedge, now the giant gnarled bole of a tall old willow, but rarely illuminating the road before them. This, together with the sighing voice of the wind which deadened the engines' rattle, gave to their progress an effect of stealth which Amanda found vaguely exciting. It seemed to fit in with the mystery of the house towards which they were creeping through the dark evening.

"I hope Peggy warned you that you might have to walk? The old Squib's very temperamental nowadays," shouted Oliver, in his cheerful voice above the sounds of car and wind.

"Nonsense. The Squib will get us there quite well," said Peggy placidly. "You humour the old thing far too much, and give her ideas."

"You're bound to stick up for her," said her husband. "You remember I told you that if we had a baby we couldn't have a new car, and you chose the baby."

"Of course. So did you," was Peggy's contented answer. "I'd rather have a *tricycle* and young Oliver than a Rolls without him."

Amanda remained silent, for she knew which she would have chosen; and at that moment Oliver stopped the car on the crown of the bridge over Glede Water, and switched off his engine. At first their ears, grown used to it, heard only the wind; then gradually there rose the endless song of the little river, muttering below them—a soft hushing sound, broken by a louder gurgling note as the water eddied round the piers of the bridge or sucked at the banks. Through a rift in the flying clouds appeared a wisp of new moon, far down the sky in front of them, lying on its back as if cradled by the clouds which in a minute would swallow it up. The wan light fell aslant on the valley, glinting on the dark coils of Glede until it looked as if it carried a silver water-snake down its length. Then it was all blotted out again by the greedy clouds, and the Squib, stuttering with indignation, broke into life and bounced forward on the last few yards to Gledewaterford.

Once between the tall stone gate-posts, they found themselves in a line of other cars, and movement became very slow, giving Amanda ample time to anticipate her meeting with Larry Heriot, the first since he had dragged from her the secret of her unhappy marriage. Her heart began to beat unevenly, she bit her lip hard, wishing that she had not come. If Larry were to show, by the faintest sign of look or tone, that he shared what she had kept so well hidden from everyone else, she never wanted to see him again. Even if he did not, she still dreaded having to see him. They moved, stopped, moved jerkily again. The startled head of a young cart-horse, with wild eyes and flowing dark mane, appeared over a fence, caught by the lights of the car in front, disappeared, and once more was lit up by tbe Squib's capricious head-lamp, only to vanish finally as they passed it. "Like the Cheshire cat, only without the grin," murmured Peggy. "Oh, are we at the door? Come on, Amanda."

She skipped out, followed by the others. "I thought we were at the door?" said Amanda, staring at the glimpses of farm-buildings revealed in the wheeling flashes of headlights, and the wide space on which cars were parking. "Where is the house?"

To herself she admitted that she would be rather relieved though not in the least surprised if the house had simply vanished; but Oliver, taking her and Peggy by the hand, led them to a small gate set between evergreens, piloted them, stumbling, up two slippery steps, and landed them, after a short walk over very knobbly gravel, at an open doorway from which issued an inadequate trickle of light, a hum of voices, and the occasional bark of a large dog.

The narrow entry, floored with square flags not only dirty but undeniably damp, took a right-hand turn almost at once, to show them an inner hall, also stone-floored, and divided from the passage by a glass door. Not a soul was in sight, nor had anyone answered Oliver's hearty tug at the bell. "Broken, probably," he now said without astonishment, and pushed open the door beside them.

From the back of the hall rose a flight of uncarpeted stairs, and half-way down these stood a lurcher with one eye and a ragged ear, watching them suspiciously. "Here, Jock," said Oliver, snapping his fingers; but the dog, although he wagged his tail, did not come to meet them.

"Welcome to the party!" muttered Oliver. "I don't know which of these doors it's hidden behind, but we'll have a shot—"

"On your left," suggested a voice, and they turned to find passage and hall rapidly filling with puzzled guests.

"Well, most of the noise seems to be coming from there," Oliver said rather doubtfully, as a shrill yell rent the air, followed by a chorus of guffaws.

"Och, come on, man, let me try if you don't like to risk it," said the man who had spoken, a burly quick-tempered-looking person, brushing past Oliver. "I didn't come here to hang about a cold passage all night."

"By all means," he said, with a cordial readiness which struck only Peggy as suspicious, and stood aside.

The burly man turned the handle with violence, flung the door open, and roaring, "Well, here we are, and a damn' poor welcome we got!" stormed over the threshold, only to stop in his tracks so suddenly that those behind him were almost knocked down in his retreat.

Over his shoulder or under his arm the bewildered crowd could see into a cavernous kitchen, dim with smoke, richly redolent of oil-lamps and frying herring, which appeared to be filled with people. From a far corner proceeded the discordant strains of a mouth-organ, to which a couple of youths was solemnly dancing, their nailed boots squeaking horribly on the stone floor. A game of cards was in progress round the huge solid table, on which stood several bottles of whisky and a heterogeneous collection of cups and glasses; and at the fire, enveloped in a cloud of hot odorous smoke from an enormous frying-pan, stood a large bare-armed woman, engaged in cooking herring with one hand and warding off the amorous advances of a stout man in long rubber boots with the other. Just as the group in the doorway took in this scene, the ardent swain dived under the cook's threatening hand, which hovered like a ham above his head, and catching her about her waist, succeeded in planting a number of smacking kisses on her hot face.

"What the . . ." began Oliver, his eyebrows drawn together in a single ominous line above his nose. "If this is what Larry's asked us to, it's not my idea of a good joke. And where the devil is he?"

The clear irate voice cut through the mingled noises of the kitchen as a wire cuts cheese. "Megsty! It's gentry!" yelled the cook, and with a screech of dismay flung the herring which, well dipped in oatmeal, she had been about to consign to the frying-pan, on the floor, where it was instantly trampled by her admirer's rubber boots, and proved as treacherous as a banana skin. Lurching and staggering, he threw out his arms desperately in search of support, and clutched the fat cook. The two, to the accompaniment of the mouth-organ, which ceased not to jig throughout, tottering, locked together as if performing some intricate measure, wove their way madly towards the door, where, as if by intention, they suddenly collapsed in a sitting position, side by side, to face their amazed and disconcerted audience.

"Is it the Big Apple?" asked Peggy, in a whisper.

"I *think*," Amanda answered thoughtfully, "that this must be one of the country dances Oliver recommended to Miss Pringle, don't you?"

The cook, regaining her breath, uttered another bloodcurdling yell and rose to her feet, levering herself up by the simple method of planting one hand in her partner's face and pushing with all her might. Then, with considerable presence of mind, she slammed the door, and the guests for the sherry-party were once more in the hall, shattered by the almost choked by the fumes of burning fat and black twist tobacco.

"Not the right door, evidently," Oliver was beginning blandly, when Jed's voice fell like an angel's from heaven on their ears.

"Aren't you coming in? They'll have all the sherry drunk if you don't look sharp," it said. "What are you all standing here for like sheep? You must have come in by the back door."

Behind him, across the hall, they now saw a doorway which gave a glimpse of another hall, square, still with the flagged floor which made Amanda think that if it had been tidier and cleaner it would have been like some institution; beyond that were lights, voices, and the welcome tinkle of glass.

"Come on," said Oliver, setting a brisk pace towards this haven. "I've had about enough of fun in the kitchen for one evening."

As the others streamed gladly after him, Amanda found that she had been steadied by the absurd incident, and her smile, her murmured greeting of her host, were amiably conventional. It was only when he had turned away to fetch her a glass of sheriy that she realized how his own off-hand manner had helped her to keep her poise. Nothing in it suggested that they had ever exchanged more than a few polite remarks on the weather. Indeed, so impersonal was he, that she felt an illogical prick of most unreasonable resentment. She had denied herself the luxury of this sort of feeling for a very long time, schooling herself to be temperate and reasonable since Cocky was so determinedly the reverse, and now she did not make even a half-hearted effort to restrain it. A delicious sensation of youthfulness sparkled in her eyes and added an unusual vivacity to her manner, which brought men crowding about her, eager to be introduced to a woman whom they had not noticed a few moments before.

III

There are hardly any women who have not at least once in their lives experienced this glorious irresponsible feeling of power, far more intoxicating than any sherry. Amanda had always had her share of it, but so often it had been a bitter triumph, merely enjoyed with the mean design of getting even with Cocky; now at last she could flirt delicately and without any aim but that of present amusement and no harm to anyone. While Larry, delayed by the arrival of other guests, was still making his way back to her, she had been supplied with at least three glasses of sherry, and had gathered a small court in her corner of the room. But though her bright eyes appeared to be entirely occupied in causing a temporary devastation among the stalwart Borderers about her, she had not failed to put them to another use. Her curiosity to see Gledewaterford, increased as she had come to know Larry Heriot, sharpened her glance, and very little had escaped it since she had entered his house.

The room in which they stood was nobly proportioned, the halls and stair were in keeping with it; but the whole place bore obvious

signs of neglect, almost of decay. Walls and ceilings were dirty, disfig-
ured by damp, and the few pieces of necessary furniture, the total
lack of ornaments or flowers, the windows bare of curtains, gave it a
desolate air that hurt her. Here was a house lovingly planned, built
by some master craftsman, made to be the home of happy people
who would care for it as it deserved, and it had been allowed to fall
into this pathetic state.

Amanda, whose feeling for places had always been stronger
than for people, wanted to stroke its walls, crying for fresh paper;
to touch with a loving hand the beautiful mantels and doors which
its ungrateful owners so evidently did not appreciate. By the time
Larry had reached her, a brimming glass in one hand and a plate of
biscuits in the other, she was ready to flay him with her tongue for
cruelty to the house which had so strong a personality that it felt
alive. Instead, she turned her shoulder on the men who had each
imagined that all her attention was for him alone, and smiled up at
her host provocatively as she accepted sherry and refused a biscuit.

"What a beautiful house this is," she said.

He looked about him with a startled air, as if seeing it the first
time. 'I suppose to him it's just a place where he can eat and sleep,"
thought Amanda indignantly; 'but how can his sister, even if she
does look like a horse, bear to let it go like this?'

"Do you like it?" he asked doubtfully.

"Not in its present condition," Amanda promptly replied. "I could
love it, I think, if it looked and smelt less like a dirty barracks. That's
very rude," she added. "But I don't care. You're so fond of hearing
the truth in your family, aren't you? You deserve it, for letting it
get so—so dishevelled. Don't *you* like it?"

"I used to, as a boy, when my mother was alive," he said slowly.

"Well, what about your sister? Doesn't she like it, either?"

"Ruth? I don't believe she cares a tinker's curse about it, or
anything except those infernal dogs of hers," he said.

"How very, very odd!" murmured Amanda; then, remembering
that she intended to punish him for behaving as she had hoped and
expected he would, she proceeded to exert all her charms on him
with that purpose in mind.

Susan, watching, felt suddenly anxious. She did not know why, but she thought that there was danger for both Amanda and Larry if she chose to flirt with him; and her uneasiness was not lessened by observing that Miss Jelly and Miss Cissy, prowling on the outskirts of the animated throng, fearfully and wonderfully adorned with bows and frills, had also noticed Larry's absorption with little Mrs. Cochrane. Last time they had seen her, she had been hanging on his arm on the road, in floods of tears, and now she was behaving as if she considered herself a widow, and a merry one at that. Quite obviously flighty, and not the sort of person they liked to know. 'Oh, dear!' thought Susan. 'How naughty and tiresome of Amanda! I wanted her to have her mind taken off her troubles, but not quite like this.'

It would have comforted her a little, though not much, if she could have heard what Larry Heriot was saying as he gazed at Amanda with every appearance of grave admiration.

"Stop that nonsense at once," he was saying. "Or party or no party, I'll put you across my knee and spank you as you deserve, my girl."

"Mr. Heriot!" cried Amanda, outraged, and furious at being seen through so easily.

"No good. I've told you already you needn't try those tricks on me. Better play with these other fellows. They don't know you."

"And you think you do?"

"Yes," he said. "I do know you, Amanda."

"You brute!" breathed Amanda, a sweet smile on her face. "I suppose you're taking advantage of having forced me to tell you things that I never should have. I might have known you would."

"That's rot, and you know that too."

"Please don't start telling me again that we're two of a kind, or something equally tiresome and untrue," said Amanda.

"I won't. I don't need to tell you what you know as well as I do."

"Isn't this where you say you're not drunk, and I try to look as if I believed you?" said Amanda unpleasantly.

He shook his head. "No."

"Please go and talk to someone else. I don't like you very much this evening."

"No. I'm going to show you some more of the neglected house, as you've taken such a fancy to it," he told her.

"But I'm not coming. I don't want to see it," she said instantly, aware that she did want to see the house, but suddenly afraid to be alone with him.

"Oh yes, you are, and you do," he said coolly. He took the glass from her hand, set it down, and turned to the door beside him. "Come on."

"You realize, I suppose, that I am coming against my will?" asked Amanda with dignity, as she passed out into the hall.

"Oh, lord, yes, I know," he said, and smiled at her grimly. "You don't want to face the music, and it was only because you were afraid I'd drag you out of the room by main force that you came." He had, it seemed, no intention of going farther, but stood leaning against the discoloured wall, here patterned by finger-marks as well as damp, and looking down at her.

"What about showing me the rest of the house, then?" she suggested at last, a little breathlessly, when the look had become a stare, and he still did not stir.

He moved then, so quickly that he had caught her by the wrists and twisted her hands behind her before she knew what was happening. He held her so, facing him, and at the look in his eyes Amanda was frightened in earnest.

"Please . . . Larry . . ." she began uncertainly.

He said harshly, "You know you ought to be beaten for playing me up like that. Beaten—or kissed. That's what you were asking for." He drew her closer and bent his head, bringing his face very near to hers. "Weren't you asking for it?"

"Yes. I was," she said, hardly above a whisper. "I beg your pardon. But please don't kiss me, Larry."

His grip hurt her wrists, his sombre eyes were like blue fire in his dark face. "Don't pretend. You've been kissed often enough—and liked it," he said. "Why shouldn't I?"

It was true, of course, and whether she had liked it or not, these other kisses had been unimportant; but she knew that for Larry to kiss her now would be a catastrophe for both.

This isn't—isn't the same," she murmured desperately.

She thought he had not heard her, but after a moment which seemed to stretch to unbearable lengths, he released her with a slight shake. "If you knew that, why did you try to flirt with me?" he said. "Don't ever do it again." And in the same composed voice, "Do you really want to see the house?"

"Well, actually, I suppose you oughtn't to leave the party. It's yours, remember," said Amanda, recovering herself and speaking only a little more lightly and quickly than usual. "And you can't show me the kitchen. There's a rival entertainment going on in there."

"Oh, that?" he laughed. "It's only Big Maggie celebrating her engagement to the cow-man. She seemed to think it was an occasion for rejoicing, and I knew that if I didn't let her have them here she wouldn't be in till all hours, and I'd have to go without breakfast as well as supper."

"Is—er—Big Maggie your entire domestic staff?" asked Amanda, no longer wondering at the condition of the house.

"One of the women from the cottages comes in to give her a hand, do the washing and make the butter and so on, I believe," he said carelessly. "It isn't my part of the show, you know. Ruth sees to all that."

"Don't you care *how* you live, Larry?"

"No. I don't give a damn," he said, his face darkening again. "It doesn't matter to me. Let's go back to the party, shall we, as you think I ought to?"

"It's a good party. Won't your sister be annoyed with you for having it while she's away from home?" said Amanda, not without interest.

"She'll be annoyed, all right, but not because she's missed it," was all he said, and she knew that it was useless to ask any more, though she longed to do so.

"Oh, Mr. Heriot!" piped Miss Cissy Pringle, pouncing on him as soon as he entered, and darting looks of devouring curiosity at Amanda. "We've *all* been wondering *where* you were! Did you know—such a strange coincidence—that our sister has been staying at the same house as Miss Heriot?"

"Was it a coincidence?" he said, without trying to hide his disbelief. "Your glass is empty. Let me get you some sherry."

Thus silencing Miss Cissy, he went in search of a decanter, leaving her to prattle into Amanda's unwilling ears. "*So* strange of him to have a party when his sister isn't here, don't you think, Mrs. Cochrane?"

"I hadn't thought about it at all," was Amanda's mendacious reply. "But in any case, from all that I've heard of Miss Heriot, she doesn't care for parties."

"Oh, poor Ruth!" said Miss Cissy, with a gusty sigh. "That's what she *says*."

"She ought to know, surely?" said Amanda, more indifferently than she felt.

"The truth is, of course, as Bell always says," broke in Miss Jelly's deep, trenchant tones, "that she is afraid to have a party in case he gets intoxicated!"

"Then I can only suppose," said Amanda, losing patience and making them her enemies for ever, "that either you are braver than Miss Heriot, or that you *hope* your host will be drunk before his party ends."

Without giving them a chance to reply, she walked away and joined Susan at the other side of the room. "What dreadful women!" she said angrily. "Yes, Jed, please give me some sherry, I need it badly to take the taste of the Miss Pringles out of my mouth. Can you imagine a mentality like theirs, so lacking in common decency that they'll come to a man's house and blackguard him while they drink at his expense?"

"What ails you at the old ladies?" asked Jed irritatingly. "Fine characters they are, and not ashamed of saying what they think. I like them. I'm going to speak to them myself."

"It's a waste of time to lose your temper over them," said Susan rather wearily. "They aren't in the least likely to change, especially as they consider themselves a great deal better than the rest of us."

"Well, I'm glad to think they will leave this party disappointed," Amanda said. "For if they wait to see Larry intoxicated, as they call it, they'll have to wait for a very long time."

"Oh, they're harping on that string, are they? But I didn't expect to hear you defending Larry quite so strenuously," said Susan.

Amanda looked a trifle taken aback. "It's—it's so unjust, that's all. It makes me angry," she muttered. 'Must every dog that is given a bad name be hanged? I do hate it so, Susan; and they can do quite a lot of damage, the old vultures. . . . Susan, has it never struck you as queer that Larry's sister doesn't do something to stop these rumours?"

"Possibly she knows that they aren't rumours," said Susan quietly. "After all, she sees more of him than anyone else, Amanda. And I don't really care to discuss them like this, when we are his guests. It makes us just a little too like the Pringles, don't you think?"

Her smile robbed the gentle reproof of any smugness; and Amanda, contrite, nodded. "You're right, of course. I was so angry that I forgot where I was, and it really isn't my business in any case." She looked at Susan and said suddenly, "Are you awfully tired, Susan? You look so pale."

"I hope you aren't telling me in a kindly way that I am looking extra *plain*," Susan said.

"No, far from it. You look wan and interesting. But you shouldn't be looking wan. Do you feel all right?"

"I feel a bit *waff*, as Jed would say," Susan confessed. "I'm all right, really. If there happened to be a chair—"

"Here's one." Amanda turned and pulled at a heavy mahogany chair of the plain pleasant type known as 'Scotch Chippendale', only to find the arm loose in her hand. "Just what I might have expected!" she murmured viciously, ramming it home in place and dragging the chair forward by its sturdy back. "I should sit on it gingerly, if I were you. It may fall to bits!"

But apart from one slight protesting creak as Susan sat down, the chair seemed quite safe, and she leaned back in it gratefully. "Thank you, Amanda. How stupid of me not to see it before, when I was standing close to it."

"I should think it was almost time to go home," said Amanda, still looking rather anxiously at the dark shadows below Susan's eyes, the pallor which made her face seem so small. Lots of people have left. Where are Peggy and Oliver?"

"They had to go early. Peggy's maternal instincts couldn't keep her away from her son. But don't say anything to Jed, please, Amanda. You see, I know he wants to wait till the end, just to—to keep an eye on Larry."

"Jed wouldn't wait another minute if he knew you felt so rotten," said Amanda.

"I know. That's exactly why I don't want him told," said Susan impatiently, and Amanda felt more worried than ever. Susan impatient and irritable was quite a new experience, and if her looks had not given her away, her temper most certainty would.

"You'd better keep away from him, then, or he can't help noticing it," was all that she said; but she made up her mind to drop a hint to Jed as soon as she could, and her eyes sought him across the room, where not more than a dozen people still lingered, wondering what excuse she could make for leaving Susan. If Larry would come and talk to them, she could slip away, she thought, and caught his eye just as the door opened, to show framed in its oblong the gaunt tweed-clad figure of Ruth Heriot.

IV

An audible gasp ran round the room, and Larry, hearing it, wheeled about. There was a petrified silence which was somehow terrifying, and Amanda's horror of scenes, almost forgotten since she had come to Reiverslaw, or at least pushed to the background of her mind, came back to her in a wave of nausea, so that she had to hold to the back of Susan's chair to steady herself. Only Jed, it seemed, was unmoved. Leaving Miss Jelly and Miss Cissy, he strolled over to the stony-faced woman still standing in the open doorway, and said with amiable gruffness, "Hullo, Ruth. You see we've stolen a march on you. Pity you didn't get here a bit earlier."

"It is," she said, her deep voice almost as gruff as his own. "A great pity. And now, perhaps you'll all be kind enough to go." The restrained ferocity of her tone had its effect on the more nervous, who now, with subdued murmurs of thanks and farewell to Larry, by this time as hard-faced as his sister, began to sidle to the door, to ebb silently through it, and to vanish like mist before the rising sun. A few bolder spirits—one or two men, the Misses Pringle, with Jed and Susan and Amanda herself—remained where they were for various reasons. The Misses Pringle because curiosity was stronger than fear, the men out of a wish to stand by Larry and a dislike of sneaking out like whipped curs, Susan because she was both tired and angry, and Amanda because she knew that her trembling legs would never carry her to the door. It seemed to her that Ruth Heriot's baleful eyes rested with peculiar loathing and disgust on her, and she was more than glad of Jed's presence, for he was like a rock against which the rage of this unbalanced woman would beat in vain. He saw no reason for going until he was quite ready.

"Will you go?" said Ruth Heriot again, pointing to the door, undeterred by politeness or hospitality.

"It's Larry's party, you know," said Jed quite calmly, but with a gleam of anger in his eyes. "If you don't like it, I'm sorry; but he asked us, and we accepted his invitation."

"He had no right to ask anybody to this house," said she. Her restraint was wearing thin; the terrible temper so close to the surface was beginning to show in her raised voice, her colourless face, her eyes of insane fury. "He knows as well as I do, as well as all of you do, why I don't have people here—"

"Yes. Because you're so taken up with your damned whelps that you've no time for anything else," said Larry, speaking for the first time. "This is my house, and if you don't like to be civil to my guests you can leave it." Turning from her as if she were not there, he added to the silent others, "There's no need to go. Ruth's a bit tired, and doesn't know what she's saying. Don't go, any of you." He spoke low, but his blazing eyes, his paper-white face, made it a command rather than a request. Picking up a decanter, he moved to the man nearest him and filled the glass which his guest still held. "Plenty of time yet—and plenty of sherry," he said.

Perhaps it was the brutal indifference to her expressed in this action which was like a lighted match thrown on petrol, no one was ever sure; but the result was horrible to see, if only because very seldom in these days of so-called civilization does any person so completely lose their self-control as Ruth Heriot did now. Springing forward, she snatched the heavy decanter of cut-glass from his hand and threw it against the wall, where it smashed like an egg-shell. For a moment the sound of falling glass and the splash of the spilt wine were all that broke the paralysed silence. It seemed as if people had forgotten to breathe. Then Susan, rising from her chair and coming forward, took the distraught woman by the arm.

"Ruth," she said, her cold clear voice dropping like a shower of rain, "Ruth, you must pull yourself together. Let me take you to your room. After all, we are your friends and neighbours, there is really no need to treat us like this. You'll be sorry when you have had time to think it over."

It seemed as if her words had some effect. Ruth Heriot's livid face quivered, and she looked at Susan almost piteously. "Why did you all come here, sneaking behind my back?" she muttered hoarsely. "Larry might have known I'd lose my temper if I found you here."

"That's nonsense," said Susan, crisply yet not unkindly, "There is absolutely no reason why we shouldn't be here if Larry asked us to come. It would be much better for both of you if you saw more people instead of living like hermits and forgetting your manners and common sense. Come to your room with me, now. The others will excuse you. They know you're tired after your journey."

"Yes. Yes, I'm tired," she said sullenly, but she did not try to shake off Susan's hand; she had even turned towards the door, when her attention was caught by a slight involuntary movement of relief from Amanda, who until then had stood as if turned to stone by her medusa-stare, not flinching even when the decanter struck the wall beside her head. At once Ruth Heriot's fury blazed up again.

"What's she doing here?" she cried. "She needn't think she'll ever get Larry, even when she's the widow she wants to be! I suppose it's fun to women like her to watch him drink himself to death? If I'd been at home she would never have been allowed inside this house!"

"Ruth . . ." began Susan warningly, but it was Amanda who now stood forward, choking down the sick faintness which threatened to overwhelm her. She had thought more than once that in many sordid scenes with Cocky she had reached depths lower than which it would be impossible to sink; she knew now that this was worse than anything that had gone before, if only because it was witnessed by these others, strangers, acquaintances. . . .

"Miss Heriot," she said, "you may be quite certain that I shall never come to Gledewaterford again. As for your brother, he seems to me far less likely to drink himself to death than you. Unless you are mad, which seems the kindest thing to suppose." Then her voice changed, sharpened, rose to a cry. She forgot Ruth Heriot's eyes of hate, forgot the staring Miss Pringle, the fidgeting men, forgot even Larry's stricken look, for Susan, swaying, had turned deadly pale. "Susan! Susan! Watch her, Larry, she's fainting!"

But it was Jed the slow-moving, Jed the placid and sweet-tempered, who caught his wife as she fell, and picking her up as if she were a child, shouldered Ruth roughly aside and made for the door.

"Lay her down for a minute, Jed," begged Amanda, holding one of the limp hands, and he glared at her over Susan's dark head, from which the hat had fallen.

"I'll not put her down anywhere in this damned house!" he said between his teeth, and without another word he walked out, pushing past the scared party from the kitchen who, attracted by the noise, had gathered in the hall, and laid his wife tenderly in the back of the car.

"Get in beside her," he ordered Amanda. "I want to get her home to Reiverslaw at once."

V

The drive at top speed through the darkness was a nightmare to Amanda; but she had no time to think about herself as she crouched on the floor of the car, supporting Susan as best she could, and rubbing her cold hands. She had the unreasoning terror of illness which only a perfectly healthy person knows, and furiously though Jed drove, it was not fast enough for her. At last they whirled up to the familiar entrance, and light streamed out from the hall as Jed gave instructions to the fluttered maids.

"What—what *is* all this fuss?" said Susan in a weak voice while she was being carried upstairs in the powerful arms which were her delight and her haven. "Has everyone gone quite mad?"

Amanda burst into tears of relief, and sobbing, flew to the telephone to summon the doctor, to ask Peggy to come up from Easter Hartrigg at once.

"Goodness gracious, Amanda dear!" said that practical young woman an hour later, when the doctor had been, and the disturbance had died down, leaving the house quiet once more. "Surely you know what's the matter with Susan? She's going to have a baby, that's all, and she is delighted."

Amanda was too much shaken by the scenes in which she had taken part to do anything but cry helplessly and without shame, until Jed, coming down from his wife's room with a face of mingled joy and anxiety, forced a quantity of neat brandy down her throat.

"No more crying, now," he said threateningly, as Amanda gulped and spluttered. And to Peggy: "She's got some excuse, poor girl. Ruth Heriot appeared at Gledewaterford and made the devil's own row. That woman is a bitch. She should have been drowned at birth."

"Is . . . Susan . . . all right now?" asked Amanda shakily, drying her eyes.

"Yes, she's fine. Of course she shouldn't have been let in for that business, but it's done her no harm, or so the doctor swears. She wanted to come down for dinner, but that isn't to be allowed this evening," he said.

"Dinner!" said Amanda, in a wondering tone. "I'd forgotten all about dinner."

"Had you? It's what you need, anyway. Come on, Peggy," said Jed. "*We're* hungry, aren't we?"

But Peggy wanted to go back and set Oliver's mind at rest, and would not wait. "Besides, the Squib will never start again if she once gets cold," she added, and left them to dine alone together.

"I'm sorry you were mixed up in all that scene," said Jed suddenly, pausing as he carved a pheasant to look at Amanda's face which still bore traces of tears. "But of course you don't need to pay any attention to what she said. Woman's mad, or bad, or both."

"We left Larry there with her. I hope they won't quarrel more," said Amanda apprehensively. "It was—horrible, Jed, to see two people in such a rage. I don't believe either of them knew what they were doing."

"Well, you can't interfere between brother and sister unless you happen to be a member of the family—which, thank God, I'm not," he said, placid once more and stolidly easting roast pheasant as if his life depended on it. It was difficult to believe that he was the same man who, dumb with anger, had walked out of Gledewaterford only two hours or so earlier, carrying his senseless wife. "So don't go on worrying about them," he ended, unconscious that her thoughts had been about himself. "There's nothing you or I can do about it."

"No. Of course not," Amanda agreed meekly, and said no more.

But she could not bridle her thoughts so easily, and long after she had said good night to Susan, lying pale but radiant in her wide bed, and had gone to her own room, she was still wondering what had happened after they left, what might be happening now in that lonely house above Glede Water, between the half-crazed woman and the brother whose name she so persistently blackened. For Amanda was certain, after the melodramatic end to Larry's unlucky party, that not only did his sister drive him to drink more than was good for him, but deliberately and of set purpose painted his character in the darkest colours possible. Leaning at her window, staring out as if her eyes could pierce not only the blanket of night but the intervening hills also, Amanda thought of Larry Heriot, with a distress so personal that it frightened her, for it argued an interest in him which she had hoped and intended never to feel for any man again. Why he allowed his sister to dominate him, she could not imagine, but Ruth Heriot must have some hold over him from which he had not the energy or the heart to break free.

"But you *must*, Larry!" she said aloud, in her intensity beating on the window-sill with her clenched hands. "You must, you must, or you'll be a prisoner all your life!"

A little comforted by her own vehemence, feeling that some echo of it must reach him and sustain him, she went to bed at last.

At Gledewaterford, where Big Maggie had removed an untasted and unappetizing meal from the badly laid dining-table and gone to bed with her single candle to dream of the cow-man, the other two occupants of the house were not thinking of sleep. It seemed that Amanda's cry had been useless, for while Ruth Heriot padded to and fro, to and fro in her grim bedroom, restless and dangerous as a tigress behind bars, her brother sat downstairs motionless save for the periodic mechanical stretching out of his hand to a whisky-bottle, and the increasingly unsteady refilling of the glass on the table in front of him, and the lift of his elbow as he drank to drown thought in the burning spirit, and drank again, all through the long quiet night.

CHAPTER NINE

I

THERE had been rain in the night, and the road, shining wet, was like a broad, curved sword-blade lying between the two rows of houses which composed Kaleford. Down the village, on her way to the Emporium, Kaleford's only shop, which was also the post-office, tripped Miss Cissy Pringle. Her pace was a trifle less girlish than usual, for her eldest sister was coming home that evening, and the thought of the sherry-party at Gledewaterford, which she and Miss Jelly had so defiantly and lawlessly attended, hung a guilty weight on her conscience. The worst aspect of the whole disgraceful but exciting affair was that they were debarred from telling about it in all its richness of detail to Miss Pringle. She would instantly have leapt to the fact that they had been present, and Miss Cissy actually trembled at the mere idea of the consequences. Reluctantly she and Miss Jelly had reached the sad conclusion that they would have to remain dumb on the subject for ever.

"If only we hadn't gone," she mourned. "We would have been able to tell her! Only then, of course, we shouldn't have known about it. Poor Bell, if she only knew what she will be missing!"

"Don't be ridiculous, Cissy," Miss Jelly had snapped—the final discussion had taken place not long before at the breakfast-table. "Of course we can't tell her. Besides, it is really Bell's own fault for not allowing us to go."

"Suppose she ever finds out, Jelly?"

"Then," said Miss Jelly grimly, "the fat will be in the fire. But she won't. Who is going to tell her? Not the Armstrongs nor that fast little Mrs. Cochrane, for their own sakes. You remember what Ruth Heriot said to *her*. As long as you are careful, Cissy, and try not to babble, we are perfectly safe."

Safe they might be; but Miss Cissy, going down the village street, trembled with not altogether unpleasant fears. There was a delicious sense of daring, of conspiracy, about it all—and after all, Bell had had Larry Heriot in the house, had even given him tea, in spite of her frequent threats that he should never set foot within her doors. 'But they are our doors too,' thought Miss Cissy, soaring to even dizzier heights of boldness. 'Bell is just a little inclined to forget that. If Jelly and I, or one of us—were to go off on our own, she wouldn't be to afford a house as big as Kaleside. I wonder if I would like to live by myself. . . .'

This idea, however, smacking as it did of ingratitude, treason, heresy, really alarmed Miss Cissy; and as she had reached the open door of the Emporium, painted a loud Reckitt's blue, she dismissed conjecture from her mind, and prepared to buy soap and matches in a practical manner remembering that her eldest sister's critical eye would see these purchases and notice without fail if there had been the slightest variation in brand or price from what she herself approved. Rebellious but resigned, Miss Cissy ordered the dull household necessities, told Mr. Dyce to send them to Kaleside, and started to walk home.

Half-way along the village, a sudden burst of wild musical sound, like bells rung madly, or wild geese crying, struck her ears, and she stopped. "Hounds!" she said aloud. Miss Pringle never allowed them to follow hounds, not even on their bicycles; she would rather have died than let them run after the hunt on foot—in which decision she was quite correct, for they would have looked exceedingly foolish. Now, however, with a reckless gesture, Miss Cissy twitched the shapeless felt hat farther on to her untidy faded hair, and hurried down a narrow lane between two cottages, where, as she knew, there was a gate into the fields behind the village. The gate was shut inexorably by means of a twist of barbed wire, but Miss Cissy bravely climbed it and fell rather than landed on the farther side. Even while she collected her wits and tugged at her hat, there was a renewed clamour from the covert in the hollow below, the clear sweet notes of a horn floated high above the tumult, and simultaneously with a roar of "Gone awaay!" two female bodies arrived with a crash beside her.

"Come *on*, Cissy!" panted Miss Jelly impatiently. "What does your hat matter? This is your only chance of hunting, and you stand there finicking with your *hat*! Well, I can't wait for you. Come on, Martha!" She plunged heavily downhill, the other figure, whom Miss Cissy, dazed, suddenly recognized as their sedate maid-of-all-work, thundering at her heels, blue print dress, white apron, cap and all. Miss Jelly was hatless, she had not waited even to throw a coat over her aged ginger-coloured cardigan and navy-blue skirt, and as she ran she waved a piece of drab knitting in one hand. Of course they had all gone mad, Miss Cissy reflected, rushing madly after them, while her hat flew unheeded from her head, to be retrieved later by 'daft Wullie', the village half-wit, who crowned a scarecrow with it, not inappropriately. Little did Miss Cissy heed, as, the joy of the chase thrilling through her, she ran and climbed and panted after the hunt. For a brief glorious hour the two younger Miss Pringles threw off all the repressions from which they had never even guessed they suffered, so complete was their bondage, and revelled in their freedom. Their return to earth was brutally sudden.

"Good God!" said a harsh voice somewhere above their dishevelled heads, when a check gave them a welcome opportunity to lean against a fence and try to recover their breath. "What guys you look! I thought Miss Pringle wouldn't let you do this, and now I've seen you I don't wonder, or blame her!" Ruth Heriot, from her tall hunter, was smiling maliciously down at them, her haggard face twisted.

They could only gape dumbly at her, as much taken aback by her effrontery, after the scene which she had made when they had seen her last, as by the covert threat in her words.

"When the cat's away, what?" she continued. "What with following hounds, and sherry-parties! It's about time Miss Bell came home!"

She gave them no time to reply, but moved off, splashing them with mud; and the two sisters were left gazing horrified at each other, the glory and excitement ebbing fast from their faces.

"Your hair's come down, Cissy," said Miss Jelly at last, in a mere uncertain echo of her usual determined voice, "And you've got mud on your nose."

"So have you, Jelly," Miss Cissy almost whimpered. "And you've torn the hem of your skirt to ribbons. And *look* at your knitting!"

"My knitting?" Miss Jelly stared in a distracted way at the ragged strip of uneven material, with streamers of unravelled wool dripping from it, which hung on two broken needles. She gave her sister a last look of defiance and flung it over the hedge. "There!" she said. "We'd better go home now, Cissy."

They turned and started to plod drearily back towards Kaleford. The church, peering above bare trees, seemed a very long way off. Miss Jelly was lame, Miss Cissy had a cruel stitch in her side, and of Martha the handmaiden there was no sign. She had vanished as utterly as the fox, as completely as the splendour of the day. Only two foolish elderly women, ludicrously untidy and muddy, were left, creeping home.

"Have you seen hounds?" suddenly called a voice, and they saw that it was Larry Heriot who had approached them. His dark face still bore a faint trace of his prolonged drinking-bout of several nights before, but they had eyes for nothing and no one but themselves now that they had been so rudely awakened to their disreputable state. Miss Jelly, who never wanted to see the Heriots again, tramped on without speaking; Miss Cissy pointed vaguely in the direction from which they had come, and added, "We've seen your sister."

"You're welcome!" he shouted, reckless of who might hear him. "She can break her neck for all I care, if she'll only keep out of my way!"

Miss Cissy, overtired and shocked, burst into tears as she stumbled after her sister. "Oh, Jelly! What will Bell say if she hears about all the things we've been doing since she went away? Oh, hadn't we better just tell her and get it over?"

Miss Jelly, whose mind was also running on the possibility that Ruth Heriot might easily tell their eldest sister about their insubordination, out of pure malice, shook her head. "No. We'll leave it to chance, Cissy. And I only hope that she will have so much to tell us that she won't notice how little we have to tell her. She'll be full of her visit, you know, and won't bother so much about home news for a day or two."

It seemed a forlorn hope to Miss Cissy; but the habit of argument had never been allowed to grow on her, and she was too weary to protest.

II

As the weary day dragged past towards evening, and the hour which would see the eldest Miss Pringle once more in her own home approached, her heart sank lower and lower; nor did Martha's air of sympathetic conspiracy help her at all, for it seemed a confession in itself.

"You might try at least not to look so guilty!" Miss Jelly irritably exhorted her. "Bell will guess that something is wrong as soon as she comes in, at this rate."

Miss Pringle always drove from Abbeyshiels in the Kaleford local taxi; but unless her sisters cared to walk or bicycle in, they were not permitted to meet her, for to pay for the double journey was a gross extravagance and to be sternly discouraged. The taxi-hirer could not charge both ways when he went empty to Abbeyshiels, and on many an occasion the younger sisters had had to watch his car trundling past their gate without passengers, and know themselves the victims of Miss Pringle's economy. This, which had so often been a hardship to them, was welcomed now. At least they would not have to sit cooped up together for several miles in the bumpy old vehicle, while Bell put piercing questions to each of them in turn, thought Miss Cissy, mechanically straightening the crochet mat on her eldest sister's dressing-table.

"Here's the car, Cissy!" called Miss Jelly's voice from the hall, and she went slowly downstairs with a smile of sorts on her face. If only Bell had had a comfortable journey, free from children and cigarette smoke! If only she herself did not feel so bowed down with deceit! She joined Miss Jelly on the door-step in the chill dusk as the car rattled up and stopped. A light flashed, showing in its cavernous interior not only Miss Pringle but two other persons, of whom she was taking an impressive farewell. One was a fair, lean, moustached young man, the other a plump woman with white curls and a babyish rosy face.

"Who *can* they be?" she breathed.

"I don't know, and I don't care," hissed Miss Jelly. "But they have given her—and us—something to talk about!"

Majestically Miss Pringle descended, saw her fibre suitcase handed out, and embraced each of her sisters in an absent-minded fashion, keeping a hand free to wave at the two still in the car as it moved off again. Miss Jelly and Miss Cissy, well versed in the rules of the game, made no comment on these strangers, but assured their returned traveller that she looked all the better for her little holiday, and that everything was all right at home, while, burning with curiosity, their guilt forgotten, they bore her with them into the drawing-room. Not until Miss Pringle, with an air of devil-may-care enjoyment, had drunk a cup of strong tea and eaten several slices of seed-cake was the subject broached.

"A dee-lightful journey!" then said the mistress of the house, brushing crumbs heedlessly off her skirt on to the carpet. "Such a charming woman. That was Mrs. Carmichael, girls. Yes, Amanda Cochrane's mother."

"Is she going to Reiverslaw? We heard nothing about her being expected there," said Miss Jelly suspiciously.

"No, she is going to pay them a surprise visit. She has news," said Miss Pringle impressively, "of Mrs. Cochrane's husband. Thank you, Cissy, another cup of tea. I haven't had anything but dish-water—China—since I left home."

With an obedient start her younger sister began to pour tea into the cup handed to her, but she could not restrain her impatience any longer. "What news has she got?" she asked breathlessly, the tea-pot in her unsteady grasp wavering over saucer and tray as well as cup. "And who was the *man* with her, Bell? It isn't—it can't be—the husband himself?"

"Look what you are doing, Cissy. There, you have slopped tea into the saucer, and you ought to know by this time how I dislike a cup that *drips*," said Miss Pringle. Then, with unexpected lenience: "Well, of course I must remember that you and Jelly have been at home, where so *little* ever happens. I must make allowances for your excitement."

The two younger Miss Pringles exchanged a guilty, hurried, side-long glance. At home, where so little happened, indeed! If Bell only knew. . . . Fortunately their sister mistook the glance for envious curiosity, and stirred her tea with complacence.

"That young man in the car is *not* Amanda Cochrane's husband," she informed them, "but a great friend of his, wealthy, who has done a lot of flying for pleasure, who has left no *stone* unturned to try to find out Lloyd Cochrane's fate. He has come north with Mrs. Carmichael to tell Mrs. Cochrane that a white man has been found in an Indian village in some out-of-the-way part of Brazil, who has been taken to hospital suffering from fever and loss of memory induced by exposure. There seems to be very little doubt that he is Lloyd Cochrane!"

"Oh, Bell, how thrilling!" exclaimed Miss Cissy, almost throwing the tea-pot, which she had been clutching in mid-air, on to the tray with a tremendous clatter.

"Has this man, this friend of poor young Cochrane's, been there to see for himself?" demanded Miss Jelly, still practical even after hearing such an unusually choice morsel of news.

"Not yet. I understand that his object in coming here with Mrs. Carmichael was to persuade Amanda Cochrane to go out with him to South America. And though," said Miss Pringle severely, "I do not approve of a young married woman travelling alone with a man not her husband, in this case I cannot help feeling that it is all for the best. Amanda Cochrane is, in my opinion, a fast little minx who has been behaving as if she were already a widow. It passes my comprehension how a sweet woman like Mrs. Carmichael should have a daughter so unlike her, and I cannot help feeling sorry for the poor young airman, Cochrane, also. Apparently the Armstrongs have noticed nothing of their guest's curious behaviour, but *I have*, and so has someone else."

"Oh, *who*?" cried Miss Cissy, rushing on her fate with unwitting eagerness, suddenly quenched by the name now uttered in portentous tones by her eldest sister.

"Ruth Heriot," said Miss Pringle, with increased severity, "has been *most* distressed by the blatant manner in which Mrs. Cochrane has been pursuing—yes, *pursuing* is the only word for it—her brother Larry. So much so, that when I found Ruth at the Brocklehursts' as my fellow-guest, I felt it to be no more than my duty to give her a hint or two. About meeting those two on the road—you remember the occasion, and how very odd it looked?—and about the sherry-party which Larry Heriot was having in her absence, and to which he had the brazen impudence to ask *me*. Poor Ruth! She was so gravely upset that she did not even *thank* me, though I need not tell you I did not do it for thanks; she rushed away *at once* in her car, breaking short her visit when it was hardly begun, in the hope that she might be able to stop the party, or at least be in time to prevent her worthless brother from making a fool of himself. I wonder how she succeeded. And *that* reminds me: have you not heard anything of what happened at Gledewaterford? In my eagerness to tell you my news, I mustn't forget that you may have some nearer home to tell *me*!"

Miss Jelly, shaking her head dumbly, looked to her younger sister for help, and Miss Cissy literally rose to the occasion. For she left her chair so precipitately that the tea-tray, together with the rickety small table which held it, was overturned, and the tea-pot, pouring out a stream of thick dark liquid and tea-leaves, landed in Miss Pringle's lap, its contents spattering her travelling dress—a serviceable snuff-coloured garment of great antiquity, but valued by its owner for its magnificent wearing properties.

With an anguished cry, so shrill, so powerful, that it might almost have been described as a yell, that lady also rose. *"Cissy!"* she screamed. "Of all the clumsy, awkward women I have ever met, you are the worst! My dress is *utterly* ruined!"

"Bell, I'm so sorry," faltered the culprit, feebly dabbing at the damaged skirt with her handkerchief. But as her eyes met Miss Jelly's, there flashed between them a glance of chastened triumph. The danger had been averted for the present, and the rating which fell on Miss Cissy's meekly bowed head seemed to both a small price to pay.

III

Click-click went Amanda's typewriter, tap-tap-tap, faster and faster, as if by speed she could escape her thoughts. Susan, passing the door, felt that she knew the reason for this feverish concentration. The scene at Gledewaterford, which she had brought to a sudden end by so conveniently fainting, must have been peculiarly trying to Amanda, since she had been so plainly the object of Ruth Heriot's venom. Ruth was madly jealous of Larry, of course; and Susan could not make herself believe that the jealousy was caused by affection, however warped. There was something malignant in it, and it was most unfortunate that she should have chosen Amanda on whom to wreak her murderous temper, in front of those other people too, especially the Pringles. Susan sighed. She would have preferred that Amanda's eyes should have been opened more gently, and by someone who liked her; but at the same time, if she was really beginning to have a fondness for Larry, it was as well that she should be shown where she was trending in good time to halt and beat a retreat, for legally she was Lloyd Cochrane's wife still, however impossible his return might be.

"Just as well," said Susan firmly, in answer to the quick light tapping of the typewriter in the little empty room at the end of the passage. "It wouldn't do at all. A man like Larry would never marry."

Click-click went Amanda, her eyes reading old Mr. Makepeace's meandering and frequently ungrammatical sentences, her fingers automatically transferring his scrawl in corrected form to neatly typed pages. If only it kept her mind as fully occupied as her hands and eyes, what a blessing it would be; but she worked mechanically, with, at the back of her head and constantly obtruding itself, the burning shame of that evening at Gledewaterford, the accusation flung at her by Ruth Heriot. Entirely unfounded though it was, how many who had heard it would believe that? Only Jed, who probably had not taken it in at all; and Susan, who did not deal in ideas of that kind. The rest, the men with whom she had flirted so carelessly, the Miss Pringles, would be only too ready to say that there was no smoke without fire, and all the other stupid things which could never be contradicted because they did not take the form of actual statement. Who could contradict a nod or a shrug?

"Oh, hell!" said Amanda, rapidly typing. "'The grandest horse I ever had the luck to train was . . .' What does it matter what they think or say? And at least they must all know that Ruth Heriot is practically mental. . . ."

All through the short chill November day she continued to type steadily. After a deceptively bright morning, the weather turned sulky and offered no inducement to go out, sending sudden wild flurries of rain to beat at the windows, raising a wind with a thin complaining voice that whined continuously round the house. She went down to tea, pale and heavy-eyed and Susan said with guile, "Could you bear to go out for me, Amanda? I took Bawtie for a walk this morning, and I'd rather not struggle against this wind again. It's just to the farthest of the cottages. I want to know how old Mrs.

Roxburgh is, because Jed tells me she has a 'bad leg' and hasn't been out in the fields working for three days now. Would you?"

"Yes, of course." Amanda was glad of the excuse to leave her typewriter. To go out on a definite errand would be a joyful relief, and she put on her thickest shoes and a tweed coat which Susan insisted on lending her, though it was much too big, and with the delighted Bawtie leaping about her like an animated rug, she set forth, head down, into the windy dusk.

It was bitterly cold now, the wind had blown the rain away, and if Amanda had been country-bred she would have smelt coming snow in the keen air. To the south-west, where the sun had gone down behind a wooded hill, and long golden streaks still splashed the sky, great banks of rose and lilac cloud, heavy with snow, floated in the cold green depths. Trees bare of all but their last leaves stood stark and black against the flushed tender colours, and above their clearly drawn topmost twigs flew some late-homing crows, beating into the wind on their ragged black wings. Stars were beginning to twinkle, brightening every minute; even the puddles in the road were luminous as though moonshine rather than rain had brimmed them. Battling against the wind braced Amanda mentally as well as physically, whipping the blood faster through her tingling body, blowing the hazes of anger and distress and worry from her brain, so that never had she felt so confident that there must soon be an end to her troubles. Breathless, exhilarated, she struggled along, calling to the wildly capering Bawtie, who looked like a mad creature with his eyes rolling and both long black ears turned inside out. Yet all the time she was aware of a great peace, for high above the tearing wind lay those serene cloud islands in the starry sea of the skies, infinitely remote, so far removed from the little fret and stir of the world and human cares that even the wind, it seemed, could not reach them.

She was sorry to leave it all when, arrived at the last cottage in the row, she knocked on the door and walked into the small bright kitchen, where two china dogs glared haughtily from a dresser at Bawtie. Mrs. Roxburgh, her rosy cheeks a network of tiny wrinkles like the skin of a withered apple, her blue eyes astonishingly bright and youthful under a thatch of short-cut iron-grey hair, was lying below a patchwork cover on a bed opposite the dancing fire. But she was fully dressed, and raised herself on one elbow to greet Amanda with such cordiality that she felt rewarded for coming.

"Ye'll excuse me no' risin'," she said, with a composure and courtesy worthy of a duchess. "Draw up a chair tae the fireside. It's a wild night."

Amanda, feeling strangely young and shy before the calm and simple dignity of Mrs. Roxburgh, who had worked in the fields most of her days, and worked hard, as her rough hands bore witness, sat down on a wooden chair, the seat highly polished by age and wear, beside the fire, and looked about her with open pleasure. The room was spotlessly clean and neat; the light from an oil-lamp shone on the white and gold of the supercilious china dogs, and showed the pink-washed walls hung with bright, cheap coloured prints. A gaudy calendar, the photograph, much enlarged, of a noble Border Leicester ram, were among them, and the Royal family, evidently cut from the pages of some magazine and framed with loyal care, hung in a place of honour above the bed. The two small princesses, the crudeness of their representation softened by the yellow lamp-light and the warm glow of the fire, smiled out across the old woman who lay below them. A ham hung from an iron hook in the ceiling, a red geranium stood in front of the curtained window. Bawtie, with a groan of doggish pleasure, stretched himself out on the rag rug before the fire, on which a kettle purred softly like a contented cat.

Amanda, having told Mrs. Roxburgh that she had come as Susan's deputy and heard the history of the 'bad leg'—which was caused by an ulcer, now, owing, as its owner said with pride, to the purity of her blood, rapidly healing—fell silent, wondering a little what to say next. Mercifully, Mrs. Roxburgh was not one of those women who rejoice in detailed accounts of illness and operations, and when she had explained about her leg and sent messages to Susan, she did not enlarge further on the subject. This was a relief, but at the same time it left Amanda at a loss. She knew that it would not be etiquette for her to leave immediately, but she did not know how to continue the conversation, which a country-born young woman, accustomed from childhood to knowing everyone in the place, could have carried on so easily. Her mother's avowed interest in 'the dear working classes', which manifested itself in a condescending curiosity as to their most intimate affairs, had always made her writhe with shame; her own dealings with them, mainly consisting of pacifying indignant tradesmen clamouring for payment of the accounts which Cocky so gaily and irresponsibly ran up, combined to give her a feeling of awkwardness in their presence. Until she came to Reiverslaw, she had concealed this by a haughty manner; but Susan's friendliness, which never became familiar or idly curious, with everyone living near her, their obvious liking and respect for her, had had its influence on Amanda. Remembering her mother's insistence that 'the lower classes must be kept in their place', she was at first doubtful of the wisdom of this frank *camaraderie*; then, when she realized that the country people, so strongly individual in character that they were not yet all cast in one mould like their town-dwelling contemporaries, had a sturdy independent pride in their 'place' and would not, from self-respect, have forgotten it, she became less cautious in her dealings with them, and enjoyed the visits which she paid them in Susan's company. This, however, was the first time she had ever gone alone into one of the cottages, and it found her almost tongue-tied.

She had forgotten her hostess's complete ease of manner, and was exceedingly grateful when Mrs. Roxburgh, with a wave of her hand which sketched the kitchen's narrow confines, said, "Ye'll not have been used wi' a hoose as wee as this, I'm thinkin'?"

"I don't believe my mother's flat in Southsea is much larger. It never looked big enough for the furniture," Amanda answered simply, a memory of the drawing-room crammed with furniture and overloaded with ornaments crossing her mind's eye.

"A flat? I've never been in one o' *them*. There'll be nae gairden, likely?"

"No. There isn't a garden at all, only a tiny green at the back of the house, and the ground-floor flat had it. My mother's is at the top, you see," said Amanda.

"I dinna think I could dea wantin' a gairden" Mrs. Roxburgh said. "For a' this hoose is no' verra big, I've a bonnie bit gairden tae it."

"I'd rather live in a house that had a garden, no matter how small it was," said Amanda. "But of course you can't always choose what you would like."

"Weel I ken that." Mrs. Roxburgh's grey head nodded emphatically in sympathy. "You an' me, that's been mairret, we've had tae gang wi' oor men. I was far, far frae Tweed for mony a year; but I'm hame noo, an' here I'll bide. An' yersel', Mistress Cochrane, that's but a lassie, I doot ye've lost yer man. If he was as guid as mine, I'm vexed for ye. But guid or ill, yer life's no' yer ain when ye're mairret. Mind, it's no' that I dinna miss John Roxburgh, whiles I'm that lanesame I could greet; but the wind's aye tempered, an' there's compensations. When ye're a widdy, there's nane can say ye never got a man, like an auld maid; but ye can gang yer ain gait an' no' a body tae hinder ye. Ay. It'll seem hard tae ye, but ye maunna think there's nae compensations."

Amanda knew only too well that she could think of compensations as to make the state of widowhood, painted in sober hues though not sable by Mrs. Roxburgh, appear quite indecently rosy. But as she was not able, especially to anyone so genuine, to pretend a grief which she did not feel, she contented herself with saying gravely, "I expect there are," and rose to go.

IV

The wind had passed on its way eastwards to scream round the walls of Berwick and lose itself finally over the North Sea leaving the dark sky clear of cloud and sown with stars. It was colder, with a nip of frost in the air, and already the road echoed Amanda's light steps ringingly and keen. She hurried along the ridge towards Reiverslaw, passing the tiny church, seeing the loch glint like a polished shield ahead. As she turned in at the shadowy gateway an owl hooted from the dim mass of the trees round it, so dolefully that she shivered and murmured, "It is the owl, the fatal bellman'," as she passed; and at the same time a man's figure detached itself from the shade where it had been standing, and said hesitatingly:

"Amanda?"

Bawtie growled, Amanda stood stock-still, her heart beating unevenly, while the owl, unseen above, hooted again mockingly, and almost a second crawled by.

"Amanda . . ." he said again. "Don't you know me?"

Then she found her voice. "Of course I know you, David, but it gave me a—a shock to see you, that's all. What are you doing here, anyhow? Oh!"—with a sudden cry. "You've brought news! I know you have. Tell me quickly, don't start trying to *break* it to me—"

"Yes, I've got news. Cocky's found," he said at once, and took a step nearer her as if afraid she would faint. But Amanda was entirely calm; she knew now that she had been expecting this from the moment she had seen him.

"You mean, I suppose, that they've found his body, or the wreck of his 'plane?" she asked, in a hard clear voice.

"Good God, no!" said David White, horrified at what must have been clumsiness on his part. "He's alive, Amanda. Cocky's alive!"

For answer Amanda began to laugh, and the sound seemed to shock even the owl to silence. Bawtie whined uneasily, and David White exclaimed in great distress, "I've done it so badly that I've made you hysterical, you poor child. After all, it would have been better if I'd let your mother tell you, as she wanted—"

"My *mother*?" Amanda's laughter ceased as abruptly as it had started. "Do you mean to tell me that my mother is here, at Reiverslaw?"

"Yes, she's in the house, waiting for you. Come on, you'll be all right once you've seen her," he urged. "I'll leave her to tell you everything."

"Why did you let her come?" demanded Amanda, in the cold quiet voice of extreme but ineffectual anger. "Wasn't it enough that you should come barging in here, without bringing her?"

"But, Amanda, I couldn't stop her. How could I? And I thought— she said—your mother seemed to be the right person to be with you."

"I know, I know. Can a mother's tender care cease towards the child she bare? Of course you couldn't stop her, my poor David," said Amanda; for after all, what could a decent, stupid, blundering Saint Bernard of a man like David, who had never seen through Cocky in all the years he had known him, do in face of Mrs. Carmichael's determination to fly to her daughter's side at this crisis? It would have taken someone like Oliver Parsons, she thought, someone like Jed, to frustrate her—or Larry Heriot.

"Well, it's no good standing here, we'd better go in," she went on, starting to walk along the drive.

"Take my arm," he said anxiously, as if she were too frail to walk alone.

"Please don't be ridiculous, David. And you haven't explained to me why you thought it necessary to come here, instead of telephoning, or getting Mother to ring me up," Amanda said, walking fast towards the orange oblong, half-way up the dark side wall of the house, which was the uncurtained window of the staircase, shining like a beacon, and laying a patch of soft light over wet gravel and sodden turf. "Rushing off in this headlong manner is just the sort of thing Mother would do, but I thought better of you."

"I don't understand you, Amanda," he said. "Here I am, with the most wonderful news, and all you can do is to ask me why I brought it to you."

"Well, never mind. Call it shock," said Amanda. "Call it anything you like, but you *still* haven't told me why you came."

"I came to see if you'd be ready to start with me next week," he said apologetically. "And it seemed to your m—to me that there'd be so much to explain, it would be easier to come and do it at first hand."

"To start where next week?" said Amanda, still keeping with desperate determination to these surface matters because she could not bear to think of the really important fact that Cocky was alive.

"To Brazil," he explained patiently. "We'll have to identify the poor old chap, you know—he's ill, and been fearfully knocked about, from what I can tell—and look after him, and bring him home as soon as he's fit to travel."

"Then you don't *know* it's Cocky?"

"I'm sure it is, I've been waiting for something like this," he said. "And you can be sure too, Amanda."

"Yes. I am sure," she said drearily.

"It's just that they seem so stupid at the other end. That's why I want to go myself—with you, of course. I won't bother you, though," he added hastily, "on the voyage. You can be alone as much as you like."

'No,' thought Amanda, 'you won't bother me, because I'm not going; but I won't begin to argue about that now. There's Mother to face still. . . .' "David, we must go in, they'll be wondering what on earth has happened to us. We'll discuss everything later."

To her eyes, confused by the dim starlight, the sitting-room seemed dazzlingly, unbearably bright. Jed, pouring out sherry in a corner, Susan, hovering behind Mrs. Carmichael's advancing rush, faded into shadows as Amanda was embraced by her mother. The room was full of her, somehow, all its peace shattered.

"My darling child! You've heard the wonderful, wonderful news about dear Lloyd? I always knew he was alive, after all!"

Dutifully returning her kisses, Amanda wished that she did not so much dislike these physical contacts; probably there was something wrong with her, or she would not shrink from them. "Yes, Mother, David told me," she said; "but surely you—and he—didn't have to come all this way to bring the news. Why didn't you ring up? I'd have heard sooner."

"Amanda!" Deepest reproach echoed in Mrs. Carmichael's voice; her baby mouth drooped, only her eyes remained sharp and calculating as ever. "Of *course*, your mother had to come, dearest! Surely no one has a greater right to share your joys as well as your sorrows?"

'This is terrible,' thought Amanda. 'It must be the contrast with Susan that makes her sound so artificial and insincere.' She felt intensely grateful to Jed for sparing her the necessity of answering.

"Have some sherry, Nora?" he said, pressing a glass-full of the shining topaz wine into her hand. "You must be tired. It's a beastly journey, with that slow train from Berwick at the end of it."

Mrs. Carmichael, who always appreciated it when she was recognized for a brave little woman, accepted the wine with an air of courageous but pathetic weariness, and began to describe to him the tedium of the run from King's Cross although it appeared that she had travelled in luxury with David.

'First class! That means that David paid for her ticket,' thought Amanda, 'and her lunch, and the taxi from Abbeyshields too, no doubt. Mother is a parasite, the ivy clinging so confidently and gracefully to the tree and killing it; she wore Father out that way, and Cocky is exactly like her. They both think that money, no matter whose it is, must be for *their* use. I won't go back to that sort of life, now that I've had a taste of something different.'

Susan, making heavy weather of conversation with the stupid, well-meaning young man who had come with Mrs. Carmichael, noticed that Amanda's face had sharpened and whitened until, in its narrow pallor, it looked like the new moon dimly seen through a wisp of cloud. Her eyes, watching her mother's little fluttering gestures, were hunted and shadowed. Yet very little could be done to help her, for how could anyone interfere between mother and daughter without making matters worse? Amanda would have to struggle out of it by herself with only a little moral support from Jed and herself.

"That's the most dismal thing about a situation of this sort," Susan said aloud, quite forgetting that David White was speaking to her, and only reminded of it by his stopping abruptly in mid-sentence, his innocent mouth open, his china-blue eyes, round and vacant as marbles, faintly worried, faintly resentful.

"Have I said the wrong thing?" asked Susan. "I'm so sorry, I'm afraid I missed that last remark of yours completely."

"I said," he answered stiffly, speaking a little louder as if she were deaf, "that I wouldn't have landed on you like this except that I wanted to persuade Amanda to come out to Rio with me."

"Can Amanda afford it?"

"I can, and she knows I'm only too glad to do anything for old Cocky—and for her," he added rather hastily.

"Then," said Susan deliberately, "I think that what I said, though I didn't hear you, was quite apropos. I can't believe that Amanda's husband any more than Amanda herself would want to be so indebted to you, Mr. White."

"Oh, Cocky wouldn't mind," was his innocent reply. "And Mrs. Carmichael thinks it's a wizard plan. She'll talk Amanda over, you'll see. Why, Cocky often . . ." And he broke off, suddenly realizing that his tongue was running away with him on to dangerous ground, and his ingenuous face reddened distressfully.

"She won't talk Amanda over, David," said Amanda herself, completing his confusion; even his ears were scarlet as she looked at him. "You may as well know it. I'm not going to South America with you. I can't possibly afford it, and"—with a gallant attempt at lightness—"it's too long a trip to make as a stowaway.'

"Amanda, you know it isn't a question of money," he began, recovering slightly at the power generated by even the mention of his wealth.

"Of course it's a question of money," she said impatiently. "And I haven't got it! Now don't start arguing, David, or you may say something, and that will end our—our friendship altogether." She spoke temperately but firmly, and Susan admired her composure as much as her sense and spirit. Unfortunately, Mrs. Carmichael, whose sharp ears had overheard the end of this conversation, did not share Susan's feeling of admiration.

"Amanda *dearest!*" she cried, deserting Jed in spite of his attempt to keep her beside him. "The shock has been too much for you, or you wouldn't be so unkind to David, who is only trying to *help* you in the most generous way! Don't try to arrange anything this evening! David, can't you see that she is quite overcome? Oh, my darling, your mother knows what you are feeling, what gratitude and relief—this miracle that has given dear Lloyd back to you; though I always knew he was alive, I never lost faith! Perhaps, who knows"—casting her eyes reverently upward to the ceiling as if in expectation of seeing a crowd of approving cherubim gazing down—"perhaps my *prayers* have done their tiny bit in helping to preserve him for us! No, David. There is a time for discussion of such things as money; but there are times, and this is one of them, too *sacred* for that. Amanda darling, I know so well what you want—to come up to your room with me and have a good cry to relieve your feelings."

"No, thank you, Mother. I don't want to cry in the least, and if I did I shouldn't do it," said Amanda, aware that she sounded brusque and harsh after her mother's soft gushing accents. "But I think I'm going to have hiccups, if that's any good?"

Mrs. Carmichael, ruffling, swelling and gobbling like a enraged turkey-cock, burst into rapid incoherent speech. "Heartless, unnatural, callous . . . break your mother's heart . . . *no* proper feeling . . . your poor husband . . . poor David . . . poor—"

"Poor everyone," said Amanda wearily, and at that point Susan felt that an embarrassed audience in the shape of herself and David White was not required. Giving Jed a meaning look which said, 'Settle this awful woman and make her shut up,' she took David firmly by the sleeve, and drew him quickly but silently from the room.

V

"I ought to stay, I don't think she should slate Amanda like that when the poor girl's so strange and unbalanced," he muttered unhappily, shying away from her light touch.

"My husband will stop her much better than you could," Susan said tranquilly. "And it is his business after all, Mr. White. Don't forget that Amanda's father was his first cousin. It's always best to leave these unpleasantnesses to be dealt with by the family rather than an outsider, however kind." She spoke with meaning, and knew that he understood by his flush and uneasy shifting of feet; so she said no more, but led him into the drawing-room, a rather chilly apartment which she and Jed rarely used except in hot summer weather.

As she shut the door, they could hear Jed's deep voice growling something. Mrs. Carmichael was apparently temporarily silenced, and Amanda's only contribution to the discussion came regular as a clock's ticking in the form of the threatened hiccups.

"I don't suppose for a moment," said Susan, sitting down on a sofa and waving him to a chair near at hand, so that she could grab him if he showed signs of wanting to rush back to the sitting-room and Amanda, "that one of them will think of making any arrangements about where you and Mrs. Carmichael are to stay tonight. Had you thought of that? Do help yourself to cigarettes, there should be some in that shagreen box beside you."

"We left our suitcases at Abbeyshiels station," said David, who seemed to have been hypnotized into obedience, for he made a dive at the cigarette-box as soon as she mentioned it.

"We're going to stay at the pub there. I wanted the taxi to wait for us, but Mrs. Carmichael said no, we could 'phone for it when we were ready. It came from Kaleford—at least, I think that was the name of the place. We shared it, part of the way, with an old lady. Mrs. Carmichael met her in the dining-car."

"An old lady? Who got out at Kaleford? *Not* Miss Pringle?" said Susan faintly. "Oh, this is the last straw!"

"Yes, she did get out there, and her name was something like that," he admitted. "What's wrong?"

"Oh, nothing, nothing. Only that Mrs. Carmichael has spent several hours in happy chat with the most virulent gossip in the whole neighbourhood. I suppose they became all cosy and confidential?"

"They—yes, they did seem to be talking nineteen to the dozen," he said. "You see, I thought that as Mrs. Carmichael had found someone to talk to, I could leave her for a bit, and have a smoke and a drink and so on. I wish I hadn't now."

"My poor young man, do you suppose that you could have prevented them from talking?" Susan said pityingly. "Short of gagging them both, you couldn't do a thing. It's just plain bad luck that they were in the same train, and worse that they should have met and presumably liked each other. I always did mistrust people who talk of their affairs to strangers on a journey. So Miss Pringle knows all, does she? About Lloyd Cochrane being found, and about your suggestion Amanda should go off with you to Brazil?"

"I expect so."

Susan groaned. "So do I. Then Mrs. Carmichael can't be allowed to go and stay in Abbeyshiels, however much she may prefer it. She'll stay *here*, under my eye; and if she sees Miss Pringle again, which heaven forbid, it will be chaperoned by me. You'd better stay too, there's plenty of room. I'm sorry if I sound unenthusiastic, but I can see so well that Amanda doesn't want either of you."

He looked chastened and did not contradict her. "Very well, if you think that's the best thing to do," he said, with sulky meekness. "But our things will have to be brought here from Abbeyshiels, which is a bit of a bore."

"Not at all. You can take our car and go for them," Susan said briskly. "And there's nothing to prevent you from starting at once. Then you will have time to dress for dinner."

She rose and rang the bell, and when Elspeth, too correct to betray vulgar curiosity by even the flicker of a well-trained eyelash, answered it: "Elspeth, please show this gentleman where the garage is, and then tell Robinia to get two rooms ready for the night."

"Very good, madam," said Elspeth. "This way, sir." She showed him out, and David White found himself on the road to Abbeyshiels in Jed's car before he had time to recover.

Susan went back to the sitting-room, where Mrs. Carmichael sat dissolved in tears and dabbing at her eyes with an ineffectual scrap of handkerchief, while Jed leaned against the mantelpiece, his face so bleak that she instantly wanted to kill his cousin Wat's widow, the boy David, and even Amanda, for all helping to make him look like that. Amanda, she saw, had disappeared.

"Has Amanda gone to her room?" she asked, to be answered by a nod from Jed and a fresh outbreak of sobs from Mrs. Carmichael.

"Surely you oughtn't to be crying, Mrs. Carmichael, after bringing such news to Amanda," said Susan, with a fine irony quite lost on Amanda's mother.

"Oh, it's Amanda I am crying about!" wailed the afflicted parent. "So *cold* to me, so reserved, after all the love I've *poured* out on her. Sharper than a serpent's tooth. It seems *impossible* sometimes that she is my child at all!"

"You are not very much alike, and I don't think it is ever any use trying to force anyone into giving you their confidence," murmured Susan.

"But a *mother*—surely—"

"Even your child is a separate human being," said Susan, rather dryly this time. "And when all's said and done, one person can only know a very little of another. We hardly know ourselves. How are we to know other people, or they us?"

"Ah, if you were a *mother*," sighed Mrs. Carmichael, with a superiority all the more irritating because of the sniffles accompanying it.

Susan bit back the retort that motherhood, after all, however sacred, was not such a peculiarly rare condition, and said, "Mr. White has gone to fetch your luggage. Of course you and he must stay here. It would be quite ridiculous for you to go to an hotel when there is plenty of room in the house."

Mrs. Carmichael stopped sniffing long enough to say gushingly, "How very kind of you, my dear Susan—I really can't call you Mrs. Armstrong when we are connected by marriage—but how can I stay here, when my child so plainly doesn't want me?" She resumed her air of martyrdom. "You *saw* how she greeted me, her *mother*! My only child!"

"Amanda's all right," growled Jed, "if you'll let her alone. She must have had a bit of a shock, y'know, Nora."

"So strange, so cold!" lamented Mrs. Carmichael. "One would almost have thought that she didn't care to hear that poor dear Lloyd is alive!"

One would, thought Susan grimly; one would have guessed long ago that there was the trouble, if only one were not quite so crass an idiot as her mother. And she wondered what Amanda was doing, alone in her room with her dread and fear. . . .

Not being the heroine of a melodrama, Amanda was neither pacing the floor wringing her hands, nor lying face down on her bed racked with tearless sobs. She was only a young woman who had made a great mistake, for which further payment seemed about to be exacted; and she stood by the window staring out at the dark night. From time to time a tremor shook her—but that might have been the cold air blowing in, bringing with it the first few flakes of snow to melt on the sill. Was it only an hour since she had heard old Mrs. Roxburgh say that a married woman must go with her husband, and she had thought that it was over for her and she could go her own way now? She had no doubt that it was Cocky who had been found, from the moment that David told her. She had always felt that he must be alive to come back and 'have the laugh on her', as he had so often said when he had got the better of her before. This was quite his best effort, it must surely be the ultimate peak of achievement. Amanda could imagine Cocky's mirth—that impish, heartless mockery of honest laughter which it made her shiver to remember. To go back to all that . . . and from divorce she had come to shrink since being at Reiverslaw. She realized that marriage had taken on an entirely new aspect for her, had attained a value which in her Southsea days she would have considered preposterously high. It was not that she had any illusions that her own marriage could ever have reached the standard of Susan's with Jed; but she had seen now what it could be and should be, with an added bitterness of regret for having married Cocky.

It hadn't been fair to him either, for he was obviously a man who should have remained single, only she had not known it in time. 'Bird-man' had become a term of ridicule rather than admiration, but that was what Cocky was—a cock-pheasant, bright-plumaged, vain, arrogant and bold, needing a harem of hens to keep him contented. It was his nature, and only an idiot could expect him to be fundamentally changed by a serious crash and a long illness. Death might change Cocky, but life never could. . . . And what was she going to do about it? Having endured seven years, and tasted a few weeks of uneasy doubting freedom, was she to go back to it? It seemed a monstrous price to pay for a passionate mistake which they had made together, but there was her promise. Though he had broken his side of the agreement as soon as made, she was bound. . . .

"I won't make up my mind about anything until I've seen him, until he is back in this country," was her final decision. "And I won't go out to him at David's expense. All that will have to stop if—if I go back to him. And if he has changed at all, he'll understand."

But in her heart she knew that Cocky would not have changed.

CHAPTER TEN

I

TRAGEDY may stalk the house overnight, but unless the cook has been its victim, breakfast, in a well-regulated establishment, will be set on the table at the appointed hour next morning.

Susan, asking her guests how they had slept, anxious superintending the coffee-machine as if the fear of its bursting was her most pressing care of the moment, thanked heaven for one of civilization's most obvious blessings, the ordered ritual of meals. The great god Convention had the power to force people to sit and eat, or pretend to eat, and to shelve as ill-bred all discussions on matters of importance. This was particularly true of breakfast, when the protagonists were apt to forget all other differences in one great one. Whatever their views or feelings later in the day, they gathered for breakfast divided into two basic groups: those who greeted the morn with song and daily dozens, coming downstairs ravenous and cheerful, stimulated by the fragrance of coffee and bacon; and the others whose condition at that hour was of profound gloom, which the scraping of knives as crisp toast was lavishly buttered only served to irritate.

Both were represented at Reiverslaw this morning—the former by Mrs. Carmichael, chirping platitudes with a conscious brave gaiety very hard to bear; the latter by David White, unexpectedly transformed from a well-meaning, tiresome and talkative young man to a morose individual who silently devoured porridge and cream opposite her. Amanda, looking tired but resolute, crumbled dry toast and ate very little of it; while Jed, rather less placid than usual, swallowed a hearty meal.

The most optimistic could not have described it as a festive board, and Susan was thankful that she had the coffee-machine behind which she could eclipse herself when she needed a rest from looking like a hostess. She foresaw that this was going to be one of the days when, to borrow an expression from Peggy's mother, the grasshopper was a burden. In her present state of strange qualms and sudden nausea, she did not feel fit to cope with Mrs. Carmichael; and it was a tremendous relief when she heard Jed say, as he rose from table, "I've got to go to the sale at St. Boswells, and I'll take the lot of you with me—not Susan, though, she's busy. You can have a look at Dryburgh Abbey if you get tired of waiting, and we'll be back here in time for tea."

"Oh, but I say, sir!" cried David, spurred into speech at last. "I've got to get the night train to town, and there's a lot I want to talk to Amanda about."

"You can talk at St. Boswells, or on the road there," replied Jed, in the tone which Susan thankfully recognized as final.

"Nora, you and Amanda had better get ready. We're starting in half an hour."

"I must pack," fluttered Mrs. Carmichael, as if she had to deal with luggage for a world cruise instead of one small suit-case. "If Dave and I are leaving tonight—"

"Plenty of time when we come home," Jed told her, while Susan said politely, but without regret:

"Must you really go so soon? It seems a pity to have taken that long journey for only one night."

"I felt it to be my duty," said Mrs. Carmichael, glancing at her daughter's unresponsive countenance. "But I really must get back to Southsea, as I am playing in an important charity bridge tournament the day after tomorrow, and it is only fair to my friends that I should be *fresh* for it. I make it a rule never to let a bridge four down. To be able to be depended on not to fail is so wonderful, don't you think?"

"Indeed, yes," murmured Susan, marvelling at her mentality.

"Mother, we must go and put on hats and things. Jed doesn't like to be kept waiting," said Amanda, speaking almost for the first time, and swept her mother from the dining-room.

It was not long before the carload of reluctant sightseers was driven away by Jed, and Susan was left to a day of blessed peace. Alternately busy and idle, the hours drifted pleasantly past, and the afternoon brought Peggy armed with a quantity of soft white knitting, and announcing that she had come to tea, "To help with Mrs. Carmichael and her young man"

"Oh, dear! I'd forgotten. They'll be back quite soon" said Susan. "Never mind, it's only till this evening. Let's sit down and make tiny garments as they do in nice books, Peg. The trouble is that the tiny garment I'm working at is big enough already for the elephant's child, and according to the book of words it isn't *half* done. What can be the matter with it, do you think? I'm sure I'm following the rules slavishly."

She displayed an enormous piece of rather uneven knitting and a tattered page covered with mystic instructions which looked like some secret code.

"It's all this 'p. one, k. one, p.s.s.o. and m. one' that puts me off," she complained. "Why can't they write it down so that I can understand it?"

Peggy gave it an expert glance, decided that it would have to be taken down and begun again, and Susan immediately tore the needles out and proceeded to pull it to pieces.

"This is much the most satisfactory part of it," she said happily, "if only I didn't have to do it all over again! Look at the dear little loops and how curly the wool is when it comes out of them, like one of those big fluffy clouds. It never looks so pretty when it's knitted."

"It won't look very pretty for long if you don't wind it as you undo it. . . . Oh! Look out! Take care! Here comes Bawtie!" suddenly shrieked Peggy, just an instant too late, as the faithful hound sprang on to the window-seat beside his mistress, landing in the very middle of the cloud of wool, and tangling himself in its curly coils with incredible speed. One moment a black dog like a sheepskin rug was leaping up, the next a curious cocoon of dubious whiteness, with portions of black dog appearing through it, was hurtling down to the floor again and rushing madly round the room, involving chairs, tables and sofa in an outsize game of cat's-cradle. Peggy, after her one warning scream, broke down and wept with laughter; Susan sat as if paralysed, murmuring weakly:

"The *wee* man!"—and still holding to her ever-diminishing knitting, which Bawtie, in his frantic efforts to free himself, was unravelling faster than she could ever hope to.

"Peggy, can't you do something to stop him?" she asked helplessly. "I don't want to drop my knitting."

But Peggy's only reply was to laugh harder than ever, pointing to the frayed remains in Susan's hand. Finally she gasped between paroxysms of tearful mirth, "I'm all wu-wound up too, and so are you! We c-can't do a thing until we're rescued!"

It was only too true. Bawtie's mad career had taken him several times round their legs, and they were as inextricably caught as everything else in the sitting-room.

"So that's why my legs are so nice and warm," said Susan. "I wondered. Well, we must sit here and wait for Elspeth with the tea-table. And one beautiful thought is that I can never start the tiny garment with *this* wool now."

"Nun-never!" wailed Peggy, waving a trembling hand at Bawtie who, exhausted at last, had lain down in the centre of his web, and with rolling eyes and savage growls was proceeding to bite his way out.

"He seems to be getting on very nicely with the job," said Susan rather enviously, after a period of determined chewing and growling on Bawtie's part. "Why shouldn't we try to untangle ourselves, too?"

Encouraged by his example, they bent down and tugged at the many strands of wool which bound them; but unfortunately Bawtie chose to take this as a sign that an exciting new game had begun, and, hung with disgusting wet pieces of half- bitten Shetland three-ply, rushed towards them, bringing in his wake two small chairs and a table.

"Go back, Bawtie! Sit *down*, sir!" cried Susan wildly and unavailingly, as everything became chaos once more. The table overturned on top of Bawtie, who began to back furiously; and Peggy, springing to the rescue, forgetful of her bonds, at once added herself to the struggling heap on the floor.

"The Misses Pringle, madam," said Elspeth, ushering in the three sisters without a glance at the turmoil near her feet.

"How do you do?" screamed Susan, above the tumult raised by Bawtie and Peggy. "Don't come any nearer for your own sakes, Miss Pringle; and I can't come to you. Elspeth, please bring the big flower-scissors at once."

"Very good, madam," said Elspeth, withdrawing in excellent order, entirely unmoved.

"I'm so sorry," Susan went on, with admirable calm. "We're in a—a bit of a muddle, but Elspeth will soon put everything right."

Peggy, now silent except for broken sounds which might have been laughter or sobs, was sitting up among the ruins face to face with the bewildered Bawtie. Both were wound from head to foot in masses of dirty wool; and Miss Pringle, glancing from them to their disordered surroundings and back again, inquired disapprovingly, "Has dear little Peggy been having a romp with your doggie?"

"Not—not exactly," said Susan hurriedly, fearing another explosion of ungovernable mirth from her sister-in-law. "Oh, here is Elspeth with the scissors."

The perfect parlourmaid flitted in, bearing a small silver salver at exactly the right height and angle, and apparently avoiding the obstacles in her way by sheer force of conscious correctness, advanced towards her mistress. Peggy declared afterwards, and stuck firmly to her story, that Elspeth rose a few inches into the air and floated over wool, chairs, and everything else in her way.

"No, no, Elspeth, I don't want the scissors," said Susan, waving her off. "Cut Mrs. Parsons and Bawtie out for me."

"Cut them, madam?" said Elspeth, for once shaken from her frozen composure, and speaking in tones of distaste, as if commanded to a revolting act of butchery which was not her job.

"Yes, cut the *wool*, I mean of course. Can't you see that they're all tangled up in yards of it?"

Elspeth, still registering disgust, stooped elegantly and applied the scissors. It was a little unhappy that the first cut should have freed Bawtie from his table, Susan thought, while leaving him with plenty of wool hanging from his person, for after shaking himself violently, he flew to greet the three Miss Pringles, and running round them, drew them all into a new net. The situation now assumed the improbable horror of a nightmare. Miss Pringle and her sisters clung together squeaking, to keep their balance, while Bawtie raged joyously about them and made playful snatches at their large feet.

Peggy, having succumbed again to shameless hysterical laughter, was quite useless. Susan tugged and pulled to get herself free, and all the time Elspeth quietly and respectfully cut through every bit of wool within reach by single strands, with the thoroughness which she gave to cleaning silver or polishing the best glass. It began to seem that they must spend the rest of their lives in this absurd spider's web, when the door opened again, to admit Jed and his convoy returned in the nick of time from St. Boswells.

"What are you all playing at?" he demanded, without more ado seizing Bawtie, tearing the wool from him and bundling him out of the way into the unready arms of David White. After that, release became simplicity itself. Elspeth rose from the floor, her hands full of odd lengths and streamers of the former half-made baby's garment, and melted away; Peggy wiped her eyes and picked up the chairs; and Susan, tearing the remainder of the wool from herself and the Miss Pringles, consigned it thankfully to the fire. It blazed for a second, died down, and was gone.

"And now let's have tea," said Jed. "I'm sure you'll all be wanting it, after the game you were playing."

II

"The wool has broken the ice, anyway, and that's a good thing," Peggy, blissfully unaware of the imbecility of this remark, murmured to Amanda as they went into the dining-room for tea, the size of the party and the state of the sitting-room making it the only possible place. Though it might have been worded better, what Peggy said was quite true: the party sat down in a polite babel of conversation, the Misses Pringle and Mrs. Carmichael emulously striving to outdo each other in remembering other like circumstances; and the fact that neither narrator nor audience noticed the total lack of similarity apparent in almost every instance was a proof of the general amiability. For the quite alarming suavity and good humour of the Misses Pringle, Susan had to acknowledge she was indebted to Elspeth, who had spread the table with the appalling tea-cloth which had been their wedding-present to her and Jed, and provided Indian tea in the silver pot, murmuring, "Miss Pringle prefers the Indian, madam, so I thought I would just infuse the smaller tea-pot for her," as she placed it firmly on the tray at Susan's elbow. Elspeth, thought her mistress guiltily, pouring out the potent brew which the Misses Pringle favoured, was quite wasted at Reiverslaw. If, being a woman, she could not grace the diplomatic service, where her talents would have made her an ambassador at once, she should at least be in the service of someone who appreciated them better, and did not deplore her lack of human failings.

In the meantime, all, like the famous ball at Brussels, went merry as a marriage bell, and there seemed no reason why it should not continue to do so, until David White, the well-meaning but clumsy, dropped enough bricks to have built a small modern bungalow with a crash which resounded through the whole room.

"Who was that fellow who was speaking to you at St. Boswells, Amanda?" was his innocent-sounding question, uttered without malice. "Queer sulky-looking fellow, Larry Something."

"I think you must mean Larry Heriot," said Amanda, beautifully undisturbed by the ominous silence of the Misses Pringle. "Will you pass me the black-currant jam, please?"

"Do you know him well—ow!" said the tactless David, breaking off in anguish, as a vicious kick, launched by Peggy, reached its objective too late to stop him. "Someone's kicked me!"

"It was me. Sorry." Peggy, scarlet with shame at having been found out, sounded anything but sorrowful; and the Misses Pringle, scandalized by this confession of schoolgirl hoydenishness so unbefitting a young matron, seemed for a moment to be side-tracked.

But Peggy's misdemeanours had been familiar to them from her not far distant childhood, and they were not long to be distracted by any red herring. Back to the trail they came in full cry, and immediately started to regale the pleasurably shocked Mrs. Carmichael with a highly seasoned account of Larry Heriot and his short-comings. Susan's offers of tea and cake could not stem the torrent of thinly veiled hints, darting glances from Amanda to her mother, sighs, shakings of the head and pursings of the lips, which Mrs. Carmichael, well versed in the use of innuendo, found perfectly comprehensible.

Just as Susan had reached the conclusion that she would stop this slanderous talk, even if it meant being openly rude, the matter was taken out of her hands by Mrs. Carmichael herself.

"*Now*, Amanda," sbe said meaningly, "perhaps, if you haven't the sense of duty to go gratefully with David to poor dear Lloyd in South America, you will at least see that you must come home with me, and not lay yourself open to gossip here *any* longer. And in connection with a man of *that* character!"

"Mother!" exclaimed the outraged Amanda, in a low, furious voice. "Have you no decency at all?"

Mrs. Carmichael, bridling, prepared to make a shattering reply; but Miss Cissy was before her. "And *aren't* you going out to South America to your husband, Mrs. Cochrane?" she piped. "I'm sure he must be counting the days till you arrive, poor young fellow!"

"No, Miss Pringle," said Amanda quietly, "I am not. I can't afford to, you see; and I know that David, who has known him even longer than I have, will look after him and bring him safely home."

"Of course I will, dear old chap," said David.

"*How* touching! What a beautiful friendship!" cried Miss Cissy, and both she and Mrs. Carmichael looked ready to burst into sentimental tears.

Miss Pringle, made of sterner stuff, returned to the original theme. ("I know, like a dog to its vomit," said Oliver when Peggy was describing the scene to him. "And don't tell me not to be disgusting, darling, because it's true, appropriate, and in the Bible.")

"I shall never regret," she announced severely, "having advised poor Ruth to hurry home and stop the sherry-party organized by her brother. No doubt it developed into an orgy—oh, I am *sure* not while *you* were still there, Mrs. Armstrong"—in a voice which expressed certainty of the exact opposite—"but later, when you had left."

"Difficult to know how that could have been managed, as we were about the last to go," said Amanda, in an off-hand tone which concealed burning rage.

"I had it from Ruth *herself*," said Miss Pringle, with triumph, "that he drank *all night* afterwards."

"Since we seem doomed to talk personalities, though I think it's a deplorable habit of small minds," said Susan cuttingly, with an edge to her voice which none of those present had ever heard before, "perhaps Ruth also told you, Miss Pringle, that she arrived at a perfectly harmless and happy party and made a most unpleasant scene?"

"Well—no . . ." Under her steely look even Miss Pringle floundered a little. "But can one wonder? Consider what she has had to bear from her brother, Mrs. Armstrong. I know you are prejudiced in his favour, but I cannot accept your description of his party at Gledewaterford as perfectly harmless, however *happy* it may have been. I should have to be convinced by some less biased eye-witness." Gathering confidence from the sound of her own voice, she rolled sonorously to the finish of her sentence.

'Can I be *really* rude to her in my own house?' thought Susan longingly and answered her own question. 'Yes, I can, and I will. Here goes.' And then, almost to her disappointment, so ready was she to give battle, she heard Jed speak.

"Good God!" he exclaimed in the simple wondering tone which she always expected the worst to follow. "Haven't you got two unbiased, unprejudiced eye-witnesses here all ready for you? D you mean to say they've never told you about how they enjoyed the party, and what a fine time they had at it?"

"I don't know who you can be talking about, Mr Armstrong," said Miss Pringle, while her sisters, who knew only too well, and saw too late whither their love of gossip had led them, wilted until they almost disappeared below the table.

"Why, your sisters. Miss Jelly and Miss Cissy were there. Weren't you?" he asked, appealing to his miserable and voiceless guests. "Drinking sherry with the best of 'em. If you'd asked *them* they could have told you it was a respectable party."

For a whole second there was silence. Then Miss Pringle rose. "I think it is time for us to go home," she said, with awful meaning. "Good-bye, Mrs. Armstrong, Mrs. Carmichael . . ." with a series of rapid bows to the appalled spectators. "Come, Jelly; come, Cissy. You can tell me *all* about the party on the way home."

With Miss Jelly and Miss Cissy, too shattered for any farewells, crawling behind her, she swept from the room escorted by Jed, who all the way to the front door could be heard assuring her that it had been a grand party, and she shouldn't have missed it.

III

"Amanda?"

"Yes, Mother?"

"Amanda dearest, Mother must talk to you very seriously for your own good," said her mother impressively, and Amanda sighed.

They were up in the spare bedroom which had been so hastily made ready for Mrs. Carmichael on the previous evening, engaged in 'a nice quiet talk' while the older lady packed. So far, the talking had all been done by her, the packing by Amanda, who was glad to have something to do while the cascade of half-sentimental, half-mercenary speech poured over her. She heard it vaguely without paying very much attention, but as she had heard variations on the same theme countless times before, that hardly mattered. Now, however, she closed the suitcase with a snap, faced her mother, and said firmly, "Before you begin, Mother, there's something *I* should like to say to you."

"Yes, dear, of course." Mrs. Carmichael, seated in a comfortable chair with a cushion at her back, assumed the expression which she considered suitable to receive girlish confidences, perhaps apologies for her brusqueness, even. . . .

"You must remember," Amanda was saying—and she did not sound either girlish or apologetic—"that although I've allowed you to interfere with my affairs all my life, I still don't think that they are any business of yours, unless I ask your advice, which I'm not in the least likely to do. This probably sounds unnatural and heartless"—she used her mother's own words gravely and without irony—"but it's true, and I feel the time has come for us to speak out to each other frankly. Up till now, I've never bothered, because I simply didn't care, and because your interference didn't seem to make things any worse than they were, but now it has got to stop. If Cocky comes home and I decide to stay with him, there must be no more plotting and scheming between you, because if there is, I shall leave him at once and for good."

"Amanda!" whimpered Mrs. Carmichael, already weeping copiously. "How *can* you be so cruel?"

"Yes. I was afraid you'd take it that way. Here's your handkerchief," said her daughter. "I don't really like to make you cry, you know, Mother, but it comes rather easily to you, doesn't it? Surely you can see my point?"

"No, I can't," wept Mrs. Carmichael. "When I *think* how I've watched over you and *prayed* for you, I despair of ever—and you call it interference! A mother's love for her own only child! Interference!"

"That's what it is, in plain English, Mother. If I were unmarried there might be some excuse for your constant poking and prying, though I don't think so. But as it is, you seem to forget that I have a husband, and when I married him, my life was—or should have been—his concern, not yours."

"Oh! Oh!" cried her mother, still weeping. "You call it interference, when all I want to do is warn you against making yourself conspicuous with that terrible man! If you're a married woman, you don't seem to remember it!" Her voice, muffled with sobs and the handkerchief held to her eyes, was more vindictive than maternal, and Amanda smiled without mirth.

"I'm answerable to Cocky, not to you, and I think you can trust me not to make a fool of myself with any man," she said coldly. "But it seems that you'd rather believe that horrible old gossip Miss Pringle than your 'own only child'. I won't argue the point with you, only don't forget what I said. If you interfere once again after—after Cocky comes home, I leave him. And it will be your fault."

"Of course you will blame *me*, whatever happens," sighed Mrs, Carmichael, with martyred dignity. "Well, go your own way, Amanda. You must buy experience for yourself, but never forget, my poor mistaken child, that your mother loves you!"

"Thank you, Mother," said Amanda more gently. After all, tiresome, affected and self-seeking though she might be, she was her mother, and presumably loved her daughter in some strange fashion of her own.

"And you *will* be discreet about this man, this Heriot, who drinks?" said Mrs. Carmichael, throwing away her advantage without ever recognizing it as such. "You shouldn't have spoken to him today, in such a public place, where *everyone* could see you hobnobbing with him! And I can't imagine what you had to say to him if you don't know him well?" Inquisitiveness shone bright in her eyes.

Amanda said shortly, "If you must know, I was telling him that Cocky had been found. That was all."

"*Ah!*" said her mother significantly, pouncing on it. "And why should it mean anything to *him*?"

"Merely ordinary sympathy and friendly interest," Amanda told her. "You and the Miss Pringles wouldn't understand."

As she listened to her mother's offended cluckings, her conscience pricked her, though only very slightly. Had it been absolutely truthful to say that Larry had shown friendly interest in the news about Cocky? Hardly, perhaps. It had been both more and less than that. . . . Meeting him at St. Boswell's, in the slippery, odorous alley-way between pens of shouldering, heaving, frightened bullocks, where she had gone with Jed, and where her mother, with a delicate lady-like repugnance, had refused to follow, had been unexpected. She had not seen him since that evening at Gledewaterford, and found herself horribly, furiously ashamed and embarrassed.

Jed had moved on almost at once, and though they were constantly passed and jostled and spoken to by men in heavy, dirty boots, they seemed to be alone, watched by the dull soft eyes of the cattle on either side. He had said at once, 'Forget all about it. Ruth says things like that. They're never worth bothering about." There was no attempt at apology, probably he thought it had gone past that; no confusion, only the statement which had done more to put her at ease than any apology. The unpleasant incident had overshadowed all her thoughts, had loomed to gigantic proportions during wakeful hours in the night, but now, under the cold grey sky, at the busy sale, noisy with men shouting and thumping the bellowing bullocks along with stout sticks, with the barking of collies and the continual stir and hum, it suddenly dwindled away to unimportance. In any case, it had been forced to the back of her memory to lie there until it made an unwelcome reappearance as it had done on seeing him, by her mother's descent on Reiverslaw with David White.

Quite honestly she had answered, "It's all right, Larry. I've had— other things—to think about since yesterday."

"Other things!" His glance had been sharp, he had leapt to the truth at once, unerringly. "You've had news of your husband."

"Yes. News of Cocky. He's alive."

"And what exactly will that mean to you?"

"I haven't quite made up my mind yet, but I think it means that I'll go back to him, Larry."

"The eternal self-sacrifice of women!" he had said with an ugly smile. "Do you suppose he'll thank you for it? Most men aren't really so keen on living with a perpetual burnt-offering, you know."

"I don't intend to be one."

"Will you be able to help it?"

"I don't think there's anything to be gained by this rather pointless discussion," she had said; and he had pulled her aside against the rails to avoid a rush of bullocks being urged towards the sale-ring.

"Poor driven beasts," she had said—how well she remembered saying it, and feeling the unreasonable anger that man should make a business of breeding them only to slaughter them for his food. And his answer:

"Isn't that just what we all are? Driven beasts?"

"I thought you and I were storm-cocks," she had said, with an attempt at lightness. "Cocky and I certainly are, I've just realized it. And we can't be both storm-cocks and driven cattle."

"Of course we can. Even the storm-cock is driven by weather, need for food, blind instinct," he had said roughly. "What living creature is there that can fight against it?"

"That's a dismal, defeatist philosophy and I refuse to agree with it," she had said with spirit. "And you should never have let yourself believe it, Larry. Why should you sit down and—and—"

"Drink like a fish?"

"I wasn't going to say that. I was going to say why should you let your sister rule your life? It's your own, and she has hers to live. You ought to live apart, and you know it."

"I don't care what becomes of me, and life isn't worth making a fuss about. As for living apart, it can't be done. Not enough money, for one thing. And there are other reasons. Give it up, Amanda, and never mind me. You'll have your own troubles now that your husband's alive."

After that he had gone into the ring, and she had wandered back to the hotel to find her mother and David drinking rather nasty sherry in front of a comforting fire.

Looking back on it dispassionately, Amanda had to admit that there had been little or no 'friendly interest' about Larry, but after all, it wasn't her mother's business. Let it stand. . . .

"I don't believe you've heard a *single* word that I've been saying to you, Amanda," said Mrs. Carmichael fretfully. "What an absent-minded vague creature you are! I should think you might pay a *little* attention to your mother!"

"I'm sorry. I was thinking. There's rather a lot to to think about, isn't there, Mother?" Amanda said, smiling rather piteously.

That was all Mrs. Carmichael needed. "My poor darling child! Such a shock—though good news, of course—and no one realizes it but me! A mother always knows!" And the interview ended just as it should from her point of view, in tears and embraces.

IV

"What a fine free feeling there is about seeing the post come and knowing you've offended Miss Pringle so frightfully that she can't possibly have 'post-carded' you," said Susan a few mornings later.

"It's all my fault," said Amanda remorsefully. "But for me you'd have been invited to all sorts of festivities by her! I don't mind that so much, but think of all the other things that can't ever have happened when I wasn't here. Rows at sherry-parties, flocks of my relations appearing unasked out of the blue and dumping themselves on you—"

"Does one mother and a friend-in-law constitute a flock?" asked Susan. "I shouldn't have thought it made even a brace, myself. And don't be so conceited. Do you imagine that nothing ever happens unless you're here?"

"You are a pet," said Amanda, and was startled by a scream of rage from Susan.

"What's the matter? Have you run a needle into your finger?"

"I—will—not—be—called—a—pet," said Susan slowly and distinctly. "Anything else in the world, but not a *pet*!"

"Very well, you aren't a pet," Amanda assured her, laughing. "Oh, here is Elspeth with the letters."

"Here is Bawtie with one of them at least," said Susan, as the black dog pranced in, carrying a somewhat moist and crumpled envelope in his capacious mouth. Behind him rushed not Elspeth but Robinia, a stick in one hand, the remainder of the morning's mail in the other.

Casting the letters unceremoniously into Susan's lap, she attacked Bawtie with her stick, crying, "Eh, ye wee ruff-yun, then! Wait till I get a hold o' ye!"

Bawtie promptly retired under the sofa, where he lay growling enjoyably, one paw planted on his letter, while he tried to seize the stick in his teeth, evidently regarding Robinia as an admirable playmate.

"That will do, Robina," said her mistress, as Amanda, seeing Bawtie fully occupied with the stick, meanly made a sortie from the rear and rescued the letter, a little mangled and minus its stamp, but otherwise intact save that most of the address had been licked off. "And where is Elspeth? Why have you brought in the letters?"

"Elspeth's greetin', an' she dina want tae come in—mem," said Robinia, swelling with the importance of one who brings news of trouble.

"Crying? *Elspeth?*" exclaimed Susan incredulously. "I hope she hasn't had bad news from home?"

"Her an' her lad's cast oot," said Robinia. "An' he's wrote tae her tae break aff his engagement. She's jilted!"

"Oh, dear. Poor Elspeth. I hope she isn't really badly upset?"

"Och, it's mair her pride. Cook's sent her tae hae a bit lie doon wi' a nice cup o' tea an' twa pills. Aspirings is it ye ca' them?"

"Very sensible of cook," said Susan rather repressively. "And you must do the best you can to help Elspeth, Robinia."

"Ay, mem." And with eagerness: "Wull I get waitin' the denner?"

"We can see about that later on. In the meantime you can clear away breakfast."

When Robinia, a little subdued, had gone, shutting the door behind her in a slow, painstaking imitation of Elspeth's noiseless manipulation of the lock, Susan said with a sigh, "I don't want to seem heartless, but I sincerely hope that Elspeth's sense of what is due to her forlorn state won't prevent her from appearing by dinner-time. It's Robinia's prime ambition to wait at table, and after one experience of it, at her own passionate desire, I am quite determined that it won't happen again."

"What was she like?" asked Amanda, who found Robinia highly refreshing.

"*Awful.* She chatted to Jed about cross-bred hoggs so interestedly that she allowed gravy to dribble from the sauce boat down on to his shoulder all the time; there were people dining with us, I can't remember who, but I could see that they were thinking all the time that poor Jed had married a wretched housewife. If they didn't help themselves at once she nudged them with the vegetable dish; when some woman refused wine she said sympathetically, 'Are ye T.T.?' And when it came to the sweet I heard her say to a horrified guest, 'That's an awfu' wee help ye've got. Tak' anither spoonfu', there's plenty mair in the kitchen.'"

"Well, she was being kind and helpful," protested Amanda when she had stopped laughing.

"Far too helpful. Can you make out who this letter is for, Amanda? Bawtie's removed all the ink except one small smudge which may or may not be 'Reiverslaw', and it doesn't help us much."

"No," said Amanda. "I can't. But it looks like one of Mother's envelopes. It's probably her bread-and-butter letter, so you'd better open it."

"All right," said Susan, ripping the envelope neatly open with a small paper-knife. "You can read it too. In fact, you'll have to. Her writing is quite beyond me."

"It's beyond most people," said Amanda, taking the single sheet of note-paper covered with sprawling characters. "Including herself, and she has a telegraphic style, just to make it more difficult. I'll skim through it first and then read it to you without any mistakes. . . . Susan! Susan! Oh, this is beyond even what *Mother* is usually capable of! She's going with David to South America! How can she let him pay for her when she's only Cocky's mother-in-law? She says she looks on Cocky and David—both of them—as if they were her own boys, and as my false pride won't let me accept a favour from one who has been like a brother to me, she isn't above using one son's wealth in order to go to the sick-bed of the other. Oh, it's too *awful* of her. What can I do?"

"Nothing whatever," said Susan tranquilly. "From the only bit I can read I see that they are sailing today. I think it's an excellent thing, Amanda. You'll be left in peace now until they let you know from Rio how they have found your husband. Don't look so shocked, my poor dear, because I'm going to laugh, I'm afraid. I can't help admiring her for having stolen such a march on you."

"It's all very well," began Amanda angrily. "How would you like it if you had such a shameless mother?" But presently she started to laugh too. "Poor David!" she said at length. "He's bored me so much, and I should have had such a frightful trip if I'd gone, with him hovering round me like a St. Bernard, all complete with a little barrel of brandy to revive me! And now he'll have to revive Mother, and she'll give him no peace. Poor David. I think, you know, that he was delighted to have an excuse for the voyage, and he was going to enjoy it and be able to feel noble at the same time."

"And now he'll only be able to enjoy the nobility?"

"That's all," said Amanda, adding pensively, "I wonder if he realizes what a rotten sailor Mother is? *Poor* David!"

CHAPTER ELEVEN

I

THE excitements and alarums which had culminated in Mrs. Carmichael's departure for South America in charge of the unwilling David White died away as the slow weeks passed and winter closed in on the countryside. Each small town and village, even each farm in the lonelier districts, seemed to draw into itself in an isolation more spiritual than actual though it sprang from a habit of thought which was traditional and belonged to times of difficult transport and impassable roads. Within their own bounds these places were cheerful, the dark evenings saw hardy folk trudging the roads from cottage to school or tiny village hall, where dances or a church 'swarry', a meeting of the W.R.I., or even night-classes drew their appropriate patrons; there was the added attraction of feeling that each parish was the hub of its own small world, that affairs outside it had faded away to a distance not measurable in miles.

Amanda, who until this year which had changed her life so greatly, had always looked on 'the country' as a place of purely summer residence, was charmed by the quiet winter days, the long chill nights made brilliant by stars. Every time she went out she discovered fresh beauty in the soft neutral tints, the duns and browns and greys of the bare fields with their infinite variety of shadow and light; in the lovely outlines of leafless trees, the tremendous sweep of the hills. Fitful blinks of sunshine, the more prized for their rarity, touched a haystack, a beech-hedge, to momentary splendour as if Midas had laid his hand on it; clouds sailing over the wide sky sent their huge shadows chasing each other across the rolling fields below. It was a time of waiting, of unseen growth not guessed at in towns, and Amanda, herself waiting for news of David's arrival at Rio de

Janeiro, felt her whole being in harmony with nature as she never had before.

She still told herself that her final decision about Cocky was yet to be made, but in her heart she knew that she would give him another chance. She could afford to, now that she had found her balance and could no longer be thrown off it by him. This quiet certainty was what helped her through the weeks of patient waiting, and she felt a new interest in living, even in such ordinary things as food and sleep, a walk with Susan, a tramp beside Jed's striding figure round the marches of Reiverslaw. Now she was beginning to enjoy meeting people, even when, as inevitably happened in a small community, they included the Misses Pringle, or, more rarely, Ruth Heriot, sullen, lowering and openly rude to her. Occasionally she saw Larry but he seemed to avoid her, and she was forced to admit that it was as well for her own peace of mind.

Too honest to pretend to herself that they could be only friends, she knew that she could do nothing for him, though it distressed her to hear that he was drinking harder than ever.

She could not stop thinking of him, he was constantly in her thoughts, ill-temper, harshness, all his many faults which had no power to make her dislike or despise him now. She was thinking about him one December morning as she walked fast along the road on her way to Easter Hartrigg.

There had been what the country people called so graphically an 'onding' of snow in the night, and a thin sprinkling, crisp with hoar frost, lay on the ground. A bitter wind, promising a further fall, was blowing from the west, but the sun shone bravely between fast-driven clouds. Cheviot, soaring into the chill pale blue of the sky, was gleaming white, his crest clear, and all the distances eastward were an exquisite melting violet-blue. Everything was clean-cut, sharply defined, the long fir wood behind the village of Muirkirk dense black, a row of stacks in a field shining palely. Only the high hawthorn hedges against purple-brown ploughland looked like a drift of smoke. Sheep were feeding quietly, and caught by the sudden sun the frozen grass turned silver-gilt, every sheep had a fleece of gold. Then clouds swept over the sky again, and Amanda saw only the snowy pasture, with greyish ewes. The glory had departed and she knew a slight chill of depression which increased as she looked along the road to see a tall, thin woman riding towards her.

Meeting Ruth Heriot face to face, alone, with no third person to act as buffer, was not unlike what she imagined a man must feel on a grey morning when he saw his opponent in a duel approaching the rendezvous. To turn back was useless as well as cowardly, since she would easily be overtaken. Amanda held steadily on, wondering what happen, prepared to be cut and pass in silence, but when she had drawn quite near, Ruth Heriot turned her horse across the road so that, to get by, Amanda must walk in the ditch.

She stopped, looked up, and said composedly, hoping that her wild heartbeats would not make her voice uneven. "Good morning, Miss Heriot. May I pass? It's too cold to stand."

"You'll pass when I'm ready, not a minute sooner," came the harsh answer, hoarser than it had been, as if her vocal chords were strained by constant railing. "I suppose you're out trying to catch Larry?"

"I don't know why you should suppose anything of the kind. I haven't seen him, and don't know where he is," said Amanda.

"Don't try to fool *me*. I know you're out after him. You want him because you're sick of your own husband," said Ruth Heriot unforgivably. "Women like you should be shot on sight."

'And women like you ought to be in a mental home,' thought Amanda, eyeing her with steady contempt, saying nothing. Her silence seemed to infuriate the other. She bent down until her face was not far above Amanda's own and said, "If you knew as much as I do you wouldn't be so keen to get him, let me tell you."

"The fact that he's your brother is against him, certainly," agreed Amanda, beginning to find a horrid pleasure in this word battle, the joy of the swordsman when steel meets steel. "But it wouldn't be fair to blame him for that."

"Do you know why he drinks? Why he always looks so hag-ridden?" went on Ruth Heriot as if she had not heard. "I'll tell you."

"I don't want to hear. It's no business of mine."

"You shall hear, if I have to shout it to the whole county," she cried, and her eyes, mad with hate, glared at Amanda's white face. "You're going to hear it, I tell you! He's haunted, haunted by the wretched girl he seduced and wouldn't marry, who drowned herself because of him!"

Amanda stood very still. "So that's his ugly skeleton," she said, speaking to herself, but Ruth Heriot heard her this time.

"Yes, that's it," she said with such hideous satisfaction in her voice that Amanda shivered as if with malaria. "That makes you think, doesn't it?"

"It makes me—terribly sorry for him," said Amanda, shaken. "He must have been so young! Poor, poor Larry! What a secret to have to carry about with him all his life! And yet, after all, it was a long time ago—"

"He'd have forgotten it. Men have such conveniently short memories, haven't they?" said his sister, laughing loudly. "*I* see that it's kept fresh in his mind! He doesn't have a chance to forget. He never will!"

Amanda said faintly, "You're his *sister*—"

"Yes, I'm his sister. And I hate him! I hate him!" Her voice rose to a hoarse, triumphant cry; she wheeled her horse and rode past Amanda like a fury.

The road was clear now, but Amanda found that she could not walk any farther on it, marked as it was by the horse's hoofs. Feeling sick and dazed, she turned aside, plunged blindly downhill across a grass field, and came to a standstill beside the burn running dark between the snow-sprinkled banks. Here she leaned against an ash, clinging to it, her arms about it as if it were alive and human, her face pressed to the rough bark, while she shuddered from head to foot.

And Larry Horiot, who had seen the meeting from the same field through which he was slowly walking with a gun under his arm, looking for Jed's elusive cock-pheasants, watched her grey-faced, burning-eyed. 'So Ruth's told her,' he thought. 'She'll never look at me again. Well, it's better that way. Easier for her.'

He glanced down at the gun, its shining barrels chill to his hand, and wondered if it would not be the simplest way out to shoot himself. Only he had always considered that the last resort of desperate cowardice, and he probably deserved to go on living and suffering, so he stayed where he was until he saw Amanda start to walk back to Reiverslaw, and then continued his slow, aimless wandering, the loaded gun as harmless to game as a child's toy pistol.

II

Half-way to Reiverslaw Amanda changed her mind and turned back once more in the direction of Easter Hartrigg. She could not face Susan, whose serenity ought to be tenderly guarded now more than ever before, looking as if she had just seen a ghost. Peggy's matter-of-fact cheerful kindness would not be so easily disturbed; she would say it was only Ruth Heriot after all, and prescribe tea and young Oliver's company as an antidote, which would probably do Amanda more good than anything, and save Susan needless distress.

So it came about that taking the short cut down the side of the fields, she saw Larry a short distance ahead of her, standing so listlessly looking at his gun, that she was frightened. Quickening her pace to reach him, her foot caught a stone, and the slight noise roused him. He looked round sharply, and involuntarily threw up his free hand as if to ward off a blow. Then he let it drop, his face hardened. He said recklessly:

"Well, you know now. I can guess what you think of me. No need to tell me that."

"Oh, Larry! I'm so sorry! It's been so—so unspeakably awful for you! Why didn't you tell me yourself?" Her look, her voice, the gesture she made, told him quite plainly what she felt, but he seemed unable to comprehend it. Speechless he stared at her, the blood mounting in a dark tide to his forehead.

At last, "You—you—I don't understand. Wasn't Ruth telling you on the road just now? She's been threatening to, the first time she got you by yourself. Didn't she tell you?" he muttered.

"Yes, she told me." Amanda's eyes flashed indignantly. "And I can't think why you've put up with her all this time, Larry."

"Oh, that!" He dismissed it carelessly. "I couldn't help it."

"Surely you aren't afraid of her? Larry, surely it wasn't because she threatened to tell everyone about that poor girl that you've gone on letting her make your life a misery?" cried Amanda. To her it was desperately important that he should contradict this accusation of cowardice.

"No, that wasn't the reason. I'll tell you, if you really want to know."

"Larry, I must know."

"I promised my father," he said slowly, "to keep Ruth with me at Gledewaterford as long as she lived. She was always—queer, even as a child, and he was afraid for her. He thought that if she was on her own she might get into mischief and have to be shut up, and it would have killed her."

"And what about you? Didn't he think what it would mean to you?"

"Well," he answered temperately. "He was devoted to Ruth, you see. A man nearly always makes a pet of his daughter, especially if she's the only one. Besides, she wasn't anything like so bad in his lifetime, we were still hoping she'd grow out of it. It was just her mad rages that made her not like other people. But I think she hated me even then. She was jealous of me, and it's grown on her since she hadn't my father to show that she was his favourite."

"What a dreadful life for you," almost whispered Amanda. "I never dreamed it was as terrible as that. So you've stuck it out for her sake and never married, and this is the way she repays you!"

"She's not normal, remember. You can't judge her by other people."

"Yet I've never heard it suggested that she wasn't, even by the Miss Pringles. In fact, they seem to think that you're the odd one!"

"Oh, well, of course she rather laid herself out to give that impression. You can't blame them," he said, still in that reasonable impersonal tone as if discussing someone with whom he had no concern beyond a mild pitying interest. "What with my own beastly temper and drinking so much, I was just the man for their money, if they wanted to talk about the Heriots. I deserve it, you know. To all intents and purposes I'm a murderer."

"Don't!" cried Amanda sharply.

"It's true. I might as well have pushed the girl into the water myself, poor thing. Her name was Marion Hume," he ended simply. "She was a damn' bad lot, but she must have cared more about me than I thought."

Amanda said nothing, and he looked at her for a moment. Then he said, quietly and soberly, "I didn't want it to end this way, with you thinking me a blackguard. But I dare say it's best after all. You'll appreciate your husband better now, perhaps."

Amanda's eyes, wet with tears, were like drowned wallflowers in her small pale face. "You've paid over and over again for what you did!" she said. "Most men go scot-free. Cocky always has, he's luckier or cleverer than you with his women. But as for appreciating him— oh, can't you see how small and mean you make him look to me?"

He took her hand in his and held it hard against him. Amanda thought that she would remember the feel of the rough tweed on the back of her hand all her life. "My dear," he said, "I've no right to say anything to you. We both know what I feel about you, but if you want me to tell you, I will."

"No." Amanda shook her head. "I haven't got the right to listen to what I—I want to hear more than anything in the world, Larry. So good-bye. We'll see each other again, of course, but this is really good-bye."

"Yes," said Larry Heriot, letting her hand fall. "Goodbye."

Amanda gave him one long searching look, as if to print his haggard face, his well-knit spare figure on her memory, then turned and ran down the frosty meadow to the boundary hedge. Once over it, and on the upward slope which ended at Easter Hartrigg, she glanced back, to see him still there watching her. She waved, he lifted his cap from his head and held it until she was out of sight among the rhododendrons beside the gate which led to the house.

"Please, Peggy, don't ask me anything just now," she said, rather wildly, when Oliver's wife greeted her with tactfully averted eyes. "Could—could I wash my face and hands? Is Oliver at home?"

"No, he's out. Did you want him? There's nothing wrong at Reiverslaw, is there?" asked Peggy, tacitly acknowledging that only questions relating to Amanda herself were barred, as she led her upstairs to a bathroom obviously used by young Oliver, as a number of blue celluloid ducks and green frogs and red fishes mingled with soap and sponges bore ample witness.

"No, Susan's all right, and so is Jed. I'm glad Oliver isn't in. I don't want him to see me looking like this," said Amanda, plunging her face into a basin of cold water, pressing chill wet hands to her hot eyes, drying them on the towel which Peggy silently handed to her. "I met Ruth Heriot," she said at last, when she had smoothed her hair. "She—she was rather more unpleasant than usual, and it's upset me. I'll be all right in a minute. Would it be very troublesome of me to ask for a cup of tea?"

"No, of course not." Peggy brightened at the thought that she could supply comfort in this easily attained and practical form. "But Oliver said I was to be sure to offer people sherry. I always forget it, and it makes him quite cross. Are you certain you wouldn't rather have sherry?"

"Quite certain, thank you, Peggy. Tea is what I really want. The thought of sherry doesn't have its usual appeal this morning."

"I like tea better myself," Peggy confessed. Then, shyly, "I'm so very sorry about Ruth Heriot, Amanda. She seems to be even nastier to you than to most people. I think it's because she's jealous. You're so pretty and dainty, and she is so dreadfully like a rather ugly horse herself."

'Blessed innocence,' thought Amanda, that saw the jealousy and at once unthinkingly put it down to the obvious reason. It made Peggy, on this occasion, much easier to talk to than Susan who, older as well as more perceptive, would have gone past the obvious at once, searching deeper for a cause.

"Would you like to see young Oliver?" asked Peggy, who considered the mere sight of her son a cure for all ills. "I'll get Janet to bring him down before she makes our tea."

"How is Janet? Any more breakages?" asked Amanda, glad to change the subject.

"Oh yes, but mostly Woolworth's, so I don't mind. She's beginning to have very grand ideas about laying the table, though, which are rather trying sometimes. I like little mats instead of a cloth, but I do draw the line at having my best ones put into the saucers at tea for the cups to drip into," said Peggy. "Oliver thought it was a lovely idea, and says that a set for the drawing-room, one under each ash-tray, would be the last word in refinement."

"Absurd creature! What fun it must be being married to him, Peggy."

"It is. The best fun in the world," said Peggy happily. "Of course he isn't always being amusing or playing the fool. He takes his job as factor at Wanside *very* seriously indeed, and then, he's sometimes in a bad temper—but not often," she added with loyal haste. "Anyhow, I couldn't be bothered with a husband who hadn't a temper, could you?"

"No," agreed Amanda absently, but she was not thinking of Cocky.

The door was thrown open so violently that it crashed against the wall, and Janet entered with a tread which shook the room, proudly carrying young Oliver.

"Put him down, Janet, and will you make us some tea, please?" said Peggy, unmoved by the noise of their arrival.

Janet rushed away, banging the door behind her, and young Oliver, dumped unceremoniously on a rug near the fire, pulled himself to his feet by means of a convenient chair, and edged his precarious way towards his mother's outstretched hands.

"Peggy! He's *walking*!" cried Amanda, as if witnessing a miracle.

"Of course he is," said his mother proudly. "Look at his lovely red shoes. Real shoes made of leather!"

"Soos!" shouted young Oliver, roaring with laughter at this exquisite witticism. "Soos!" and looking hopefully at Amanda, added: "Baba?"

"No, darling, that's not a baba. That's Aunt Amanda."

"Baba," said her son firmly.

"I don't mind. It's rather a compliment," said Amanda. "I've never been taken for a baba before—at least, not since I really was one. Oh, Peggy, how quickly they change. It's almost frightening. He isn't a baby any more, he's a little boy."

"I know." Peggy's bright face clouded for a moment. "I'm missing my helpless baby, however adorable Oliver is getting, and we won't be able to afford another for simply ages. I don't know how people can do without them . . . oh, Amanda, I'm sorry! I quite forgot you hadn't any!"

"It doesn't matter, Peggy. I don't want you to feel that you have to be careful not to say things. It—it wouldn't have been much fun for me to have a baby when Cocky's job is so risky and dangerous."

To herself the explanation sounded thin, and it evidently worried Peggy. She said slowly, "Wouldn't it? I should have thought that you'd have wanted all the more to have a boy, to remind you of his father, whatever happened."

To have a boy who would remind her of Cocky! That must never be, Amanda thought. One Cocky loosed on the world was quite enough; but she could not bear to disillusion Peggy, and only said, "Perhaps. I didn't see it that way. But you'll be having a new baby in the family soon, even if it's only a nephew or niece."

"Yes. Darling Susan! How are the tiny garments getting on?" asked Peggy, dimpling as she remembered Susan's knitting.

"Well, they're improving both as to size and shape," said Amanda. "But it isn't any use pretending that Susan is an expert with knitting needles. Even my attempts look better than hers. I've made some ridiculous woollen boots with holes to run ribbon through, and a sort of vest, though it doesn't look much like the pattern. I'd call it more of a petticoat myself, so I'm rather meanly hoping that the baby will be a girl, and be able to wear it without disgrace."

"I expect Susan is hoping it will be a boy."

"Probably. It's the natural thing, isn't it? Most women want a son."

"So do most men. And then they make far more fuss over their daughters," said Peggy, "and squabble with the sons they wanted, when they grow up."

"I suppose," murmured Amanda, "that was what happened with the Heriots. The father spoiled Ruth and didn't get on with Larry."

Peggy, though puzzled, followed this lead. "I think it was more that old Mr. Heriot paid very little attention to Larry," she said. "He was his mother's favourite. I've heard Father say so."

"Do you remember them, Peggy?"

"Not Mrs. Heriot. She died before I was born, but old Mr. Heriot had a red face and a beard, and I can just remember meeting him once when I was in Abbeyshiels with Father. He patted me on the head so hard that I nearly fell down, and told Father he had a fine lassie for a daughter. I felt very pleased with myself," said Peggy, smiling.

"Poor old man. He probably wished he'd had the luck to be *your* father instead of Ruth's."

"Oh, I don't think so, Amanda. I was a very ordinary little girl."

"Ordinary little girls turn out the best," said Amanda. "What was Ruth like then?"

The conversation, punctuated as it was by the clattering entrance of Janet with the tea, and constant short expeditions about the room, guiding young Oliver's staggering voyages of discovery, was spasmodic, which made it easier to talk on the subject of Amanda's thoughts without seeming to give it undue importance.

"I don't know. She must be about fifteen years older than me, you see," said Peggy, taking from her son the teaspoon with which he was delightedly stirring the various articles on a low table, and substituting half a biscuit. "I mean, when I was seven or eight, she was a young lady helping the mothers at children's parties. I was terrified of her," she added, as she hurriedly removed a box of matches out of young Oliver's reach and placed it on the mantelpiece. "No, darling, *not* good. Eat your nice bikky instead. And Larry, of course, didn't appear at those functions at all. He must have been about twenty. Ruth is two or three years older."

"Oh, I see. You can't have known much about them, then." Amanda put down her empty cup and rose. "Peggy, I shall have to fly. I've been here much longer than I meant to. Thank you for being such an angel. I felt horribly low when I came."

She left, blowing kisses alternately to young Oliver and his mother at the drawing-room window and hurried home. Comforted she might be, but she was no nearer to finding out anything which might relieve Larry a little of the sense of guilt which had been a crushing burden for so long. It was quite evident that Peggy could know nothing.

'I'll find out somehow, if I have to gossip like the Miss Pringles,' she vowed, cheered by the prospect of having something definite to do for him. 'It's the only way I can help him, and before I go—if I have to go—I'll do it.'

III

"If you really want to give Elspeth that perfectly good hat, Amanda, the one you said didn't suit you, I think this is the moment," said Susan a few days later, wken they were drinking coffee in the sitting-room after lunch. "Robinia tells me that she has 'got over' the defection of her young man, and is seeking fresh prey. Don't you think that a new hat might help?"

"Well—" Amanda sounded more than a little doubtful. "I can't believe that Elspeth will look her conquering best in blue, particularly that shade of blue. I know I don't; but I dare say it will give her that lovely feeling of satisfaction, which is what counts really. I'll present it to her now, if she'll take it."

"As a favour to you, remember. That's the line to take," called Susan after her.

Amanda fetched the hat, a peacock blue felt bought by Cocky, and presented to her, she had always been certain, because he had quarrelled with the girl-friend for whom he had intended it. It was smart, expensive, and, to her eye, hideous, and she hated it. She had kept it more as a reminder of Cocky's fickleness than for any other reason, and now, ashamed of her spite, was glad to hand it on to the gratified Elspeth, whose sallow face and rather prominent artificial teeth would look their worst under its brim.

"I've done it, and I feel a criminal," she said to Susan. "She looks too awful, and she's so delighted with it! She's going to wear it when she goes out this afternoon."

"Oh, that reminds me, I promised that she should be taken to Abbeyshiels," said Susan rather guiltily. "Jed darling, would you—"

He shook his head. "Nothing doing. I've got some fencing to see to."

"This is very difficult of you, and I suspect it's just because you don't like Elspeth."

"You're not so keen on her yourself," he pointed out.

"No, but she's such a good parlourmaid, and I couldn't help being sorry for her about her young man. The poor thing will never get another. And now she's pining for the bright lights of Abbeyshiels, and you won't take her there," said Susan reproachfully.

"Let Amanda drive her," was Jed's reply. "I know she thinks she's far better at it than me. I might put Elspeth in the ditch. You never know. I wonder you like to risk her with me if she's so precious."

"*Would* you, Amanda?"

"Yes, I'd love to. Jed has never let me put a finger on the wheel yet," said Amanda, who liked to drive. "Will you come too, Susan, or don't you trust yourself with me?"

"It isn't a question of trusting myself, dear. After all, I've been driven by Jed for several years, I can bear anything. But I'm not coming," said Susan, raising her voice a little so that her husband, who had composed himself for an after-luncheon nap in his enormous chair, should hear her. "I'm going to stay and see that Jed goes out and does his fencing, if I have to lead him to the field by the ear!"

Amanda was relieved when Bawtie jumped up beside her, leaving Elspeth, in all the splendour of her new hat, which was almost more unbecoming than the donor had feared, to occupy the back of the car alone. However perfect she might be as a parlourmaid, Elspeth was no easy conversationalist. Probably she considered it beneath her dignity, thought Amanda, driving Jed's ill-used car along the winding road to Abbeyshiels. Every now and then she caught a glimpse in the mirror of Elspeth's prim face, crowned by the vivid blue confection, which she wore at quite the wrong angle, bearing an expression of solemn pleasure, softening almost to a smirk whenever they passed a roadman or a ploughman leading a horse to the nearest smithy to be shod. There was no doubt about her satisfaction, no fear that she did not look her absolute best in a hat from Paris crossed her mind. Amanda found her rather pathetic, and her hope that Elspeth would have a good time was uttered heartily when she stopped the car in front of tbe Town Hall in Abbeyshiels. Elspeth, who privately looked upon Amanda as a figure of romance equal to the heroine of any film drama, though disappointed that she had turned out not to be a widow after all, responded much less stiffly than she ever did to Susan, and tripped away down the Horse Market.

'I hope she paints Abbcyshiels a refined shade of pink and wipes everyone's eyes with her hat," thought Amanda, going across to Mr. Hush, the draper's, to buy more wool for Susan. It was rather an embarrassing errand by this time, and Mr. Hush, with his bedside manner and insistence on the fine soft quality of his wools, made it abundantly plain that he suspected what he called a Happy Event in the near future; but Amanda was quite hardened to his solicitude, and made her tell-tale purchases blandly, assuring him of Susan's excellent health.

'She might just as well have put a notice in the *Abbeyshiels Advertiser*,' was her thought, as she escaped from the shop with its rather hot stuffy smell of cotton goods and wool at last. 'Everyone knows all about it already.'

Everyone might know, or at least have a shrewd guess at the truth, but their genuine kindly interest would never betray them into open questions, which would be a deplorable breach of etiquette until some official announcement had been made. Amanda liked both the interest and the delicacy which veiled it, and she was smiling as she threw her bulky parcel into the car. She could not start home again until various other messages had been loaded in by their appropriate shops, and was wondering a little how to pass the time when, glancing across at the high façade of the 'Plough and Horses', she saw Watson hovering in the doorway, obviously anxious to catch her eye. Amanda, who liked the cheerful little landlord, walked over the cobbled street, calling to Bawtie, who was exchanging greetings with a number of dogs of his acquaintance round a lamp-post; one or two were of recognizable breeds, but the remainder quite as odd as Bawtie himself, and in most cases not so good-looking.

"I was wonderin', madam, if ye'll excuse the liberty," began Watson in his voluble way, "as it's a sharp afternoon, would ye not come ben and wait for yer parcels? Forbye my old faither's that eager to have a crack with ye, madam, having been shepherd to Mr. Wat's faither, that'll be yer grandfaither, up at Staneyett in the old days."

"I should like to meet him," said Amanda promptly. "Though I don't remember my grandfather at all, and my father died when I was a small child, so I hope he won't expect too much of me."

"Oh, he just likes to get somebody that'll listen to him," said Watson with devastating candour. "An' the wife ane me, we're ower busy. It would be a real kindness to all o' us, madam."

Thus encouraged, Amanda went into the hotel, and led along passages to a small room behind the office, where a gnarled old man, bowed over two sticks, stood in front of a hot fire. Twenty idle years lived in the 'Plough and Horses' had not wrought the slightest change in him beyond that of increasing age; he was a hill-shepherd still, bent by years of tramping the moors in all weathers, keen of eye and stouthearted as ever. His body was spare still, and tougher than his son's, as his features were both stronger and more refined than the landlord's; it was another case where the softer man had not worn so well, showing even in face the effects of town life, until there was by now very little resemblance between them.

As Amanda put her hand into the dry bony one which he took from his stick to offer her, the old man said, "Ay, I kenned yer faither well, an' *his* faither afore him, lang syne. Ye dinna tak' efter them, lassie."

"No, and I'm not like my mother either," said Amanda. "No one seems to know where my looks came from."

"I'll sune tell ye that. Ye favour yer grandmither, Maister Wat's mither," he said. "I can see her in yer e'e, and the turn o' yer heid."

His speech, broader and rougher than his son's, flowed like a hill-burn over stones, and though a great part of what he said was like an unknown tongue to Amanda, she liked the sound of it, the pure Doric, rich with native words, once the daily speech of gentle as well as simple. Watson, giving her an apologetic look, took himself off and left them together, an oddly assorted pair.

"Sit ye doon an' gie's yer crack," said the old shepherd, lowering himself with difficulty into a chair beside the fire. "I'm an auld done man, but in yer grandfaither's day I was as soople's a wand. Dae ye mind yer grandfaither?"

"Do I mind?" began Amanda uncertainly, to realize in time that he was not asking if she objected to a grandparent whom she had never seen. "No, I'm afraid I don't remember him," she finished.

"It'll be lang afore yer time. Ye're but a lassie, but mairret, they tell me, on a young chap that gangs aboot the skies in a flying-machine. Ye'll hae been in ane o' them likely?"

"Yes, I've been in an aeroplane," said Amanda. "Only on short flights, though."

"Man! It maun hae been a wunnerfu' experience, up in the skies like ony bit bird," he said, his eyes keen with interest. "Were ye no' feared?"

"No, I don't think I was. It doesn't feel so very wonderful when you're a passenger—at least, it didn't to me, but I don't believe I'm air-minded," Amanda told him.

"Tae luik doon an' see the country like a map spread oot!" he marvelled. "Yer grandfaither wad never hae thocht it possible."

"Tell me about my grandfather and the old days," said Amanda. "I can just remember hearing my father talk of Staneyett when I was a very little girl. He spoke as if it were Paradise."

He gave a dry chuckle. "I wadna gang sae faur as that. It was a gey lanesome bit in the back-end o' winter, wi' the snaw lyin' deep; but it's a bonny place i' the simmer, an' hot eneuch forbye at the clippin' o' the sheep. Ye'll ken Staneyett? It lies in at the back o' Gledewaterheid yonder."

"Near Gledewaterford?" asked Amanda quickly.

"Ay, it mairched wi' Heriot o' Gledewaterford. That was anither o' the auld sort. Him an' yer grandfaither was chief."

"Surely my grandfather was much older than old Mr. Heriot?"

"Na, na. There wasna mair nor ten years atween the twa, if as mony. Heriot o' Gledewaterford mairret late in life, ye ken. Young Heriot'll no' be forty yet."

Amanda sat very still, letting the old man's voice run wandering on, hearing little of his reminiscences. Was it possible that she was going to get a clue to lead her to the source of Larry's trouble, so quickly, so easily, as this? Two days earlier she had been wondering hopelessly how she would ever find out, and now, by one of the coincidences which govern human affairs so much more than the so-called realists will admit, she had found someone who probably knew all about it. Even the matter-of-fact materialist has occasionally been jolted out of his rut by some happening beyond his experience, the most common form of which is the sudden mention, by a stranger, of a mutual friend or a subject in his mind at the moment. What causes these inexplicable happenings? Chance, perhaps, which is given the credit by the sceptic, and covers so much with comforting vagueness; or perhaps that wireless of the mind which sends out

urgent waves of thought to another in sympathy; Amanda, no sceptic, but no bigot either, was sitting in the Watsons' private room in
the 'Plough and Horses', opposite an old man of whose very existence she had been ignorant until that afternoon, who was babbling
freely of Larry Heriot and his sister Ruth. She could well believe
that it was telepathy, that her mind and heart, so full of Larry, had
communicated their need to Watson's father. . . .

"I'm an auld done man noo," he was saying. "Fair crippled wi'
the sciaticky, an' there's nane heeds me. Ma son Jone's a dacent
lad, an' ma guid-dochter's a kindly wumman, but they dinna heed
me. I hear them gaun on aboot 'puir Maister Heriot' that's drinkin'
himsel' silly, an' I could tell them baith whit's wrang wi' him, but
they'll no' heed me, I've juist tae haud ma tongue. Wild the Heriots
a' were, even the best o' them, but I never heard tell o' them drinkin'
mair than the lave. I mind Larry when he was a wee callant, toddlin'
aboot, an' yon wild hempie o' a sister o' his. The faither made a pet
o' her, but it wasna eneuch, she had aye tae be firrst wi' a' fowk,
an' that's no' guid for onybody. Whiles I think it mebbe turned her
head a bit, for she seemed tae me tae hae a *want*."

He paused to sigh and shift his aching bones in the well-cush-
ioned chair. Amanda, hardly daring to breathe, said very softly,
"Mr. Larry Heriot must have got into trouble of some sort to make
him drink like that, don't you think?"

"Think? Lassie, *I* ken," said the old man. "I ken, if nae ither body
does, an' I've never let on, a' these years. Let them that's sae dooms
clever at explainin' clash on. They'll never heed me, an' I'll no'
tell *them*. But I'm auld, an' I aye likit the lad, an' I'm ettlin' tae gie
ye a seein' that ye're a Carmichael, an' the leevin' image o' the auld
mistress, ye're fit tae be trusted. Mebbe Reiverslaw wad ken what
use tae mak' o' the information. . . . I'm no' yin tae speak ill o' the
deid, but yon Merren Hume, her that he got into trouble, was a bad
wumman. She wasna a silly lass that had slippit the ae time, ye ken.
There's a word in the Bible for her, but I'll no' fyle yer ears wi' mair
nor's needfu'. Mistress Carmichael"—Amanda realized that he had
forgotten who she was, he was speaking to her grandmother—"as
God's ma witness, yon wumman wad never hae drooned hersel' for
a wee thing like bein' disappointit o' a waddin' ring. She didna want

it. She wasna ettlin' tae get wed. The verra day afore she was fund in the Lily Loch abune Staneyett she tellt ma dochter Jessie, that's deid these ten years, that she never wantit tae mairry, no' if the King speired her. It's no' the likes o' *her* that kills theirsel's for shame."

"It—it certainly doesn't sound like suicide," murmured Amanda.

"It does not, an' I canna prove it wasna, but I ken as well as if I was staundin' by the waterside watchin'. I've been a lang, lang while thinkin' it a' oot, an' noo I ken. It wasna easy tae see what was the best, but I'll leave that same tae you, mistress. When ye come near the end o' yer days, ye whiles get a clearer sicht o' mony things that aince ye saw through a glass darkly."

"Then what happened? Did she just fall in?"

"I wadna say that. I wad say she was pushed in," he answered slowly but with no uncertainty in his voice.

"Oh no! No! Surely Larry never—"

"Wheesht noo. Whae's talkin' o' *him*? It was his sister did it. I tellt ye she was daft, an' I met her that nicht on my way doon aff the hill, comin' tearin' doon the path frae the Lily Loch like a mad thing. She never saw me, she was mutterin' in tae hersel', ay, an' lauchin' tae mak' yer blood rin cauld."

"Oh, but it's too horrible! She couldn't have done such a wicked thing!" cried Amanda. "Why, she wanted her brother to marry the girl, she told me he'd refused—it's so *wicked—*"

"If ye'd let me get feenishin' while I've the strength," he said testily. "There's plenty wickedness in the warld if ye ken whaur tae seek it, ay, an' in places ye'd mebbe no' expeck tae fin' it. Ma dochter Jessie was ben the hoose when I won hame. She was warkin' tae them at Gledewaterford, an' it was her day oot. It seems she heard a terrible row gaun on atween the twa o' them—the brither an' sister. Ye couldna help frae hearin' it, she said, for they were roarin' a' up an' doon the hoose, Miss Heriot at her brither tae mairry Merren Hume an' mak' an honest wumman o' her, an' him refusin'. He was richt eneuch, tae, for the Lord Himse' wad hae had a warstle tae dae that same. Syne, when she was hoarse wi' flytin' she begood tae threaten him, the warst thing she could dae wi' a stiff-necked lad as a' the Heriots aye were, tellin' him he'd be sorry if he didna, she'd shame him some ither way. He banged oot the hoose in the end, an' awa' doon tae Abbeyshiels, an' sma' blame tae him. If it hadna been her ain efternune oot, Jessie said she'd hae rin hersel' that meenit. I thocht mebbe he'd gane aff tae see Merren oot o' spite, but Jessie said na, that couldna be, seein' she'd met Merren awa' up tae the Lily Loch tae pu' white heather for luck.

"Weel, ye ken the luck she had. An' the neist day, what a tirravee! She hadna been hame that nicht, an' her drooned body was there in the loch, wi' a bit o' white heather in the ae haund, an' a wee bit cloath in the tither. It was me found her, an' I took awa' the bit tweed cloath. It was like a jacket I minded o' Maister Larry wearin', ye see. I didna ken at the time his sister had got the tailor tae mak' her a coat o' the same. . . . Some said she'd been bendin' doon tae see her face in the watter, for she was vain o' her luiks, or for a drink, an' had slippit in; an' some said the kelpie got her. It was Miss Heriot said she'd drooned hersel' the way Maister Larry wadna mairry her. But I ken better, an' noo I've tellt *ye*. Mebbe ye'll ken what tae dae, mistress. I'm an auld done man, an' I'm wearit noo. I'll bid ye guid-day, Mistress Carmichael."

His head drooped forward, he fell into the light doze of old age, and Amanda, her mind a whirl of horror, anger, relief, and sick disgust, stole out of the room and got to the car without meeting Watson.

Bawtie, sitting patiently beside it, gave vent to a long musical yawn, wagging his tail forgivingly and grinning up at her. She stooped and stroked his broad black head. "How much nicer dogs are than people," she said. "Oh, Bawtie, you don't know what dreadful things you miss. You don't have to be diseased with jealousy and repressions, and commit crimes for no other purpose than to make someone else wretched all their lives. What am I going to do about it, I wonder? Tell Larry . . . it can't help being a shock to him, even if it's a relief as well. To know that your sister hates you so badly that she'll murder someone so that she can have a hold over you. . . . How can he go on living with her after this? She ought to be shut up, she might try to kill him. . . . I wish I knew what to do!"

Bawtie was in no doubt as to what she ought to do next. "Home!" he said plainly, jumping up at the door of the car. *"Home!"*

"You're right. We'll go home and think it out," said Amanda, letting him in, following him, and driving slowly away.

When she got to Reiverslaw she could hear Jed at the telephone. "No, she's not in yet. What's that? It's you, is it, Watson? Your father? I'm sorry to hear that, man. He was a fine old fellow. There aren't many left like him."

He turned as Amanda came into the room.

"Watson of the 'Plough and Horses'," he said briefly. "He was afraid you might be upset. Were you in seeing his old father?"

"Yes," said Amanda, her eyes widening and darkening. "What—what's happened? He fell asleep while I was there, and I crept away, not to waken him. I thought he was so tired."

"You wouldn't have wakened him, Amanda. He died in his sleep, it must have been just after you left."

"Isn't it strange?" she murmured in a dazed manner.

"Strange? No, I don't think so. He was an old man."

"That's what he said—'an old done man'. But I meant it's strange that *always* something happens when I'm there. I must be an unlucky person, Jed, a storm-cock, just as Larry says. The poor old man, he was only just in time—"

"Look here, Amanda," said Jed, alarmed by her tone. "Do you feel bad? D'you want some brandy? Will I call Susan?"

"No, Jed, thank you, it's quite all right. I'm—I'm only so thankful that I did go and see him today. He had something rather—important to tell me, you see. It had been on his mind. I don't think he could have died in peace without telling it. He took me for my grandmother Carmichael. . . . It means a lot to me that I was the one to hear it."

CHAPTER TWELVE

I

LIKE a great many other people who set themselves to do something difficult, Amanda had found the hardest part of her self-imposed task quite easy of accomplishment. After racking her brain for a means of discovering the truth about Marion Hume's alleged suicide, and almost despairing, fortune, in the shape of old Watson the retired shepherd, had stepped in and handed her the whole story, dying immediately afterwards, so that she was the only person who knew.

It should have been the easiest thing in the world to see Larry and tell him, and yet she could not bring it about, even after overcoming her first scruples. She could not go to Gledewaterford when Ruth Heriot was at home, and equally she could not sneak there to lay information against her when she was out. To arrange to meet Larry, after they had taken leave of each other, would be to raise impossible hopes; naturally he did not come to Reiverslaw, and she could not ask Susan to invite him. It was a maddening impasse; perhaps she was being over-scrupulous, but she mistrusted her own judgment in this, and there was no one whose counsel she could take.

For several days, following on three patient weeks of waiting for news from South America, she had lived at the peak of nervous excitement, strung up by the scenes with Ruth Heriot and Larry, carried out of herself by her determination to lift his burden at least if she could not make him happy; the means had been put in her way by the old man whose peaceful death she had missed by minutes, if indeed he had not actually been dying when she left him, as she thought, asleep; and after that—nothing. As each idle day slipped away, she thought that she could not endure another.

"*Why* don't they cable me?" she burst out one morning to Jed, finding herself alone with him in the course of a chilly walk round the fields, with a cold wind whimpering in the hedges. "They left at the end of November, and it's nearly Christmas now! And their boat got in a week ago. Jed, what do you think has happened?"

""Well," he said slowly, after his usual pause for consideration, serious blue eyes fixed on the black bullocks gracing near at hand. "The only thing I can think of is that your husband is too ill for them to cable either way. The papers would get hold of it, and there'd be a stir, and maybe nothing really definite to go on, and you upset more than you need be. It's hard on you, Amanda, having to wait like this. We'll go in and see if the post's brought any word."

As they tramped back to the house through half-frozen tussocks of coarse grass left uneaten by fastidious cattle, Amanda said, trying to laugh, trying to speak lightly, "Even the weather doesn't seem to know what it wants to do! It keeps on trying to snow, and then nothing comes of it except a few flakes and a colder wind than ever."

"Makes you feel all strung-up. I know," he agreed, with a weather-wise glance at the leaden skies. "But there's snow coming, and it won't be long now. It can't hold off much longer."

Susan met them in the hall. "There's an air-mail letter for Amanda, from Brazil," she said quickly. "In the sitting-room." She motioned Jed to wait with her, but Amanda said at once, "No. You come too. I'd rather you were there when I read it, if you don't mind?'

The letter was from David, his round, unformed schoolboy scrawl had achieved two pages, a tremendous feat for him, whose pen was not that of a ready writer.

It was no good cabling (he wrote). *The old boy was too bad and I didn't want to raise your hopes for nothing. He's a lot better today and the Drs. said I could tell you he would live alright, but he can't talk yet and is all mufled up in bandadges with only his eyes showing and he's never opened them when I was with him. Your mother hasn't seen him yet. They say it's a miracle he's alive. The papers have got hold of the story of course. I hope they won't bother you to much. I've told them what I could.*

Yours,

David.

"You know," Susan said thoughtfully, after a short silence, "that's a very decent young man, Amanda. It's a pity he's so dull."

"The decent ones often are," Amanda murmured absently.

It was strange to think of Cocky lying with closed eyes unable to talk, all 'mufled up in bandadges' (poor David!). Cocky, whose abounding vitality had often made her feel exhausted and drained of energy, whose helplessness now roused in her a faint impersonal sympathy.

"It's taken almost a week for this letter to come," she said. "I may get a cable any day. I hope so. I should like some more definite news."

"The papers are definite enough, anyway," said Jed dryly, displaying a sheet with 'LLOYD COCHRANE FOUND' splashed across the top, and below, in slightly smaller capitals, 'Airman's wife, unable to travel, sends David White, wealthy amateur aviator and sportsman, to husband's bedside.' 'Lloyd Cochrane, whose attempt to set up a new record between England and South America narrowly missed success, is on the road to recovery in a Rio de Janeiro hospital, where his devoted friend David White identified him', said the second paper. 'TWENTIETH-CENTURY DAVID AND JONATHAN' was another headline.

"Good heavens!" said the astonished and indignant Amanda, throwing down the page which informed her that *the airman's blonde young wife'* was *'unable to leave this country for reasons of health'.* "They've made it sound as if I were going to have a baby! I see Mother's fine Italian hand sticking out all over this!"

Then the telephone rang, and having rung once, continued to ring. The airman's blonde young wife, having been tracked to her hiding-place by the indefatigable press, was asked in varying accents, both male and female, to give her exclusive story to whichever newspaper the voices represented. By mid-day Amanda, hoarse with saying, less politely every time, that she had nothing to tell them except that her health was excellent and she hoped to have her husband home soon, was talking in a desperate whisper of packing and going to Skye or the Faroes.

"I'm damned if I'll stand any more of this. We're all worn out," growled Jed. "I'll have the telephone disconnected."

"Heaven forbid!" wailed his wife. "They'll only come here in droves if you do that, and camp all round the house to waylay us."

"I'll shoot 'em if they do," he said, and he looked so capable of carrying out his threat that both Amanda and Susan gave a cry of alarm when they saw a man dismount from a bicycle at the door and ring the bell. Elspeth, entering with a note on a salver, found them clinging to Jed and imploring him to wait and see if it really was a reporter before filling him with small-shot.

"A note from Miss Pringle, madam. The man will wait for the answer," she said, and for the first time since meeting her Amanda's feelings towards Miss Pringle were not of dislike. They warmed almost to friendliness as Susan said in wondering tones:

"She wants us *all* to go to tea this afternoon! My dears, it's the olive-branch, it's a whole grove of olives. . . . Oh, Elspeth, you needn't wait. Take the man into the kitchen and give him some beer or what he likes. I'll ring for you when I have written to Miss Pringle." As Elspeth, concealing acute disappointment, faded from the room:

"Amanda, it couldn't have come at a more opportune moment, even if it *is* curiosity and the longing to entertain you because you're News today with a capital N! At least we'll have a rest from the telephone, so I'm going to accept, politely but no gush—you know. And, Jed, you must come too, she's asked you specially."

Jed, grumbling that he'd rather wait and have a pot at the journalists, was persuaded into accompanying them, and shortly after luncheon, a meal eaten furtively and with one eye on the window, and constant interruptions from the telephone, they left thankfully for Kaleford, Jed driving and casting many a wistful glance at every available scrap of cover where an enterprising newspaperman might conceivably be expected to lurk.

"Are you satisfied with your morning, Amanda?" he asked, as the car went slowly down a long, straight hill, which he habitually chose as a good place to take his hands from the wheel to light his pipe. "After grumbling to me because nothing had happened! I hope you feel pleased? I'd sooner have shawed an acre of turnips than gone on bawling into that telephone."

"It served me right for complaining," Amanda said meekly, finishing her remark with a sigh of relief as Susan quietly put her hand on the wheel from her place beside Jed, and saved the car from running into the ditch. "But I'm truly sorry that you and Susan had to suffer as well, poor innocents."

"I rather enjoy a little excitement," said Susan meaningly, as her lord, after two attempts, both of which failed, to get his pipe going, left the car to its own devices again and struck another match. Her hand had gone to the wheel automatically, and once more she steered it out of the ditch, on the other side this time, for their progress had described a series of stately curves all down the hill. "Though I must confess that after this morning I feel rather as if I'd been put through a mangle several times. This 'little outing', as Miss Pringle would call it, is a welcome relief."

"I'm glad you find it so," Amanda said with a shudder, as Jed, taking over the car, whirled them round the sharp bend at the bottom of the hill, announcing genially as he did so that he had once gone straight on through the hedge. "Your nerves must be much better than mine. I shall be thankful to arrive at the Miss Pringles'! By the way, what is the reason for her sudden change of heart? Just my notoriety? It's only a flash in the pan. Perhaps she is wise to take advantage of it at once."

"Her note said that she felt, after her sisters had gone to Glede-waterford, she ought to put things on a proper bearing and invite the Heriots to Kaleside, and to make a thorough job of it, she's asked all of us who were at tea at Reiverslaw, when Jed betrayed poor old Jelly and Cissy, to witness the formal reinstatement of Larry as a respectable member of society once more. Oh, it's an Occasion," said Susan. "Even when Miss Pringle has to climb down she must make capital out of it by doing in the grand manner. She will be in her element today."

"It'll fall a bit flat if the Heriots don't turn up." was Jed's comment. "I must say I'm damned if I see why they should go near her house. I'd refuse to if I were Larry. I'd like to see the letter she sent to them. It must be a masterpiece if it brings 'em."

Amanda shrank into the very corner of the car so that her reflection could not be seen in the driving-mirror, which Jed consistently kept at the wrong angle, by the two in front. She might see Larry. In a few minutes she might be looking at him, feeling the touch of his hand, speaking to him. . . . Cocky was as completely forgotten as her fear of loving a man, as her vow that never again would she think of one except with cool friendliness, or equally cool dislike. Such a wave of love for Larry, such a certainty that they were two of a kind, swept over her, that she was shaking from head to foot. In vain did reason whisper coldly that there was not the least likeli-hood of either Larry or his sister accepting Miss Pringle s invitation; Amanda, lost in dreams, refused to listen as she sat staring out at the passing landscape, quiet fields dun beneath dull skies, bare trees, colourless distant hills. She saw them all irradiated by an unearthly light, over-arched by a rainbow of transcendent bril-liance, loud with bird-song, gay with many flowers. Only as the car drove through Kaleford village and turned in at the entrance to Kaleside, did she waken with a shiver to reality, remembering that Cocky was alive and recovering, that Larry was bound by a promise to took after his sister, that her own interest in meeting him must be confined to the only thing she could ever do for him, to telling him old Watson's story.

"I believe Amanda's been asleep," said Jed complacently stopping the car with violence before the door. "It shows what a good driver I am over rough roads, whatever she likes to make out."

"Dumb with terror, afraid even to shriek, more likely," retorted Amanda, inwardly amazed at the toughness and resilience of the human heart, which might ache, or even break, if hearts do break, under cover of backchat and careless-sounding laughter, and no one be any the wiser.

Oliver and Peggy came up in the Squib just behind them, and they all went into the hall, through which drifted a faint but unpleasant composite odour of parrot, baking, and damp mackintosh. An astonishing number of persons, the majority of whom had been at the Gledewaterford sherry-party of awkward memory, was crammed into the small drawing-room, but neither Ruth Heriot nor her brother was among them. At the upright piano Miss Jelly was giving an emotional and inaccurate rendering of the first movement of the Moonlight Sonata, which was mercifully only audible in snatches during short lulls in the buzz of chatter. Her sisters, awe-inspiring in trailing robes of velveteen which put to shame their tweed-clad guests, moved about among them with a constant clashing of beads and bangles, unerringly separating persons who wanted to talk to each other and reforming the groups so that presently no one would talk at all, but stood in sulky silence waiting to be moved on once more.

"You know, Delly's a grand old girl," murmured Oliver, from the retired corner to which he had succeeded in leading Amanda. "Look at the ruthless way she's tearing 'em apart. Everyone expected to find her draped in sack-cloth and ashes, and instead she's in cracking form and doing what no other hostess would dare. There's only one snag, as far as I can see. The principal performers haven't shown up. No offence meant, I'm shaw!"

"And none taken, Commander Parsons," said Amanda amiably. "I didn't expect to be the star of the afternoon."

"Oh, but you will be," he told her encouragingly. "This is one of those all-star pictures, and as the airman's blonde young wife you—I say, Amanda, here's Larry, at any rate. never thought he'd come, did you?"

"I—I didn't know what he would do," murmured Amanda, above the suffocating beat of her heart. " Is Miss Heriot with him?"

"I don't see her. She wouldn't be likely to be, though. If she thought it would gratify the Pringles if she came, she'd stay away. Watch old Belly being gracious to the prodigal. Joy in heaven! Now he's been formally received back into the fold! What a joke. I thought she was going to imprint a chaste salute on his alabaster brow just then, didn't you? I say . . ." Turning, Oliver discovered that his companion had slipped away while he was absorbed in watching Miss Pringle greet the real reason for her party, and was no longer visible.

'Oh, lord!" he thought, rather uneasily. 'I quite forgot how she was mixed up in Larry's party and how vilely Ruth treated her. I hope she didn't think I was showing very bad taste. Or perhaps I was boring her, and I'm not sure that isn't worse. I must find Peggy and be reassured."

He made his way between the restless crowd in search of his wife; while Amanda, who had left him simply because she was in too prominent a position and did not want to catch Larry's eye right across the room—did not, indeed, want to speak to him at all under the raking fire of so many curious glances—was almost concealed by a heavy maroon curtain hanging over a doorway. It was a good place, she realized, for she had not the appearance of trying deliberately to efface herself; but again she had reckoned without her hostess, and just as she congratulated herself on having chosen an ideal skulking-ground, the door beside her, which she had innocently supposed led only to a cupboard, opened, the curtain was pulled aside, and she was confronted at these close quarters by Miss Pringle and Larry.

No believer in half-measures, and determined to show that she approved of both her embarrassed and angry victims, she now said in her most gracious manner, "I brought Mr. Heriot round this way, Mrs. Cochrane, as I know he won't want to waste any time in wishing you joy of your husband's *wonderful* recovery!" And, waving a large hand benevolently in the air over their heads, she swept on her devastating way, leaving them face to face in an oasis of quiet amid the noisy desert of the drawing-room. Though her remarks had been made as loudly as a public announcement from a platform, no one heard and as the entire party had quickly turned its back on the second door as soon as it saw her appear there, no one even saw the two who stood there so silently.

II

"Your—your sister didn't come with you?" asked Amanda, ridiculously nervous, for the sake of saying something.

"No."

"I—somehow I didn't expect you, either. This sort of thing is hardly in your line, is it?"

"Do you want to know why I came?" he asked directly, his voice hard.

"No," said Amanda, breathing fast. "No, I don't."

"I came partly out of spite," he said, smiling at her discomfiture. "Because Ruth made such a song and dance about my daring to show myself here. But that was just eye-wash, really. I came to see you. I never expected a chance of talking to you like this, but I had to see you."

"Yes," said Amanda, and suddenly remembered. "Larry, I've got something to tell you, but I can't possibly here. It would take too long, and we'll be certain to be interrupted any minute. It's important," she added desperately, for he hardly seemed to be listening.

"I'm afraid there isn't much hope, is there?" he said. "Must you tell me? Won't anyone else do?"

"Larry . . . !" she exclaimed, chilled by his lack of interest; but before she could continue, a body of women, led by Miss Cissy, rushed up to her, eager to hear *all* about her poor brave husband, and what it was like to be interviewed by the daily Press.

"Simply too terrible." Amanda answered the last question as being the easier. "Especially as I don't think they believe a word I say, and it will probably appear in a totally different version in the papers."

"*I* was interviewed once," Miss Cissy cried brightly, "but it was at a garden party, and a lady journalist asked me if I had been speaking to the Duchess, and I hadn't."

"So what happened?" someone asked tactlessly.

"Why, nothing, of course. But it was *most* interesting, though rather tiresome, just as Mrs. Cochrane says," answered Miss Cissy, associating herself with Amanda as one whom the Press clamoured to interview.

The afternoon dragged on somehow. At intervals Amanda got glimpses of Larry, handing tea and buns reminiscent of a Sunday-school treat; but he never came near her, and she had to find what consolation she could in the fact that he had not gone away early.

They were leaving at last, and still she had not told him, and this might be her only chance. Then Jed said casually, as they went down the steps, "I've asked Larry to look in on his way home, for a drink."

"That will be nice. Tve hardly spoken to him all afternoon," said Susan. "What about Peggy and Oliver?"

"I thought they'd gone. No, there's Oliver." Jed nodded towards a limping figure approaching them, lighted by the wayward beams of a car, backing and filling in the congested space. Just as he reached them, Larry came up to ask:

"Does any of you want a lift?'

"I don't think so, Larry," Susan was beginning, when Oliver said hastily:

"Yes, we do. The Squib's let us down, won't start, blast her. There's something gone wrong with the mag. Peggy and I will have to be taken as far as Reiverslaw, Jed, where I'll ring up for a man to tow her to Abbeyshiels. We don't want to stay *here*."

"Well, Amanda, what about coming with me?' Larry suggested carelessly; and as carelessly she said:

"I suppose I might as well. There won't be much room in Jed's car."

Sitting beside him, shut into the narrow darkness so close that her arm brushed his, they were more alone than they had been before. Jed passed them, his lights died away along the road, and there was nothing in the world but the cold windy evening, and two people in a car. Larry drove fast and silently for a mile or two, then, drawing into the side, where the County Council had considerately left a space to accommodate spare road-metal, he stopped, turned to her and said:

"Now you'd better tell me—whatever it is you want to. We'll never get a better chance than this."

Amanda drew a deep breath. Stumblingly at first, but gaining eloquence as she went on, she told her story without interruption. He sat like a man in a trance, and even after she had ended, there was silence for a second before he said;

"*You* did this—for me?"

"There was nothing else I could do for you," said Amanda, trying to keep her voice steady. "Can't you see I wanted to do something? And, after all, it only meant listening to an old man talking. It was so easy, and I'd almost hoped it would be difficult—just to satisfy my conceit, of course!" She finished on a broken laugh.

"You did it. That's what matters."

"Larry! It matters far more than that. It clears you, and you're free. Is that nothing?"

"Not so long ago," he said, slowly and heavily, "it would have been the biggest thing that could have happened to me. But now—are you blind or silly? *You* ought to know why it hardly matters—now—Mandy . . ."

His tone, the pet name which no one had ever used before, by which he must have been in the habit of thinking of her, were too much for Amanda's composure. She gave a sob, and hearing it, he turned and caught her in his arms.

"Nothing matters to me but you, and you say you're going back to that rotten hound of a husband," he muttered savagely. "I'm damned if you shall, Mandy—Mandy. . . ."

For a moment of exquisite pain and delight, sword-sharp, her head rested against the hard strength of his shoulder, his lips were on hers. If one could die like this, or the world end now! But the world went steadily on its course round the sun, and she gathered courage to push him gently away.

"Don't, Larry, my darling. Please. It only makes it so much harder—"

"I won't give you up," he said again. "You belong to me, don't you? Aren't we two of a kind? What has he done to have you back? Do you expect me to let you go—to the power of the dog?"

"He happens to be my husband," she said.

"You were going to divorce him before."

"It was different then. I didn't care what became of me. Now—can't you see, Larry, that he'd always be between us? And it isn't only Cocky. There's—your sister."

"Ruth! My God! I'd forgotten her!" he said, with a groan. "It makes me sick to think of her; and I've got to go back to Glede-waterford and sit at table with her, live under the same roof with her, until one of us dies."

"It's far harder for you than for me, poor Larry," said Amanda, weeping.

"That's as it should be. I'm a man, and anyway, I deserve most of it."

"But you'll never have to feel that awful weight on your conscience any more. What she says to you will mean so little, now that you know . . ." Then a thought struck her. She put out her hand to touch his sleeve, almost timidly. "Larry, you'll be careful, you know what a temper you have. You—you won't quarrel with her?"

"There's no sense in quarrelling or losing your temper with a mad woman," he said wearily. "I've always just let her rave on, and I won't stop her now. I thought you were going to ask me to stop drinking. Most women would have grabbed at the chance of getting a man to do something in return for what they'd done for him."

"It seems too mean to take advantage, and I was never meant for a reformer," said Amanda.

"I've knocked it off already. I never enjoyed making a senseless brute of myself," he told her gruffly, taking her hand in his, crushing her fingers unconsciously. "It was just to get a little peace."

"I know."

"So we're sunk, and there's nothing to be done about us, is there? We've got to go on."

"We're *both* sunk, though, remember."

"Poor comfort, to know that you're unhappy as well as myself," he said. "But I'm far too selfish to want you to be happy with him. Maybe I'll come to a better frame of mind later on. . . . I'll need to take you back to Reiverslaw now, Amanda, or they'll think we've crashed in a ditch. Tell Susan I had to get on, would you? I can't come in and drink and talk to them tonight."

He dropped her at the gate, after a silent run; his only farewell was to hold her hand to his cheek for an instant before he drove on. As Amanda went stumbling and faltering along the drive like an old woman, the snow began to fall in a steady purposeful manner as if, this time, it meant to lie.

"Where are Oliver and Peggy?" she asked, struck by the silence of the sitting-room.

"They walked home, Amanda," said Susan.

"Have we been so long? I didn't know." Indeed, she had no idea of how much time had passed since she and Larry had left Kaleside. It might have been years or minutes.

"No. We've only been in about twenty minutes." This was Jed at his gruffest, and Amanda looked at him.

"Something's happened. I hope you haven't shot a reporter?" she asked, with a nervous attempt at lightness.

"Amanda dear, there was a cable, sent to Jed. I'm sorry, but—but your husband—Cocky is dead," said Susan.

"Dead. Cocky—dead," said Amanda wonderingly. "It doesn't seem possible, somehow. I never thought he would be dead. Poor Cocky, he will hate it. He was so fond of life, you see." Then, rousing herself: "But David said he was getting better. The doctors said he would live!"

"There's been a mistake in identity all along, Amanda," said Jed, clearing his throat, and preparing to make a statement of more than one sentence. "If young White had seen this fellow in hospital without all his bandages, he'd have known at once that it wasn't Cochrane. The man had your husband's papers and things, and was too ill to say anything, so they all took him for the missing airman. It was natural enough."

"Then we're back where we were a month ago?" Amanda, deadly pale, spoke quite steadily. "And Cocky hasn't been found yet?"

"Yes, he was found by this fellow in the hospital. He was dying, gave all his things to this man, who saw him buried, and then, on his way to Rio with the news, got badly smashed up somehow, and was brought in by native porters with such a garbled tale that the hospital authorities got hopelessly mixed. White's sending you the details, of course, and your mother'll be writing for certain." He stopped speaking, not knowing what else there was to say. "And that's all," he added helplessly. "Have a drink, Amanda? You need one." He left the room, thankful for an excuse to get away decently and without the appearance of craven flight.

Susan looked at Amanda, then went to her and put her arm about the slight drooping figure. "You don't need to pretend, Amanda," she said gently. "I guessed how you felt, long ago. And I only want to say that your husband died as an airman should, on a flight, before he got too old to fly and had to spend tbe rest of his time on the dull earth."

Amanda's tears began to run down her white cheeks, washing away the bitterness which had never been absent from her thoughts of Cocky. "It seems so terrible," she said brokenly, "that I'm not sorrier about him. But I know that if he'd come back, poor Cocky, he'd have been just the same, just as bad as ever. And he used to say he'd die in the air, when he had to die. Poor Cocky. David will be so dreadfully cut up about him!"

Poor Cocky indeed, thought Susan, whose wife's tears were mainly of relief and pity, whose only real mourner was his friend. And yet, perhaps, all things considered, fortunate Cocky—for all his failings had not alienated faithful, stupid David.

III

All that night the snow fell, and morning saw the countryside shrouded in white, lighted by the strange eerie glimmer, blue-grey like faded mother-of-pearl, which the snow reflects back again to grey skies.

"We're going to have a bad fall," said Jed after breakfast, experienced anxious eyes searching the sky for weather-signs. "We'll need to get the beasts into the closes as soon as we can."

He tramped out, pausing only to tap the barometer hanging in the hall, and went off towards the steading. Susan and Amanda were left to wander aimlessly about the warm sitting-room, filled with the foreboding and uneasiness which threatens even human beings as well as the wiser animals, before a coming storm.

"I must write letters," Amanda said at last, sitting down resolutely at the desk. "They'll have to be done sometime, and it's never any use putting it off."

"Are there many? I wish I could help, but this is the kind of thing that no one else can do for you."

"No, not many. Cocky's parents are dead, and he was an only child of only children. He was the most relationless person I've ever met. It was always rather a boast of his," said Amanda. "I shall have to write to Mother and David, and the lawyer, and one or two flying people, and notices for the papers. That's all. It won't take me long, and I'm getting off very lightly, Susan. No funeral, no hordes of distressed relatives to contend with—and pretend to— even Mother at a safe distance. None of the conventional trappings of death. Even if we have a memorial service for his friends, it can't be until David and Mother come back. Am I an unfeeling monster to discuss this so calmly? It is an unspeakable relief to be able to talk about it openly to you at last. I only kept it from you because I was afraid you'd be distressed."

"I know. I understand, " said Susan. "There isn't anyone to be shocked because you can't feel as if your life had come to an end with his death. Have you thought at all what you are going to do with yourself?"

"Only that I'm not going to live with Mother. I can't help it if she is hurt. I shall have to get a job as soon as Mr. Makepeace's book is typed, and it is very nearly finished now."

"Don't be in too much of a hurry to leave us. We should miss you very much, Jed and I. And now I'm going to see cook, and you can write your letters in peace."

For an hour Amanda's pen moved swiftly over the paper. She found it unexpectedly easy to write except to David, and on his letter she spent much trouble. It was due to him that she should not spoil his innocent faith in Cocky by any hint of coldness or relief. Cocky was dead: let him remain, to this one friend at least, a flashing figure of gallantry and gaiety. She was sealing the last envelope when Elspeth brought in the mail.

"If you please, madam," she said decorously, but subtly conveying her knowledge of events by a tone of muted sympathy, "the postman said he would wait for any important letters you want sent off. He says there will be a storm, and if the roads are blocked, you might not get them away after today."

"Thank you, Elspeth. That was very thoughtful of the postman—and you, because I'm sure it was your idea to ask me. Will you give him these, please? And I want the two South American ones to go by air-mail."

Dismissed with a smile, feeling as though she were taking part in a deliciously sad film, Elspeth tripped out. The cinema was almost her only weakness, but she had cultivated a taste for it which had become a passion. Now, as she handed Amanda's letters and instructions to the patiently waiting postman, she compared their writer to Greta Garbo, Norma Shearer, and Joan Crawford, her three prime favourites—to none of whom Amanda bore the slightest resemblance in any way. It was, however, a harmless foible; Amanda never knew what honour had been done her, and Elspeth floated through the day's work, in a mellowing haze of tragic romance which amply compensated her for the loss of her prosaic and singularly un-Clark-Gable-like young man,

"Amanda," said Susan in a worried manner, seeing that the letters had been written, "do you think it would be any easier to *sew* things for this wretched baby? If it has to depend on what I can knit for it, there won't be any wardrobe for it on arrival. There's no blinking facts any longer. I simply and plainly can *not* knit."

"I don't know." Amanda was doubtful. "There must be some things that can be sewn—dresses and such, but the others almost have to be knitted, wouldn't you think?"

"Then Jed must do it. After all, he's the child's father, or will be. I shall set him down with a ball of wool, a pair of needles, and a book of instructions this very day, and see what *he* makes of our old friends 'k. tog.' and 'w. fwd.'" said Susan, with finality.

Amanda laughed. "It will be a most inspiring sight, Jed knitting," she said. "But you're remembering that he's liable to fling the whole affair into the fire if you provoke him, aren't you?"

"The fire, in my opinion," Susan said darkly, "is the only place for it. Amanda, do you remember in *The Virginian* where they're baiting the wretched Baldy with having knitted a pair of slippers for the schoolmarm? How does it go?" She turned to the nearest book-case, picked out a rather battered red volume and flipped over the pages rapidly. "Here it is. I knew it was a pearl. . . . 'Baldy, yu' know, he can stay on a tame horse most as well as the schoolmarm. But just you give him a pair of young knittin'-needles and see him make 'em sweat!'"

"I'm very sorry," said Amanda gravely. "But my imagination totally refuses to see Jed making any knitting-needle sweat, or vice versa. Does yours?"

"No. Not really," Susan agreed reluctantly. "Another beautiful idea wasted. If the baby is a boy, he shall be taught to knit immediately; and then, instead of lisping hymns or something equally useless and priggish at an incredibly early age, he'll make all his mother's pull-overs."

"And if it's a girl?"

"I'll leave her to Jed to bring up. Jed would be an education in himself for any girl. . . . Amanda, where *is* Jed? The wind's risen, and it's beginning to snow again."

Amanda followed her to the window, where they both stood looking out at a dazzling whirling dance of snowflakes blown to and fro by a vicious wind. Snow already on the ground rose in clouds to meet the fresh fall, until the whole world was blotted out in the storm of tiny white particles which could so quickly transform it to a ghostly landscape of black and white and grey. A dim figure, looming even larger than life, came staggering round the corner of the house to the door, and Susan said with a sigh of relief, "Here he is at last!"

Jed came in on a blast of icy air and a scud of following snow, which seemed loath to lose a possible victim; he and Bawtie, who was at his heels, were covered with the soft powdery stuff, clinging to Jed's moustache and eyebrows as well as his rough tweed coat, caked on Bawtie's feet and hanging in hardened lumps from the woolly hair of flanks and belly.

"God, what a morning!" said Jed, as he and the dog shook themselves and raised a miniature snowstorm in the hall. "We've got them all in, and only just in time, too, by the look of things. I wouldn't like to be on the hills today."

"Look at Bawtie. He's like one of those old-fashioned draperies on a mantelpiece, with rows of bobbles hanging down," said Amanda, stooping to pull one of the 'bobbles' off, a kindness rewarded by Bawtie with a yell of agony.

"Let the poor beast alone, and they'll melt," said Jed. "If he sits in front of the fire he'll soon thaw."

The truth of this statement was discovered all too soon, for Bawtie, thawing, left large dirty pools of half-melted snow all over the sitting-room carpet.

"The *wee* man!" murmured Susan resignedly, as she fetched a cloth, while the culprit did his best to help by eating the solid portions encrusted with his own fur, crunching and smacking over them as if they were peculiarly choice tit-bits.

The weather grew steadily worse, the wind blew from all points of the compass at once it seemed, the barometer fell below 'stormy', and every window was plastered thick with furiously driven snow. By the middle of the afternoon lights were needed, and they settled down beside a fire heaped high with coal and logs in the yellow lamplight. Susan doggedly began to knit, Jed pored over his cross-word, Amanda brought down the last chapter of Mr. Makepeace's reminiscences to look through for possible mistakes in typing. In the warm kitchen, cook triumphantly cut a large plateful of superlative Swiss milk 'tablet' into neat squares, arranged half of them in a silver dish, and invited Elspeth to take it to the sitting-room.

"Cook thought, madam, that you might fancy a piece of her tablet as it is such a bad day," said Elspeth, breaking on the rather dismal quiet like a sudden sunbeam—the resemblance of course, as Susan hastily added later on, making this picturesque simile, being due solely to the contents of the dish which she set conveniently near at hand on a small table.

"Thank cook, Elspeth, and tell her she's saved our lives from death by boredom," called Susan dramatically, a message transmitted by Elspeth as 'the mistress was real pleased to have it, cook', while she elegantly accepted a bit of the dainty herself from the kitchen dish.

After a short burst of spasmodic comment on the weather, the occupants of the sitting-room relapsed into silence, this time cheerfully broken by a gentle rhythmic crunching. Time passed pleasantly to the click of knitting-needles, the soft rustle of turned pages, the crackle of the fire; and the telephone, trilling suddenly, made them all start. In that quiet lighted room, with the world outside cut off by the soft relentless snow that blotted thickly against the panes, the sound was almost shocking. Susan dropped her knitting, and several stitches promptly slid off the needle; Amanda was sitting bolt upright in an instant, thinking, 'It's news of Cocky', before she could remember that there would be no news of Cocky any more. Jed, the least perturbed, got up slowly, growling in duet with Bawtie, who had been as startled as his human belongings.

"Infernal din that thing makes. I don't know why the devil they have to have such a brute of a bell."

"Because they know that unless its voice was so revolting that you couldn't bear to let it go on ringing, people like you would never answer it at all," suggested Amanda.

Susan, picking up her work, merely uttered a wailing cry. "Six, no, *seven* stitches lost for ever, and they've left a thing like a ladder behind!"

"Hullo," growled Jed, lifting the receiver. It was evidently a call from no great distance, and he never held the receiver close enough to his ear, so the others could hear the answering:

"Hullo. That you, Jed?"

Amanda stiffened. Her hands, tightening unconsciously on the typed sheets which she held, crumpled them past repairing. It was Larry who was speaking, in a voice loud with urgency.

"Is Ruth at Reiverslaw by any chance, Jed?"

"Ruth? Good God, Larry, look at the weather!" said Jed reasonably. "Of course she's not here."

There was an inarticulate sound at the other end, and Jed's own voice had sharpened when next he spoke. "You don't mean she's really out in this, Larry? What's that? Gone since before lunch? Well, man, don't worry yourself. She's got storm-bound somewhere, that's all. You'll not get her back to Gledewaterford today, though. Aren't you pretty well snowed up?"

The two women, still seated in comfortable chairs by the fire, turned wide eyes, from which all appreciation of that comfort had fled, on each other. "Ruth . . ." murmured Susan. "And she's as mad as a hatter. She might have gone anywhere. Weather wouldn't stop her if she wanted to go out."

Amanda said nothing, but listened with straining ears to Jed; she could no longer hear Larry's voice at all.

"I can't make it out." Jed was both puzzled and worried now. "We've been cut off. Where's that rotten exchange? Why the hell don't they answer?" There was a pause, during which he violently jiggled the receiver-rest up and down. At last: "Here, exchange! You've cut us off. Gledewaterford was on the line. Connect us again, will you?"

"Ay'm sorray, Mr. Armstrong," came exchange's clearly heard imperturbable tones, infinitely refined. "Ay'm afrayd there is no connection to the Gledewaterhead laynes. Thayre exchange doesn't annswer. The snow must hev brot down the laynes, We were expecting this, Sorray."

Jed, pausing to hurl the receiver down, came stalking over to the fire again, his weather-beaten face set and anxious. "I don't know what to make of it," he said heavily. "You heard some of it, didn't you? Larry was shouting, poor devil. He's rung up every place he could get where he thought she might have gone, but drew a blank each time. This was his last hope. God knows where she is, or what we can do. I can get the men, and we'll have a look round about the place, but it'll have drifted deep by now, and we'll not get far."

Susan started to say something, bit her lip, and started again more mildly. "You'll be careful, Jed? You won't go far?"

"We'll not be able to, I tell you." He took her face very gently between his big hands. "I'll be careful, lass," he said.

Amanda looked away, towards the windows which let not a hint of dying daylight in through their snow-crusted glass. When Jed, muffled in great-coat and scarf, his cap pulled down to his eyebrows, went to the door, she was close behind him, peering out as he opened it, only to draw back with a cry of alarmed surprise. Howling wind, dancing swirling devils of snow which cut the skin they touched . . . there was no sky, no earth, nothing but this wild waste, confusing the senses, blurring sight and hearing.

"Oh, Jed, *don't* go out!" Accustomed only to snowstorms in a town, she was frankly frightened. "It will worry Susan so—and how do you know Ruth Heriot ever came this way? I don't believe she would. Did Larry say she was walking? How could she get all this way with snow on the ground?"

"I'll only go up to the steading and the cottages," he promised. "In case one of the men has seen her. But of course, if she was walking, she must be much nearer home. You go in now, Amanda, or you'll catch cold."

He was not gone long, but the minutes seemed like hours to the two left in the house. Susan sat very quiet, knitting with a sort of steady ferocity, her eyes on it as if it required intense concentration.

"She couldn't be here, you know," Amanda said suddenly, in an argumentative tone. "For one thing, it's the last place she'd come to, because of me. And she must have been walking—"

"Why must she?" Susan asked, without looking up.

"Because Larry didn't say anything about the car or a horse, did he? Not that she could have been riding today."

"No, but he seemed to expect her to have got as far as this."

"Didn't he tell Jed that this was his last hope?"

"Amanda, so he did! How comforting of you to think of it. And you take it to mean that he'd tried all the nearer places first," said Susan, laying down her knitting at last, and staring at Amanda.

"Of course. I may be quite wrong, but that's what I thought," she answered.

"Then she may quite well be in one of the cottages not far from Gledewaterford? Oh, I hope that's the solution! They aren't on the telephone. She's probably in the shepherd's house, there or at Staneyett."

It was Amanda's turn to say nothing. She could not help thinking that Larry would have gone himself to every house within reach before he started to ring up, but there was no need to add to Susan's worry by these fears. And when Jed came in, worn out with struggling even the short distance to the cottages, and soaked to the skin, she still avoided saying a word which might betray her own alarm.

"I walked into a drift up to my neck. It's level with the top of the hedges just a little along the road," said Jed. "We're snowed up, and you'll have to make the best of it. Let's have some wireless to cheer us up."

"Wireless!" said Amanda. "Do you know, I'd forgotten, actually forgotten, that such a thing had ever been invented? This afternoon we seem to have taken a long step backwards in time."

"Yes, I feel the same," said Susan, as the radio burst into light music, provided by some hotel orchestra for its tea-time patrons. "It's odd to think that people are sitting listening to that at Bournemouth, or wherever it is, and if there's any snow, it won't be more than can be swept up off the streets quite quickly and easily. Jed, stop fiddling with the knobs and go and change *at once*."

Jed, unnaturally obedient, nodded and went upstairs, and Elspeth came in with the tea-table.

"Thank heaven we aren't cut off from civilization's cosiest blessing," said Susan devoutly, as she made the tea. But though they all talked and pressed one another to eat, it was noticeable that the only unspoiled appetite belonged to Bawtie who found himself plied with delicacies normally withheld or only given him in tiny pieces, to an almost embarrassing degree.

"How can we be expected to feel hungry?" said Amanda defiantly to no one in particular, as if answering an awkward question. "We haven't been out all day, and we made pigs of ourselves on cook's tablet!"

"Of course. I knew there was a reason for this feeling of repletion." Susan, snatching at the excuse, looked gratefully at her.

The evening dragged on endlessly. They dressed slowly and carefully for dinner, made a pretence of eating it, returned to the sitting-room to drink coffee thirstily.

"What about a hand at cut-throat?" Jed suggested, and although it was a form of bridge abhorred by all of them, they played it with feverish intensity until they could bear it no longer.

"It must be late," said Susan at last. "What time is it? Quarter past *nine*? Nonsense, Jed, the clock has stopped."

But the clock was ticking placidly on, unmoved by weather or human fear and feelings.

At twenty to ten Jed went to the telephone. "I'm going to try to get Larry again. The line may not be down at all. Those lazy devils in Abbeyshiels will say anything to save themselves trouble."

"Oh, do, Jed!" implored his wife, who usually listened to his attacks on the exchange with ill-concealed disapproval. He lifted the receiver, listened with a queer look on his face, then replaced it quite gently. "No good. We've gone down too," he said.

When they went to bed, weary but far from drowsy, at the early hour of half past ten, the snow had stopped falling, and stars were shining coldly out of a polished dark sky on a world so deeply blanketed in cruelly glittering, whiteness that every inequality in the ground was smoothed out. Amanda, tossing miserably between her warm blankets and glossy lavender-sweet linen sheets, could not sleep. They were safe in the house, Susan had Jed at her side, where she only needed to stretch out a hand to touch him; but Larry must go on searching, if he had not already found her, for the sister who hated him.

IV

Two more days, leaden-footed, crept by, without news of their own little world—although the wireless kept them needlessly informed of villages isolated by the snow-storm which had swept Scotland and northern England, and of a terrible railway accident in the blizzard—without letters, without the telephone, whose bell they had so often cursed, which mocked them now by its silence. They could go out along narrow paths dug, one shovel-wide, through two feet of snow, as far as the steading and a few yards beyond it; but until the overworked snow-ploughs could clear the road, they were entirely cut off. Children, unable to get to school, rejoiced in the unexpected holiday and celebrated it by making a snowman of such noble proportions that his diminishing body, crowned by an ancient Balmoral bonnet which sank nearer the ground every day, still stood by the roadside as a memorial a week after the snow had disappeared from the fields around. Two more wakeful nights, haunted by ghastly details of the railway crash, followed the weary days; but on the third morning Robinia, bringing Amanda's tea to her bedside, announced cheerfully, "The snowplough's awa' alang the road this meenit!"

"Oh!" Amanda sat up. "Then we can get out, and the post can come!"

"Ay, the post can come, but he'll be late," warned Robinia. "The roads'll be heavy, ye ken, an' he'll need tae stop an' gie a' the news on the way."

The post was very late indeed. It was afternoon and they were all growing irritable with strain by the time he arrived, laden with mail and three days' newspapers, one of which bore the brief announcement of Cocky's death. He lingered in the kitchen, regaled by powerful tea and cook's best fruit cake while he told a tale of minor disasters, telephone wires down all over the country and fallen trees. Besides these there were graver results of the storm: sheep had been lost by the hundred, and as well as the death-roll of several accidents, at least one human life had been taken by the snow nearer home for Miss Heriot of Gledewaterford, after a desperate day-and-night search by her brother and every man whom he could collect, had been found frozen stiff in a deep drift up in the hills above her own house. It was Elspeth, swelling with importance, who carried this news to the sitting-room, where it was received in utter silence.

"Stunned with horror, cook," she reported pleasurably, "And Mrs. Cochrane, poor thing, as white as the snow itself. What with all the shocks she's had and her husband's death in the paper and all, I wouldn't wonder if she ended with a nervous breakdown."

Cook, sympathetic, and not wishing to be out of things, prescribed tea at once, "for the mistress, in her state, would be the better of a wee stimulant, an' there's nothing like a nice cup o' tea, Elspeth."

"What for are they in a state aboot yon Miss Heriot?" Robinia wanted to know. "I wad hae run a mile tae get oot her road!"

"Whisht, Robinia," said cook severely. "An' dinna talk that way. Ye may say things ye might live to regret. It's ill work speakin' against them that's dead."

This admirable sentiment prevailed in the sitting-room, where Jed contented himself with saying, "Well, poor thing, she didn't do much good to herself or anyone else in her life."

"Poor Ruth!" murmured Susan.

Amanda said nothing at all. She was thinking of Larry alone in that haunted house, with his sister lying dead, almost unregretted, and wishing that she could see him to comfort him.

"I ought to go to the funeral," Susan said, two days later. "I know it isn't considered necessary for a woman to go, Jed, but the poor thing had so few friends, and she didn't hate me."

"You'll not go a step in this cold," Jed answered flatly, "if I have to lock you up to keep you here. I'm going, and that will have to do."

Then Amanda summoned all her resolution. "I know what Susan means," she said. "And though she *did* hate me, I'll go to Ruth Heriot's funeral instead of Susan—if it wouldn't look strange."

"Bless you, Amanda! Whatever it looks like, it would be kind," said Susan. "I can't bear to think of her—so unloved, so unliked, even—going to her grave without a woman to follow her. It may be ridiculous, Jed, but I'm licensed to be ridiculous and unreasonable just now, and it will haunt me if you don't let Amanda go as my deputy."

So Amanda went, to stand with the small group of sombrely clad people whose black clothes and the dark earth of the open grave marred the brilliant purity of the little kirkyard of Gledewaterhead, listening to the solemn words echoing through the bleak air, hoping that Ruth Heriot's hatred had died with her, and that the wild mad spirit would find rest.

The Misses Pringle, red-nosed and pinched and oddly subdued, were there also, and came up to speak to her afterwards while Jed was talking apart with Larry.

"Mrs. Cochrane, it was *noble* of you to come," said Miss Pringle, in a hushed voice. "After what the girls told me that—"

"Oh, please, Miss Pringle! Let that be forgotten. It's the only thing we can do for her," said Amanda, distressed. "I really didn't come here to flaunt my nobility. I don't feel noble at all, only thankful to be alive!" And for once Miss Pringle was silenced, and went away discomfited and strangely ill at ease with herself, a state of mind so rare that she bullied her sisters without mercy throughout the rest of the day to restore her confidence.

V

"Jed has asked me to come back to Reiverslaw with you. Do you mind?" said Larry, leaning in at the car window, where she had gone to wait.

"Mind? Of course not," Amanda said, shaken out of her composure by his nearness, taking in every detail of his face seeing the lines graven there by bitter years, the grey hair at his temples, seeing his haunted eyes peaceful at last, though very tired.

"I'd like to tell you about it. You're the only one who knows what she did—that time, long ago," he went on, very low. "If I could tell you, and then it can all be forgotten."

"Of course," repeated Amanda, unable to say more, knowing that the stilted condolences which he had received from others must only sound false if she spoke them.

At Reiverslaw, welcomed by Susan with her grave cordiality, he sank into a deep chair and sighed gratefully. "This is a peaceful place," he said. "It was good of you to have me, Susan. Jed gave me your message."

"My dear Larry! Aren't we your friends? You know I'd have been there this afternoon if Jed hadn't asserted himself; but Amanda went for me—"

"Amanda. Yes—yes, of course. . . ." Neither of them, Amanda thought, sitting silent in her favourite corner of the sofa, seemed able to say anything but 'Of course', this afternoon!

Tea was brought, and as soon as it was over, Susan said to her husband, in a tone which brooked no denial, "Jed, I want you to come and look at—at a hole in the pantry. Elspeth says there's a mouse."

Jed, bewildered, for she was not in the habit of bothering him with such trivial household cares as mice or their problematical holes, followed her meekly from the room, and silence lay heavy over the two who sat there as if tongue-tied.

"She was found on the path that goes up to the Lily Loch, you know," Larry said suddenly. "All the evening before, she'd been worse than usual. She was furious with me for going to the Pringles' tea-fight, and when I got back she started telling me I'd have to marry that girl, as if the years had gone back. I could do nothing to stop her, I just had to let her rave. . . . And, then, next day, she went out like that. Amanda, she must have forgotten that it happened fifteen years ago. She went out into the snow to—to do it all over again, to push Marion Hume into the water again." His voice shook uncontrollably, and Amanda, leaving her corner, came swiftly to sit close by him on a low stool.

"Don't, Larry. Don't look back. She was—stopped in time, this time. Who knows that she hadn't thought better of it? We can't tell now. She may have gone thinking in her poor muddled mind that she could save the girl."

"No one but you would have thought of that," he muttered. "It's like you. And when I saw you there, this afternoon, after the way she treated you—"

"Don't," said Amanda again. "It's over now, and you are free, and so is she. Think of that, instead."

"The trouble is, I don't know quite what to do with my freedom," he said, with a painful smile. "I don't want to bother you by dragging it all up again, but I told you it meant very little to me now."

And with a curious contraction of the heart, Amanda realized that he still thought Cocky was alive. She got up, went over to the fire, and playing with Jed's pipe, which he had left on the mantelpiece, said, her back turned to him;

"Larry, Cocky is dead. I'm—I'm free, too."

"Mandy!" he said uncertainly, and repeated it as if to give himself heart. "Mandy!" This time hope rang in his voice. He was beside her, he had turned her to face him, his eyes blazing. "You mean it? You're sure?"

"Quite sure, Larry."

"You won't mind giving up your freedom to marry me? You know what I'm like, and that you'll have to live at Gledewaterford? God, how can I ask you to come to that haunted place?"

"I know you. You've got a horrible temper, and a neglected house," she said. tears and laughter struggling for mastery. "But it won't be haunted any more. The trouble with me, you see, Larry, is that I love you."

He took her into his arms, and there was no more need of words.

VI

I don't know what Mother will say about this, my getting engaged so soon," said Amanda, but she did not sound at all distressed.

A fortnight had slipped away, taking Christmas and New Year with it, bringing a letter from David White, but no word from Mrs. Carmichael since the garbled cable which had reached her daughter three days after the great snow-storm.

"It won't bother you very much, seemingly," was Jed's comment, but his teasing grin was friendly.

"I wonder what Miss Pringle will have to say," said Susan, who was sitting in the window-seat, and now ended her remark with a faint moan: "Talk of the devil . . . !"

An angular form on a bicycle moved jerkily towards the house, large feet in sensible shoes pressing the pedals as if to show that they would stand no nonsense from them, and a few moments later Elspeth announced, "Miss Pringle."

"You're just in time for tea," observed Jed, rising not too willingly to greet the uninvited but never wholly unexpected guest.

"I am so lucky to find you at home," said Miss Pringle, who brought into the room with her a miasmic blast of eucalyptus oil. "*Both* the girls are confined to the house with bad colds, and I felt I wanted a change of air and society. I passed Commander Parsons and little Peggy on the road. Do you suppose *they* can be coming here, too?"

"More than likely," said Jed. "You're not the only one who comes looking for a free tea."

"Jed!" said his wife, but fortunately Miss Pringle decided to take it as a joke and laughed gaily.

"How amusing of you, Mr. Armstrong! I always say to the girls that marriage has done such a lot for you, not that you weren't always very, very *jolly* and *cheery*, but nowadays you have quite blossomed out!"

'That's one for Jed!' thought Amanda, stifling laughter with difficulty.

"Now, if only poor Larry Heriot could find a nice little wife, I think *everyone* would be pleased, don't you?" pursued Miss Pringle, with a beady glance at Amanda which betrayed curiosity and suspicion. "Why, *here* he is, too. You will be quite a *party*, Mrs. Armstrong. Perhaps, though, you don't feel up to entertaining so *many* of us, and I should mount my trusty steed—ha-ha!—and ride away?"

"By no means, Miss Pringle," said Susan. "I feel splendidly fit, and a tea-party is just what I'd like this afternoon. Come in, all of you!" she called, as voices were heard in the hall. "You're making a draught, with the door open. Oliver, just tell Elspeth that there will be seven of us for tea!"

"*Such* a dee-lightful gathering of friends and neighbours," said Miss Pringle, when they were all sitting at tea in the dining-room, her wedding-present cloth hurriedly put on the table by the invaluable Elspeth, who had substituted it for a harmless white embroidered linen. "I was just saying, Mr. Heriot, that you ought to get married *too*!"

"Good idea, Larry. What about it?" said Oliver, winking openly at him.

"By Jove, yes, Miss Pringle! You're right. I believe I will,' cried Larry, as if the idea in all its brilliance had struck him that moment. "Who would you recommend as a bride?"

Miss Pringle, to everyone's incredulous joy, succeeded in looking arch; and Peggy promptly and disgracefully choked on a crumb and had to be thumped on the back by her husband until her eyes were swimming in tears.

"I know. I'll marry Amanda!" said Larry.

"Oh, Mr. Heriot! This is so *very* sudden," said Amanda, simpering.

Miss Pringle's mouth fell open and she forgot to shut it for quite half a second, during which, Oliver said afterwards, he appreciated the feelings of a man in a small boat with a hippopotamus opening its jaws to engulf him.

"So it *is* true?" she gasped at length. "I had heard, but I didn t believe—"

"So you very wisely came to find out. Yes, it's perfectly true," said Oliver briskly. "Of course you will understand, Miss Pringle, that in the circumstances, *nothing* is being announced as yet, until the bride's mother has given her blessing on the approaching nuptials. We can *rely* on you, I know, to *respect* this confidence." He spoke with portentous gravity and an almost perfect mimicry of the lady to whom he addressed his words.

"Of course, of course." Miss Pringle, nodding like a mandarin, forgot the felt pudding-basin which she called a hat and which fell forward on to her long nose in her vehemence.

She was still straightening it when Robinia, who had no business to bring in the letters—or, indeed, to appear in the dining-room at all—thrust a tray under Amanda's chin, muttering hoarsely, "Here's a letter for ye, by the efternune post—mem. Seein' it's got a foreign-eerin' stamp on it, it'll be frae yer mither!"

"That will do, Robinia," said Susan sternly. Amanda looked at the envelope as Robinia, crestfallen, left the room much more quietly than she had come, and said to Susan:

"Shall I open it now? Robinia seems to think I ought to read it at once."

"Yes, go on, Amanda. We're dying to know whether it's a parent's blessing or an I-wash-my-hands-of-you note," said Oliver, with a wicked glance at Miss Pringle's nose, quivering with eagerness.

Amanda skimmed through it, looked dazed, turned to the beginning again, then raised her head and said, "Yes, she's quite pleased. At least, she doesn't say she isn't."

"A bit luke-warm, I must say," said Oliver. "She seems to have expressed this dubious view at great length."

"Oliver, I am *ashamed* of you," said Peggy, blushing. "Such vulgar curiosity!"

"Oliver can't help being vulgar, poor lamb," said his sister kindly.

"Oh!" suddenly shrieked Amanda. "Susan, Jed, Larry, all of you! What *do* you think? Mother's *married*!"

"Sensation in court," murmured the irrepressible Oliver.

"To an Argentine cattle millionaire!" went on Amanda. "What do you think of that?"

"No wonder she hasn't bothered much about your engagement," said Jed. "She's done a damn' sight better than you, and been quicker about it into the bargain!"

Miss Pringle rose, simmering with suppressed excitement. "My *most* sincere congratulations," she said, to Larry and Amanda. "And be *sure*, my dear, to send them to your dear mother also! Mrs.

Armstrong, I feel I must *tear* myself away and return to my poor invalids. Good-bye, and thank you for a *most* enjoyable tea. *Good-bye! Good-bye!*"

"Those words had the ring of absolute truth," murmured Oliver, as they all trooped into the hall to see her off. "She is off and away over rock bush and scaur to tell the others!"

Miss Pringle, leaping on to her trusty bicycle, which wobbled perilously as it received her weight, was hardly aware of their presence. *What* an afternoon Jelly and Cissy had missed, what a rich haul of news, through their own faults, for if they had worn their thicker woollen scarves, as she had advised, they would not have caught cold. Now, perhaps, they would pay more attention to their eldest sister! Now she would regain, at one swoop, all the supremacy which she had loved so long and lost awhile! Wrapped in delightful anticipation, Miss Pringle bicycled away along the drive, and was lost to view in the gathering darkness.

THE END

FURROWED MIDDLEBROW